Jane Thynne was born in Venezuela and educated in London. She graduated from Oxford University with a degree in English and joined the BBC as a journalist. She has also worked at the *Sunday Times*, the *Daily Telegraph* and the *Independent*, as well as for numerous British magazines. She appears as a broadcaster on Radio 4. Jane is married to the writer Philip Kerr. They have three children and live in London. *The Winter Garden* is Jane's fifth novel.

Find out more at www.janethynne.com, connect with her on Facebook, or follow her on Twitter @janethynne

Praise for *The Winter Garden*:

'Thynne's fifth novel is an absolute cracker of a read . . . her tale of pre-war intrigue is fast-paced and gripping from the start. She expertly maintains the suspense, while evoking the tension of Berlin as the city gathers its strength for war' *Sunday Times*

'This tale is so convincing, one forgets it is a piece of fiction' *The Lady*

'A thoroughly enjoyable read: fast-paced, atmospheric and genuinely suspenseful' *Mail on Sunday*

Praise for *Black Roses*:

'It was a clever idea to hone in on the Nazi wives and girlfriends, and the crosscurrents and dangers of the build-up to war are established with expertise and not a little menace. Terrific' Elizabeth Buchan, *Sunday Times*

'An exciting story and a subtle, original portrait of the early days of the Third Reich . . . Jane Thynne's smooth writing, sensitive understanding of the era and sharp observations combine into an excellent historical thriller. Good news: it's the first of a planned trilogy. I'm eager for the next'
Jessica Mann, *Literary Review*

'Thynne's thriller is strong on the city's paranoia, and its exploration of the Third Reich's bizarre attitude to women gives it an original take on Nazi Germany' *Mail on Sunday*

'Enthralling novel of love and divided loyalties. Storytelling at its best' Fanny Blake, *Woman & Home*

'Thynne takes us on an inspired tour of the rarely examined female side of the Third Reich . . . she has managed something quite remarkable . . . this is the Third Reich seen backstage and from the dressing table, with make-up both on and off'
Peter Millar, *The Oldie*

'This divine novel is almost unbearably exciting and the love story would melt a heart of stone . . . Gripping stuff'
Saga Magazine

By the same author

Black Roses
The Weighing of the Heart
Patrimony
The Shell House

The Winter Garden

JANE THYNNE

SIMON & SCHUSTER

London · New York · Sydney · Toronto · New Delhi

A CBS COMPANY

First published in Great Britain by Simon & Schuster UK Ltd, 2014
This paperback edition published by Simon & Schuster UK Ltd, 2014
A CBS COMPANY

1 3 5 7 9 10 8 6 4 2

Simon & Schuster UK Ltd
1st Floor
222 Gray's Inn Road
London WC1X 8HB

www.simonandschuster.co.uk

Simon & Schuster Australia, Sydney
Simon & Schuster India, New Delhi

A CIP catalogue record for this book
is available from the British Library
PB ISBN: 978-1-84983-989-1
EBOOK ISBN: 978-1-84983-990-7

Typeset in Bembo by M Rules
Printed and bound by CPI Group (UK) Ltd, Croydon, CR0 4YY

For William

'Woman's world is her husband, her family, her children and her home. We do not find it right when she presses into the world of men.'

Adolf Hitler

'Take up the frying pan, dustpan and broom and marry a man.'

Hermann Goering, Nine Commandments of the Worker's Struggle

Prologue

Berlin, October, 1937

The flash and dazzle of fireworks, like multicoloured shrapnel, studded the night sky. Vivid bursts of phosphorus erupted in the damp air, bloomed into extravagant showers of stars, then fizzled and died against the dark sheet of the Wannsee below. A faint plume of smoke drifted across the lake as the fireworks fell quiet and night closed in again.

From where she stood, in the deep shadow of the garden, Anna Hansen tried to work out which of the big villas on Schwanenwerder Island had something to celebrate. Fireworks were nothing special here. There were always parties going on in the grand houses. They all had large gardens stretching down to the lake from where, across the water, loomed the inky mass of Grunewald's eastern shore. Between the shores the dip and ripple of small boats could be heard, rocking in the wind as the water slapped against their sides.

Anna shivered in the night air. It was cold standing here, surrounded by softly dripping shrubs. She shuffled her slippered feet and clutched her dressing gown more closely around her. Though it might have been the bangs and whistles which woke her, in truth she had scarcely been able to sleep, despite an exhausting day. But then, it was always an exhausting day at the Schwanenwerder

Reich Bride School. It seemed there was so much to learn for women who were about to marry members of the SS. It wasn't like being an ordinary German bride, though, heaven knows, those girls had their work cut out. But as the Führer said, the women who were to marry the cream of German manhood needed to be something special.

Not that Anna had much choice when she arrived at the Bride School, a stately villa with pillared gates proudly topped by a pair of swastika flags and screened from the world by a ridge of tall pines. A course there was compulsory, it had been since 1935, on Himmler's orders, and you needed to submit the certificate you gained to the SS Race and Settlement Office before your marriage could go ahead. In some ways the School was like a military training academy, with a regime which started at five thirty in the morning and didn't end until the shattered brides dropped into their beds at nine o'clock at night. That morning, for example, had begun with the usual outdoor bath, to take advantage of the island's fresh, pine-scented air, followed by energetic gymnastics in shorts and vests. After breakfast came Sewing, and then a visit from the local Mother and Child branch for Childcare instruction, before lunch, which was made on a rota by the brides themselves, wearing headscarves and spotless aprons.

Today they had been focusing on 'Cooking Without Butter' because of the shortage, and very dull it had been too. Though that was no bad thing, Anna thought, because all these regular meals were making her plump. After lunch came Culture, consisting of a talk on fairy tales. All brides needed to learn fairy tales because the German mother was the 'culture bearer' to the next generation. Today's lecturer had explained how in Cinderella it was the prince's Germanic instincts that led him to reject the stepsisters' alien blood and search for a maiden who was racially pure.

Culture should have been what Anna enjoyed best. She had been a dancer after all, not so long ago. Chorus line at the

Wintergarten. Standing there amid the shadowy shrubs, she ran an absent hand over her rumpled, shoulder-length hair. Her dark roots were showing badly and the bleached curls were already turning to frizz in the damp air. She sighed. It was hard to imagine a greater contrast between her previous life and the one she was living now. Her old friends would die laughing if they could see her. But then Anna's circumstances had changed. Changed drastically. And by some miracle, just as she had needed to escape from a difficult spot, SS-Obersturmführer Johann Peters, six foot two with a jaw like granite and eyes as blue as the Baltic Sea, had walked into her life. From the moment Johann had come up to her in that dank little nightclub, she hadn't looked back. If it hadn't been for Johann she might even have resorted to answering one of those depressing advertisements you saw in the newspapers. '*54-year-old lawyer, pure Aryan, desires male offspring through marriage with young virgin, hard-working, low heels, no jewellery.*' So when Johann had requested a dance, and shortly afterwards her hand in marriage, she had taken him up on it without a second thought, even if it meant spending six weeks at Bride School in preparation.

The villa that housed the Bride School had been occupied by a single Jewish family until it was transferred into the ownership of the Deutsches Frauenwerk. As Anna walked between lessons, she would look wistfully at the grandeur of the décor, the folded mahogany panelling of the hall and the line of little bells in the kitchen which were connected to different rooms in the house. The whole place was full of colour; pistachio paint in the hall, almond white on the dado rails, and deep burgundy red in the library, which still smelled of leather and cigars. The music room – an entire room devoted to music! – was painted daffodil yellow, and the ballroom, which was lavender blue, had a ceiling like a wedding cake, moulded with plaster roses, from where great chandeliers were suspended. Anna liked to imagine the life that had existed there before – all the parties and the fun and the elegance.

There were patches on the walls where gold-framed oil paintings had hung, and if you stood quite still you could almost sense the family that had gone before, evanescent as a waft of perfume down a corridor, or the faint sound of laughter in the air.

Now, though, the ballroom had been fitted with desks and its damask curtains taken down in the interests of cleanliness. Cleanliness was all important at the Bride School. Everything had to be hygienic and disinfected, smelling of soap and polish. Dirt, and all soiled traces of the past, must be scrubbed away. Dust was disgusting, the instructors said. It was almost unGerman.

Anna's dormitory, where eight girls slept, was a long room on the top floor. It must have been the nursery originally, but it had been redecorated in the same plain, brutal fashion as the rest of the house. Iron bedsteads flanked the walls, and the floors were bare boards. The wallpaper had been whitewashed over, but if you tipped the wardrobe slightly you could see a remnant of it, pale pink with knotted posies, in a spot that was difficult to reach. Anna was observant like that. She had an eye for detail; she always liked to know what lay underneath things.

It had been hard to leave her bed and slip out of the house unnoticed. Strangely for an organization which believed so fervently in fresh air, the dormitory window was kept locked and after bedtime the corridors were patrolled by the sewing mistress, Fräulein Wolff. Brides were encouraged not to leave the room except in cases of emergency. Luckily the only person to notice Anna waking that night was Ilse Henning, a good-hearted country girl with a shelf of a bosom and a face as scrubbed as a pine table, who blinked at her in puzzlement, then rolled obediently onto her side. Ilse probably assumed, quite correctly, that her roommate was going into the garden to smoke an illicit cigarette.

That much was true. Yet it was a deeper restlessness which was troubling Anna Hansen. All day she had had the curious sensation that she was being watched. It was nothing obvious. Just a brooding self-consciousness that crawled across her skin, raising the minute hairs on her neck, making her tense, the way a gazelle tenses when it scents the approach of a predator. Several times during the day, both in the garden and the house, she had the distinct feeling of someone's eyes upon her, only to wheel round and find nothing there. She had repeatedly attempted to rationalize the sensation. Perhaps it was the sorry shortage of nicotine that set her nerves jangling. Or maybe the ugly gardener, Hartmann, the one with the limp and the hedgehog haircut, was spying on her. He was always hanging around eyeing up the Reich Brides. What was a man like him even doing in a place like this? Why couldn't he be sent to the Rhineland or something?

The feeling came on her again as she lay trying to sleep in the dormitory, listening to the distant crump of fireworks, and to shake it off she had risen and crept out into the chill October air.

The moon was obscured by a bank of heavy cloud as she progressed down the garden, avoiding the gravel path and hugging the shrubs at the edge of the lawn. Behind her in the distance the house was a shuttered and slumbering hulk, with only a single lamp burning on the ground floor, and ahead lay the leaden expanse of the lake, visible only by the lights which glimmered from the few yachts and pleasure boats moored at its edges.

She stopped at the trunk of a large pine tree and pulled out her cigarettes. Around her a dim tangle of laurel receded into a pool of deeper shadow. There was dense vegetation underfoot. Flecks of water from the lake blew against her face and she hugged her arms to her chest, wishing she had worn something warmer than an old silk dressing gown. Because of the rigid dress code at the School, nightwear was the only area where brides had any self-expression. Most of the girls opted for a floral tent of scrubby towelling, but Anna's was creamy silk with ivory lace inserts with a matching negligée which smelled of smoke and perfume and acted as a consoling, luxurious reminder of the good old days.

Suddenly she sensed a glimmer of movement in the bushes, a spectral flicker accompanied by a rustle of leaves. She froze, her senses on the alert, straining to filter the night sounds. The fireworks had subsided now and the night's silence was penetrated only by the whine of the high trees swaying and the thrum of a car making its way along the lake road. More faintly, the soft rattle and groan of boats, their timbers creaking and the water slapping on their sides, carried on the breeze.

There it was again. A distinct crackle of leaves, a couple of yards to her left. Anna stiffened, her heart lifting in her throat, and turned to see a white shape and a pair of golden circles trained on her. She almost laughed with relief.

'God, Minka. You gave me a fright. Hiding from the fireworks are you?'

The cat approached and rubbed against her leg. She was a friendly animal and much loved by the Bride School inmates. Anna squatted down to stroke her head, then took out her lighter, an elegant silver lozenge engraved with her initials. God forbid anyone should find her with it. She had had to smuggle it in here, because smoking was strictly forbidden at the Bride School. The Führer called cigarettes 'decadent' and said smokers were unfit to be German wives and mothers. All brides had to sit through a lecture on the poison of nicotine and how the Jews had brought tobacco to Germany to corrupt the native stock. She snapped the lighter open, the flame leapt up, lit the cigarette and she took a deep drag, impatient for the first delicious hit to coil down her throat, then rested her back against the bark of the tree. This was a long way to come for a smoke, but it was worth it.

Beside her the cat froze and lifted its head. It had seen something, but what? A mouse perhaps, or a bird? A fox even? Following its gaze she stared blindly into the murk.

'Is someone there?'

A sudden screech heralded the launch of a single rocket that flared and dissipated in an emerald shower, lighting up the sky. The cat's pupils contracted to slits. As the sound died away, Anna heard something else. The soft crunch of a footstep on the wet earth.

'Who is it?'

The words choked in her throat. As she stared desperately around her into the darkness, frantic thoughts raced through her mind. It had been a mistake to come out here. She should never have left the dormitory. Perhaps it was the creepy gardener, spying on her.

'Hartmann? Is that you?'

Two more steps and then a face was looming up before her. As she peered through the darkness, terror engulfed her. Her knees almost buckled, and it took everything she had to summon a tone of coy flirtatiousness.

'Well, hello stranger.'

The man raised the Walther 6.35-calibre pistol and Anna's eyes widened a moment, but the sound of the shot was drowned in an exuberant volley of fireworks. A spume of scarlet sparks arced and spangled the sky. The man with the gun watched Anna languidly as she fell, then he turned away and melted into the shadow. For a moment Anna's hand clutched frantically, as if she were trying to haul herself up on empty air, then it dropped back and the lighter slid out of her opened palm, down into the damp grass.

Chapter One

Clara Vine swung her car through the wrought-iron gates of the villa and braked violently to avoid a peacock crossing the drive. As the bird strutted onto the lawn, dragging its magnificent lapis lazuli tail, she was sure she divined an arrogant glint in its beady eye. Still, she was relieved she hadn't hit it. It wouldn't do to damage any property belonging to the Reich Minister for Enlightenment and Propaganda, even if it did happen to be an unwanted pet. The birds were a leftover from Joseph Goebbels' magnificent Olympics party the previous year, when Peacock Island in the Wannsee had been turned into a fairy-tale playground for two thousand guests, filled with dancing and fireworks. Film stars, singers and all kinds of celebrities mingled with diplomats and high-ranking visitors. The papers had been full of it for days. After the balloons and the banners had been packed away some of the birds had ended up here, even though Frau Doktor Goebbels detested them. Their jewelled crowns and magnificent displays concealed a nasty temper, and the stillness of Schwanenwerder was constantly pierced by their raucous cries.

Not that the neighbours would have dreamt of complaining. The Goebbels' villa, at Inselstrasse 8, was in the most desirable position on this tiny, exclusive enclave. Though it was called an island, it was actually a peninsula, which stretched out from the

Grunewald into the lake, connected by a single, narrow road. Surrounded on all sides by water, and wooded with oak, birch and pine, Schwanenwerder was only a few kilometres from the centre of Berlin, yet it might have been another country. It had been colonized a hundred years ago by the very wealthiest of Berlin's society, the bankers, industrialists and department-store owners, who had competed among themselves to build the most tasteful, luxurious country houses and take advantage of Schwanenwerder's restorative air. Since then, in the space of four years, a new élite had emerged to replace them. On the day Hitler came to power, Nazi stormtroopers flocked onto the island and raised the swastika flag on its water tower. Most of the homes were now occupied by senior party figures. Number eight had been bought by Goebbels at a price far beneath its genuine value from the chairman of the Deutsche Bank, who had been all too keen to sell before his enforced departure abroad. It had a panoramic view of the Greater Wannsee, extensive lawns running down to a boathouse and a garden ringed with oaks, pines and fruit trees.

Clara parked the red Opel next to a Mercedes Benz cabriolet with beige leather seats, checked her lipstick in the rear-view mirror, and smoothed her hair beneath her hat. She sat for a second, waiting for her trepidation, like a surge of stage fright, to come under control, then stepped out of the car. As she made her way to the front door a pear, like a tiny, unexploded bomb, dropped down beside her into the grass.

The maid showed her into the drawing room, whose French windows at one end led to a stone-flagged terrace circled by a balustrade, beyond which was a magnificent view of the lake, edged by the gloomy, impenetrable Grunewald. Now, at five in the afternoon, the sun was a molten orb in a streaked caramel sky, turning the waters of the Wannsee into a sheet of hammered gold. At the end of the garden Clara could see a private beach and a jetty, where Goebbels kept his motor yacht, *Baldur*. Seagulls squawked and wheeled in the sky and, further out in the lake, a couple of fishermen drifted in their boats, hunched over their tranquil lines waiting for pike, like figures from a nineteenth-century painting.

Clara crossed her arms and waited, affecting a nonchalance she did not feel, as she tried, yet again, to work out what Magda Goebbels could possibly want with her.

The message had come that morning out of the blue. A studio runner brought the note to Clara directly onto the set at the Ufa film studios in Babelsberg where she was filming a romantic comedy called *A Girl For Everything*. He shouldered his way through the make-up girls and the script man, right into the dazzle of the arc lights, to deliver it. The boy's face was a picture of urgency and intense curiosity, as befitted a summons from Magda Goebbels, wife of Hitler's right-hand man and the woman informally known as the First Lady of the Reich. The other actors had looked on avidly as Clara quickly scrutinized the message, then folded the note and stowed it in a pocket. Her face, she knew, gave nothing away.

Now Clara walked around the drawing room, assessing the pictures and furniture on display. Last year Goebbels claimed he was embarrassed to have moved into such a large villa because he hated luxury, yet for the sake of the Reich he could not be expected to receive distinguished guests in his old apartment. One look at this room, however, revealed that his aversion to luxury did not run very deep. The place was furnished in solid bourgeois taste; rich Persian rugs and fat sofas upholstered in satin and watered silk, side tables in restrained, nineteenth-century style on a parquet floor polished to a high shine. A Gobelin tapestry hung on the wall and a Bechstein piano stood in the front window. The standard portrait of the Führer, *de rigueur* in any Party home, hung above a mantelpiece crowded with family photographs, most of which Clara had already seen in the newspapers. There was

Goebbels in open-necked shirt and sunglasses, at the wheel of his motorboat. The four Goebbels children, Helga, Hilde, Helmut and Holde, the girls in matching white dresses and ribbons, and Helmut in a sailor suit, sitting in their miniature pony carriage. Goebbels, it was said, insisted on one baby a year. Four children may be enough for a string quartet, he joked, but not enough for a National Socialist. He had publicly promised another five babies for the Reich.

Catching sight of herself in a gold rococo mirror, Clara scrutinized the picture she presented with a critical eye. She was wearing a buttoned ivory blouse beneath a fitted serge navy suit with a fur collar, her chestnut hair freshly cut in a neat bob. A new, fashionably tilted navy velvet hat. Red Coral lipstick by Max Factor. Lizard-skin clutch bag. Every inch the screen actress whose career was on the rise, though not so successful that she would be recognized in the street. And all of it a façade. Clara was used to a life of deception now. Sometimes deception seemed like an extension of her own being, moving bodily with her as she walked the streets of Berlin or sat with friends in bars or crossed the sets of the Ufa film studios. The Clara Vine she saw in the mirror was both herself and not herself. What the real Clara Vine might look like, she could no longer say.

Though she couldn't fault the image, still Clara felt anxious. The near miss with the peacock had done nothing to improve her nerves. Behind her she heard the creak of the door and the heavy tread of her hostess.

'You haven't changed a bit!'

It sounded more of an accusation than a welcome. As Magda Goebbels entered the room, permitting a transitory smile to twitch across her crimson lips, Clara tried to conceal her surprise at the change in her. Even if she had wanted to return Magda's compliment, it was impossible. Four children in five years had done Magda no favours. Clara had seen her often enough in the newspapers, of course, decked out in satin and pearls, hosting grand Party occasions alongside Hitler, presiding at the Mothers' Union and the Winter Relief charity, partying with foreign dignitaries at last year's Olympic Games. But close up it was a very different picture. Magda was still elegantly turned out in the height of fashion; she wore a Chanel dress in peach silk and her platinum hair was scalloped tightly against her cheek. But beneath the rouge her skin was putty-coloured, her mouth lined and the dress bulged at the belt. Her body was waging a war between elegance and middle-aged spread and it seemed the spread was winning.

They sat on low chairs looking out onto the garden while a maid shuffled in, straining under the weight of a tea tray laden with brown bread spread thickly with butter, sponge cake and Lebkuchen. Magda aligned the handles of the cups precisely and gestured to the girl to pour the tea, wincing as her trembling hand spilled tea into the saucer. Impatiently Magda waved her away.

'I'm sorry about that. She's training. There's a Bride School on the island and we like to help out by giving their girls a little practice with serving. But I have to say I feel sorry for those poor husbands-to-be.'

She waited until the girl had left and closed the door behind her, then turned.

'So, Fräulein Vine. Your career is blossoming, I hear. My husband tells me you are quite the rising star at Ufa now.'

'Thank you. And how are you, Frau Doktor?'

'Not too good. I've been at the clinic in Dresden again.'

Like most women in Berlin, Magda Goebbels was obsessed with her health. She was always visiting spas and clinics to receive injections which purported to calm her nerves.

'I'm afraid I haven't kept up with your films.' She gestured at the family photographs. 'My life is rather busy.'

So this was how it was to be. From the first line of the script,

Clara could judge the expected dialogue, and she was glad of it. Their conversation would be confined to pleasantries. Magda was icy as ever. There would be no reference to what had gone before.

'I've been busy too, fortunately.'

'Indeed. You have a new film out now, I see.' In her lap, Magda's hands were a tight fist of nerves. 'I'm trying to remember what it's called?'

'*Madame Bovary*. It's directed by Gerhard Lamprecht. I'm just finishing another, called *A Girl for Everything,* and in a few weeks I'll begin a new film with Ernst Udet: *The Pilot's Bride*. He plays a Luftwaffe pilot who is shot down and I'm his wife.'

At the mention of Ernst Udet, Magda Goebbels responded the way everyone, from small boys to middle-aged women, tended to respond. Her eyes brightened and her attention was captured. The subject of aviation in general and Ernst Udet in particular was an exciting one just then. The handsome fighter ace, with his strikingly blue eyes, deep cleft chin and jovial smile, was not just a war hero but a national celebrity. He had been the best friend of Manfred von Richthofen, the Red Baron, and after the war he became a film star, moving to Hollywood and taking up stunt flying for the movies. Now back in Germany, in his forties and unmarried, he was something of a playboy. His lean frame had rounded out, but it suited him and besides, German women liked their men with some flesh on them. His autobiography had sold millions. Lessing and Co, the cigarette company, had even produced a special Ernst Udet brand, which came in a pretty cobalt tin, bisected by a soaring scarlet biplane.

In the past year, however, Udet had been dragooned into the service of the Reich. At Goering's insistence he had been appointed head of the technical division of the Luftwaffe. He was supposed to be too busy overseeing aircraft manufacture and development to waste his time stunt flying, but still he couldn't resist it. He was coming into the studio later that week to discuss filming *The Pilot's Bride.*

'Generaloberst Udet! What fun for you! We saw him flying at the Olympics. Such a clever man. Will he be performing any of his stunts?'

'Of course. We've got a day's filming out at Tempelhof.'

The fact that Udet's stunts were to be filmed at a real airport, in the real sky, was unusual. Hardly anything was shot on location now. All movies were filmed in the studio. It was as though the Nazis wanted to present their fictional world, perfect in every way, without any interference from the real world and all its complexities.

'Then I shall make certain to see it.' Magda speared a slice of lemon and suspended it in her tea. 'And I'm grateful you could spare time in your schedule to see me.'

'It is a pleasure, Frau Doktor,' said Clara neutrally. But her mind was racing. She took a bite of sponge cake and waited for Magda to come to the point.

'I have a little request for you. About a party I'm hosting on Saturday. I wondered if you might like to attend?'

A party at the home of the Propaganda Minister? Clara could think of nothing she would like less. And no offer harder to refuse.

'How kind of you.'

'I have an ulterior motive, I'm afraid. There are some English guests. Their German is not quite as proficient as one would hope, and I think they find conversation quite exhausting. As you have an English father I thought you might be able to speak to them and make them feel relaxed.'

'I would be delighted.'

'Excellent.' Her mission accomplished, Magda glanced around restlessly, as if in search of small talk. Her fingers hovered over a biscuit, then withdrew. 'And how is your family? You have a sister, don't you?'

'Angela.'

'Perhaps I will meet her one day. I imagine she is most interested in the country where your mother grew up. Your mother's family came from, where was it again?'

'Hamburg.'

'Ah yes.'

Clara wondered how long these cordialities would continue. Their words hung between them like mist drifting over deep waters. Frau Goebbels avoided her eye, tapping her fingers on the arm of her chair like a pianist trying to recapture an elusive melody.

'I wonder . . .' ventured Clara, 'could I ask who these English friends are?'

'Oh, didn't I say? You know them, I think. Unity Mitford and her sister Diana.'

The Mitfords. Diana and her younger sister Unity were notorious in London for their fascist sympathies. Diana had caused a scandal by leaving her husband to set up house with Oswald Mosley, the darkly handsome leader of the British Union of Fascists, whose rallies were frequently the opportunity for violent clashes between his gang of black-shirted followers and their opponents. Though Clara had indeed met Diana and Unity, they were Angela's friends really, part of a set that adored fancy dress, cliquish societies and wildly extravagant parties. How curious that their politics should share some of the same characteristics.

'We've met, yes. But it was a while ago.'

'Diana's a Mosley now, of course. She married her husband last year in our apartment in Hermann Goering Strasse.'

Magda's face softened as she recalled the occasion. 'They wanted a quiet ceremony, you see, because Mosley's first wife had only recently died. So they decided to marry here in Berlin and the Führer graciously agreed to attend. Diana wore golden silk. Unity and I were her witnesses and afterwards we drove out here for lunch, down by the lake, and my little girls presented her with posies of wild flowers. We gave them a twenty-volume set of the works of Goethe. It was so romantic.'

At this, it was as if Magda realized she had confided something she shouldn't have. As if she had stepped into some territory that had been declared forever out of bounds. A blush bloomed momentarily in the pallor of her complexion and her whole body stiffened.

'Anyhow, they're coming over for the day. I had planned a whole day of sightseeing, only . . .' she hesitated momentarily, as if uncertain over imparting any further information. Clara concealed her curiosity with careful sips of scalding tea.

'Only I've had to cancel a local outing I had planned for them. I had hoped to show them round the new Bride School just down the road from here, but unfortunately there's been an incident. Well, a bit more shocking than that, actually.' She flicked an eye towards the door as though the maid might be eavesdropping and lowered her voice. 'One of the brides was found murdered.'

'Murdered?' The word rang harshly in the tranquil, teatime air.

'Yes. In the garden, apparently. A girl called Anna Hansen. Terrible, isn't it? It's so sad for her fiancé.' Magda grimaced in annoyance. 'And rather inconvenient for us. The visit can't possibly go ahead. It's obviously cast a cloud. It wouldn't be the right atmosphere.'

Anna Hansen. For a second, the name snagged in Clara's mind. Then she realized she used to know a girl of that name, though it could hardly be the same one. The Anna Hansen Clara knew was an easy-going, bottle blonde from Munich who would be more at home in a negligée than an SS Hausfrau's apron; indeed, when Clara first met her, she hadn't been wearing any clothes at all. She had been a life model for the artist Bruno Weiss, whom Clara had met through Helga Schmidt, the small-time actress who had been the first person to befriend Clara when she arrived in the city. After Helga died in 1933, Bruno and Clara had become good friends and Clara would often drop into his Pankow studio to watch him working and bring him meals he might otherwise forget to eat. Since Helga's death Bruno had been working with feverish intensity, his canvases becoming bloodier and more grotesque, his hatred for the regime erupting in livid clots of paint. It was on such a visit one day last year, bearing a couple of rolls and some sausage, that Clara had encountered Anna. Her naked form was arranged obligingly on Bruno's crusty velvet sofa, her legs splayed and a cigarette dangling from a long amber holder in her hand. She had the kind of flexible, muscular limbs which came from a dancer's training. The idea of Bruno's Anna Hansen marrying an SS officer was too incongruous for words.

The inconvenient death of the Reich bride seemed to have caused a chill in the room. Magda rose with unexpected haste and clacked across the parquet floor. 'Anyway, Fräulein Vine, don't let me keep you any longer.'

She held the door open.

'The party will be next Saturday at seven p.m. Only twenty or so people. Is there . . .' she hesitated, 'a guest you might like to bring? A fiancé perhaps?'

'No, there's no one.'

'Then we shall be most pleased to see you.'

With a peremptory nod she disappeared across the hall and up the stairs.

Clara walked back to her car, her mind working furiously. Her mouth was dry with nerves and she found herself unexpectedly shaking. An invitation after all this time? Magda had said it was her idea, but could it be really? She tried to analyse the request. There was nothing especially strange about the Goebbels' entertaining English visitors. There were plenty of high-ranking Britons arriving in Berlin, even now when Germany's march into the Rhineland and her backing of Franco's faction in Spain had opened the eyes of most British people to the intentions of the regime. Last year, during the Olympics, Berlin had been full of tourists and last month's Nuremberg rally had attracted another clutch of politicians and dignitaries. Yet much as the Nazi élite enjoyed meeting them, conversation could be strained. The truth was, the British were lazy about learning the language. Many of them had nothing more than a few phrases picked up from a *Baedeker* guide to help them. They could order a beer in a restaurant and find their way to a nightclub, but that was not much use when discussing the delicate matter of friendship between Germany and Britain in an increasingly difficult international situation.

As she backed the car out of the drive Clara told herself that her role would be simply to chat to those guests and perform a little polite translation to oil the conversational wheels; she would be no more than an accessory, a party decoration, like those peacocks. Her task would last a couple of hours, at most. How difficult could that be?

Making her way back round the single road that skirted the island, Clara craned her head to glimpse the houses she passed. Most had fences and forbidding gates, or signs announcing that they were patrolled by dogs and security guards. Others had long drives, screened with trees. Between the branches she caught snatches of handsome, turn-of-the-century villas, with balconies and impressive porches and well-kept lawns. It hadn't taken long for the occupants of this slice of paradise, the Rothschilds and Israels and Goldschmidts, to yield to the offers of high-ranking Nazis and pack up their belongings. One villa had been purchased by the Reich Chancellery and reserved for Hitler's own use. Another was occupied by Hitler's doctor, Dr Morell, and Albert Speer, the Führer's young architect, had been seen house-hunting on Schwanenwerder too. It was hard to connect such men with this idyllic place. Now murder, too, had tainted this paradise.

It was fifteen minutes before Clara's Opel Olympia passed through the dense Grunewald, reached the leafy avenues of Wilmersdorf, and moved along Königsallee into the clanging bustle of Kurfürstendamm, Berlin's smartest shopping street, known to all as the Ku'damm. The noise was always what one noticed first at the heart of Berlin. The high-decibel blaring of car horns, the screech of brakes, the calls of the newspaper boys. Then the smell, the fumes of traffic and hot oil, the spicy scent of a pretzel cart or a wurst stall. Normally the pavements outside the fashionable cafés were crowded with customers, sipping coffee and watching life go by. Today, though, the tables were largely empty. The cold of the past few days had reminded everyone that another bone-chilling Berlin winter was approaching fast, and shoppers passed quickly, huddled into their coats and scarfs.

At the junction with Wilmersdorfer Strasse Clara braked as a traffic policeman stepped forward with his hand extended to allow a detachment of soldiers to pass. There was always some kind of military procession now. Either it was troops or a formation of the Hitler Youth or the BDM, the League of German Girls with their flaxen plaits and navy skirts. The storm troopers, the SS or the Hitler Jugend, all with their different uniforms and insignias. War was constantly in the air. Even the collecting boxes and the banners talked of the 'War on Hunger and Cold' as though the most charitable of enterprises must be undertaken with military aggression. There was a stirring of something just over the horizon that people preferred to ignore and pedestrians, looking forward to the weekend, kept their heads down, their faces as blank as the asphalt underfoot. They hurried on, hoping that no motorcade of Party top brass would be following the soldiers, requiring everyone to halt and raise a respectful right arm. The Führer supposedly trained with an expander so he could perform his own salute for two hours without flagging, but most people found even a few minutes a trial. Clara wondered where the soldiers might be heading. These days, that was all anyone was thinking.

She recalled the British newspapers she had flicked through that summer. The dispatch in *The Times*, informing the world how a special German flying unit, formed to support the Nationalists in the Spanish civil war, had bombed the ancient Basque town of Guernica. For more than three hours Junkers and Heinkel bombers unloaded bombs and incendiaries, while fighter aircraft plunged low to machine-gun those of the civilian population who had taken refuge in the fields. The town was razed to the ground and hundreds of women and children were killed. The evidence of three small bomb cases stamped with the German Imperial Eagle had proved to the world that the official German position of neutrality was a sham. Looking up now at the bone-white sky, Clara tried to imagine the bombers screaming out of the stillness of a spring morning and the terror of the people fleeing as they were strafed from the air. Then she pictured the same happening in England, Hitler's bombers raining their payload on the House of Commons or Westminster Abbey, or Ponsonby Terrace where her father lived. On Angela's home in Chelsea, or further out in the quiet suburbs, in Hackney and Greenwich and Barnes. On the Wren churches and Nelson's Column and the National Gallery. She imagined the raid sirens, the women and children hurrying out of their houses, the fighter planes diving low to finish off those stumbling figures who had escaped the incendiaries. The horizon lit by the red glow of a thousand fires, gas bombs sending coils of poison into family homes. She shook her head. That could never happen.

As she waited for the traffic policeman to clear the road she looked across the street, to where a crane was poised like a giant bird, pecking at another excavation. Berlin these days was like a patient under constant operation. Every street was subject to extracting, filling and fixing. You couldn't move for heaps of bricks, plank ribbing laid over holes in the earth and skeletal steel structures rising into the sky. Everywhere there was the roar of cement mixers and the rattle of drills, erecting the monumental, neoclassical buildings deemed suitable for the new world capital of Germania. There was something grand and futile about these buildings of the Führer, Clara thought. They were like an empty boast, designed to make human beings feel like ants in their long passages and echoing halls. Goering's Air Ministry had seven kilometres of corridors apparently, and it was said that for his centrepiece Hitler wanted Albert Speer to build a dome that rose a thousand feet into the sky, capable of holding a hundred and eighty thousand people. Nonetheless, the Führer had also ordered Speer to equip all Government buildings with bulletproof doors and shutters, just in case the people should ever lose their enthusiasm for his grand plans.

Chapter Two

It would be hard to find a greater contrast between the Goebbels' home in Schwanenwerder than the worn, ochre-painted nineteenth-century block in Winterfeldstrasse, where Clara lived on the top floor. A heavy wooden door led from the street into a hall painted institutional brown and lined with pocked tiles. To the left was an arthritic wrought-iron lift and behind it a stairwell for when the lift all too frequently refused to function. To the right, secreted in a cubby-hole furnished with a chair and lamp, Rudi the caretaker could be found. Try as she might to enter silently, Rudi would always dart from his cubicle with some piece of information or greeting. He was a Party member with a prestigiously high number – signifying that he had joined the Party in the early days, well before they closed the ranks to new membership – and in his role as National Socialist block warden, every Saturday he donned his brown shirt and attended a Party meeting. That was the only time one could be sure he was not around. Rudi knew everything that went on in the building, and Clara suspected he had seen every film she appeared in. He smelled of unwashed clothes and styled his sparse hair in imitation of the Führer. His oyster eyes bulged from a face as pinched and mottled as a crab's claw and his breath reeked like old carp, but Clara knew that nothing and no one escaped him.

'Good evening, Fräulein Vine.'

He sidled up unctuously and handed her some mail. There was an invitation to a lecture on the Semite in film – probably dispensed to all Ufa employees – and a routine flyer appealing for contributions to the Winterhilfswerk. The money raised was supposed to provide coal and food for the needy, but everyone knew it went on armaments. Herr Kaufmann, her neighbour, had put a sticker on his door, testifying that he already contributed to the Winter Relief Fund and was exempt from doorstep collections, but that only meant that when the Hitler Jugend came round with their collecting tins, Rudi ensured his was the first door they knocked on. Also in the pile was a letter with a London postmark and the curly female handwriting that belonged to her older sister Angela.

'May I ask how filming is proceeding?'

'Well, thank you, Rudi. We're almost finished. Though we had a late script change, which has meant a delay.'

The change had come down at the last moment from Goebbels' office, just a few days before the wrap. The Minister went through the script of every film made at the Ufa studios and issued alterations whenever he felt like it. In this case, he had decided that the actress playing an unfaithful wife should die at the end of the film. *'It would not be right for us to encourage the propensity to adultery at a time when young men are separated from their families by the call to arms. Infidelity must be publicly punished!'* the notoriously womanizing Minister had scribbled on the director's script. The director had read out the comments to the assembled actors deadpan. That was the greatest test of acting skill at Ufa – managing not to laugh.

'Just to mention, Fräulein, our official collection point.'

Rudi gestured at a bin he had installed in the lobby. This was a new idea. Clara had heard about it on the wireless. Citizens were to donate anything they didn't need that was metallic: cutlery, old toothpaste tubes, soup cans, razors or tinfoil, for the greater good of the Reich. Clara wondered how many toothpaste tubes it would take to build an aeroplane, then abandoned the speculation as far too much like the maths problems she used to face at school.

'Of course, Rudi. Thank you.'

'And to warn you, there are men coming in to mend the lift.'

There were always men coming in to mend the lift.

There were six apartments in the block, and hers was on the top floor. She climbed the steps and, reaching her door, she paused and put out a forefinger to examine a fine, dusty coating of powder on the ebony handle. It was a habit of hers, whenever she left the apartment, to give the handle a swift dab with the Max Factor compact in her handbag. Entering, she locked the door behind her, and surveyed her private domain.

If Berlin was being rebuilt according to an architectural fashion for gigantic size, Clara's apartment was the precise opposite. There were four rooms, all of them small. To the right of the dingy hall was a bedroom, to the left, a minuscule kitchen with a porcelain stove, its surrounds tiled in black, and a pine table, on which stood a red geranium. Further on was a bathroom so cramped you had to close the door before undressing. The bedroom was dominated by a large painting of a jazz trumpeter which Clara had positioned directly opposite the bed so it was the first thing she saw in the morning. It was not a beautiful picture. Its clashes and jagged lines expressed something of the fear that encircled the city and suggested not harmony, but screeching, discordant notes, yet she loved the painting because it reminded her of the artist, her old friend Bruno Weiss. Beside it was a tallboy, containing several evening dresses as well as the linen blouses, dark skirts and bright jumpers that were her working wardrobe.

The sitting room had views over the rooftops towards Nollendorfplatz a few blocks away. Clara had covered the wooden floors with rugs and with her scant wages had assembled a collection of deliberately modern furniture, not the heavy, dark stuff of so many Berlin apartments but low armchairs, a modern glass-topped table, a huge mirror and bookcases that ran the length of one wall. The entire décor was designed to maximize space and light. Clara loved this apartment. It was her refuge. It was the only space in Berlin that felt entirely secure, and the only place she could really relax.

She went into the kitchen and boiled water for coffee. For anyone with an addiction to coffee, Berlin was the ideal place to nurse it, even though it had risen shockingly in price and most places sold ersatz concoctions with the bitter tang of chicory. The watered-down stuff in the cafés had acquired its own contemptuous street name – *Negerschweiss* – Negro Sweat, but Clara liked to buy the best, Melitta Kaffee, which she found in a specialist shop just north of the Tiergarten. She adored visiting the cramped aromatic space, surveying the hundreds of different beans heaped in drawers behind the counter, like gold and amber gems. She lingered happily as the rich roasted scent rose like incense from the coffee machine and the proprietor weighed out her order in a priest-like ritual. A trip to the coffee shop was as good as any pilgrimage, Clara thought.

Waiting for the coffee to filter she opened the window and reminded herself, as always, how lucky she was to get a place in this part of town. She had inherited the apartment from an American journalist, Mary Harker, who had needed to make a quick exit from Germany. It was a departure for which Clara was indirectly responsible. When Helga Schmidt plunged to her death from her apartment window, Clara, convinced it was not suicide, but murder on the orders of the Nazi high command, had confided her suspicions to Mary. The ensuing article in the *New York Evening Post* so enraged Joseph Goebbels that he gave Mary forty-eight hours to leave. That was the last Clara saw of her, yet she still missed her friend's warmth and dry wit. She had received the occasional letter, full of Mary's trademark deprecation about life in suburban New Jersey – *undoubtedly the seventh circle of hell for any woman with a brain* – but in the past year there had been nothing.

When Mary left, the surrounding streets had been home to bars full of artists, intellectuals, singers and actresses, but now the Nazis had closed most of the bars down and if she ever came back, she would be hard put to recognize the area. Nollendorfplatz was still the same though, the busy square straddled by an elevated track and the great dome of a railway station. It was criss-crossed day and night by trams, and clattering above them the maroon and yellow carriages of the trains, sliding into the station. At the south end of the square was the Neues Schauspielhaus, a theatre which had once been home to Expressionist artists like Georg Kaiser and Ernst Toller, but was now consigned to revue shows and the kind of light operetta that the Nazis adored. Its granite façade was decorated with chunky Teutonic nudes, their taut calves and rippling muscles rising from the grey wall, the frigid opposite of the curvaceous dancers who could be seen performing in increasingly skimpy costumes inside.

Rising above the tangle of traffic sound and shouts, from a nearby window issued a familiar shriek. It was Joseph Goebbels on the radio, reprising his talk from the Nuremberg Party rally.

The Jew is a parasite, the ferment of decomposition.

All his speeches were the same. You hardly needed to listen to them. Even when you tried to block out the content, the same word emerged again and again, *Juden*, spat out like a curse. Goebbels was on the radio almost every day now. He timed his later broadcast for when people were sitting down to their evening meal, but even if you switched it off, there was no escape. Loudspeakers throughout the city obligingly blared the thoughts of Hitler and his Propaganda Minister. You would hear chunks of speech whenever you passed an open shop, or waited in line at the bank. Their words hammered into your brain like construction workers' drills, whether you liked it or not.

Quickly Clara closed the window and took the coffee to her desk along with a sandwich made with the last of her cheese, and a square of Ritter Sport chocolate. As she ate, her thoughts turned away from Joseph Goebbels and back to his wife.

Magda Goebbels, aloof and neurotic, was Hitler's favourite among the wives of his top men. She had indeed caught the Führer's own eye before he decided that marrying would be a bad career move and encouraged Joseph Goebbels to take his place. Magda liked to invite actresses to her parties for the pleasure of the Führer and a couple of times a year Clara would routinely be summoned to these events. Yet until today Magda had never addressed a word to her since the time, four years ago, when Clara, newly arrived in Berlin, unwittingly became a go-between in Magda's clandestine love affair with a Jewish man. Burdened with Magda's secret, Clara had concealed a deeper secret of her own. She became a spy on the private life of the Third Reich, passing snippets of information and gossip to Leo Quinn, assistant at the British Passport Control office and agent for the British Secret Service. It was Leo's idea that Clara should feed him details of the Nazi women's lives, reporting on their feuds and conflicts while masquerading as an actress without a political thought in her head. Leo had impressed on Clara how crucially the British needed information about the top figures in the Nazi regime. He had taught her everything he knew about surveillance and observation, how to keep herself safe and move with ease amid those she hoped to deceive. He had taught her the precautions every informer must take to avoid the paranoid suspicions of the Nazi state. He had schooled her and drilled her and inducted her into a dangerous new world. He had also fallen in love with her.

Leo. The thought of him still sent a shard into her heart.

Tall, with a penetrating green gaze and upright bearing, Leo

Quinn possessed a reserve that Clara assumed she would never overcome, until she discovered the intense passions that lay beneath. He loved poetry and translating Ovid. Part of him hankered for an academic career in some remote, ivy-clad quad, yet he was driven by the urgent need to help Jews escape from Berlin. He was the man who had turned Clara's ordinary existence into one fraught with danger and deception, yet he had also helped her escape the confines of her life in a way she could never have imagined. Leo was the only person in Berlin to whom Clara had confided her most dangerous secret – the fact that her own German grandmother was Jewish, and so, by maternal line, was she.

To begin with, when Leo left for London, Clara's first waking thought would be of him. Now it was more like a scratch that had healed and only hurt when certain things came to mind – a view of rooftops, a snatch of Latin inscription, or whenever she had reason to pass Xantener Strasse, a block off the Ku'damm, and look up at a third-floor window above a bakery to the safe house where they conducted their affair. She still missed him though. Sometimes she strove to hear the ironic lilt of his voice in her head or conjure up the frank intensity of his gaze. On a purely physical level, her skin craved the touch of a man, the trace of fingers across her skin and the heat of a body close to hers. The rush of desire would come upon her quite suddenly, when acting in a love scene, or meeting the glance of a handsome stranger on a tram. After they had separated, she and Leo had agreed not to contact each other. In the early days she had needed physically to restrain herself from calling the consulate and asking for his forwarding address. There were times when she had stood here, biting her lip and hugging her arms round her chest to avoid lifting the telephone. That didn't happen any more. The hurt had ebbed. For all she knew Leo was married. Indeed, that was how she liked to think of him. Back in London, married with a child. Besides, she had her own child to think of.

She moved over to the mantelpiece and examined a small photograph. It was of a boy, aged around six, gap-toothed, with a broad grin; Erich, the son of Helga Schmidt. As Helga lay dying on the pavement Clara had promised she would look after Erich and she had been true to her word. Every month she sent part of her wages to the grandmother he lived with. When he won a place at a top Gymnasium in Berlin, Erich and his grandmother had moved to a cramped apartment next to a brewery in Neukölln. Erich was almost fourteen now, and the broad grin had vanished. Though he had his mother's dark eyes, he lacked her sunny disposition and had grown into a serious, intelligent child, who concealed his anxiety with acts of bravado. Clara had seen him a lot over the last summer. They had driven out to the beach to sunbathe, and they had taken boats onto the lake. Clara had surprised herself by learning how to row. She had indulged his passion for aerobatic displays and he had tolerated her enthusiasm for the theatre.

Erich's birthday was coming up soon and he had asked for a Hitler Jugend knife. He had even given Clara a picture of the one he wanted, torn from a magazine, with *Blut und Ehre!* etched on the blade and an enamel swastika on the black checkered grip plates. He was very precise about these things. Clara sighed. She would much rather give Erich a book than a knife. Children were like that, she supposed. Always wanting unsuitable presents.

She finished her sandwich and cleared away. How unpredictable life could be. Five years ago, as a jobbing actress living in London with her father and sister in a tall Georgian house close to the Thames, she could never have imagined that at the age of thirty she would have made a life in Berlin, with an apartment and a contract at the Ufa studios, and a teenage boy to look after. The more conventional path for her life, the path her late mother had passionately hoped for, lay in marriage and motherhood. A safe alliance with the son of one of her father's political friends and a home in one of the creamy, stucco terraces which fanned out like chunks of wedding cake into Kensington and Chelsea. Her children would no sooner grow up than be sent away to school. Her life would be a round of cocktail parties, dinners, theatre and Conservative Party fundraising events. Deference to a husband who had invested in a set of opinions at boarding school and saw no reason to equip himself with new ones. Respectability, convention, tedium.

Clara gave an involuntary shudder. It bored her just to think of it.

But nor could she have imagined either that she would discover her own grandmother, Hellene Neumann, was Jewish, a fact that had been concealed throughout her childhood until she contacted her German cousin. Or that her father had received funding from the Nazi regime to finance his own pro-Nazi group in England, a cause her sister Angela had enthusiastically joined.

Angela's envelope lay on the desk unopened. Whenever they exchanged letters, Clara stuck to sketchy accounts of her time at Ufa, the parties, the nightlife and the apartment.

'Last week there was a premiere for *Love Whispers* and afterwards we all went out to Gustav Fröhlich's house – he's just about the most famous star in Germany!'

Clara never gave a hint of the horrors she saw every day. The ugliness on the streets, the arrests of colleagues, the terror that laced the air. Angela reciprocated with fulsome details of her social life, seemingly unaware that Clara was not transfixed by the doings of the Belgravia cocktail party set and the Kensington Ladies' Tennis Club. Right now, Clara decided, Angela's letter could wait.

It had been a tiring day. She had been called for filming at nine tomorrow morning which meant she would need to catch the S-Bahn out to the Babelsberg studios by seven. She was longing for a bath. She ran the water and as the scented steam rose about her she unbuttoned her blouse and stepped out of her skirt.

Slipping off her underclothes, she stood naked at the heavy porcelain basin, smoothing her hands over her hair. She took out a tin of Nivea cream and began removing her make-up with rhythmic, automatic strokes. With its high, arched brows, strong cheekbones and straight nose, her face had a neat symmetry that made her photogenic. She examined the fine tracery of lines at the side of her eyes, the blueish tinge beneath them and the faint brackets of smile lines. She pursed her mouth, with its pronounced cupid's bow, and ran her hands down her body with a secret regret that no one else did. Her body was still as slender and smooth as it had been at eighteen. Not that being an actress in Berlin meant starving yourself any more. Marlene Dietrich-style slenderness had disappeared about the time that Dietrich herself left for Hollywood and all the top actresses now boasted voluptuous curves. But every actress worried how long their screen career could last and Clara was no exception. She tilted her face left and right, lips slightly apart, the way you did for press photographers, staring critically. Then she leaned forward and spoke.

'I am a thirty-year-old woman who has no lover or husband, and only another woman's child. I pose as a friend to the National Socialists, while informing on them for British Intelligence. My father admires the Nazis, though my own grandmother was Jewish. No wonder I like going to the studio. Being an actress is the only time that I'm not acting.'

These thoughts she uttered very quietly. All truths in Berlin nowadays were expressed beneath the breath. It was only the lies that were broadcast at maximum volume.

Chapter Three

Ilse Henning had known something was wrong from early on. She had been woken before dawn by the shadows of car headlights swooping over the ceiling of the dormitory and the crunch of hard-soled boots on the gravel drive. Then, at five o'clock, when it was still dark and Fräulein Wolff paraded the length of the corridor with an old cattle bell, Ilse reached across to prod the familiar hump of Anna beneath the bedclothes, only to discover empty sheets. Normally Anna was the last to get up and Ilse often had to cover for her when Fräulein Wolff was on the rampage. It was unknown for Anna to be up and about early. Once Ilse had given her face a perfunctory scrub in the freezing basin, squeezed her plump form into the sweaty serge dress the brides had to wear, tied on her white apron and braided her hair, there were signs that Anna's disappearance was not the only unusual thing at the Reich Bride School that day.

In the dining room, where the brides not on kitchen training awaited their bread and muesli, there was a strict rule of silence. Yet today, along the long benches, the women whispered among themselves. Frieda Müller, collecting the eggs from the chicken roost, had seen men at the bottom of the garden, and they weren't gardeners. What could that mean? Further signs that things weren't right came directly after breakfast when the brides were abruptly informed that the fresh-air bath had been cancelled. They proceeded to lessons unwashed, agog with speculation. During Cookery that morning there was a talk on thrift and the economic situation, and how to pad out sausage-meat with breadcrumbs, but Ilse was too worried to concentrate. After a swift break for coffee came Childcare in which they were to learn a prayer for mothers to say with their children each night. It was based on the old-fashioned 'Our Father', only it began 'Mein Führer'. *Ich kenn dich wohl und habe dich lieb wie Vater und Mutter.* 'I know you well and I love you like my father and mother.' Ilse sat at the back, hoping to remain inconspicuous, but the gimlet eyes of Frau Messer fell upon her and she was asked to stand and recite it. Ilse opened her mouth obediently, but the words had gone straight out of her head. She sat down again, the admonishments of Frau Messer ringing in her ears, her mind too full of foreboding to care.

What had Anna done now? Had she been caught smoking and got herself suspended? If so, she would never be able to get her marriage certificate and that meant she wouldn't be able to marry Johann. She would be devastated. Anna was always talking about the wonderful life she was going to have with Obersturmführer Peters after they were married, in a big house in the west of the city, Zehlendorf she fancied, with a BMW 328 convertible and a wardrobe full of clothes. Ilse had no such grandiose hopes for her own married life with Otto, most likely starting off in his parents' three-room apartment in Kreuzberg. But Anna was a real dreamer. A surreptitious tear of sympathy fattened and rolled down Ilse's pillowy cheek.

The worry continued past lunchtime. She was so distracted on her cleaning duties that Fräulein Horder lost her temper and made Ilse scour all the wash basins and bathroom floors a second time. Coming down the back corridor with the buckets she was sure she caught a glimpse of a couple of unfamiliar men in overalls in the scullery, but when she dawdled past them a door was closed firmly in her face.

By two o'clock, news that the police had been called to the premises spread like wildfire, but there was still no word of what had happened to Anna. At two thirty Household Budgeting, the lesson Ilse detested most because it involved balancing all the Reichmarks she was going to spend with her husband's income and allowing for emergencies, was moved from the ballroom, which looked out on the back of the house, to the library whose windows gave onto the front. Staring unhappily into space, trying to work out how much sugar and flour a family of four would need to keep them a week and what fraction of Otto's monthly income that would cost, Ilse's eye fell on the dolls' house. It was a wonderful little thing, which had been made for visiting children to play with, but had been moved to the library to stop them playing too much. The man who crafted it had lavished his work with loving detail. The walls were papered with specially made National Socialist *Toile de Jouy*, featuring little Bund Deutscher Mädel girls skipping alongside Hitler Jugend boys, erecting tents and waving banners. The furniture was hand-carved oak, and the dining table set with plaster ham and bread. In the bedrooms a girl played with miniature dolls and a boy with bomber aircraft. In the sitting room the father smoked his pipe and listened to the wireless, a portrait of the Führer above the fireplace. In the kitchen, amid her pots and pans, a mother in a flowery apron rested from her ironing, with a microscopic cup of Kenco coffee. Why couldn't real life be like that? Ilse wondered, with a dear little house and a cupboard full of food and children playing tidily in their rooms? That was how it was meant to be, wasn't it?

It was as these thoughts were passing through her head that a commotion on the drive made everyone turn round. Ilse looked out to see a fast-moving huddle of men, in the midst of which was

Hartmann, the Bride School gardener, his bewildered face mouthing a cloud of words into the icy air. But no one was listening and as she watched, Hartmann's head was rammed brutally down as he was bundled by the policemen into a waiting car.

Chapter Four

Unter den Linden, like so many things in Germany now – the sludgy coffee that was padded out with chicory, the butter that was half whale blubber and the bratwurst that was full of bread – did not quite live up to its name. The Linden trees that had stood for hundreds of years had been cut down on Hitler's orders so that his troops could march along the main avenue twelve abreast and the spindly saplings that replaced them were dwarfed by lamp posts. The result was that Unter den Linden was now nicknamed Unter den Lanternen and Berliners grumbled that it would take decades for their glorious greenery to grow up tall again.

Clara threaded her way through the Mitte district of central Berlin as the last light leaked from the sky. She was pleased to walk. She needed the exercise after a day in the studio and, besides, it was a chance to think. Buttoned up in her trench coat, hair bundled beneath a felt hat, she walked all the way up to the Lustgarten, passed the gloomy, soot-stained Dom and crossed one of the little bridges over the Spree. The Spree was not the prettiest stretch of water, always crowded with barges and tow boats carrying coal and bricks, its walls all streaked with ash, but Berliners had a great affection for it. That evening the water's gun-metal grey was lit by sulphurous yellow lights that shimmered on the surface while the wind whipped leaves in jittery circles like Brown Shirts at a brawl. In winter, Clara thought, Berlin was a Braque painting; full of sharp lines and awkward perspectives coloured in an entire palette of greys and browns.

Making her way northwards, past the labyrinthine alleys of Hackescher Markt and up Orianenburger Strasse, she came to the Jewish quarter, where shops with spiky Hebrew lettering offered window displays jumbled with jewellery, stockings and electrical devices. There was a hurried bustle in this area, among the pharmacies and the clothing workshops. The people here looked shabbier, smells of frying food hung in the air. Narrow alleys, webbed with washing lines, led into dank courtyards where children played and old men in the long, black coats of the Ostjuden congregated. She passed a cigarette-stub seller, with his goods laid out on a battered tin tray beside him and a card offering three stubs for a pfennig or two pfennigs for a half-smoked cigar. Through an opened window she glimpsed a piano, on which a couple of girls in matching horn-rimmed glasses were performing a duet, but as she passed their mother hastened to draw the shutters, glancing anxiously at Clara as if piano playing was the latest pleasure to be outlawed in this part of Berlin.

The echo of last month's Party rally down in Nuremberg still resounded here in a rash of posters decorating the walls, warning that *'Every crime begins with the Jew'* and *'The Jews are our Misfortune.'* A hoarding attached to a shop front suggested in loud, red letters that all Germans should '*Unite against the Jewish Bolshevist World Enemy*'. Despite herself, Clara shuddered. The previous year, during the Olympics, there had been a brief hiatus when the streets billowed with green garlands and red ribbons all the way down from Brandenburg Gate to the Olympic stadium and loudspeakers everywhere dropped their regular propaganda broadcasts for updates of the sporting results. Goebbels had been obliged to choke down his hatred of the Jews for a few months and ordered the removal of the brown cabins, plastered in swastikas, from where the most vicious anti-Semitic paper, *Der Stürmer*, was sold on street corners. The posters with their crude caricatures of hooked-nosed Jews were torn down and authors like Marcel Proust and Heinrich Heine, whose books had been burned on the Opernplatz, were allowed on public shelves again. But now, a year later, things were back to normal, or rather the new normal of the Third Reich. There was no longer any ambiguity about the plans of the regime. Already the Nuremberg laws had stripped Jews of citizenship. No Jew might vote, hold office, practise medicine, teach Gentiles, marry or have sex with them. The fact that the Führer decided to devote his speech at the Party rally to the theme of Jewish Bolshevism was a sign that a fresh round of trouble was in store.

Clara turned into Koppenplatz. It was a pleasant, unremarkable square with a patch of grass, dotted with benches. She checked her watch – 7.30 p.m. – and looked around for Koch's café.

She had never been to this place before. All she knew was that a bouquet of yellow chrysanthemums had arrived at the studio earlier that day bearing the label of a florist with exactly this address and a Berlin telephone number ending 1930. There was no other message, but she didn't need one. Flowers were the preferred method of communication of Archie Dyson, attaché at the British Embassy and agent of the British Intelligence service, and she had received several bouquets from him over the past couple of years. It sounded romantic, but really it wasn't.

The fact that her every movement must be accountable was one of the first things that had been impressed on Clara when she began working for British Intelligence. She must have a perfectly innocent reason to be where she was, and she must assume she was watched every hour of the day. Wherever she went, there must be a perfectly rational explanation. More rational, of course, than supplying information to the enemies of the Nazi regime.

To this end, she walked with a purposeful pace and carried a newspaper in which she had circled the timings of *La Habanera* with Zarah Leander at a cinema just north of Rosenthalerplatz which she had absolutely no intention of seeing.

She pushed open the door, exchanging the haze of mist outside for a grainy fog of cigarette smoke.

To most eyes, Koch's café was a typical Berlin tavern, an ill-lit, low-ceilinged dive where men drank to get drunk, and sometimes accessorized their beer with a plate of sausage, bread and pickles. But due to the cooperation of Herr Felix Koch, a bull of a man in braces and collarless shirt who stood wiping the wooden bar, flicking a bored eye at his customers, the café was also safe. Herr Koch was considered entirely trustworthy, a trust that was cemented by the fact that his daughter had married an Englishman and lived in Brighton. It was entirely understandable, as an agent of British Intelligence had assured him, that he should be concerned for her well-being and Mimi Koch's happiness would be greatly enhanced if her father were on friendly terms with His Majesty's government. Despite this, Clara gave a quick instinctive scan of the room as she entered. There were only four other customers, two slumped over a window table, and a pair in factory uniforms, sinking foamy steins of beer.

Archie Dyson, Eton and Cambridge, in loden overcoat and silk scarf, was sitting at the back of the tavern behind a screen of fretted wood, trying to do the *Times* crossword, folded into a copy of that day's *BZ am Mittag*. Clara leaned over and saw him hovering over '*Break one's word, 9 letters*'.

'Hyphenate.'

Dyson started visibly and put the newspaper down. 'Goodness, Clara, I didn't see you coming. How did you learn to do that?'

'Someone taught me.'

'The crossword, I meant.'

'Oh that. I always enjoyed crosswords.'

She had discovered that as a child. The thrill when her brain, against all the odds, began to fizz, plucking words like 'crepuscular' and 'cruciverbalist' from its store of vocabulary with no problem. The way words flickered together in segments, then parted and repaired, whirring through split-second computations. She thought of Angela, legs thrown over the side of her armchair, frowning at the paper then tossing it towards her. *'Oh, you take it, Clara. Puzzles are more your thing'*, her tone implying that crosswords ranked somewhere between jigsaws and knitting in the realm of human endeavour. That was the way the Vines operated – compliments and insults were delivered in a sidelong fashion, never outright, because boasting about one's abilities was not done and showing excessive enthusiasm was seriously bad form. But Clara recognized that crosswords, like chess, were the kind of intellectual activity at which she could beat others fair and square.

'I'm a little rusty, I suppose,' said Dyson, quickly folding the paper away. The attaché to the British ambassador was a patrician figure with a narrow moustache who couldn't have looked more English if he had been wearing a bowler hat and carrying an umbrella. Everything about him reminded Clara of England, of limp cucumber sandwiches, Twinings tea and cocker spaniels with damp fur. In another life Dyson would have been the secretary of a golf club, or a city stockbroker. He seemed entirely unsuited to subterfuge. That was obviously the point, Clara realized. Dyson is not at all what you expect. None of us are.

'Summer's over.' Dyson always started with the weather. It was engrained deeply within him, as instinctive as walking on the outer side of the pavement or saying the Lord's Prayer. It was the conversational equivalent of clearing his throat.

Clara slipped off her trench coat, noting that Dyson's tan had intensified and there were small patches of pink on his nose where the skin had peeled.

'And I'm guessing you went sailing again?'

'Spot on. I just got back. A little trip with my wife on a friend's yacht in the Med. Very pleasant.'

Although Dyson spoke in his usual languid, upper-class drawl, Clara deduced from his heavily bitten nails that he was suffering from a certain amount of inner stress. He paused as Herr Koch brought over a glass of beer.

'Und eine Berliner Weisse mit Schuss, bitte.'

This drink was a local favourite, made by adding a shot of raspberry syrup to mask the acidity of the pale, golden Berlin beer. Dyson always ordered it for Clara, presumably thinking a dash of sweetness was what women liked, and Clara had never had the heart to contradict him.

She knew Dyson felt infinitely more at home drinking a gin fizz in some glittering hotel in Berlin's west end than in this scruffy bar. But given the nature of their meetings, Dyson had been obliged to familiarize himself with different, and quite unexpected, places around town.

Dyson waited until Koch had moved away and addressed Clara in English.

'So how are you, Clara? Any news for me?'

'Yes, as it happens. Magda Goebbels has asked me to a party. It's in honour of the Mitford sisters. You know of them, I suppose?'

'Of course. The daughters of Lord Redesdale. One of them, Unity, is obsessively in love with the Führer by all accounts. She's moved to Munich and installs herself in his favourite restaurant whenever he's in town.'

'I heard she said that sitting next to the Führer was like basking in dazzling sunshine,' said Clara.

He snorted. 'Presumably with the odd thunderstorm thrown in.'

'There's another sister here too. Diana.'

'Indeed. Given that she's married to Oswald Mosley we do keep an eye, as you can imagine.'

Clara took a sugary sip of her beer. 'Magda wants to introduce them to some of her friends, but she's worried their German isn't up to it, so she's asked me to translate.'

'It's not the first time Diana's visited Berlin this year,' said Dyson. 'She's already been over to talk to Hitler about constructing an English-speaking radio station on German soil in Heligoland.'

'A radio station?' Clara was baffled.

'A commercial station. To raise funds for the fascists. We've got a chap in the British Union of Fascists who's very helpful about their plans. The idea is, Hitler should subsidize it and the whole enterprise will assist Mosley's movement by broadcasting fascist propaganda to southern England. Diana has had several private late-night meetings at the Chancellery already, and apparently he's invited her to Bayreuth.'

'I'll pass on whatever I hear,' said Clara.

'Yeees . . .' The door banged, bringing with it a gust of chill wind, and Dyson fell silent as he assessed the raddled figure in a worn overcoat making his way to the bar. 'It's appreciated, Clara, though—'

'Though what?'

'I suspect the Mosleys are a bit of a busted flush now.'

'Why's that?'

'We're hearing that Goebbels in particular is annoyed at the amount of money they're asking for. He'll be suggesting to Hitler that they're spoiled goods. He knows that any political influence they had at home is rapidly dwindling. But he'll do it subtly, because he realizes how much the Leader likes young English maidens. Unity is the only foreign woman allowed in his inner circle.'

Dyson tapped out a cigarette and offered one to Clara.

'And the fact is we've got some rather more important visitors on our agenda.' He paused. 'Well, I say more important, but in another way, they're not important at all.'

'I'm not that good at puzzles, Archie.'

Dyson cupped his chin and fanned his fingers out, masking his mouth, a gesture, Clara noticed, that was instinctive to him. He hesitated, she was sure for effect.

'It's a little bridal party. The ex-king and his wife are about to arrive here on honeymoon.'

Clara could not suppress a gasp of astonishment. Edward VIII, the Duke of Windsor as he now was, had abdicated the previous December to marry an American divorcée, Wallis Simpson, in a scandal which had blazed around the world. The couple settled in France and their wedding in June had been covered obsessively in all the magazines. Like everyone else, Clara drank in the details and pored over the photographs. The Duchess, slender as a reed in her box-shouldered Mainbocher dress – in a shade now rechristened Duchess Blue in her honour – reclining with her husband against the balcony of the Château de Cande. Sapphires and diamonds at her throat, her hair violet black with an inky shimmer. Wedding photographs by Cecil Beaton. Roses and lilies by Constance Spry. For the wedding breakfast they ate lobster, salad, strawberries and, with a certain poignancy, chicken à la king.

'They're coming here? Why on earth?'

Though she asked, she knew the answer. The Duke's mother was German, he spoke the language fluently, and his past comments suggested a robust admiration for the Nazi regime.

'You may well ask. The Foreign Office is absolutely hopping. The whole thing has been arranged behind their back by the Germans. It's a massive propaganda coup for the Reich. They're going to make enormous capital out of it and it's going to be terrifically embarrassing for Britain. They arrive at Friedrichstrasse Station on the sixteenth. The ambassador has been ordered not to attend.'

'Ordered?'

'Prime Minister's orders. They're not to be treated as having any official status. No official interviews, no special ceremonies. Not so much as a gin and tonic and a cocktail onion at the Embassy. The Government don't want anyone getting the idea that this is any kind of official visit, rather than an entirely private occasion. The result being that yours truly has been deputed to greet them.'

Though he affected a jaded weariness, Clara could see that Dyson rather liked the idea of meeting the former king.

'Not that we'll be rolling out the red carpet, exactly. I'm sure the Nazi top brass will be doing that for them. Apparently Robert Ley, head of the Labour front, will be there. The Reich is paying for the entire thing. The fact is, the couple are going to be mobbed wherever they go.'

'Where will they go?'

'It's a nine-city tour. And the American press are reporting that the Duke wants to discuss "Hitler's hopes for the future".'

'Let's hope the Duke's a good listener.'

Dyson rolled his eyes.

'Precisely. He doesn't know what he's in for. The plan is that the Duke should inspect working conditions throughout the Reich. Factory visits and so on.'

'Wouldn't be my idea of a honeymoon,' said Clara, casually.

For some reason this remark caused Dyson to fix his gaze more intently upon her. She was a curiosity to him, she knew. Her presence seemed to make him uneasy, as though he was unsure whether to treat her as an employee or a social equal. She was different from the women he knew back home, neither one of those upper-middle-class girls waiting to get married, nor a determinedly spinster secretary or a bluestocking. She was nothing like Lettice, Dyson's wife, a brisk redhead who spent her time organizing cultural outings with the other Embassy wives, serving coffee and shortbread biscuits to visiting dignitaries, and who fully intended her husband to be an ambassador himself one day.

Clara had love affairs, Dyson knew, yet she had shown no desire to marry. Her sharp brain, as evidenced by her facility with crosswords and her formidable memory, were traits that the Service treasured in their agents. Her looks, social confidence and acting talent gave her access to circles that would otherwise be hard to penetrate. Yet it was her willingness to place herself in danger that he found hardest to fathom. Dyson simply couldn't work her out.

'Do you ever think about leaving, Clara? Going back to England?'

What could she say? Only last week she had received a letter from an old schoolfriend, Ida MacCloud, expressing astonishment that Clara was willing to stay in Germany while the Nazi regime gathered pace. Wasn't she by staying there in some way tacitly supporting what they did? Ida asked. How could Clara justify that?

'Occasionally.'

'You must miss your family.'

She gave him a narrow look. Dyson knew, as did everyone in the Berlin station, that Clara's father, Sir Ronald Vine, was a key member of London's Anglo-German Fellowship and a strong Nazi sympathizer. His coterie was rich, influential and determined that Britain should place itself in alliance with rather than opposition to Hitler's Germany. Sir Ronald himself had received funding from Hitler for his political lobbying. Clara's shock in discovering her father's activities and the fact that he was being shadowed by domestic security in England had been part of her motivation in approaching British Intelligence four years earlier. It was important that the security service chiefs felt they understood Clara's motivation. They needed to be able to trust her. Yet she saw no reason to confide in Dyson the Jewish part of her background.

'As it happens I had a letter from my sister yesterday saying that she and my father are coming to visit. Though you probably knew that already.'

Dyson gave a little smile.

'So you did know.'

'I imagine the German authorities know too.'

'Why are they coming over then, Archie?'

'I may be many things, but I'm not a clairvoyant, Clara. Ask them yourself. That's not why I asked you about going home.'

'Why then?'

Dyson fiddled with his glass for a moment, as if weighing his words. The hesitation made Clara's heart pound. Something had happened. She forced herself to wait for him to explain.

'Actually, it's what I wanted to talk to you about. It might be nothing.'

Dyson's mouth twisted unhappily, reluctant to impart the news. It may be nothing, but Clara knew from the gravity of his expression that it almost certainly wasn't. She kept her face composed, despite the small detonations of panic inside her.

'We had a hint that you might have aroused suspicions. I just wanted to say . . . don't do anything out of the ordinary. Tread carefully.'

'I always do. Where did this hint come from?'

'A friend. He let us know that in the past couple of days your name had come up in conversation.'

'Whose conversation? Where?'

'At Prinz Albrecht Strasse.'

Though Dyson uttered it without flinching, this address more than any other had the power to strike terror into a citizen of Berlin. The blank Prussian façade of the former Arts museum at Prinz Albrecht Strasse 8 gave no clue to the horrors within. Since 1933 it had been the headquarters of the Geheime Staatspolizei, the Gestapo, who had the power, without the intervention of the courts, to arrest, interrogate and send prisoners to SS concentration camps like Dachau, Sachsenhausen, Buchenwald and Lichtenburg. Beyond its austere, vaulted entrance hall hundreds of bureaucrats spent their days combing files and reports on citizens.

Beneath them, in the basement, lay the interrogation rooms, a warren of white-tiled cells where information could be extracted in a more direct manner. Once you arrived in Prinz Albrecht Strasse, no amount of acting talent could save you from what they had in store.

A wave of fright hit her, like a blast of icy air. Deliberately she hesitated, taking out a cigarette, fixing it in a holder and inhaling.

'Who exactly is this friend?' He had to be either a policeman or a Gestapo member if he had access to Prinz Albrecht Strasse.

'He works for them. He says an informer passed on your name.'

An informer. That could be anyone. All Gestapo agents had their own network of informers, fanning out through every layer of society like a malign web enmeshing anyone who crossed its path. The service depended on them heavily for denunciations of suspect or illegal activity. They were not always the obvious candidates. An informer could be a quiet neighbour, or a friendly butcher. Postmen, shop owners, even children. Anyone with a secret to keep or who might be susceptible to blackmail. In one way or another the Gestapo viewed the whole population as an amateur police force to assist in enforcing control. The idea was that nothing should escape the Gestapo's net.

Dyson was uttering calming words, like a doctor who had just delivered terminal news.

'Look, we're not worried. Nobody has talked about an arrest order. You speak German like a native. In their eyes you're no different from an actress like Lilian Harvey – she was born in Muswell Hill, wasn't she? And, most importantly, they know your father . . .'

They knew her father. It seemed incredible that the same nepotistic class structure which had governed Britain for hundreds of years might also hold sway among the Gestapo agents of Nazi Germany.

'And you take routine precautions?' Dyson was saying. 'You

don't talk on the phone? You vary your routine, you write nothing down. Don't drink in doubtful company.'

'I take precautions, Archie.'

'Fine. It may be nothing. But I would say you're almost certainly being tailed. So I wanted to warn you to keep your guard up. And more importantly still, to lie low.'

Lie low?

'So should I attend the Goebbels' party?'

'You'll have to go because you've been invited, and not to turn up might attract attention. But don't do anything more at the moment. Do nothing. Enjoy your filming.'

'There's a break in filming. I've finished my last film and we don't start rehearsals for another few weeks.'

'Enjoy your break then. Remember what I said.'

While Dyson got up and went over to the bar to pay the bill and engage in some finely judged conversation with Herr Koch, Clara drank the syrupy remnants of her Weisse and tried to collect her teeming thoughts. An informer had passed her name to the Gestapo. Who could it be? A lowly staffer at the studios, perhaps, or someone closer to home? How bizarre it was that just as she had received an invitation to the Propaganda Minister's home, another part of the regime was thinking of inviting her to Prinz Albrecht Strasse. Clara's previous sense of security, the confidence that had grown and developed over her time in Berlin, was badly rocked. She felt the clench in her stomach that always came with anxiety, like a tight belt squeezed around her middle. She scanned the bar quickly, as though the informer might be watching her right now, but saw only the regular customers, slumped at their Stammtisches, their regular tables, growling in Berlinerische, the thick local dialect, and Archie telling Fritz Koch about the delights of Brighton Pier.

Lie low, Archie said. *Do nothing.*

Dyson returned and picked his hat up from the table.

'On the subject of breaks, Fritz is talking about taking a holiday in Brighton, going over to see his daughter. I told him it's restorative at this time of year. Sea air can be very bracing. My sailing hol was immensely good fun. If I were you, Clara, I'd give it some thought.'

Chapter Five

Photography was the ultimate art of the Reich. Joseph Goebbels said if you told a lie big enough for long enough people would believe it, so he must have reckoned if you showed them enough pictures they would believe those even more. Because whatever the occasion, be it a quiet lunch on Hitler's terrace at the Berghof, a military march, a rally, or even a routine health and fitness session with a hundred fresh-faced BDM girls in the park, a camera would be right there too. Several cameras usually, straining against the official cordons, unleashing a dazzling fusillade of flash. All kinds of cameras: cumbersome official equipment with tripods and lights, or the Speed Graphics which the press men used, or the new roll film cameras from Leica and Zeiss. These days in the Reich there was always a lens poised to capture a fleeting image. To smooth rough reality with a soft focus and a monochrome glow. To fix the whole of Germany, like a film actress, in a glamorous quicksilver glare.

That bright Thursday morning Goebbels was posing by the monumental gates of the Ufa film studios for a newspaper feature in honour of his approaching fortieth birthday. He had ordered the photographer to shoot from street level, ostensibly to include the whole of the overarching gates in his picture, but actually so that his five-foot-four frame with its withered foot should seem as imposing as possible.

'He's very particular about the way he's photographed, isn't he?'

'Wouldn't you be? If he had more sense he'd keep out of shot altogether.'

Clara was gazing from the window of a production office in the Babelsberg studio lot, a sprawling assembly of halls and editing rooms and carpenters' warehouses and sets tucked in the thick pine woods outside Potsdam, ten miles from Berlin. The office belonged to Albert Lindemann, an executive producer she had known since her first week in Germany. Back then Albert had been a harried junior producer, with sparse hair and even sparser promotion prospects. Now he was a sleek and powerful man, his wiry form encased in a silk shirt and purple bowtie with cream suede shoes stretched out before him on the desk. Since the Aryanization, when anyone of Jewish extraction was barred from working in the Ufa studios, Albert's career had flourished. He had been given increasingly important projects to produce. He had a flashy new car and an apartment in Schöneberg which was dripping with chrome furniture, blond wood, big mirrors and thick white carpets. Albert loved gossip, possessed an acid humour and a highly developed sense of the absurd. He had no interest in women whatsoever, yet he was never seen out without a young actress on his arm. Much as she might want to, Clara refrained from asking questions about Albert's private life. It was safer that way. Except for casual badinage about Nazi officials, they avoided politics. When news came that an actor had disappeared from the studios, as often happened, or a director had been taken for interrogation, their eyes would meet, but they rarely discussed it. Just that week, an actress both had worked with, Gisela Wessel, had been arrested for 'organized activities and Communist demoralization' and taken in for questioning. Albert had merely raised his eyebrows and murmured, 'Gisela's gone.' He didn't need to say any more. He was the closest thing Clara had to a friend in Berlin and they understood each other perfectly.

'Thanks for lending me the car.'

It was Albert who had taught her to drive the year before, sitting beside her nervously as she swerved her way around the streets of Berlin, cursing theatrically as she slammed on the brakes, relaxing only when they reached the empty vistas of autobahn stretching into the countryside. She passed him the keys but he waved them away.

'Keep it for a while, darling. I'm not using it at the moment and your life is so much more glamorous than my own. I imagine a car comes in handy.'

Albert always tried to balance his raging appetite for gossip with the discretion that politics demanded. On the subject of Clara's encounters with the Goebbels, he accepted that the less he knew the better.

'I just hope your trip to Schwanenwerder was successful.'

'I don't know about successful. It was interesting.'

Albert stretched out and helped himself to a bottle of schnapps which rested in the bottom drawer of his desk. He knew Clara far too well to worry about drinking in front of her, though she noticed that the bottle had taken quite a hit since she last saw it. Everyone had their own ways of coping with the atmosphere at the studios. Albert took a deep swig and surveyed her, his eyes crinkled in concern.

'You seem a bit jumpy this morning, darling. And rather pale. Not in any kind of trouble, are you?'

'Trouble?' Clara gave a light laugh. 'Quite the opposite. I'm getting plenty of work, aren't I?'

It was true. Clara had been in almost continuous demand since her arrival in Germany. The advent of the talkies meant actors were discovering that their voices mattered just as much as their looks. Some stars dropped out of fashion overnight, because their voices were too high, or their accents too comical. Others complained that they couldn't party at night any more, because of all the lines they had to learn. Clara's first film, *Black Roses*, had been one of the innovative, tri-lingual talkies shot in German, French and English, but that experiment didn't last long. Foreigners lost their appetite for the films being shot in the new Germany. Especially now that war films, starring brave German soldiers ready to die for their country, dominated the screens.

Albert abandoned attempts to probe her mood. 'Did you hear our Master's latest theory?' He waved the latest issue of *Filmwoche*, compulsory reading for everyone in the industry, which contained a lavish profile of Goebbels. 'He says in here that the ideal woman should be composed of the three Ms – the Mother, the Madonna and the Mistress.'

'I thought he preferred to keep them separate.'

'So did I. But if what I'm hearing about Lída Baarová is true, he's thinking she might like to combine two roles.'

Lída Baarová was Goebbels' latest girlfriend. A sultry Czech actress with stunning Slavic cheekbones, she had been propelled to stardom by her devoted admirer. Her new film, *Patriots*, about a brave German soldier befriended by a French girl, was to be the subject of a lavish premiere later that month at the city's plushest cinema, the Ufa Palast am Zoo.

'So it's serious this time?'

'He's really smitten. Obsessed. He vets all her leading men. I've heard he makes her leave her phone line open so that when he's at his desk he can pick up the earpiece just to hear her breathing.'

'Her breathing!'

'Romantic, isn't it? Or perhaps he wants to hear if she's packing her bags for Hollywood like everyone else. They say he's so desperate to keep her he's going to ask Magda for a divorce.'

'I thought Lída was already married.'

'What's marriage? A piece of paper. Goebbels is good at fixing paperwork.'

Clara moved away from the window. Even though he was a

hundred metres away at the studio gate, she had the sudden feeling that Goebbels might have eyes in the back of his head. Albert laughed.

'You don't need to worry, darling. You're obviously doing something right. Looking forward to your first title role?'

The part in the new film, *The Pilot's Bride*, was technically Clara's first major role. She was playing Gretchen, the young wife of a Luftwaffe flying ace, known for his heroics in the sky, until he was tragically shot down. The story was a simple one. Gretchen alone refused to believe her husband was dead and daringly, she learned to fly so that she could seek him out and bring him home. Evading enemy guns she landed on hostile territory and found her husband injured but alive. So far, so standard. Brave Luffwaffe, long-suffering heroine, happy ending. There were any number of films that like being made right now, but this one would be a sure-fire, cast-iron, guaranteed success. Because of Ernst Udet.

She smiled. 'We all know who the real star is.'

She moved over to Albert's desk and flipped through a stack of postcards featuring Udet's beaming figure in a variety of poses. Udet was a born celebrity. During his time in Hollywood, he liked to perform his stunts in a full dress suit and top hat. One of his favourites was to fly at zero height scooping objects from the ground. The press had been ecstatic when he won a bet with Mary Pickford to pick her handkerchief off the grass with his wing tip as he flew past.

'The sad thing is, this is his last part,' said Albert. 'They say the Führer's banning him from filming or performing any more stunts.'

'I thought his film work was supposed to be great propaganda for aviation?'

Udet's last film, *The Miracle of Flight*, the story of a boy who wanted to be a pilot, had been box-office gold.

'It is. But now he's too important to the Luftwaffe. They can't risk anything happening to him. He's so miserable about it I heard he's talking about going to America.'

'Does he not like his job?'

'Hates it. He's a real duck out of water. He sits at his desk all day doodling and making paper aeroplanes.'

Goering was so determined that his old war colleague should be at the forefront of the Luftwaffe's rapid expansion he had made Udet head of the entire Technical Division of the Luftwaffe, responsible for the development of all fighter and bomber planes and other specialized aircraft. Udet's trouble was, he hated paperwork and Party politics as much as he loved women, alcohol and planes. Nor did the public seem to understand that he was now a dignified Party bureaucrat because they persisted in begging him for autographs whenever he walked down the street. The studio was making the most of Udet's celebrity status. That morning he was due to sign a number of promotional postcards and posters for the forthcoming film.

The phone rang. Albert picked it up and semaphored to Clara.

'That's it. He's arrived. Want to come and meet your screen husband?'

They hurried through the offices and took a short cut through the Great Hall where all the filming took place. It was the size of an aircraft hangar and housed a dozen sets crammed in back to back, preparing a dozen different versions of reality to distract the German public from military manoeuvres and butter shortages. Skirting the tattered backs of the sets, behind the wooden props, they passed a group of bishops chatting to some men in powdered wigs and lace cravats. Ropes and electrical cables snaked over the floor. A director complained about the sound of drilling and shouted '*Ruhe!*' for silence. They exited the other end of the hall and crossed the lot to a redbrick reception office where a robust figure in his early forties stood, wearing a slate-grey Luftwaffe uniform which emphasized his dazzling blue eyes.

'Herr Generaloberst, may I introduce Clara Vine?'

Udet had a smile hovering around his lips as though engaged in an elaborate practical joke. He clicked his heels and kissed Clara's hand with old-fashioned courtesy.

'My sweetheart. On film at least. And, may I say, an excellent choice.'

'We're delighted you could make time for this, Herr Generaloberst,' said Albert, obsequiously.

'I'm delighted too, let me tell you,' he said, winking at Clara. 'I nearly didn't make it. I had an accident the other day. The plane was a complete shit crate. I escaped, but another inch and I'd have been singing soprano.'

Behind Udet Clara saw a pair of secretaries stop and signal to each other, covering their mouths and giggling. Those girls saw famous actors every day of the week, so if they went weak at the knees over Udet, he had to be a big star. Everything Clara had heard about Udet's charisma and the easy-going jollity that prompted people to besiege him in the street seemed true. She warmed to him instantly.

'Ever done any flying?' he asked Clara.

'I'm afraid not. But I saw your Olympics display last year.'

Like everything he had a hand in, Hermann Goering's Olympics gala for seven hundred guests at his Leipziger Platz home could not be called understated. A swimming pool had been built in the garden, complete with swans. There was a miniature French village, a carnival, shooting galleries and a merry-go-round. An entire *corps de ballet* was brought in to dance on the moonlit grass, while above them Udet's plane had performed a series of gliding acrobatics, swooping and circling in the sky.

Udet beamed. 'You enjoyed that, did you?'

'It was the most amazing stunt I've ever seen.' It was the truth. The sight of the plane curving down in the night sky, twisting through beams of light with balletic swoops, had transfixed her.

'I'll arrange a flight for you, if you like.'

'Oh, I don't know . . .'

'You'll love it! It'll help you get into character. Isn't that what you actresses say?'

'In that case, it's very kind of you.'

'Leave it with me. I'll see what I can do.'

Albert gestured to the pile of promotional material he was carrying.

'We were wondering, Herr Generaloberst,' he said unctuously, 'if you could spare the time, whether you could come to my office and sign some of these?'

'And,' Clara intervened, 'may I ask you for an autograph for a young admirer? He's a friend of mine called Erich. He's seen you fly and he wants to join the Luftwaffe when he's old enough.'

Udet peeled off a postcard from the top of Albert's stack. It was a shot of himself standing next to a Ju 87 Stuka dive bomber, wearing his cap at a jaunty angle. With a flourish he scrawled on the back,

'To Erich! Best wishes, Ernst Udet!'

Then he took another postcard, wrote on it, and handed it to Clara with a mock bow. She read:

'*Fräulein Clara Vine is invited to a party at Pommerschestrasse 4, Berlin-Wilmersdorf. 18th October, 8 p.m.*'

'I hope you can come and meet some of my friends. We should get to know each other, considering you are going to be my bride. Bring Herr Lindemann with you. But be warned, I make a pretty formidable cocktail.'

Chapter Six

A sharp breeze corrugated the surface of the Wannsee, setting the water dancing and nudging the boats against their moorings. Until a few years ago these boats had names like Edda or Ute or Gretel on their bows, but these names had now been painted over and replaced with grander, National Socialist aspirations like Courage or Victory or Endurance. Clara turned away from the view and shivered. It might have been the chill breeze blowing through the opened French windows of the Goebbels' drawing room, but more likely it was the company that was gathered around her.

The furniture had been cleared to make way for a crowd of women in bright sheath dresses, the glint of their jewellery competing with the gleam of silver death's heads on black SS dress uniforms. As always, it was an unnerving experience being in close proximity to a bunch of SS officers. The bark of German conversation was interspersed with the familiar bray of the English upper classes, but so far no one had taken up the offer of Clara's translation. The Germans pretended they already understood, and the English assumed that speaking their own tongue both louder and slower would make them perfectly comprehensible.

'It's a lovely spot, you have here, Frau Doktor,' said one. 'I hear the Führer sometimes prefers Schwanenwerder to Berchtesgaden.'

'Nothing could be better than Berchtesgaden!' interceded a

gawky Englishwoman with a straw-coloured bob. 'Berchtesgaden is the nearest you can get to heaven.'

Unity Valkyrie Mitford had a stolid, impassive look, which reminded Clara of the stone women on the theatre façade on Nollendorfplatz. Her face with its high, plucked eyebrows, was like a blank pool into which you longed to throw a pebble. The girl who had asked a German newspaper to let everyone know she was a 'Jew-hater' had a sullen air, like a cow that has been thwarted at a gate. Though she was only twenty-three, she had left England and relocated to Germany to be as close to Hitler as possible, basing herself in Munich and hoping each day for an invitation from the Führer to lunch, or the opera, or just to take tea at his apartment. Occasionally she was asked to make speeches or write newspaper articles, in which event she would turn out a tirade against the Jews as dull and plodding as a twelve-year-old schoolgirl's essay.

Unity's awkward woodenness only served to emphasize the beauty of her sister Diana, who was four years older, smaller by a head and exquisitely dressed in cream Dior, with milky blonde hair and eyes of bright, hostile blue. The two had the same broad brow and high cheekbones, but the features which produced Diana's loveliness were cast more coarsely in Unity. Looking at the two sisters together made one wonder how birth could fashion such different outcomes from identical raw materials. The same thought must have occurred to Heinrich Hoffmann, Hitler's personal photographer, who was circling the guests with surprising nimbleness armed with a Leica.

'Don't mind me. Please don't let me disturb you!'

Hoffmann was a dapper character with the practised charm and ingratiating smile of the professional hotel manager. His hair was slicked with pungent pomade and a silk handkerchief bloomed extravagantly from his top pocket. The fact that he had for many years been the only photographer permitted to take official portraits of the Führer meant he was the VIP photographer of choice at gatherings of senior party figures. That evening he had abandoned lights and tripod in favour of a handheld camera, but his efforts to remain unobtrusive were quite unnecessary because the Mitfords ignored him entirely. Being photographed was, for them, entirely routine.

'The Berghof is terrifically homely,' agreed Diana, who had just returned from a break at the Führer's hideaway in the Bavarian Alps. 'The view is glorious, though it is just the teensiest bit like staying in a bed and breakfast in Bournemouth. The cushions have little slogans embroidered on them, can you believe?' She had a sharp, tinkling laugh, like a champagne glass being smashed. 'There was even one that said, *The German Woman is knitting again!* And the cushion was knitted itself! Isn't that funny! If there hadn't been so many great big guards around I would have popped it in my bag and taken it home.'

'That's a terrible thing to suggest,' objected Unity humourlessly. 'Guests wanting souvenirs from the Berghof are a frightful problem for him, poor Führer, but he can hardly say anything. His spoons get stolen by everyone. Even the brushes and nail files from the bathroom. Just because they're engraved with his initials.'

'Perhaps he should be more careful with his guests then,' concluded Diana brightly. 'I must say, some of those women at dinner the other night seemed of doubtful origin. And not much to look at either. I don't know how the darling Führer can stand to look at them. Figures like the Hindenburg, didn't you think?'

Diana's body by comparison was as fine and delicate as a whippet's. In profile her face had a freakish perfection, like a Greek goddess. Beside her Magda Goebbels, in a white dress and striped cardigan, an ashy film of powder on her face, looked stout, her ankles swollen. The sisters began talking to Hoffmann's daughter Henny, a vivacious girl who they knew from Munich, as her father took another photograph. Henny spoke in a low, gossipy whisper.

'You were lucky to be sitting with the Führer at the Berghof. I was stuck next to Herr Bormann. He was boring on about his grand plans for matrimony in the Reich. He wants to institute mass weddings with fifty couples getting married at the same time. Can you imagine anything worse?'

'I think it would be rather a hoot,' said Diana. 'Just think of all the brides' mothers, competing in pastels.'

Clara wondered if Archie Dyson was right in his assessment of the Mitford sisters as a busted flush. They seemed to her to occupy an extraordinary place in the Nazi hierarchy. They were respected guests of Hitler, privy to intimate conversations among the top brass at his Bavarian retreat. They listened first-hand to the Führer's plans for Europe's future and in turn fed him a vision of England that was eccentric in the extreme. Contemplating this, she sensed Diana's clever eyes travel over her, as if reading her thoughts.

'Clara! How lovely to find you here. I haven't seen you for too long. How's your divine sister Angela?'

Diana knew Angela, but was closer to Angela's new husband Gerald, a stolid barrister who had political ambitions and, in Clara's eyes, absolutely no redeeming features. Gerald had flirted with joining Mosley's British Union of Fascists, though in the end he had opted for the Conservative Party as a safer bet.

'Angela's very well, thank you. She's coming over soon.'

'Frightfully good fun, your sister is. It's a shame she couldn't have come in time for the rally. It was terrifically impressive. Did you make it down to Nuremberg?'

'Not this year, I'm afraid.'

So far, Clara had managed to avoid attending any of the Party rallies, though she guessed sooner or later she might have to accept an invitation. The talking point of that year's Party congress in Nuremberg had been the 'Cathedral of Light' designed by Albert Speer, in which a hundred and fifty searchlights reached up into the night sky, like the pillars of a holy building.

'It was awfully naughty of you to miss it, Clara,' butted in Unity. 'It was just the best Parteitag ever. The Führer was thrilled with it. I can't believe you've never been. All the rallies and the marches are absolute heaven and the Hitler Youth boys look like angels.'

Clara laughed lightly. 'There are plenty of marches in Berlin to be going on with.'

'Maybe. But I think it's a crime to miss it. You've never seen so many people all in one place. It culminates in the procession of the Blood Flag – that's the flag held by the young Nazi struck down in the Putsch – and all the other flags are consecrated by touching the Blood Flag. It's the most sacred moment. You can't really describe it. You have to see it for yourself. It's monumental.'

'Not as monumental as the Herr Doktor's speech,' teased Diana. 'Fifty pages on the evils of Bolshevism!'

Magda laughed uneasily at this joke at her husband's expense, but any further embarrassment was prevented by the entrance of three tiny Goebbels children, five-year-old Helga, three-year-old Hilde and two-year-old Helmut, who were ushered in to dance to a tinkling piece of Strauss on a music box. The girls, in white pin-tucked party dresses and ankle socks, shepherded the toddler Helmut between them around the floor. The adults gazed on their performance in silence, then broke into a ripple of applause as the children ended with tiny Heil Hitler salutes and posed obediently for Hoffmann to take photographs. The solemnity was broken when Hilde kicked up her leg and said, 'Look! I have new shoes!' prompting a ripple of benevolent laughter.

'Heini Hoffmann,' hissed a voice in Clara's ear. 'The Führer's own photographer. We are honoured.'

Clara turned to see Annelies von Ribbentrop, wife of Germany's Ambassador to the Court of St James. The Ribbentrops, it was said, were returning to Germany, with hopes that he would be made Foreign Minister. Holding her cigarette to one side she proffered Clara her cheek for an air kiss.

'Frau von Ribbentrop. You're back from Britain!'

'At last. Though I don't know for how long.'

Annelies von Ribbentrop's square face was framed by dark hair, severely disciplined in tight braids, and her formidable form was upholstered in a type of bottle-green woollen jacket which suggested hunting, though without any of the fresh air or exercise that went with it.

She sniffed. 'I do admire you British for coping with such dreadful weather. The damp affects me badly, I'm afraid. I'm sensitive to atmospheric depressions.'

It had to be the only sensitive thing about her, Clara thought.

'But how are *you*?'

The force with which Frau von Ribbentrop enquired into Clara's well-being was always in inverse proportion to her actual interest.

'Very well, thank you.'

'Your father threw a delightful dinner for us in London.' Clara had heard about this occasion. The Anglo-German Fellowship had booked the Grosvenor House Hotel ballroom for a dinner to honour Hitler's ambassador. 'They had all the tables decorated with swastikas. So touching. You must thank him for us. He's a wonderful man. Though I must say it's a relief to be back in Berlin.' Her eyes flickered round the assembled company. 'I've been catching up on all the goings-on. What unexpected joy for Frau Goering! I suppose you heard the news?'

Everyone in Germany had heard the news. Emmy Goering, at the ripe age of forty-one, had become pregnant with her first child. The event was considered a near miracle. Many people believed the baby could not possibly have been fathered by the Reich Minister who was said to be impotent, either from his morphine use or his war wounds or his enormous bulk. The whole country was gossiping. Everyone had their own favourite joke about it and the nightclub artiste Werner Fincke had been arrested for telling his.

'Such wonderful news,' said Clara, neutrally.

Outside, there was the scatter of gravel on the drive and the purr of an engine. Clara looked out to see a figure jump out of a gleaming, low-slung Bugatti. Then the front door closed and a minute later the late guest appeared. He was a tall, sandy-haired man in his forties wearing the expression of someone who has left a casino to attend a meeting of the parish council.

'Sorry I'm late,' he said in English.

'Goodness, Ralph,' said Diana, plucking imperiously at his sleeve. 'That hat makes you look like a Jewish bookmaker. Do come in. It's very naughty of you to keep us waiting.'

As the maid took his hat and coat and Magda drew him aside, his gaze lingered fractionally on Clara, though no one thought to introduce them.

Clara was finding it hard to focus on the party. For the past two days Archie Dyson's words had rung in her head.

'We had a hint you might have aroused suspicions.'

His remark had affected her more deeply than she expected. She knew – she had known for years – that she would be under observation. Someone like her, who was half English, mixing with the Nazi élite, couldn't hope to go unremarked. She was ready for it. She had always been prepared to accept the consequences of what she did. Yet the absolute confirmation that she was being watched produced a continuous, dull tension which knotted her stomach and dragged her mind relentlessly through the same questions. Again and again she had run through her acquaintances, trying to work out which of them might have confided their suspicions about her to the occupants of Prinz Albrecht Strasse. But she could think of nothing she had done recently which was out of the ordinary. No revealing conversations which might have been overheard, no meetings with anyone hostile to the regime.

At that moment, standing amid the crowd, she detected a scent that brought her attention sharply back to the present. An astringent citrus fragrance. Scherk's Tarr aftershave.

'Fräulein Vine. What a pleasant surprise.'

No matter how often she saw him from afar at the studios, hurrying along the studio corridors with his jerky crippled gait, an actual encounter with Joseph Goebbels, arch persecutor of the Jews and the man charged by Hitler with responsibility for 'the spiritual direction of the nation', still made Clara shudder. His skin was stretched tightly over a pinched, clever face and his shrunken frame dared you to look down at his deformed foot. His smile was as dazzling and intermittent as a prison searchlight and he crackled with nervous energy. Tonight he was dapper as usual, wearing a well-cut light serge suit and navy tie. He dipped his head swiftly and kissed Clara's hand, then took out a cigarette case and offered her one.

'I saw you at Babelsberg the other day, I think. With Generaloberst Udet?'

'He's starring in our new film. He's agreed to perform a stunt.'

'Has he? I saw him in *The Miracle of Flight*. A miracle he was able to make the flight, was what I heard.'

It didn't surprise Clara that Goebbels should be fully briefed on Udet's love of alcohol. It was his job to know the weaknesses and peccadillos of all senior Nazis. No doubt the Gestapo too had a stack of notes filed away in the great bank of files that they kept in Prinz Albrecht Strasse, ready to use against Udet should the moment arise.

Clara smiled politely. 'Actually, I'm hoping he will let me fly with him.'

'Then you're a braver person than me. Perhaps you have a taste for danger, Fräulein Vine.'

'I'm sure it'll be perfectly safe.'

'I suppose. So long as you make sure it's before lunchtime!'

Out of the corner of her eye, Clara was aware of being scrutinized. It was the latecomer, the Englishman called Ralph, who was standing between Magda and the Mitford girls, or rather towering over them, a good six foot two. He had a broad-featured face and a bump in his nose that suggested a break on some distant playing field. His hair receded over a high brow and he cupped one elbow in his hand as he smoked. Clara noted the clean ovals of his fingernails and the gold signet ring on the little finger of his left hand. For a split second, as their eyes met, a spark of connection flickered across the distance between then.

Diana called across to Goebbels.

'We're playing a game, Herr Doktor, and you must join in. We're talking about the deadly sins. I think the old ones are all terribly passé. There should be new deadly sins. Or perhaps we should have deadly virtues instead!'

'How about chastity?' suggested the Englishman.

'A sin or a virtue?'

'It's pretty deadly either way.'

A burst of laughter filled the room. 'Well if you can't decide, Ralph, you'll have to think of another,' Diana persisted. 'What do you suggest?'

'Secrecy.'

'A sin or a virtue?'

'A virtue, definitely.'

While Diana's bright laugh glittered out, Goebbels was glowering. He was refusing to join in the joke. It might be that he detested this kind of English party game, but more likely he suspected in his guests' banter some humorous reference to his love affair with Lída Baarová. What had Albert said?

'He's really smitten this time. They say he's contemplating divorce.'

His expression set, Goebbels turned his attention to the Englishman.

'On the subject of virtue, Captain Sommers, I have a complaint to make about your English newspapers. They are constantly handing out lectures on our morality, like some dried-up old governess scolding away at our young Reich. Tell me, are you happy for them to continue spouting their lies or are you going to put them right?'

'I'm afraid you overestimate my influence on the denizens of Fleet Street, Herr Doktor,' Sommers replied pleasantly. 'Though I'm surprised you find them uncongenial. Surely many British newspapers are supportive of the National Socialists? Wasn't Lord Rothermere insisting the other day that Adolf the Great will soon be as popular in Britain as Frederick the Great? And as far as I'm concerned, the faster Britain realizes her interests lie in a close association with the German Reich, the better.'

He nodded to Clara and extended a hand. A small silver swastika glinted in his lapel.

'Ralph Sommers.' At the touch of his hand a shiver ran through her.

Goebbels waved grandly in Clara's direction. 'Captain Sommers, this is Fräulein Clara Vine. She represents the perfect union of our two great nations. Her father, Sir Ronald Vine, is English, and her mother was German. She may look a little English on the outside, but I think we have won the battle for her heart.'

Sommers' eyes swept over her speculatively. 'I'm pleased to hear it. I only wish some of the people back home would follow her example. Stop talking about war and start thinking more about what our two people have in common.' He nodded at Clara. 'Don't you agree?'

'Of course.'

'We are two ancient Aryan races, who should be united in friendship. We stem from the same blood. Our royal family speaks German as a mother tongue. We have a common enemy in the

Bolshevik. There seems to me no reason why Britain and Germany should not form one of the great alliances of the modern world.'

Clara didn't need to ask what a man like Captain Sommers was doing in Berlin. The city was full of people like him. English socialites enamoured of the new regime, infatuated with the marches and the banners and the upstanding ranks of the Hitler Youth. Though his eyes were a little tired and his face shadowed with stubble, Ralph Sommers exuded the same, unmistakeable confidence she recognized from the men her sister knew, men from the most privileged ranks of society, the sleek products of public schools who felt the world was at their feet. Given his mention of Lord Rothermere, he was no doubt another of the press baron's associates, determined to befriend Hitler and bent on an alliance with Germany. She wondered what Sommers assumed of her. That she was one of those girls who hung around Nazis because they liked the uniform and the proximity to power? Clara reminded herself how important it was to be careful with other English people. They could spot mistakes that the Germans ignored. They could sense falsity.

'So what brings you here, Captain Sommers?'

'I run a small aeronautical research and sales company. Offices in Conduit Street. Here . . .' He reached into his pocket and drew out a gold business-card holder. 'Take my card. I'm over on business actually, but I took the opportunity to motor down to Nuremberg for the Parteitag and I have to agree, it was an absolutely tremendous show. It quite takes the breath away. While I was there, the Frau Doktor very kindly invited me to this evening. She really does spoil me.'

Goebbels saw his empty glass. 'It seems we're not looking after you so well tonight, Sommers. You have no champagne.'

He gave his wide smile, the one that chilled Clara to the core, and signalled to a young woman holding a bottle of Henkell champagne wrapped in a white napkin. Clara recognized her as the girl who had served tea the other day. The girl from the Bride School. Her cheeks were flushed and a drop of sweat trickled down the side of her brow. At the Minister's summons she approached and grappled with the bottle, managing to spill champagne down Ralph Sommers' sleeve. Goebbels' face twisted with anger.

'Watch yourself, you clumsy woman!'

Sommers brushed the flecks of champagne from his sleeve with a smile.

'No harm done,' he said smoothly.

Goebbels glowered after the retreating bride.

'I'm sorry. She's not one of our usual maids. She's from the Bride School.'

Diana Mosley pricked up her ears.

'A Bride School, did you say? How awfully quaint! Perhaps I should attend one of those.'

'You wouldn't last long,' said Unity belligerently. 'Given you were expelled from every school you ever attended.'

Goebbels, however, was not joining in the joke. 'God help the wretched Schutzstaffel who have to marry these women.' With a visible effort he controlled himself. 'Still. We have quite another wedding in mind right now. We are expecting a visit from other of your countrymen. The Duke and Duchess of Windsor are to arrive on honeymoon tomorrow.'

For a split second, from across the room, Clara locked eyes with Frau von Ribbentrop. There were rumours that von Ribbentrop, in his time in London, had conducted an affair with the former Wallis Simpson. After they were introduced by the society hostess Emerald Cunard, whose home in Grosvenor Square was the centre of pro-Nazi London, it was said Ribbentrop had sent seventeen red roses to the Duchess's London home every day. Annelies von Ribbentrop had handled this gossip with her habitual iron composure. At the mention of Wallis, she assumed an expression which could set concrete.

'The only shame for them is that they should be hounded from their own country for such a harmless misdemeanour,' continued Goebbels, turning to the Mitford sisters. 'I cannot get over the disdain you English have for the idea of a divorced queen.'

'Not *all* the English,' corrected Diana, who was, Goebbels scarcely needed reminding, divorced herself.

'Perhaps not. But the fact remains you were fortunate enough to have a happy young king with a most attractive wife and yet those dried-up prunes in the Government could not tolerate it. And they were abetted by the repulsive hypocrites in the Church. I regret to say, to me that's the mark of a nation on the decline.'

'The Duke feels it most awfully,' conceded Diana. 'I think the idea of the tour is that Wallis should have a little taste of being queen. If they're going to be so beastly as to deny her the Royal Highness status, he says she should jolly well experience a royal tour with all the trimmings. Rolling out the red carpet and being greeted by the British ambassador when they arrive.'

'Not the British ambassador,' said Clara, without thinking, and then cursed herself. How had that slipped out?

'Indeed?' said Sommers. He cocked his head to one side. 'And why not?'

'I imagine it would be politically difficult,' she improvised.

'Do you now?' He spoke with a slightly mocking air, his cigarette nonchalantly poised, one eyebrow raised. He seemed to be challenging her, maintaining eye contact for longer than was comfortable. 'Why?'

'I would have thought that was perfectly obvious. I do read the newspapers, you know.'

'I'm sure.' His lips curved into a smile, but his cool, green eyes were probing her. 'And with a father like yours, you must be well acquainted with politics.'

'I don't need my father to teach me about politics,' she snapped.

At her terse reply his eyes widened slightly, but he continued to smile as though he found her amusing.

'Of course not.'

Suddenly, Clara couldn't stand any more. What kind of party was it, where you detested all the guests and couldn't drink a drop? What a life this was, mixing with people whose views you loathed, associating with a regime which stood for everything you hated: intimidation, violence, brutality. Befriending people who represented a version of England you didn't recognize. The strain of being constantly on her guard, of laughing and chatting and dissimulating, of never putting a foot wrong, was exhausting. She had to be away, if only for a moment.

She drifted onto the terrace as though in search of fresh air and moved away from the French windows so that the chatter of the party receded. Easing herself into the shadow at the edge of the house she stood quietly listening to the calls of the night birds in the woods and, further off, the hum of traffic from the other side of the lake. Catching a faint, salty tang in the air she pictured the muscular strength of the current combing the surface of the Wannsee. She had adored her time this summer on the beautiful lakes around Berlin, rowing and swimming and diving into the breathtaking crystal water of the Havel, though she had been warned that even the calmest surface concealed treacherous tides beneath.

Another sound interrupted her thoughts. A man's step, it sounded like. A hard leather sole with a steel tip in the heel making its way out onto the flagstones. She shrank back into the darkness. Light spilled out of the open doors, illuminating a swathe of the terrace, and she saw it was Ralph Sommers prowling – that was the word for it – like a predator in search of its prey. He braced his shoulders backwards and stretched his arms wide, like a wild animal, then reached up a hand and massaged his neck. Even from where she was standing, she could tell he was tense and preoccupied. Clara folded herself more closely against the wall and tried to regulate her breathing. She was certain he couldn't see her, yet he still looked curiously in her direction, cupped his hand to light a cigarette and seemed to gaze right at her, before turning and going back into the house.

Chapter Seven

It was ten o'clock before Clara got back to Winterfeldstrasse and wearily parked the car. The hall was deserted, though she noticed that a couple of chicken-soup cans had been tossed into Rudi's collection point, enough perhaps to make a few bolts for an aeroplane wing tip. It was Party night, she remembered, Rudi's only evening out of the week, from which he would regularly reel back reeking of beer, and filled with SA songs.

By contrast, Clara was stone-cold sober. She had drunk nothing at the Goebbels' party, aware more than ever now that she needed to keep her wits about her. She had held a glass of champagne throughout, because that was the kind of detail Goebbels noticed. Yet even with her sobriety and her heightened state of alertness, she had managed to make a mistake.

At least the lift was mended. She sighed as she waited and rubbed her legs. Her black patent heels were killing her. She was longing to fling herself down on her bed and let herself relax. She could not get the face of Ralph Sommers, aeronautical businessman and Nazi sympathizer, out of her mind. Something about him unnerved her. The cool gleam of his eyes, the current that ran through her as they shook hands. Her inexplicable desire to see him again.

The lift shuddered upwards and stopped with a grunt at the

top floor. Pushing the cage back, Clara flicked on the hall light and rummaged in her bag for her key. But as she approached the door her senses quickened like a cat's. She hesitated. The film of Max Factor face powder on the door handle had gone. That could mean anything, of course. Rudi, perhaps, snooping around. A Hitler youth, or a girl from the BDM, selling their publications and aggressively rattling the door as they touted their collection boxes. And yet . . . Clara felt unsettled. Something wasn't right. She turned the light off again, her heart pounding as, swiftly and quietly, she inserted the key in the lock.

She pushed the door open a fraction, then stepped into the hall. An eddy of cool air against her face suggested a window had been opened. There was a distinct, indefinable fragrance that she didn't recognize. Someone had been in the apartment. Perhaps they were still there. Two steps in allowed her a view of the kitchen, where she could see a used cup on the table. A single, blue china teacup without a saucer and a teaspoon by its side. Yet the table had been bare when she left. The kitchen window was slightly ajar, but it seemed impossible that anyone should have climbed in from there. From that window into the cobbled courtyard was a sheer five-floor drop.

Clara froze. From where she stood there was no other sign of an intruder, none of the casual wreckage a burglar might create. Whoever had entered her apartment that evening did not have destruction on their mind. She slipped off her heels and stood in her stockinged feet, straining for the slightest sound. Although the apartment was silent, there was a ripple in the air. A strange, subliminal frisson that suggested the presence of another human being. Another heart beating, very near.

Walking as slowly and as silently as possible, she approached the drawing room and flung back the door. There was no light on but to her shock, there was the dark mass of a figure in the chair, framed in shadow against the uncurtained window. Even as she looked, the woman stood up and addressed her with a laugh.

'Clara Vine! I might have guessed you'd never actually be at home on a Saturday night. And looking so glamorous. You cut your hair!'

Clara dropped her bag and took up her friend in a wide-armed embrace. The adrenaline coursing through her turned to joy. Tears sprang into her eyes.

'Mary! Mary Harker. What on earth are you doing here?'

The visitor returned her hug, tightly.

'Long story.' Mary had a languid, American drawl with a bubble of humour beneath it. 'Which I have every intention of telling in great and exhausting detail, so you'd better not be tired.'

'But . . .' Clara snapped on the lamp, shrugged off her coat and dropped it over a chair. 'How did you even get in here?'

'Rudi let me in. I caught him off to one of his Nazi nights out. He was thrilled to see me back. He's a nice guy really, under all that Nazi bluster. While I waited I had a good look around to see what you've done with my apartment and I admit I'm impressed. It was never this tidy when I was here. I never even saw the floor-boards under all my junk. I love all this furniture. And I simply adore that painting in the bedroom.'

Mary Harker had aged since the day Clara had last seen her, in 1933, as she prepared to leave Germany for America. Her bosomy figure had filled out and her face had gained a few lines. Yet in all other ways she was exactly the same ambitious reporter who had briefed the readers of the *New York Evening Post* on the early days of the Third Reich. Same thick tweed suit. Same heavy glasses and earnest air. Tousled hair which she cut herself and was barely acquainted with a brush. Grey-green eyes that could switch from serious to humorous in an instant. The merest lick of make-up. Freckles, a voice that sounded like she gargled gravel and a gap-toothed smile that warmed every corner of the room.

She clapped her arms theatrically. 'But God, it's cold in here. I forgot how freezing this city can be in winter.'

'And it's getting colder. Winter's only just beginning. I'll stoke up the stove. First let me get you some food.'

Clara opened the refrigerator to find a single bottle of beer and some milk, a hunk of dark brown rye bread and a rind of cheese. Mary peered gloomily over her shoulder.

'I thought actresses were supposed to keep champagne and cold salmon in their refrigerator.'

'Not this one. I haven't been shopping in a while.'

'What do you eat?'

'I tend to eat out. Or at the studio. It'll have to be coffee for now.'

As Clara put on the kettle and got out the cups, Mary scrutinized her critically.

'You're looking thinner. Not starving yourself, I hope, for some role.'

'Oh, Mary. You're going to find a lot has changed here.'

How could you explain, to someone who had been away for four years, just how Germany had changed in that time? Now, in the autumn of 1937, food was so much scarcer. Under Goering's four-year plan, there was a new slogan, 'Guns Not Butter', to drive home the sacrifices everyone needed to make for the nation's rearmament. Not that it was such a sacrifice, given the state of the butter when you did find it.

'There are food shortages all the time. You can't find eggs. Any butter you get is rancid. The milk is so watered down they call it Corpse Juice. People have to save their crusts. On top of that, there are all sorts of rumours whirling round. Like the reason you can't buy onions is that they are being used for experiments with poison gas. And out in the country, you can be hanged for feeding grain to pigs. There's this song they sing. "*Der Hitler hat keine Frau, Der Bauer hat keine Sau, Der Fleischer hat kein Fleisch, Das ist das Dritte Reich."* Hitler has no woman, the farmer has no sow, the butcher has no meat, that's the Third Reich for you.'

'Catchy.'

'Yes, and liable to get you caught if anyone hears you singing it.'

'The place doesn't look too different to me. The restaurants are full.'

'Sure, but they only serve two dishes. Try ordering anything else and you'll find it's sold out. And the waiters scrape the plates and take the scraps home to their families. According to the Reich Food Corporation we need to make the nation self-sufficient. The only problem is, the Government says if Germany is to be self-sufficient, it's going to need more land.'

'Somebody else's land, I assume.'

Clara handed her friend a cup of coffee and tucked her feet beneath her on the sofa.

'Exactly. But let's talk politics later. First things first. I want to know everything. What's been going on in your life? What brings you back to Berlin?'

'Apart from the biggest story in Europe, you mean?'

'I mean how did you manage it? Being expelled by the Propaganda Minister himself isn't an achievement all journalists can put on their resumés.'

'Oh, getting accreditation was a nightmare. I'd gone back to New Jersey to spend time with my father, and when he died, my mother wanted me to stay on at home to entertain her. Given that her idea of entertainment is playing bridge at her country club and peekaboo with her grandchild, I was dying to escape. We never saw eye to eye. Keeping out of journalism was killing me and once the civil war broke out in Spain, I said damn it, I just have to go. Mother's always saying she wants there to be more between us. I thought, let's make it the Atlantic Ocean.'

'You went on your own?'

'Sure. I decided I was going to be a one-woman band. I took out a thousand-dollar bank loan and booked a passage. Took my Remington,' Mary tapped the typewriter case beside her, 'and my lucky hat,' she pointed to a battered black felt creation which Clara recognized, 'and set sail for Europe.'

'I can't imagine what it's like out in Spain. The reports are terrifying.'

'Words can't describe it, Clara. I went to Madrid first, while it was being besieged by Franco. The International Brigades were fighting from street to street. I'd never seen a sight like it. They saved the city from the hands of the Nationalists at the last moment. Then in February I was on the Andalusian coast, where there were thousands of refugees fleeing the advance on Malaga. I passed mothers who actually begged me to take their children, because they were so certain they would be killed. Everywhere you go there are ruined buildings and desolation. This spring I moved all the way up to the Basque country. That's where most of the Republican resistance movement is and I can't tell you the things I saw there.'

Mary stopped for a moment and passed a hand across her eyes.

'I will tell you. Only not now. Anyway, I freelanced for various outfits and filed a little copy for United Press and I begged and wheedled Frank Nussbaum, the *Evening Post*'s editor, to take my stories. But what I really wanted was to get back into Germany. This was where I wanted to report from. Then I had the most enormous piece of luck. You've heard of Charles Lindbergh?'

'Who hasn't?'

Everyone knew Charles Lindbergh. The celebrated American aviator, world famous for his solo flight from New York to Paris, had had his life torn apart when his baby son was kidnapped and murdered. To escape the hysteria of the ensuing murder trial, the family had moved to a peaceful village in Kent.

'As it happens, Colonel Lindbergh comes from New Jersey, near where my parents live, so we knew him a little. I prised the address out of my mother, went over to England, drove down to the village and knocked on the door. I dropped my family name very heavily and asked if he would do an interview and to my amazement, he said yes. I suppose I must have been talking about wanting to come to Germany, because it seems he spoke to someone and the next week, a visa came through.'

'Lindbergh must have German contacts.'

'Sure he does. He's great pals with Goering. I'm certain it was Goering who had my visa approved. Anyhow, the *Post* were ecstatic when I offered them my Lindbergh interview, and the result was they agreed to take me on at the Berlin bureau again for sixty dollars a week.'

'Sixty dollars! You'll live like royalty here on that.'

'That's the easy bit. Now I just have to find some stories. It's harder than before. Restrictions on foreign journalists are tighter. I just want a good story. Something meaty, that gets my by-line above the fold.'

'There is something,' Clara hesitated. 'I heard about it the other day, but there's been nothing in the papers here.'

The death at the Reich Bride School had been preoccupying her. Not that violent crime was unusual in Berlin. It was more of a daily occurrence. The fact that the girl's shooting had gone unremarked was hardly surprising. Why bother to report on a murder in a city where sudden death was the prime instrument of law and order? It was just that the woman was called Anna Hansen. It couldn't be the same Anna . . . could it?

'There was a woman shot last week at the Schwanenwerder Bride School. They think . . .'

'Hold on right there.' Mary cocked her head. 'Did you say Bride School?'

'There are Bride Schools all around Germany. They're Himmler's brainchild. You need to attend one if you're going to marry into the SS.'

'What do they teach? Which flowers go well with roses? Where to seat a bishop at dinner, that sort of thing? How to use an oyster fork?'

Clara laughed. 'More like herring recipes and how to hem curtains. Whatever it takes, in the National Socialist mind, to be a good wife.'

Mary rolled her eyes. 'Presumably this girl wasn't shot for her cooking skills?'

'That's just it. We don't know. There's been nothing about it in any of the papers, I've looked. And I wouldn't be interested, only the dead woman was called Anna Hansen, and I used to know a girl called that. I wondered if it could be the same one.'

'Sounds like a pretty common name to me.'

'I suppose. It was just a thought. The woman I knew came from Munich and she was the least likely candidate for an SS Bride School I can imagine. She was a model for Bruno Weiss. My artist friend. I don't think you ever met him but he knew Helga Schmidt.'

Helga Schmidt. The actress whose death had brought Mary and Clara together. Mary was shaking her head in disbelief.

'Whoever the girl was, this Bride School sounds like a story in itself. I'm sure my editor would adore the idea. I'll get onto it first thing.'

Clara stifled a yawn.

'Sorry, it's been quite an evening.'

'So which room's mine?'

Mary gazed innocently at Clara, then burst out laughing.

'Don't worry. I'm not moving in. It would be far too compromising for you to share an apartment with a journalist. I'll just need to stay a night until I find somewhere else. I'll bunk up on your sofa. You'll never know I'm here.'

Clara felt a guilty twinge of relief.

'Of course. Stay as long as you need. Whatever you want.'

'What I really want is a drink. Where shall we go?'

'Now?'

'Why not? Unless Berlin nightlife has changed out of all recognition, things are only just getting started at eleven o'clock.'

At the prospect of an evening out with Mary Harker, Clara's fatigue evaporated. Mary's enthusiasm was like a transfusion of something life-giving. The kind of substance you couldn't get in one of Magda Goebbels' clinics.

'Where would you like to go?'

'Do you know anywhere a couple of women on their own could drink a Martini without being bothered?'

'I think so. Why?'

'That's exactly the kind of place I want to avoid.'

Given they had spent such a raucous evening, it was strange that Clara should wake so early. The pearly morning light was beginning to penetrate the curtains' edge like a negative developing in its chemical bath, seeping into the room and transforming the solid black shapes of furniture to watery textures of grey. Clara lay for a while in bed in a state of exhausted clarity. Even though, for the first time in ages, there was another person sleeping in the apartment, she had never felt so alone. Her solitude seemed to envelop her in an invisible cocoon as she lay listening to Berlin waking up, car horns, the rumbling of trams on Nollendorfplatz and the metallic screech of the S-Bahn trains on the high stilts of their elevated tracks.

Mary had been full of questions last night. *How long can you stay here? Are you happy? Is there a man on the horizon?* Clara had smiled and shaken her head at that. The truth was that despite the odd flings of the past few years, she had never met anyone she was deeply attracted to. There had been love in her life once, but since Leo's departure, no man had managed to penetrate her defences. She could laugh with them and sleep with them, but she would leave in the morning without a backward glance. Perhaps it was testimony to the strength of the carapace she had erected around herself, but no one had ever had the effect on Clara that meeting Leo had. The frisson she had felt from the very moment she met him. No one, until perhaps Captain Ralph Sommers.

What about your private life? Mary wanted to know. Clara couldn't tell her that there was no such thing as a private life for someone in her position. Her private life was where her professional life, her unofficial professional life, took place. At parties and premieres she was always on the alert, always attentive for useful pieces of information. Any snippets of gossip that the women let drop about the Führer's thoughts, or the feuds between their husbands, or the grumbles about the Reich's intensifying military preparations, would be memorized until she could feed them back to Archie Dyson. Yet although Clara batted away Mary's questions, it was increasingly difficult to silence the clamour of questions in her own head. Which, thanks to a succession of gin Martinis in a West End bar, was feeling distinctly muzzy.

Her eye fell, as it always did, on the Bruno Weiss painting on the opposite wall. *What happened to you, Bruno?* When she got to know him, after Helga died, she had grown to love his mordant, Berliner humour, and his brave decision, as a Jew, to turn down a visa for England. That kind of decision was absolutely typical of Bruno. It was simultaneously bold and foolhardy, because life for a German Jew, let alone a former Communist agitator who had already been arrested for pamphleteering and whose paintings were everything the National Socialists considered degenerate, was a perilous one in the Third Reich. Other artists, like Bruno's friend Georg Grosz, had already emigrated. Otto Dix had been forced to join Goebbels' Reich Chamber of Fine Arts, but as a Jew, Bruno couldn't follow his example and retire to the country to paint inoffensive landscapes. Under Reich law, Bruno couldn't even paint, so how was he earning a living? Was he living a life in the shadows somewhere, trying to get by? Sleeping on the street and in shop doorways, risking a beating from any passing Nazi? Or had he been captured, imprisoned and sent to a camp? Bruno was the only German Clara had ever trusted to know what she did and what she was. It was impossible not to conclude that it must have been Bruno, under interrogation in some police cellar, who had aroused the suspicions of the men in Prinz Albrecht Strasse.

Clara stretched and reached a foot out of bed. Her head pounded like a marching band. She needed coffee, then aspirin, then more coffee. She should never have drunk so many Martinis, not with her low tolerance for alcohol. She stood up unsteadily, as though on the deck of a yacht, and felt the ground settle beneath her. She would make breakfast for Mary. That was the plan. Get up, find herself an aspirin and make Mary some breakfast. Then she remembered there was no breakfast.

They could have found coffee anywhere. Berlin was a whole city of cafés. Cafés were where the citizens met, disputed, wrangled and, more recently, since it had become so hard to heat a home, huddled in the warmth that the price of a cup of coffee could bring them. It was coffee that flowed through the veins of Berlin and kept the city on its feet, even now, when the stuff was more likely to be chicory or acorns or some other ersatz concoction. And Clara was longing for coffee. But Mary insisted they walk all the way to Olivaerplatz, a good twenty minutes away, to see if a bar owned by a friend of hers was still going strong.

'There's no hurry, Clara. You're not on set today and a foreign correspondent's day doesn't start until lunchtime. New York is hours behind us, remember. I don't even start sending wires until late afternoon.'

As they walked through the streets, Clara tried to see Berlin through Mary's eyes. It was true, the changes wrought by the new regime were not always immediately apparent. The flower women were still selling their little bunches of violets and roses. Berlin shop owners were still not inclined to give the Nazi salute and usually contented themselves with a straight '*Guten Morgen*'. Even when they did, Clara, like many other Berliners, had discovered that you could avoid returning a salute with the simple precaution of carrying a briefcase in one hand and a bag in the other.

Yet there were truckloads of soldiers in the streets, pennants and banners hanging from every building. The sombre edifices of Berlin blazed with scarlet, as though someone had spilt a jar of red ink across the city. And everywhere there was Hitler's face, in shops and on placards, and piled in postcard form on racks by the U-Bahn entrance. The liquorice loop of hair across his forehead, the pasty cheeks, the studied frown. Mary squinted at them and pulled a face.

'He's like a sunset, isn't he? People never get bored of looking at him. That same view, in a thousand slightly different versions. Arm up, arm down, full face, half profile.'

'Shh.' Foreigners' voices, Clara had noticed, always seemed unnaturally loud. 'Haven't you heard that phrase everyone uses? *Speak through a flower*?'

'What's that supposed to mean?'

'You hear it all the time now. It means say only positive things about the Nazis in public.'

'You won't catch me mumbling through my bouquet. I couldn't care less if people hear what I have to say. And I think it's strange they like Hitler so much here, considering he doesn't much care for Berlin. He calls it a Trümmerfeld – a field of rubble.'

'Well, he's the one we have to thank for that. You must have noticed the construction going on everywhere.'

Even as she spoke they walked past a building site, where clouds of dust rose like incense in the morning air, and a couple of workers, their moustaches matted with dirt, hacked at rocks. One of them, with braces and shirtsleeves and a glint in his eye, paused to call out a greeting in a thick country accent.

'Why do Hitler's buildings have to be so big?'

'He needs size. He thinks it enhances his own stature. Apparently he asked Speer to copy Mussolini's idea of having a gargantuan study so that visitors have to walk a long way across the floor to reach him. He thinks it makes him more intimidating.'

'God, and that's a man who needs to work on his softer side.'

'Speer is only allowing stone, marble and bricks to be used,' said Clara, 'He has a theory. Because the Reich is going to last a thousand years, one day all these buildings will resemble the ruins of ancient Greece.'

'What does it say if your architect is talking about ruins before the thing is even built?' said Mary, pushing open a café door. 'Thankfully Stefan's still here, at least.'

Stefan Hirsch, a lean man in his early sixties, welcomed Mary as effusively as was possible for a habitually gruff Berliner. His smile was like a crack in gnarled oak and his voice was as gritty as the Berlin earth itself.

'So you came back. What happened? Some other café forgot your order?'

'Oh, you know. I felt like a change. How are you doing?'

'Lucky for you I'm still in business. You want your usual?' said Stefan, turning to the shining coffee machine and clattering the cups.

'With whipped cream on top!'

'Shows how long you've been away. You won't find whipped cream in any café in Berlin now, Fräulein.'

'I'm so pleased he remembered me!' hissed Mary, as they ensconced themselves in a window table over steaming cups of coffee.

'To be honest, it would be hard to forget you.'

'What's that supposed to mean? No, don't say.'

On the railings outside Stefan's café, swastika flags fluttered in the breeze, alternating with the banner with the bear of Berlin, the city's heraldic animal, raised on its rear legs.

'Don't think I put them there,' Stefan growled, delivering thick slices of freshly baked Streuselkuchen to the table. 'It's the city's seven hundredth anniversary. A lot of fuss about nothing, I'd say. All these flags and marches and live bears.'

'Live bears?'

'The city of Bern donated them. They're building a pit for the wretched beasts in Köllnischer Park.'

'A bear pit? In the middle of the city? Erich would like that,' said Clara, biting into the rich, cinnamon-spiced dough. 'Perhaps you should cover it, Mary.'

But Mary was absorbed in a copy of the *Berliner Illustrierte*, whose front page bore a photograph of a large Mercedes, with two SS guards in the front seat, others on the running boards and behind them a small man with a dark-haired woman by his side.

'Look at this! Seems your Duke of Windsor finally arrived.'

Clara thought back to December last year, the high, surprisingly reedy voice on the wireless: '*I, Edward the Eighth of Great Britain, Ireland and the British Dominions beyond the sea, King, Emperor of India, do hereby declare my irrevocable decision to renounce the throne.*'

The abdication had transfixed Britain and sharpened the already deepening social divisions. There were people in pubs and working men's clubs across England who hoped it would mean the end of the monarchy and others, in smarter circles, who feared the same thing. Angela wrote that the whole household had sat in the Ponsonby Terrace drawing room, servants too, listening to the broadcast in silence, and the cook had cried.

'What's wrong with Wally anyhow?' objected Mary.

'She's divorced.'

'I don't think it's anything to do with that. I think it's just that you Brits can't stand the thought of an American on your throne.'

The *Berliner Illustrierte* had gone to town. There was a six-page spread with a series of photographs. The Duchess in evening gown, on a yacht, at her wedding. Then two impeccably trim figures making their way along a red carpet at Friedrichstrasse station, dwarfed by a posse of Nazis. The Duchess, in a black coat and fur tippet, gripping a bouquet of white roses and the Duke with a sour expression on his monkey face. They did not look a picture of nuptial bliss. For a moment Clara almost felt sorry for the Duke. What must it be like to give up the throne for a woman? To sacrifice your entire life's work for love? Clara had only sacrificed love for her work, so how would she know?

'It says here that Dr Goebbels personally composed a song to be performed on the royal couple's arrival at the Kaiserhof. That's over the road from his ministry. No doubt he booked them in there to keep a close eye on them.'

'Very romantic.'

'What's the betting the Gestapo has installed a microphone in the bedroom?'

'Let's hope they have and then Goebbels will get to hear what they really think of his song.'

The two women finished their coffee and made their way slowly back in the direction of Nollendorfplatz. At the centre of Olivaerplatz they passed through a little park where, between stone colonnades garlanded with late-flowering honeysuckle, sparrows hopped and bobbed. A man played his accordion for pfennigs. It was a tranquil morning, with only a couple of clouds scudding in the bright blue sky. Mary and Clara continued arm in arm, until Clara noticed with a twist of disquiet that a knot of people had gathered.

Instinctively, she avoided crowds now. There were benign crowds certainly, queuing at shops where a consignment of butter had arrived, or outside the theatre to see the stars arriving, but more often crowds presaged something far less pleasant. The chance was you would find yourself witnessing some violence being perpetrated, or at the very least be asked for your papers. That suspicion was confirmed as they approached. At the centre of the throng were the distinctive grey service uniforms of a pair of SS men. Even from behind Clara could sense the cruelty coming off them. Before them were a young couple engaged in the apparently futile task of rubbing down one of the park benches with their handkerchiefs.

'What the hell . . . ?' said Mary.

To Clara, the situation was all too clear. The jeers of the guards explained precisely the situation.

'Filthy swine! Contaminating the benches for decent people!'

'I want to see it spotless. Get all that dirt off. You're lucky we don't arrest you right here.'

The young man, in his coat and hat, was visibly sweating as he scrubbed frantically at the wooden struts of the bench. His girlfriend, who might have been a secretary in her white blouse and neat tweed suit, was kneeling on the path, running a scrap of lacy material along the wrought-iron legs, silent tears sliding down her face. Painted onto the bench were the words *'Nur für Arier'*.

'Those benches are barred for Jews,' said Clara quietly.

'Where are Jews supposed to sit then?'

'There,' said Clara simply, pointing to a bench at the far end of the park, closest to the road. It was painted a dirty yellow colour and the people who had been occupying it were moving hastily away. Above it was a sign explaining, '*Die gelben Banke sind für Juden.*'

'The Jews are only allowed on the yellow benches.'

Some of the onlookers appeared embarrassed at the display and winced in distaste, but plenty of them were smiling and there was even a mother, Clara noticed, pointing out the fun for the benefit of her young daughter. To her horror, Mary seized her notebook and made to push through to the centre of the crowd. Clara grabbed her sleeve.

'Mary. Stop it. Be careful!'

'Why? I'm a journalist, aren't I? I'm supposed to be reporting on what's happening here. This is exactly the kind of thing my readers need to know about.'

How was it, thought Clara in exasperation, that the one friend whose company she most enjoyed should be a journalist. Clara's job was to be inconspicuous, Mary's to find trouble and then wade into the centre of it. Clara avoided attention. Mary attracted it. Clara hung back as Mary approached the guards.

'What are you doing?'

One of the guards had just delivered a spiteful kick to the young man, causing him to topple sideways onto the ground. The guard looked up in astonishment as Mary addressed him.

'My name is Mary Harker,' she flourished her press card. 'And I intend to report this in my newspaper, the *New York Evening Post*.'

For a moment the two SS men exchanged glances, bemused. Clara held her breath. But their inventive taunting of the Jewish couple had put them in a good humour, so they linked arms, smiling.

'Sure. You can take our picture too, if you like!'

'Too bad I don't have a camera,' grumbled Mary, turning on her heel. Clara gripped her arm and walked quickly away.

She led the way through the park tight-lipped, crossed the road and hailed a taxi. How could she explain to Mary that while she had been away, it wasn't just Berlin's buildings that were being demolished and rebuilt? It was as though the whole of Germany had been turned inside out and the darker things which had once been hidden were now on full display.

Just then, she decided not to bother explaining.

'You've only just arrived here, Mary, and if you carry on like this you're going to get thrown out again so fast, you won't need to bother unpacking your suitcase.'

She had not the slightest confidence, however, that Mary would take her advice.

Chapter Eight

The windows of Ernst Udet's apartment in Wilmersdorf looked out onto the sedate plane trees of Preussenpark. It was a leafy, upmarket neighbourhood, close enough to the shops and theatres of the Ku'damm to be fashionable, yet far enough away that the streets fell almost silent after dark, save for the odd dog walker ambling home to his handsome, nineteenth-century villa. Currently, however, this area's reputation for bourgeois respectability was in the process of being comprehensively demolished by its most celebrated resident, Generaloberst Udet himself.

The blast of jazz could be heard halfway down the street and as soon as she stepped through the door Clara realized that nothing she had heard about Udet's private life had been an exaggeration. The dimly lit room was filled to bursting with grey-blue Luftwaffe uniforms and a scattering of young women in skimpy dresses with plunging necklines. It brought to mind the kind of clubs that were common just a few years ago in Berlin. Small, squalid places rammed to the walls with people, where smoke filled the lungs and music throbbed through the blood. You would find couples there in any combination. Men with women, men with men, women with women. Most of those clubs were closed now, or at least harder to find, but Udet's parties were a credible alternative. In the corner he had installed a cocktail bar, a modern curve of smooth wood with chrome fittings and a generous cluster of bottles, behind which a Luftwaffe general, in a barman's black waistcoat with a napkin slung over his shoulder, was concocting a Brandy Alexander. At the other end of the room a piano with a glass of beer resting on it was being played by an officer in a monocle and comically tilted Luftwaffe cap. Beside him, Udet's pet dog, Bulli, was petted by a statuesque blonde with hair rolled tightly away from her face and a bosom like the window display in a jewellery store.

In the four years since she had been in Berlin, Clara had never got used to entering a room filled with National Socialist officers. Close proximity to a Nazi uniform made genuine relaxation an impossibility. They were almost all Luftwaffe here, with a sprinkling of Wehrmacht officers in field grey. As she threaded her way through the men in their tightly belted tunics, studded with aluminium buttons and decorations, she felt the lascivious flicker of eyes upon her and guessed that many of these men had recently returned from active service. Like all men starved of female company, they were hyper-alert to the approach of an unknown woman. Especially one in a halter-necked, backless evening dress.

'Isn't that what's called a cocktail dress? Surely you need a cocktail to go with it?' Ernst Udet surfaced from the crowd and kissed Clara's hand. His own hands, she noticed, were rather small and exquisitely manicured, as he waved over a man carrying a tray of margaritas.

'It takes the Luftwaffe to really appreciate a beautiful woman. You want to know why? It's a requirement of the job that pilots have perfect vision, so it follows that we need something perfect to look at too.'

His tanned face beamed with boyish pleasure at this aperçu and Clara couldn't help laughing too. 'Herr Generaloberst—'

'Ernst, please.'

'Ernst. Thank you for inviting me. I'm so pleased you were able to spare time to make the film. You must be terribly busy.'

'I jumped at the chance! I miss the old days, you know. There was none of this office work. Just flying all day. Now I haven't practised a good stunt for weeks. The last real stunt I performed was flying my Focke-Wulf Stieglitz under the Hindenburg and hooking onto its undercarriage . . .' he gave a deprecating smile. 'Ach, but girls aren't interested in aeroplanes.'

'No, I am. It's fascinating.'

'You're lying, my dear. However, even if you think I'm an old bore, your lad Erich would like to hear about it, I'll bet. You must get me to tell you about how the famous Ju 87 Stuka dive bomber was born. But first, we should find our producer. Herr Lindemann was here, somewhere.'

Clara looked around for Albert. Plenty about this party would appeal to him. One young man was sprawled on a sofa, legs splayed, his arm flung around an older officer. There was another, whose full formal evening dress included mascara and lipstick. For a man like Albert, everything had changed since the death of Ernst Röhm, the monstrous commander of the SA, the storm troopers' unit, whose downfall had been preceded by a welter of homosexual scandal. Being homosexual was an anti-social offence now, warranting direct removal to a concentration camp. Indeed it had become a useful method of dispatch for anyone who caused offence. Neighbours with a grievance would frequently entrust their suspicions to the Gestapo with a quiet note: '*I regard it as my duty as a German to bring this to your attention*'. When a friend was arrested for homosexuality, no one even needed to mention the word. They would simply murmur *'Hundertfünfundsiebzig'*, signifying the 175th paragraph of the German criminal code. That was enough. Bars and meeting places once popular with homosexual men were monitored closely by the secret police and the result was that private parties became prime meeting places. Albert, however, was taking no chances.

'There he is.'

Standing in the midst of a group of Luftwaffe officers, Albert had the regulation blonde clamped to his arm. Clara had not seen this one before. She had a hard, calculating face with high arched eyebrows, which gave her an expression of permanent surprise. Or perhaps she was genuinely surprised at being the date of a man like Albert, Clara thought. He was holding forth, slightly drunkenly, on the subject of film production.

'We're a nation of engineers. Germans are the best engineers in the world. You people are making aeroplanes, we are making films.'

Another officer, with shaved flaxen hair, guffawed. 'Forgive me, Herr Lindemann, but with Goebbels in charge you're not exactly producing Junkers.'

Udet gave Clara a complicit wink. 'Clara, meet Oberst Heinrich von Kleist, Oberst Horst Schilling and Oberst Leutnants Rudolf Fleischer and Hans Schwarzkopf. Heinrich and Horst are test pilots and Hans and Rudolf work for me in the technical division. We often have a refreshing exchange of opinions. Take no notice. It's nothing serious. Just men's talk.'

The four officers acknowledged her with a nod. They towered over Albert with an air of confidence and authority that was enhanced by their Luftwaffe uniforms.

'Say what you like, but Goebbels is an emotional engineer,' continued Albert. 'Films produce emotions and Goebbels believes in engineering the right films to produce the right emotions.'

'Poisonous little propaganda runt,' said von Kleist, but under his breath.

'In terms of understanding the value of propaganda, Doktor Goebbels stands head and shoulders above the others,' asserted Albert, his voice slightly slurred.

'Goebbels couldn't stand head and shoulders above my dick!' announced Horst Schilling to general laughter.

'Wait, gentlemen. I will advance one defence of Doktor

Goebbels,' volunteered Fleischer. 'He's made some attempt to sort out the art from the trash. I was down in Munich the other day and I decided to take a look at that revolting Degenerate Art exhibition. All the rubbish they confiscated from museums.'

'I heard about that,' said Schilling languidly, toting a cigar. 'Jew art, isn't it? You can see that kind of thing on the walls of any public lavatory. I don't see why it needs a museum.'

'The interest was phenomenal. There were queues stretching down the street.'

'There you are then! The genius of Goebbels!' interceded Udet. 'It must be a great exhibition!'

Fleischer eyed him coldly. The way the skin stretched over Fleischer's bullet head made Clara think about the skulls at the Berlin Natural History Museum, lined up in rows according to their ethnicity. His eyes were as pale and flat as highly polished steel.

'Goebbels was right to collect it up, but he should have made a bonfire of it, just like he did with the books. Those paintings are really disgusting. They're rotten, depraved works by human effluent. The message is always the same: Man is bestial, Berlin is a sink of depravity. Germany is poisoned. Everyone is for sale. All that Bolshevik crap.'

'So which artists are appearing in this Degenerate Exhibition then?' enquired Clara.

'As Horst says, mostly Jews. Paul Klee, Picasso, Miró, Emil Nolde, Kurt Schwitters, Kandinsky, Bruno Weiss. I saw him actually, Weiss. Standing there bold as brass, looking at his own filthy artwork.'

Bruno Weiss! The shock went through Clara like a knife. This man had seen her friend Bruno. Alive, in Munich, and recently too. The surprise caused the glass to tremble in her hand and in an effort not to betray her amazement, Clara kept her eyes fixed rigidly on Fleischer's bony face.

'In fact,' he continued, 'he was lucky I didn't have him arrested straight away.'

'On what grounds?' enquired Schwarzkopf. He was by far the handsomest of the group, with a high aristocratic brow and eyes of hard, Aryan blue.

Fleischer shrugged. 'Endangering public morality, encouraging disrespect of the National Socialist state. Any fucking grounds you like. The police have a list of those offences as long as your arm, so they're bound to be able to find a few to suit a piece of Jewish garbage like Bruno Weiss. As it was, I reported him to the local authorities, so he's likely to find himself answering some questions very soon.'

'And they won't be questions on the meaning of art,' added Schilling.

Schwarzkopf laughed. 'More like the kind of questions where if he gets them right, he'll be in a camp and if he gets them wrong, he'll be wearing a wooden overcoat.'

'What were you doing there, Fleischer?' teased Udet. 'Do you have a taste for that kind of thing yourself? Decadent art?'

'I was visiting family,' said the Oberst Leutnant stiffly.

'Well I come from Munich too. Perhaps I should drop in on my next visit.'

Udet grinned at Clara, but she barely registered. She was still trying to control her astonishment. So Bruno was in Munich. He wasn't in a camp, or dead, because this man had seen him standing right in front of his own artwork. Such a notion was incredible. It would be rash, bold, and recklessly ill-advised. And exactly the kind of thing Bruno would do.

In her torrent of emotion it was hard to focus on the fact that Udet was attempting to introduce another officer, standing to her side.

'And this, Clara dear, is my right-hand man. Oberst Arno Strauss. Arno, you must meet my new wife. She has eyes you could drown in, don't you think?'

While Udet's face bore an alcoholic flush and there could only be room for a few more cocktails inside him, Oberst Arno Strauss was manifestly sober. He was ramrod straight with an athletic frame and tightly cropped dark hair. In profile, his hawkish nose and lean cheek suggested a chiselled perfection, but when he turned his head it was a different matter. The whole of one side of his face was crumpled, as though it had once melted, with a long scar that ripped and puckered the flesh from the side of his eye along the cheekbone to the corner of his mouth, drawing down the eye and raising the skin of his cheek in a silvery welt. As a result of this disfigurement, it was hard to tell whether the curl of his lip was expressive or accidental. Perhaps it was both.

He clicked his heels gallantly, bowed and kissed hands.

'So this is the Pilot's Bride.'

'Arno Strauss is the only man in Germany who can outperform me in the sky,' slurred Udet.

'Only in the sky?' queried Strauss.

'And who can drink me under the table, of course.' Udet leaned confidentially towards Clara, exuding alcohol like the fumes of a Mercedes exhaust. 'Arno makes excellent brandy cocktails. His Angel's Wing has to be tasted to be believed. Brandy, cream and crème de cacao, served without mixing. Superb. He would make the best bartender in Berlin, but the work he's engaged in at the moment is a little more useful to the Fatherland.'

'So what's this film about then?' asked Strauss.

Udet rolled his eyes, then lowered his head like a naughty schoolboy. 'To be absolutely honest . . .'

'Don't tell me you didn't read the script?'

'I read as far as the part where I did the first stunt and I told them I'd take it. I don't need to know the story.'

In a strange way, Udet was right. The Ufa films now followed such a predictable template one could pretty much guess after the first few minutes how it would turn out. In this case an audience could tell that a heroic Luftwaffe pilot would almost certainly have survived the downing of his plane, and that Gretchen's bravery in going in search of her dead husband would be rewarded, allowing her to return to housewifely duties. The conflict in which Udet was supposedly fighting was not specified, but anyone looking at the flat, sandy plains which had been painted on sets in the studio could not mistake the landscape of Spain.

At that moment, a couple of girls came and dragged Udet away, pleading with him to perform a juggling trick. Finding herself standing next to Strauss, Clara felt obliged to continue the conversation.

'And . . . where do you work?'

His cool grey eyes flickered over her as though he could barely be bothered to reply. Clara noticed a navy-blue cuffband on his arm which read *Legion Condor*.

'I suppose you know the Reichsluftfahrtministerium?'

It would be hard to miss it. Goering's new Air Ministry on Wilhelmstrasse at the intersection with Leipzigerstrasse was simply as gargantuan as its chief, though rather more sober in its décor. Indeed the building was starkly austere. It was popularly called Haus der Tausend Fenster but in reality the granite slab had not one, but four thousand windows, extending seemingly endlessly across the cliff face of its façade. Inside there was a lift without doors which never stopped, so that staff had to step out as it passed their floor.

'Ernst has room 231 and I have room 232.'

'Do all these officers work with you?'

'Somewhere.' He cast a dismissive glance at them. 'On a lower floor.'

'Do you fly much?'

He gave a bored smile. 'I get out as much as I can. Like Ernst I'm not made for desk work.'

Clara willed herself to keep the conversation going. 'So what's this work for the Fatherland you're engaged in?'

His laugh was as desiccated as leaves blowing down a blind alley. 'Ernst exaggerates. It's technical stuff. It may as well be me as anyone.'

He was plainly unwilling to talk, but Clara ploughed on, trying to look at him without staring at the scar. His face was like a sculpture on some old Roman temple, half perfect and half decayed.

'Have you known Ernst for long?'

'We met in 1916. We were assigned to the same unit flying single-seater Fokkers. We were out one day, making a routine patrol, when we came under heavy fire from a group of British and French aircraft. We were hugely outnumbered but Ernst managed to down a French plane and I downed another. These fellows made forced landings and Ernst decided to land beside them and take the men prisoner. They were terrified, as you can imagine, but Ernst strode over and shook hands with them, like a proper gentleman. When they were later imprisoned, he brought them cigarettes. I thought, that's the kind of man I would like for a friend. After the war I continued flying commercially and when Goering got the Luftwaffe going again, I rejoined.'

All the time he told her this, he had kept his head averted, as though conscious that she might not like to look at him, his gaze fixed on the middle distance. Eventually, he seemed to remember where he was. 'But enough of my work, Fräulein Vine,' he said stiffly. 'Yours is far more exciting.'

'It's quiet at the moment. We have a short break before we start rehearsals.'

'You're going to enjoy working with Ernst. He has a taste for fun. Look at him over there.'

Udet was juggling with a couple of empty wine bottles. A space had cleared around him, but his ability was hampered by a drunken girl who was getting too close, trying to hang on his neck.

'Everyone's looking forward to working with him. I hear he makes paper aeroplanes that fly as well as the real thing.'

'Just one of his many accomplishments,' commented Strauss dryly. 'He also spins plates and does cartoons as well as a street artist. Women find him irresistible. And he usually sees little reason to resist them.'

Clara wondered if this was meant to include herself.

'He's promised to organize a flight for me,' she volunteered. 'I need to fly to understand my character properly. And to tell the truth, I've always wanted to go up in a plane.'

'Why?'

'It sounds interesting.'

'Does it? I'll take you then.'

The offer took her aback. 'Do you mean it?'

'I have a test flight to make from Tempelhof on Thursday. A Henschel 126. You can come up with me if you like. As long as you sit tight and wear something warm. No female hysterics in the cockpit. Can you manage that?'

'Certainly.'

'Good then. It'll have to be early, mind. Be there at nine.'

From across the room, Udet could be heard mocking the grand new art gallery the Führer had opened in Munich. In contrast to the Degenerate exhibition, the Haus der Deutschen Kunst was a long-held ambition of Hitler's to showcase the best of German art. Udet, his face glowing with drink and wreathed in smiles, was telling an indiscreet joke about his boss. 'So Goering is visiting the House of German Art and he's enraged to find a portrait of himself as a pig. He starts to complain but the museum director says, "Oh no, Herr Reich Minister, can't you see that's a mirror?"'

There was a gale of laughter, but Strauss turned away and stared out of the window towards the dim confines of the park. From there, the ugliness of his disfigurement was hidden, yet the shade of stubble on his face seemed to echo a deeper shadow in his eyes. Clara tried to read his emotions but it was impossible to tell what he was thinking until he said quietly, 'I fear my friend Ernst has a dangerous condition.'

'What's that?'

'He damaged his hearing in the war. It means he speaks too loudly for his own good.'

There was a crash from across the room. Udet, with a tablecloth tied round his waist, was dancing the can-can on a tabletop.

Chapter Nine

'Why must we study healthy eating?' enquired the teacher, a woman with hair wound in tight braids around a face that could split wood.

'Because our bodies belong to the Reich and we have a responsibility to nurture them?'

'Good. Anything else?'

A forest of hands. 'Because we are the bearers of children and children are the building blocks of the German Reich.'

In a sun-dappled room, with a stunning view overlooking the lake, twenty young women sat in rows, dressed identically in grey dirndls over white blouses and blue checked headscarves. Ahead of them, her feet planted wide and a rod in her hand, the teacher pointed at the board.

Mary always felt a little ripple of nausea when she set foot in a school – a souvenir of her days in a New Jersey boarding establishment battling with algebra and the American Civil War. But the Bride School brought on a lurch of full-scale sickness in the pit of her stomach. There was no smoking inside – God, how did they cope? – and the corridors were infused with an institutional cocktail of cabbage and carbolic. Indeed, it would be hard to find a more spotless institution than the Bride School. The garden looked like it had been tidied with tweezers. The gravel drive was combed and the path ran down the lawn like perfectly parted hair. Even the birds on the lawn were like tiny mechanical toys, hopping like clockwork on the shaven grass.

'This really is an inconvenient time for a journalist's visit,' complained the woman alongside her, who was called Fräulein Wolff.

'Why inconvenient?' asked Mary disingenuously, but if she had hoped to eke some information out of the woman, she was to be disappointed.

'We have an administrative examination,' she said blandly. 'There is to be a visit from the Ministry. We are planning demonstrations of the various classes. Childcare, Sewing, Obedience in Marriage and so on. Also there is to be a talk on "How to be a Good German Woman".'

'That all sounds fascinating,' said Mary encouragingly. 'Perhaps I could sit in.'

'I doubt it.'

She tried again. 'Do all SS brides come to a school like this?'

'All SS marriages must be authorized to prevent SS men marrying unsuitable women.'

'In what way unsuitable?'

Fräulein Wolff gave a sniff of exasperation at being required to answer unsolicited questions.

'Health, for a start. The brides must complete forms giving all family history of tuberculosis, psychopathy and gynaecology. If an SS man is found to have contracted an unauthorized marriage, he will be expelled from the SS.'

'Expelled? Just because he doesn't have a certificate?'

The woman looked as if she would dearly like to expel Mary there and then.

'Follow me.'

She led Mary through a pair of high double doors into the marble hallway. Above the mantelpiece, facing the Führer's picture like a pair of grisly betrothal portraits, was a painting of Gertrude

Scholtz-Klink, the leader of the Women's Bureau, in grey worsted jacket, shirt and tie.

'It's Frau Scholtz-Klink you really need to see. She's away just now. I shouldn't really be the one to talk. Can I see your journalist permit again please?'

Mary flourished the pass which had been issued to her with punctilious efficiency on the day of her arrival. The Germans were still, thankfully, keen to assist American journalists in every particular in the hope of cementing an international alliance. The woman's face creased with dismay.

'As I tried to explain, this is not a convenient day for you to visit, Fräulein. Perhaps you could return tomorrow.'

'Tomorrow I will be attending a speech by the Führer,' lied Mary. 'But I don't need much. I wonder if I could interview one of the brides? Perhaps there's somewhere I could talk with one of the women in private?'

The idea of brides enjoying private conversations was plainly unheard of here. Fräulein Wolff seemed about to refuse, then the demands of the day overtook her.

'Very well. Come in here. They're preparing a wedding breakfast for one of the brides. I'll see if anyone can help.'

They entered a large, sparkling kitchen, crowded with a bevy of brides in white aprons. Either the warmth of the ovens, or the proximity of food made the atmosphere jollier here than in the rest of the house. There was a hum of chatter and a mouth-watering smell of spice and baking. In the shafts of sunlight, clouds of flour floated over a worktop where a couple of brides were bent attentively, in the act of what looked like plaiting strands of dough. Others were weaving ivy and orange blossom into table settings in the shape of a swastika with a candle at each corner. In the middle of the wide pine table, glistening in the sunshine, stood the wedding cake. It was a glorious, two-tier effort, and when Mary looked closer she saw that on its snowy top, instead of a bride and groom, a tiny, black-suited effigy of the Führer stood to attention, rendered in marzipan right down to his little moustache, and surrounded by sugar roses.

'As you can imagine, we make a lot of wedding cakes here,' said Fräulein Wolff, tersely. 'What's the matter, Ilse?'

A plump blonde girl, with greasy braids and an agonized expression, was surveying the sugar figure in dismay.

'I'm worried, Fräulein Wolff. Will it not be difficult?'

'Difficult? Why?'

'Who is going to cut up the Führer? No one will want to do that, so no one will be able to eat him. It's a waste, and the Führer hates waste.'

The teacher's face creased in contempt. 'Let's not get into that, Ilse. I need your assistance. This is Fräulein Mary Harker from the *New York Evening Post*. She's an American journalist, and she would like to write a piece about an average day at the Reich Bride School. You will accompany her to the music room.'

At this suggestion Ilse looked thunderstruck. She stared from Mary to the teacher in dismay.

'Well, go with her, girl! Be as helpful as you can.'

Ilse wiped her hands on her apron and tucked a strand of hair behind her ear. Despite the uniformity of the dreary serge uniform, she somehow made it look untidy, bulging out in places, her blouse spilling out between the laces of her dirndl. She led the way to the music room and Mary closed the door behind them.

'Forgive me, Fräulein, I'm sure I can't help you. I don't know very much.'

'It's fine, Ilse,' said Mary, pulling out her notebook. 'I'll ask the questions. All you need do is answer them.' She gave her best, most encouraging smile. The one she reserved for policemen and small children. 'Tell me about the Bride School.'

'Well,' Ilse chewed a lip and cast her eyes around the music room, as though she might draw inspiration from the posters proclaiming *'Cooking Is the Woman's Weapon'* and *'Order saves you Time and Effort'* which had been tacked to the wall.

'What do you learn?'

'All sorts of things.' She rattled off a list. 'How often to change linen, how many times to wax and polish a floor, how to can fruit, how to obey your husband, what to cook on special days.'

'And why did you choose to come here?'

'Oh but you have to. If you don't attend, then your man will be dismissed from the SS. When you get your certificate you must submit it to the wedding office of the Race and Settlement central office, so that the marriage gets official SS approval.'

'Approval?'

Ilse looked at her as if she was mad.

'Everyone in Germany needs approval to get married. Everyone needs an Ariernachweis, that's a certificate of Aryan purity. But it's stricter for people marrying in the SS. You have to report to the Race Bureau to have your racial characteristics assessed.'

'And how do they do that?'

'It's very simple really. You get weighed and they measure your nose and your upper lip. You won't get permission to marry if you don't pass that. You also need to provide birth and marriage certificates for your ancestors going back to 1750 – that's such an effort. Sometimes you have to visit all the churches they married in, to find the proof. But the SS needs to be absolutely certain you are racially pure, with no Jewish or mixed blood.'

Their conversation was interrupted by the clanging of a bell and the clatter of shoes on the stairs.

'It's lunchtime, Fräulein. Would you like to join us? It's not Sunday but the school has declared today we will have Eintopf.'

Mary had heard about this. Every Sunday, in an effort of national belt-tightening, everyone, from party leaders downwards, ate only one dish at dinner and gave the savings to the Winter Relief fund. Generally the Eintopf was a stew with floating islands of grease, into which the least glamorous parts of an animal had gone. Mary decided to pass on it.

'It's all right,' said Ilse. 'I'm not hungry either. We could take a walk in the garden if you'd like.' She cast a glance at Mary's bag, from which a packet of cigarettes protruded. 'You can smoke outside, if you want.'

They strolled into the garden and down the path. It was a crisp autumnal day and as they rounded the path they came across a workman hammering the timbers of a building, midway through construction. He straightened up politely as the women passed, then continued with his task. It was a mediaeval-style cottage, complete with flowering window boxes, beams and timbered gables. Only the roof remained to be finished. It looked like a playhouse for grown-ups.

'That could be straight out of *Snow White*. It looks like it ought to have the seven dwarves inside it.'

'It's going to be a model home,' explained Ilse. 'For the brides to practise married life.'

'Not so much of a fairy tale then.'

'Oh, it will have everything you need,' continued Ilse earnestly. 'A kitchen, an ironing board, a sewing room. They're going to bring in children from a local kindergarten for childcare practice. I love looking at it. It's going to be like a perfect little home . . .' She stopped suddenly, and Mary noticed that tears had sprung into her eyes. 'I'm sorry, Fräulein Harker. It's a difficult time for me.' She let out a sob. 'A friend of mine has just died.'

'Died?'

'Here in the garden. I don't know what happened to her.' Ilse shuddered, imagining Anna face down on the grass, a ruby line of blood leaking from her mouth and smearing the strands of her bleached hair. Then she remembered that Frieda Müller had said

Anna had been shot directly in the heart. Killed the way an expert huntsman would kill a deer, Frieda had explained to a little group of brides in a hushed voice. That's what one of the policemen had told her. The thought of Anna hunted down like an animal made fresh tears come.

'You mean Anna Hansen?' probed Mary.

'How did you hear? It hasn't even been in the newspapers.'

'I heard they arrested the gardener.'

'Hartmann. Yes, they took him away, so I suppose it must have been him. But I would never have guessed it. He's just a simple lad really. Soft in the head. And he has a lazy eye. He was always staring at us, but I thought looking can't hurt, can it? I suppose I was wrong.'

'To be honest, Ilse, I knew about the case already. That's partly why I'm here. I was planning to ask Fräulein Wolff about it.'

Ilse looked horror-struck. She stopped in her tracks.

'You can't do that! They won't talk to you about that!'

'Why not?'

'We're not allowed to talk about it. We were all told to keep quiet and not ask any questions. They said it was a tragic accident and Hartmann had been taken away, so there was nothing more to say. Oh dear,' she wailed, realizing her indiscretion. 'Fräulein Wolff will kill me if she thinks I've been talking to you about Anna.'

The thought of punishment to come brought on a fresh burst of tears, prompting Mary to put a consoling arm round Ilse's shoulder and say coaxingly, 'I would never tell anyone you had spoken about it. You have my absolute word on that. But it seems unfair that poor Anna's death should be hushed up, doesn't it? That she should be swept under the carpet as though she didn't matter?'

It was a shrewd image. The idea of Anna being tidied away in the same frenzy of cleanliness that ruled everyone's lives at the

Bride School had its intended effect on Ilse. She bit her bottom lip and swiped a sleeve across her face.

'No. You're right.'

They carried on walking down the gravel path until they reached a group of pine trees standing at the end of the grounds, overlooking the lake. Ilse stopped and looked beseechingly at Mary, as though she held the answer to the questions which had been troubling her.

'To tell the truth, Fräulein Harker, I don't really believe it was anything to do with Hartmann. Anna would never have had a relationship with him. She wouldn't give him the time of day. She loved her fiancé, Johann. She used to tell me how she met him, when she was dancing at the Wintergarten, wearing a sequinned corset and a feather headset.'

'She was a dancer?'

'Yes, and Johann came to see her. He walked up to her in a bar afterwards to tell her how much he admired her performance, and it was love at first sight. She was always writing to him. And he wrote back. She kept his letters in a special place.'

'A special place?'

Ilse froze like a trapped deer, as though Mary had laid a cunning snare for her, into which she had innocently wandered. She was the kind of interviewee who made you feel like the Gestapo, Mary thought.

'Oh dear. That's something else I shouldn't have told you. There's no privacy here, you see. They say privacy is bad for brides and leads to indolence. But Anna found somewhere.' She shot a defiant, damp-eyed look at Mary. 'A sort of hiding place, behind the wardrobe in the dormitory. If you push the wardrobe out, there's a vent in the wall where a fireplace was. It's bricked up, but there's a space at the top, where the bricks don't fit.'

'How do you know? Have you looked in there?'

'No! Well, yes. You see, I had noticed that Anna would go to the dormitory in the evening sometimes, when we were supposed to be singing, and one day I followed her there and saw her sitting on the bed, with the wardrobe pulled away from the wall and this little leather case on her knees. Well, it was not a case so much as a little portable desk, a lap desk I think you call it, with a handle at the top, and doors that open out and little places to keep your pen. For writing letters when you travel, you know?'

'Sure. My grandmother had one of those.'

'Anyhow, when Anna saw me she got terribly cross and said it was bad enough having no privacy, without having nosy brides following her every second of the day. She was so angry I thought she was going to slap me.'

'Did you read the letters?'

Ilse's cheeks blazed with colour. 'Of course not! What must you think of me? I would never have done that. But after she died I checked to see if the case was still there. I thought she probably kept her jewellery in it too, and you aren't allowed jewellery here. I knew I should have said something about it but, you see, I felt it was disloyal to her. When I asked Fräulein Wolff what they did with Anna's things, she said they had sent them on to Johann. Her clothes belong to the Bride School, so there wasn't much. Just a hairbrush and shoes and so on. I should have mentioned the case then, I suppose, but Fräulein Wolff would have been so angry. I do keep thinking about it. Someone's going to find it, sooner or later, and read all of Anna's private thoughts. I wish I could give it to Johann, or her family, but I haven't the first idea where they are. All I know is that she had a sister who lives in Munich called Katia.'

'Perhaps I could help.'

'How could you?'

Mary improvised fast. 'The woman who shares my apartment is a family friend. It was she who told me about Anna. That's how I heard about it.'

'And do you think she could return the letters to Anna's family?'

'I'm sure she could.'

Ilse flushed with joy. 'Then you *must* take the case. At least that way it'll go to someone who cares. They've already reallocated her clothes to another bride. There's a new girl in her bed and Anna's only been dead a couple of days.'

'Could you fetch it for me?'

Ilse cast a panicky glance back at the house, as if they were being watched.

'I'm late for Volksgemeinschaft anyway.'

'What's that all about?'

'Oh, um, community issues, you know. We're doing race and the national economy today. But the teacher, Frau Schneider, is very easy-going.'

'Right.'

'I'll say I need a clean apron from the dormitory. This one is covered with flour. And if anyone sees me with the case, I can always say it's yours. Wait for me in the hall.'

She was back in minutes, carrying a small case of burgundy leather by a brass handle. It was good-quality leather, supple and soft, with a brass fastening. The last worldly goods of Anna Hansen. Mary was appalled at how anxious the Bride School had been to rid themselves of all traces of their former pupil. As Ilse made to hurry off, Mary pressed a card on her.

'Take this. It has my old address on it but they know where to reach me. You must contact me if anything else occurs to you.'

Ilse scrutinized the card solemnly. The address was a street called Winterfeldstrasse that she had never heard of. She tucked it in her belt.

'Thank you, Fräulein, I will.'

The leather case was far heavier and more expensive-looking than she had expected. Mary wondered whether to open it herself, or wait till she saw Clara. As she was pondering this, Fräulein Wolff bore down on her with an expression of suspicion and dismay. Now that she had what she needed, Mary decided to broach the subject.

'I meant to ask you, Fräulein Wolff. I was so sorry to hear about the dreadful incident with one of your brides the other day.'

Fräulein Wolff flinched, as though she had been physically assaulted.

'How did you hear about that?'

'A family friend told me.'

'It was a tragic accident, Fräulein. Her family have asked for absolute privacy on this affair. And before you ask, no one will be speaking about it, do you understand? No one at all.'

Chapter Ten

The terminal building of Tempelhof airbase in the south of the city was a showpiece for the new Germany. Built by Ernst Sagebiel, the same man responsible for the monumental Air Ministry, its sprawling hangars fanned out in a gigantic arc, intended to resemble the spread wings of an eagle in flight. It was the largest freestanding building in the world. Beneath it, in five levels of underground tunnels, fighter bombers were being assembled and above, the mile-long roof was arranged in tiers with room for eighty thousand spectators to observe aerobatic displays. The whole place felt less like an air terminal and more like a cathedral devoted to the twin gods of aviation and the Third Reich.

Clara had never been anywhere so big. Standing in the cavernous Hall of Glory, still not completed, she was completely disorientated. The place was so vast, the distances between each point of focus so great, that she felt disembodied, all her senses adrift. It was like being trapped inside a Cubist painting with perspective going in all directions and an incipient dizziness from looking too hard.

Arno Strauss was striding towards her. The withered twist of his face startled her afresh, and it was hard to tell if his tense expression was mere disfigurement or if he was regretting his offer of a flight. He had goggles pushed back on his head and a cigarette clamped between his fingers.

'Good morning, Fräulein Vine.' He looked askance at the black polo-necked jumper and trousers she was wearing. 'You're going to freeze like that. Take this.'

He shrugged off his leather jacket and draped it around her shoulders. It was sleek brown leather with epaulettes and a simple winged eagle on the breast pocket. The weight of it was comforting, as was the warmth of his body still contained in its rabbit fur lining.

'Still want to come? Not nervous, I hope?'

'Only a little.'

She had been sick with nerves from the moment she woke up. Indeed she had barely slept. Silly really, she told herself as she brushed her teeth and made a black coffee. People fly in aeroplanes all the time. And this man was an expert. One of the top pilots in the entire Luftwaffe, Udet had said. Why should the prospect of flying be enough to terrify her? Nonetheless, she had been unable to eat any breakfast. That was probably a wise precaution.

'Just so you know,' he remarked shortly as they headed out of the hall, 'I'm bending the rules a little here.'

'Not too much, I hope.'

'Let's just say, for official purposes you don't exist.'

They walked out onto the tarmac, a sharp wind blasting against their faces, forcing them to raise their voices to a shout. The plane was standing ready for them, a sleek, angular, grey-blue machine, nose tilted upwards like some great rook poised to lurch forward and creak heavily into the air. As they ducked under the wing, Strauss reached up and his forefinger brushed a swastika painted on the underside.

'I always touch one for luck.'

'Do you need luck?'

'We all need luck. Though I've probably had more than my share already. We may have to rely on yours.'

The cockpit was barely big enough for one person but there were two seats, one behind the other, and Strauss propelled her into the rear, threading the buckles of a parachute harness over her shoulders and handing her a sheepskin-lined cap and goggles. His face was rigid with concentration as he fitted first her parachute, then his own. He smelled of leather, grease and petrol fumes. When he bent close to fasten her buckles she caught a whiff of alcohol, which added to her jittery nerves.

'So have you flown this plane often?'

'First time, in fact. This one's a prototype. A Henschel Hs 126. It hasn't entered service yet. They've made ten for us to try out. The idea is it's able to go fairly slow.'

'Is that a good thing?'

He gave a gruff laugh.

'Good for our purposes. Though it won't seem slow to you, I promise.'

He settled in front of a curved dashboard, slammed down the glass hatch over their heads and began to run his eyes over the instrument panel. Through her goggles, Clara looked uncomprehendingly at the blur of levers and dials. Strauss's perfect, undamaged side was towards her and she was so close to him, she was practically breathing into his neck, her knees folded up into her chest.

'Who usually sits back here?'

'It's the camera bay.'

He flicked a switch, gunned up the engines and the plane began to whine, a deafening high-pitched squeal that sent a shudder through the entire fuselage. Below them Clara saw a man run out to remove the chocks beneath the wheels and the plane crept forwards, taxiing slowly and bumpily down the runway which stretched seemingly endlessly ahead of them, lit by a narrow avenue of lights. Then it gathered speed and she felt her intestines sink within her as the plane rose with a loud thump into the air.

As the force of acceleration pressed her body back into the bucket seat, Clara thought how uncomfortable it must be for a grown man to cram himself into this tiny steel space. The dashboard had come alive now, a bank of wavering needles and glowing lights, and she saw the set of Strauss's jaw, the flinty eyes narrowed as he pulled the stick towards him and they hurtled upwards into the dense air.

Below them the city was dwindling to a quilt of red roofs and chimneys. Just outside Tempelhof, she could see a patchwork of allotments, little grids of cabbage and leeks, like a bar chart in a child's schoolbook. Around the green spaces the crossword puzzle of streets and blocks extended and on the outskirts of the city braids of smoke from factory towers twisted into the sky.

Thinking of herself and Strauss suspended so perilously high above them, Clara's heart caught in her mouth. Why had she agreed to his invitation, she asked herself, yet she knew the answer already. Some instinct within her, ingrained too deeply to eradicate, meant she was never able to refuse a challenge. Their father had instilled it in childhood, setting sister against brother, making every game of chess a competition, every outing an opportunity to test their own resources. On holiday in the Scottish Highlands, where the children would follow his austere, forbidding figure as they laboured with knapsacks through the drizzle, he would set each child a task. They would be left in a distant location equipped with only a ball of string, a compass and a shilling. That was all they required, he would say, to hike their way home. Somehow, Clara had always managed it. From an early age she had learned never to show fear and never to reveal reluctance.

As the plane climbed higher the map turned into a tapestry, with dark green forests, thick as fur, wedged between the patchwork of fields. A flash of river, like mercury. They flew through a fleece of clouds, moisture beading the outside of the glass, and out again into the empty sky. As Clara breathed in the air, sharp and cold as a knife, she felt a rush of exhilaration. Suddenly she understood the addiction of flight. How wonderful it must be to have this heart-stopping excitement in your life, to feel that in an instant you could soar above the city and leave your landlocked life behind you.

'That's the rate-of-climb indicator.' Strauss jabbed a finger at the instrument panel. 'The boost pressure indicator, the speed indicator, the altimeter. The maximum speed of this plane is three hundred and sixty-five kilometres an hour.'

None of the dials meant anything to her. Crouched behind Strauss, Clara felt like Sinbad on the back of the eagle, though her every sensation was governed by the penetrating cold. Her attempt at dressing warmly had been hopelessly inadequate. The cold burned her face and even with Strauss's jacket she felt as if she might freeze to the steel seat. She wondered how Strauss was managing without it, though she could see he was wearing fur-lined boots and a thick sweater swaddled over several layers.

They were much higher now, unimaginable thousands of feet, and below them Brandenburg spread out to the faint line of the horizon, purple with the wrinkle of the hills.

'Hold on!' shouted Strauss.

From its great height, the plane flipped in a graceful somersault, tumbling through the cloud cover before swooping downwards. Banking and turning, it rolled over and over so she could no longer tell whether they were up or down. To her horror, it seemed that the propeller had cut out and the engine was dead. As they hurtled towards the earth, trees and grass and buildings came into view. Clara could scarcely breathe from terror. A searing pain drilled in her ears and the air was knocked from her lungs as she gripped the sides of the seat, wanting to scream but unable to make a sound. The propeller was still not functioning. She squeezed her eyes shut. For several seconds they continued downwards until at the last moment, when they had dipped so low they almost touched the grass with one wing, the plane swung violently to one side, Strauss opened the throttle and the ground leapt away from them as they ascended steeply into the air.

'That's called a Dead Stick landing,' he shouted, pulling the plane into a rapid climb. 'Our friend Ernst has the copyright on that.'

For a moment she did not grasp what he was saying, until she comprehended that the terrifying plunge was intentional, and that Strauss had performed a dangerous stunt without warning her. When she understood, fury and fear mingled in her as the plane thrust its way upwards, every inch shuddering as the propeller blades, working again, sliced through the cold, white air. She was going to be sick, she knew it.

Above the cloud bank the plane dropped speed a little, levelled out and they drifted high through the sparkling morning. The ground beneath was obscured by vapour so they were entirely alone, suspended between earth and heaven. Spokes of sunlight streamed through gaps in the clouds.

Strauss brought the plane around in a vast, lazy loop as though it was performing its own graceful ballet in the air. Then he seized the throttle and brought it down forcibly so that the sky reared up towards them and the plane was almost at ninety degrees. Clara wanted to beg him not to perform another stunt but the breath was knocked out of her, as though she had been winded, and the rushing air pressed against her lips. She formed the word 'Please!' but it did not emerge from her mouth. When she felt the plane level and then tilt nose down, she knew it was already too late.

The scream of the engine was too high for her to speak, and she was consumed by a panicky vertigo. The ground was rushing towards them crazily fast. Nine thousand feet, eight thousand, seven thousand. The air speed indicators on the dashboard wheeled excitedly round in their glass cases. Wind whipped through the fuselage and red lights glowed on the dashboard. What was he thinking of, trying a stunt like this? Strauss's face revealed nothing, but his jaw was clenched as he grappled with the controls. The fuselage was juddering so violently she was certain the plane was about to come apart. They were hurtling towards earth in a steel coffin, about to sink like a stone into the hard ground. Strauss seemed to be wrenching the throttle while they continued to accelerate steeply down. She felt the nausea rising in her, and looked for something to vomit in. How awful to be plunging to your death and looking for a sick bag.

Just as they seemed certain to die, Strauss made a sharp movement with his foot, jerked the throttle lever towards him and the plane tilted ninety degrees, throwing them both bodily to the left as they rose again. Through her jangled brain the comment of Goebbels came to her.

'I think you have a taste for danger, Fräulein.'

Goebbels was wrong. She had no taste for danger. But danger had a way of seeking her out.

It took a few minutes for the plane to bank and turn again and make a slow descent towards the Tempelhof runway. Strauss taxied to a halt and the engine grunted and stuttered before it died and the propeller blades flapped to a halt. Taking off his hat he sat still for a moment, his lips compressed into a mirthless grin. Beads of sweat stood out on his brow. His eyes were dark and unfathomable, like a pool of oil.

'Were you frightened?' he said.

'No.'

'You're lying.'

'OK, I was terrified.'

He laughed. A short, joyless bark. 'So was I. I lost control there, you realize? I thought we were for it. The throttle locked at high altitude. I almost gave up. Luckily I managed to kick the stick with my foot in the nick of time.'

He helped her climb out of the plane and they walked back across the tarmac. They had spent no more than fifteen minutes in the air, yet she felt like a lifetime had passed. Her legs were shaking as though she had just got off a ship and her thoughts were a maelstrom of confusion. Had Strauss deliberately risked her life, as well as his own? Was he telling the truth when he said he lost control?

'How do you feel?'

Instinctively, as ever, she suppressed the anger and confusion churning inside her.

'I feel like a cocktail that's just been shaken,' she said lightly.

He looked at her in astonishment, but even as she said it, her mood changed. It was true. She was euphoric that she had not died. She had cheated death and was about to continue an ordinary Berlin morning, going about her ordinary, earthbound life. Did every pilot have this intense, searing sensation of being alive, every time he returned to land? If so, it was almost worth the fear you went through to achieve it.

'Well, I need a smoke.'

Strauss stopped, reached over to the pocket of the jacket she was wearing, freed a packet of cigarettes, and lit one for her and one for himself. His fingers, she noticed, were trembling.

'Sorry to frighten you.'

'I thought you said the conditions were perfect.'

'The conditions were fine. It was the throttle that misbehaved.'

'I hope you mention that throttle in your report.'

'I certainly will.'

'There is one thing I wanted to ask. When we were up there. You said you almost gave up. So why did you not?'

His face glazed over again with the absent, thin-lipped expression that she had seen before.

'It was too early for me to die. Especially with you on board.'

She laughed, as though he was joking, though he gave no appearance of it.

'You know,' he said, 'there's a poem I like. It's Irish. You might know it.'

'Try me.'

'I know that I shall meet my death
Somewhere among the clouds above;
Those that I fight I do not hate
Those that I guard I do not love.'

'That's Yeats. *An Irish Airman Foresees His Death*.'

There was a spark of interest in his eyes. 'You do know it?'

'I love it.'

'Me too. That idea has roots in our German mythology too. The old Teutonic heroes would go on a journey from which they would never return. It was called the Totenritt, the death ride.'

'Well thank God we avoided one of those.'

'We studied Yeats at school. That same teacher, the one who taught us our mythology, he loved poetry. Most German schoolchildren concentrate on Schiller, Heine, Goethe and so on. Or at least they used to. But our teacher focused on other poets too. Foreigners. Though he did point out that the Irish were Germany's allies, of course.'

As they neared the terminal they talked a little about the forthcoming film. Strauss never bothered watching Ernst's movies. Those film people always got the technical details wrong, and besides, he preferred Ernst when he wasn't pretending to be some po-faced Nazi hero humming the Horst Wessel Song. Ernst didn't need to pretend to be anything other than what he was. He already had a chestful of decorations and you could make a whole aeroplane out of the medals he'd won in real life. As they talked, the vibration resounding in Clara's bones gradually left her and she felt entirely calm.

When they reached the main hall Strauss said, 'I shall be meeting some compatriots of yours soon, as it happens. I've had an invitation to meet your former king. The Reich Minister's holding a reception for him at Carinhall.'

'That will be fascinating,' said Clara neutrally.

'Do you think so? For an actress perhaps. As a pilot I can't think of anything worse. I'm not suited to standing around making polite conversation with duchesses.' He looked at her thoughtfully then gave a stiff, ironic bow.

'Now, Fräulein, I must go and fill out my test report.'

She felt a surge of regret that he was leaving so soon, but shrugged off his jacket and held it out to him.

'I hope you got what you needed. For your film, that is.'

'More than enough.'

'Then I'm glad to have helped.'

Strauss tipped his cap and strode away into the airport building.

Chapter Eleven

When Mary Harker first arrived back in Berlin she had looked forward to revisiting all her old haunts. The Verona Lounge, on Kleiststrasse near Nollendorfplatz, which after hours turned from a chic evening club to an outrageously bohemian bar. Le Garconne on Kalckreuth Strasse, owned by Susi Wanowski, the former wife of a Berlin police chief who in a drastic life change had become the lover of the erotic dancer Anita Berber. Mali and Ingel's in Lutherstrasse, where if you ignored the sign reading 'Closed for Private Party' you would find all types of artists, intellectuals, singers and actresses. Even in the first days of the Reich, there had been lingering traces of Weimar decadence. Every night you could pass a cellar door and look down to see a dancer adjusting her bustier or a man with a saxophone in a sweaty bar. Now all these places were gone. The sly, smoky rhythms of jazz that leaked out of nightclub cellars had been replaced with light operetta, marching music and brass bands. Instructions had gone out from the Reich Chamber of Culture that saxophones should be replaced where possible with the viola, improvization was banned and any song's lyrics must be light-hearted rather than the 'gloomy, Jewish' kind. In particular, the Reich liked drums, to keep German hearts banging in rhythm. Strident music in a major key.

The nightlife wasn't the only thing that had changed. All the journalists in the world had converged on Berlin. It was competitive as hell. The crisis in Europe attracted foreign correspondents like bees to a honeypot, except there was nothing sweet about the content of the twice-daily press briefings handed out at the Ministry of Propaganda. The Nazis kept things as controlled as they could. Every morning and afternoon the journalists sat and imbibed whatever lies the Government chose, delivered either by the press chief Otto Dietrich or by Goebbels himself. At the moment it was all to do with the perfidious Bolsheviks and the need for Germany to arm itself to protect the world from Communism.

The only good thing Goebbels had done was to build a fancy new press centre on Leipzigerplatz where many of the foreign correspondents had moved en masse from the Adlon bar. It had newspapers and plush leather armchairs and mahogany desks, as well as telegraph facilities for sending copy, if anyone was mad enough to trust their copy to the in-house censors. It was, of course, staffed by Nazi informers, and there was a rumour that the seats were wired for sound, but the correspondents had evolved a complex method of semaphore if they had anything important to convey. That was where Mary sat in the dining room on the first floor, thinking about Clara.

Clara had revealed, in their long talk the other night, that she missed the presence of a man in her life. There had been a couple of men, yet sometimes she feared she had lost the chance of a serious relationship altogether. As ever she was full of lively gossip but now there was a sombre tone beneath it, and a suspicion of private heartache. She was estranged from her family and had ended the relationship which seemed most likely to lead to marriage.

But then, Mary had written the book on heartache. The man she had wanted didn't want her and the only person who had ever proposed to her was a lawyer back in New Jersey called Dirk

Phillips, who had put his case in such desiccated tones, he might as well have been cribbing from the marriage service itself. That dreary bit about marriage being ordained for the procreation of children and as a remedy against sin. As Mary didn't want any children and she didn't mind sin, she had no problem in turning Dirk's proposal down.

The arrival of a waiter bearing two Martinis and a bowl of olives returned Mary's thoughts to Clara. The truth was, whatever the state of her love life, Clara's life seemed enviable. She had that adorable apartment in Winterfeldstrasse – thanks to Mary – a car, even if it was on loan from a friend at the studio, and a wardrobe full of stylish clothes. Her career was blossoming. She looked, if anything, prettier than she had four years ago, her cheekbones more sharply defined and her beauty modulated by the grave shadows behind her eyes. Mary had always admired Clara's deep brown hair, with its hints of chestnut and honey. Mary's hair, by contrast, seemed defined by what it was not, neither brunette nor blonde, but a washed-out shade that only seemed to take on colour in the sun. She had nice eyes, but if she wanted a man to see them properly she had to take off her glasses, which meant conversely, that she could not see him. And whereas Mary had a constant battle with the bulge, the food shortages in Germany had left Clara lean and willowy, but not so slender that men did not look at her, just like they were doing now, as she made her way through the club to the table. Mary sprang up and kissed her.

'Thanks for putting me on to the Bride School. What a story! Let's hope no one at home gets any ideas. There are men in New Jersey who want nothing more than a woman who knows how to stuff a herring.'

Clara gave a wry smile.

'Frank Nussbaum loves the whole concept. When I told him they have lessons on how to obey a husband he was practically ready to move here.'

Clara guessed, though she had never asked, that Mary had given up the idea of marriage some years ago. Presumably she thought it was incompatible with her work. But then, she told herself, Mary probably assumed the same thing of her, and how accurate was that?

'How can those girls stand it?'

'You mean the prospect of marriage, or the pig-trotter stew they serve? God! Even I couldn't face the lunch.'

'So did you find out what happened?'

'A little. There was a girl called Ilse Henning who filled me in. To start with they were blaming it on the gardener. According to Ilse he was soft in the head. But when I called up the department of Criminal Police they said he had been released without charge. Rock-solid alibi, apparently. So they're combing through all the violent criminals on their books . . .'

'Which is a pretty long list in Berlin right now . . .'

'Exactly. And they still haven't found their man.'

'And Anna Hansen?'

'Looks like you were right. She was a dancer. Originally from Munich. Engaged to an SS Obersturmführer Johann Peters.'

'It must be the same Anna Hansen then. The girl Bruno knew came from Munich and had been a dancer. But she was the last person I'd have expected to find at a Bride School.'

Clara remembered what she could about the day she had come to Bruno's studio and found Anna Hansen there, a girl with a ready smile and a calculating look. When Clara arrived Anna had sat up, taken a paint-spattered sheet like it was an evening dress, and pulled it lazily over her neat, tightly muscled body. Clara had been cool towards her, thinking Anna was a romantic replacement for Helga, assuming that Bruno had forgotten Helga already, despite everything he said about being heartbroken. As a result the two women had exchanged barely a few words. And now she was dead.

'I suppose knowing that it's the same girl doesn't make much difference now.'

'Except . . . I almost forgot,' said Mary. 'There's this. It was hers. I said you might be able to give it to her family.'

She hauled out the burgundy leather case and passed it over. Curiously Clara fingered the neat tooling and the locked brass fastening. It was heavier than it looked.

'What is it?'

'It's a lap desk,' Mary explained. 'A kind of portable stationery case. Anna used to keep it hidden in the dormitory for the sake of privacy. Ilse said she used it for writing letters to the beloved Johann. She seemed to think that the letters are still in there, and Anna's family might like to have them back.'

'But why on earth did you say I'd give it to her family? I don't know them. They live in Munich presumably.'

'*Obviously* I didn't mean it! But I had to say something. No one else knows it exists. Ilse was upset that Anna's death seemed to have been brushed under the carpet and she wanted to believe that someone, somewhere, might care. I thought, if it makes her happy, why not?'

At that moment Mary was distracted by a greeting from the other end of the bar. *If that's not Mary Harker? Great to see you back! Are you planning on staying a little longer this time?* A gnarled American in a rumpled raincoat was waving a rolled-up newspaper in her direction and Mary disappeared for a chat. When she returned, Clara was looking at the case with concentration.

'You know . . . I think I will take it.'

'To Munich? That's the other end of the country! Nearly four hundred miles away. Don't be crazy, Clara. It's not even as if you know where the family lives.'

'We could find out.'

'How? As you said, Hansen is a common name. There's probably a hundred of them in the telephone book.'

'Why don't we look inside?' Clara tapped the case.

'That's more like it,' grinned Mary. 'You read my mind.'

'It may help us find an address. You said she kept all her letters. They may be private, but Anna isn't here to mind, is she? It doesn't count as snooping if someone's dead.'

'Girl after my own heart.'

'There's no key, I suppose?'

'Pass it here.' Mary had wrenched a kirby grip out of her hair and was applying it to the lock with intense concentration. Within a minute, the lock sprang open with a satisfying click.

'Ha! Little trick I learned as a kid. And much easier than I thought.'

The doors of the case opened out to reveal a miniature desk lined in worn purple plush, with a leather insert on the base for writing. Piled inside was a thick bundle of envelopes and papers, and at the back were small cubicles for pencils, pens and space for an ink bottle, which was missing. Above were two drawers with ribbon ties, one containing stamps, the other a stash of fresh envelopes. Mary took the bundle of papers, handed half of them to Clara and began to thumb through the rest.

The cache of letters had been hastily ripped from their envelopes and carelessly refolded. Most of them bore the address of the Bride School.

'Love letters,' said Mary.

They were written in a regular, unsophisticated schoolboyish hand, and from one of them dropped a small, black and white photograph of a group of SS officers, arms linked, standing outside a tavern. None of the men could have been older than twenty-five. There was no indication which was Johann Peters, but Clara could imagine him bending over the letter, the tip of his tongue protruding with concentration, as he tried to communicate with his glamorous new fiancée.

'And she kept her old programmes.'

Mary was flourishing a sheaf of theatre programmes, bundled together with a rubber band. The Friedrichspalast, the Wintergarten and the Metropol in Berlin. *Happy Journey*, Strauss's *Die Fledermaus*. A production of *The Merry Widow* at the Gärtnerplatz theatre in Munich for which Anna Hansen's name appeared in tiny print in the cast list of the chorus. Mary handed one over to Clara who peered at it, unable to make out any individual figure from the group of scantily clad women posing in a forest of peacock feathers.

'This isn't much help.'

'But this one could be.'

There was another letter, with a stamp on it, which was sealed but had not been posted. It was addressed to

Katia Hansen,

Frauenstrasse 17,

München

'Perhaps that's her sister.'

'That's good. So I have an address.'

'Seriously, Clara, I can't imagine why you would bother taking these all the way to Munich. It's not as though anyone knows we have the case. And Anna Hansen wasn't your friend, was she? She was a friend of Bruno Weiss.'

Something within Clara, some deep reserve of caution that now governed everything she did, prevented her telling Mary about the remark she had overheard at Udet's party, that Bruno Weiss had been seen in Munich at the exhibition of Degenerate Art, standing right in front of his own paintings and observing them with pride. She believed it, not only because the Luftwaffe officer had no reason to lie, but also because it was exactly the sort of bold, foolish, unconventional thing that he would do. She could just picture the satisfied smile on his face, knowing that whatever the regime thought about his paintings, Art always spoke for itself. Yet the officer had reported him to the authorities. And

Bruno was the only person in Germany to whom she had confided her own, secret activities.

If there was a chance of finding out what had happened to Bruno, it was a chance worth taking. And she could deliver the case to Anna Hansen's family at the same time.

'I have no work for the next few weeks. I've never seen Munich. Why not? It'll be like a holiday.'

Mary was looking at Clara with a level gaze. She bent towards her and spoke quietly.

'You've changed, Clara, since I was last here. You had me fooled then, and it was hard to tell what you were thinking. But it's worse now. Now I haven't got the first idea what's going on in your head.'

Chapter Twelve

For the rest of that week the cold settled on Berlin. The frost feathered the railings and softened the trees with a fur of brilliant white. The sweet smell of roasting chestnuts issued from trolleys parked on the pavement. A chill wind whipped round the grey flanks of buildings and iced the walls of the canal. All the iron that made up the city's bones, the cables that glittered in the sharp air, the girders that screeched and shivered, the tramlines, lamps, bridges and railway elevations, was frozen to the touch.

And still Clara could not shake off the sensation that she was being followed.

The feeling had been there from the moment that Archie Dyson had issued his warning. Dyson's advice had been to lie low, uttered as mildly as a bank manager cautioning against extending an overdraft. But lying low had changed nothing. In the following days the feeling had only intensified. Someone was on her tail and she was sure of it. The next afternoon, after a costume fitting for the new film – all girlish gingham dresses, dirndls and aprons – Clara decided to find out.

Babelsberg Station, a short walk from the studio, was a pretty, redbrick construction of gables and fretted wood. Looking down the tracks beneath her, feeling them grating and humming with the approaching train, Clara forced herself to consider the possibility that this feeling she had arose not from the streets of Berlin, but the depths of her own mind. She had always been self-conscious. Was this merely a sense of heightened alert that had become impossible to switch off?

Twenty minutes later the train pulled into Bahnhof Zoo and she descended the platform, making her way eastwards along Hardenbergstrasse. She walked fast, the chill slicing into her as she went. She passed peeling posters for Strength Through Joy holidays, with their blue skies, Norwegian Fjords and night sun on Baltic beaches. *Now You Can Travel Too!* The pictures would have been a mockery to passers-by, were it not for the fact that barely anyone lifted their eyes above street level, keeping their necks huddled tortoise-fashion into coats and scarves.

She turned left up Budapester Strasse, stepping purposefully as she approached the Tiergarten. There was a shiver of wind in the trees and the broad pathways were deserted, save for the dull bronze heroes who punctuated the paths. After a few minutes in the park, once she had assured herself no one was following, she executed a swift U-turn, and walked steadily south, dipping into the U-Bahn at Wittenbergplatz, and surfacing a few stops later at Potsdamerplatz.

The buildings of Wilhelmstrasse turned their drab, bank manager backs on her as the wind whipped down the streets of the government sector. She passed the Air Ministry and tightened her coat in an unconscious defensive reflex. Ahead of her, rounding the corner of Voss Strasse, where a forest of scaffolding surrounded the new Reich Chancellery, two men in leather coats approached. That was hardly surprising. The Gestapo were everywhere, and this was the very crucible of the Nazi regime. Clara passed them, eyes downcast, like any other citizen, observing them minutely all the same.

The Gestapo had only been in existence for four years, yet it had spread like a cancer through German society. Its aim was to know everything about a person, from what they wore, to how they slept, to where they went in their dreams. Its surveillance was legendary. The techniques were equally impressive but some of them, at least, she knew.

They had signals. A man bending to tie a shoelace might be signalling to his partner that he was keen to terminate the observation. A man raising his hat, a woman stroking her hair, a boy leaning against a wall turning the pages of his newspaper, all these apparently random gestures could be code for instructions or communication between one observer and another. Leo Quinn had taught her some of them, but these signals and their meanings changed constantly. What you needed, Leo had said, was to note more instinctive signals, like the set of a head or the direction of a gaze, and above all to develop a sixth sense that you were being watched.

In her mind she ran through a constant register of the people around her and studied not just their clothes but their faces, separating them out into their distinctive parts – easy elements like spectacles or a glass eye, and more subtly, the jut of a jaw, the curve of a nose, the eyes slightly too close together. At that moment, for example, there was a man sweeping the pavement, armed with a large broom, who glanced at her, revealing a mouthful of brown teeth. There was a boy of around sixteen, who seemed to be taking an inordinate length of time lighting a cigarette. Parallel to the Propaganda Ministry an old woman in a floral headscarf stood complacently while her fat little dog relieved itself against a lamp post. Ahead of her a man in a pale fedora with a dark band and a slight hunch to his shoulders turned a corner to his left. There was nothing she could see to raise any suspicion.

At the top of the street Clara jumped on a tram and took a quick glance round. Weary office workers were strap-hanging in the crowded carriage, exuding the smell of unwashed clothes. A boy in a cap and earmuffs stared at her dispassionately. Opposite, a man with a plush black hat and a silver-topped cane caught her eye with a flicker of puzzlement. That didn't worry her. She was quite used to being half recognized. She knew to counter it with stony impassivity. What she was looking out for was something more covert. Yet no one in the carriage deliberately looked away, or masked their observation beneath a newspaper.

By the time she jumped off the tram halfway up Friedrichstrasse the light was fading. The wide thoroughfare was the theatrical heart of the city, where the neon of the theatre lights reflected off the sides of gleaming Mercedes and BMWs. The street was busy with people beginning their evening out to the theatre. An operetta called *Maske In Blau* was playing at the Metropol. Past the steel arches of the station, the red neon lights of the Wintergarten announced that Das Führende Varieté, the leading variety company, was staging a magician's act.

As Clara passed she glanced in the shop fronts, looking through the displays of stockings and shoes and handbags, to the images of other pedestrians, noting the colour of their tie, or hair, or shoes. Anyone following would look utterly anonymous, so it was important to observe the details, the ones they could not easily change.

Further on she wove round the back of a crowd of people laughing and chatting as they waited to enter a cinema. With a jolt of surprise she noted that the film was *Madame Bovary.* She glanced up to see the dark eyes of Pola Negri looking across at Werner Scharf, the dashing actor who played Leon Dupuis. For once Clara was glad that her part had been so small. There was no chance of anyone connecting the figure of a nineteenth-century French village girl with the slight figure in trench coat and cloche hat lingering at the glass display cases that showcased coming attractions.

Past the cinema she stopped off at a café, and ordered a plate of bockwurst with potato salad and fried onion which she ate while observing the people outside, watching for anyone who dallied, or lingered without obvious purpose. For a while she kept her eye on a man waiting in a doorway opposite. He seemed restless and on edge, glancing over the top of his newspaper covertly, suggesting he was watching, without wanting to be watched. Then suddenly a girl ran up and joined him and they went off laughing, arm in arm.

At Oranienburger Strasse she caught the S-Bahn back down towards Nollendorfplatz and headed for her apartment. She had run a great ring round the city, with no sign of anyone in pursuit. Her aim had not been to shake off a potential tail, only to determine if they were there. But everything about her journey had convinced her: the only shadows were the ones in her mind.

It was properly dark now. Ahead of her street lamps hung like a string of pearls in the deepening dusk, casting precise circles of light on the pavement beneath. A man emerged in front of her and as he passed each lamp post his shadow loomed and wavered ahead. He was not a tail. A tail would have melted into the darkness on the other side of the street.

By the time she rounded the corner of Winterfeldstrasse, she was looking forward to a quiet night in and soaking in a hot bath with a good novel. Her feet were aching with all that walking. She should have worn more comfortable shoes.

The street was very quiet. It always was at night, even so close to Nollendorfplatz. A blind winked at a window, and she became aware of footsteps behind her. Something – perhaps that sixth sense Leo had talked about – told her to stop, and she ducked swiftly into the porch of the block to her right. A cat perched on the roof of a parked car watched her with bored yellow eyes as she shrank into the shadow, waiting for the footsteps to pass.

There were twenty paces between the corner of Nollendorfstrasse and her door. She knew. She had counted them. The footsteps were confident and deliberate. They took ten paces.

Fifteen. Then she recognized something. It was something she had heard before. A click of steel in the heel of the shoe. That was not unusual in Berlin, no one threw a pair of worn shoes away when the holes could still be patched; indeed not just patched but mended a dozen times, stitched and heeled and soled with cardboard. But there was something about this tread. Something languid, decisive, metallic. The paces came to a stop. He must be right outside her door.

She stepped out of the porch. Ralph Sommers was standing beneath the streetlight right outside her door, lighting a cigarette. He looked up at her approach.

'I must say you're awfully difficult to track down.'

'You seem to be awfully intent on finding me.'

He shook out his match, threw it away and smiled charmingly. 'That's because, Clara – may I call you Clara? – I would very much like to invite you for a drink.'

Clara was dumbfounded. She felt like she was playing a game, whose rules she didn't know. Had Sommers followed her all the way from Bahnhof Zoo? Had he tailed her right round the city, or had he come to Winterfeldstrasse by chance?

'You want to invite me for a drink?' she repeated.

'That's right. I'd be delighted if you could. Do you know the Einstein Café on Kurfürstenstrasse? Why don't we meet there? Are you free Thursday night? Say seven o'clock?'

Chapter Thirteen

Neukölln lay to the south of the city, a poor area of tenements, factories and cemeteries, crowded with East European immigrants. In the past it had been a Communist stronghold, and even now underground printing presses existed, tucked away on the top floors of shops, concealed in cellars or hidden in apartments, where the people who once had written for Communist newspapers now issued crude pamphlets with hand-lettered text containing news of people who had been imprisoned. They would paste them up at night, wearing gloves so they didn't leave fingerprints, with brushes and paste concealed in orange boxes. The penalties for distributing these *Flugblätter,* dissident political posters, was death and the Gestapo went to great lengths to analyse everything, from the papers' origin, to the brand of paint and the kind of typewriter used. Despite that, everywhere you looked scraps of flyers could be seen plastered on walls and across tram timetables, slapped onto advertising hoardings. Their messages were partially legible, where they had not been properly torn off. *German soldiers! Fight with Us for the Overthrow of the Nazi Regime! Join the Anti-Fascist Struggle!* There were stencils too: *Down With Hitler!* and more simply *Freedom!* If you wanted to know the truth about a country, better not to read the newspapers but to read the walls.

As she made her way that morning Clara wondered if her own allegiance was also evident to anyone who looked hard enough. Last night's encounter with Ralph Sommers had made her more determined than ever not to relax. Had he followed her round the city? And, if he had, was it purely to ask her for a drink? Was a drink, indeed, all that he wanted? His calm, faintly mocking demeanour, mingled with his undeniable attractiveness, had unsettled her profoundly and caused a night of restless, troubled sleep. She was looking forward to seeing him again, and dreading it at the same time. That lunchtime, however, she was due to meet Erich. They were going to his favourite restaurant, so for just a few hours she would do her best to forget the events of the previous evening and concentrate on something normal.

Erich was ready and waiting when she rang at the apartment. He ducked quickly out of the door, anxious to be away from his grandmother's nagging. Clara was touched how pleased Erich was to see her. She had feared, once he became a teenager, that his dogged, boyish affection would mutate into something more gruff and withdrawn. That a certain embarrassment and reserve would appear, along with the stubble and the broadening shoulders. And that might have been the case, if it hadn't been for his accident.

Aged twelve, away at summer camp with the Pimpf, the junior section of the Hitler Youth, it was as his mother had feared. Erich, who was short for his age, had attempted to make up for his lack of stature with an excess of ambition by scaling an almost vertical rock face. The fall badly fractured a femur and when he was brought back to Berlin to endure three months with his leg in plaster, Clara had spent many hours at the apartment reading aloud passages from some of her favourite books. They started with German novels like *Emil and the Detectives* and progressed to English works. This was partly to help Erich learn English but also because Clara had discovered there was no better way of bonding with him than over an absorbing passage of literature. He loved

Sherlock Holmes and *The Thirty-Nine Steps*. *Kidnapped* was possible, but slow. Dickens and P. G. Wodehouse left him baffled. Clara's experiments with English literature had another point. She didn't want to talk to Erich about politics or risk him absorbing any anti-Nazi views from her, in case he should repeat them at school and be punished. So she contented herself with talking about books and history. And of course, above all, film.

That day, as usual, they were going to see a movie after their meal. They made their way through to the U-Bahn, past the towering Karstadt department store, whose roof garden restaurant was a regular haunt of theirs. She loved taking Erich to places he would never normally go, treating him like an adult. Ordering anything he wanted from the menu. Besides, though he might be small for his age, he was the same height as her now, so it was all too easy to forget that he was still so young. That day, however, Clara was on edge and mildly irked. She decided it was because Erich was wearing his new Hitler Youth uniform. He had a freshly ironed brown shirt, gleaming belt and a swastika armband – an outfit for which Clara had paid a breathtaking hundred and thirty-five marks.

'Why have you got that on?'

'I've been collecting this morning.'

'Winter Relief?'

'Nope. You'll never guess what.' He wrinkled his nose. 'Bones. We have to go to households and collect bones from their kitchens. You can't imagine the stink of them.'

'Poor you. What on earth do they need bones for?'

'They grind them down for industrial use. Our leader says they turn bones into lipstick. Do you reckon that's true, Clara?'

She shuddered. 'If it is, that's the last time I wear it.'

'I have my proper induction ceremony next week. As soon as I turn fourteen.'

'Fourteen, eh? Quite grown-up.'

He gave a wry smile. He knew she was teasing. He had a watchful look which she sympathized with because she recognized it in herself. She knew Erich had been bullied at school, yet he took it as his due. An orphan was a dangerous thing to be. The only thing worse than having no mother or father was having a parent who turned out to be the wrong kind.

'So you'll come?'

'I'm sorry, Erich. I don't think I can make it.'

'Doesn't matter,' he shrugged.

The truth was, she didn't want to make it. Beside the Hitler Youth boys, with their ardent Aryan faces and their wide blue stare, Erich just didn't fit in. Erich had Helga's own dark eyes. The eyes that Clara had last seen begging her wordlessly to care for her son, as she lay broken and dying on Rykestrasse, a halo of blood lacquering around her head.

Their first meetings after Helga's death had been awkward affairs. Erich stared at his knees, his lip bitten, and barely spoke. He sat through whatever outing Clara devised – a walk, the movies, or the café – with the same, immutable expression. The only other boy Clara had ever known well was her brother Kenneth, who was the sunniest, least troubled person imaginable. Kenneth had come through the trauma of their mother's death entirely unscathed, and the worst he would do in a mutinous mood was go and kick a ball, or walk his dog, Flashman. Erich was different from Kenneth, quicker and more intelligent, but more troubled too. Clara had originally seen herself in a godmotherly role to Erich, but any thoughts she had of occasional trips to the theatre and the bestowing of improving gifts had gradually vanished. Now Erich was more like a son to her. At least what she imagined a son would be.

They came up out of the U-Bahn at Potsdamer Platz and made their way across the square to the Haus Vaterland. Kempinski's Haus Vaterland was a fantasy destination, a gigantic pavilion full of themed restaurants fitted out with astonishing detail. There was the Bavarian beer garden, which seated a thousand people, the Viennese Grinzing café, a Spanish bodega, a Hungarian eatery, Italian, Turkish and Japanese. Erich's favourite was the Wild West bar on the fourth floor. They passed through the saloon doors to find straw bales hung from the ceiling, rams' horns adorning the walls and wooden tables lit by tin lanterns. A cowboy in a ten-gallon hat showed them to a table beneath a poster proclaiming that *Law And Order's Rough And Ready In A Lawless Land*. That was the kind of slogan you saw scrawled on the walls in Neukölln. Clearly the restaurant owner had a well-developed sense of humour.

They ordered lemonade and Erich's favourite: braised pork knuckle with noodles. Clara loved indulging him. And he ate so much more now. She noticed the muscles bunching on his arms as he ate, the thickening neck, the stockiness which was gradually filling out his slender frame. Her eyes dwelt on him fondly as he tackled his plate, then she remembered an important piece of guardianship.

'I've been meaning to say, Erich. Your grandmother tells me the HJ leaders are rude to her. They undermine her authority.'

'That's not true. Oma's too sensitive. She's always interfering. She's got to understand I'm grown-up now. I'm not a child any more.'

Clara sympathized with Erich's grandmother. Everyone complained that the Hitler Jugend encouraged children to be contemptuous of their parents. For Erich, with his desperation to fit in, that tendency was likely to be worse. 'Anyway,' he continued, 'she won't see so much of me. I'm going to be away much more now. I'll be busy with the HJ.'

Clara knew how the Hitler Youth operated. Meetings every week and two hours of political instruction and sport every Saturday afternoon. Fifty-mile hikes at weekends. Camping in the holidays. The idea was that the boys should never have any peace and quiet. No time to escape the propaganda and reflect. It wasn't just the HJ, of course. The National Socialists had a group for every stage of life. The joke went that with a husband in the SA, a wife in the National Socialist Women's Movement, a son in the HJ and a daughter in the BDM, the only place a family could actually meet would be at the Nuremberg rally.

'Well, try to be more respectful to your grandmother, eh? She's an old lady now. She loves you.'

The English boys she knew of Erich's age had respect drummed into them, along with please and thank you and standing up when an adult came in the room. But in Hitler's Germany, things were different. The power lay with the youth, and they knew it.

'Yeah. I will.' He ate hungrily. 'I can't wait for next summer camp. We're going out to an island on the lake. I'm glad you taught me to swim because if you say you can't swim, they throw you in the water so you learn quickly.'

Sometimes, Clara thought, the less she knew about what went on in the Hitler Youth, the better.

'And how is school?'

'OK. Apart from Herr Klug. I hate that teacher. He has a *Backpfeifengesicht*.' It was a German word which didn't exist in English. It meant a face badly in need of a fist.

'Why do you hate him?'

Erich's face was a hostile muddle of emotion, as he sought to define the precise reason he disliked the man.

'He asks the boys what they had for Sunday lunch.'

'Why on earth would he ask that?'

'He's waiting to see who never says pork. You know, if they're Jews.'

Clara was surprised at this. She had seen the race charts in Erich's books full of photographs of children showing the difference between the Jew and the Aryan. The theme didn't just emerge in Rassenkunde, race science, but every subject. Even maths. '*Compare the percentage of Jews in different positions with their share of the total population.*'

'He's always trying to catch out Karl Meyer. Karl does fine at school. He gets top marks in maths and science. They don't let him join in the songs and all that, but everyone likes him. Anyway, Herr Klug makes Karl stand up for the whole lesson. And when Karl won the hundred metres Herr Klug said he wasn't allowed a medal.'

Clara wondered how it was that Erich could not see the connection between the odious teacher and the methods of the HJ. The anti-Semitism that made him bristle at school was openly taught in the Hitler Youth. How was it possible that he did not connect the two?

'I'm sure Herr Klug already knows who's Jewish. The Jewish boys don't Heil Hitler, after all. So what subject do you like best?'

'Still history. He's good, Herr Schnaubel, though we can't make him out. There are all kinds of questions about German history, or our future, that he just won't answer. He simply says, "We do not discuss what the Führer tells us".'

'He's right.' Clara realized Herr Schnaubel was playing a dangerous game. Most probably he hated giving the Nazi view of German history. Yet if a master was suspected of being anti-Nazi, he would be pursued by the bigger boys. Avoiding discussion was the safest tactic.

Erich finished his noodles and started to glance at the menu again, selecting, as always, Black Forest cake, sandwiched with whipped cream, topped with cherries and grated chocolate.

'I don't mind you missing my induction ceremony, Clara, but next year, if I'm lucky, I'll get to march at the Party rally and then you'll have to come and watch me.'

'I will. I promise. Now . . . I know what you want for your

birthday, and I'll give it to you next time I see you. Meanwhile, I got you this.'

Across the table she slid an envelope containing the signed postcard of Ernst Udet. Erich's eyes lit up, as she knew they would. He whistled.

'You've actually met Ernst Udet?'

'I'm married to him. In the film, at least. And yes, I've been to a party at his house.'

Erich's eyes swivelled from the card to Clara. He had quite forgotten his dessert.

'Do you think . . .? Is there any chance that I could meet him?'

'I'll see what I can do.'

He studied the picture, eyes shining.

'Perhaps they'll make a card of you soon. Like they did with Mutti.'

The promotional card of Helga Schmidt, which showed her flimsily clad and leaning coquettishly towards the camera blowing a kiss, might not have been the most appropriate image for a son to treasure, yet it was the most precious of Erich's paltry possessions. There had been a dreadful day when his schoolfriends discovered the picture, snuggled between the leaves of *Mein Kampf*, and waved it in the air with hoots of glee, taking it first for a girlfriend, and then, when they discovered the truth, with howls of cruel laughter and taunts of whore, and Mutti's boy. It was a miracle he had managed to recapture it.

'I suppose they will,' said Clara. 'I'll be on the poster, certainly.'

'I'm going to be a glider. Goering says Germany is to be a nation of aviators. I've signed up for training this summer. I can join when I'm seventeen.'

Clara wondered what would happen by the time Erich was seventeen. It might not be just gliding that awaited him. It might be war.

*

After dinner they went to the Ufa cinema in the base of the building. The first feature was a documentary about Mussolini's recent visit to Germany. There were shots of SS guards crouching on rooftops as Hitler and Mussolini rolled past side by side in an open-topped Mercedes, the Duce's darting black eyes surveying the massed storm troopers with a scowl. Fountains of coloured water had been installed in the Pariser Platz, in the red and green of the Italian flag, and white stands held aloft golden eagles on Unter den Linden. The newsreel was followed by a war film. As Erich relaxed beside her, Clara allowed herself a quick glimpse at his face. She adored him. Love had seized her with unexpected force, and Erich was not even her son. What must it be like to have a child of your own?

The film, however, was dreadful. It was one of the worst kind of war films, full of horror and violence. Yet again Clara wondered how Erich could like things like this? She supposed it was just a stage, like making model aeroplanes, that all boys went through. Perhaps even sensitive boys needed to find cruelty in themselves, to harden themselves like young African tribesmen, for what life had in store. To watch violence and death so they would know how to face it when it came for real.

Chapter Fourteen

In one way, deciding what to wear on an evening out should have been no problem for Clara. When Hitler established the Reich Fashion Bureau – which had originally been headed by Magda Goebbels – he decreed that German actresses were allowed to wear only clothes which had been made by German designers, of Aryan race, and made of pure German fabric. The result of this stricture was that German designers fell over themselves to persuade the top actresses to wear their creations. And even though Clara was far from a major star, she still received occasional dresses and jackets, and had been given a stunning violet evening gown from the House of Horn to wear at a recent premiere.

The problem was that the other part of her work involved attracting as little attention as possible. Distinctive clothes and perfume made a woman stand out. Her favourite scent, Bourjois' *Evening In Paris*, had been reluctantly consigned to the back of a drawer. Her looks made her the kind of woman that people noticed, yet she needed to be the kind that people stopped noticing.

In the end she selected a dress of soft moss green, with a sweetheart neckline and puffed sleeves. A single strand of pearls round her neck and diamond clips in her ears. Her nails were freshly lacquered, but covered by soft leather gloves. Attractive anonymity was the best she could hope for.

The prospect of a drink with Ralph Sommers unsettled her on several levels. She felt the predictable twists in her stomach, which always accompanied anxiety. She couldn't make him out. Had he followed her all that way through Berlin? If not, how had he known where she lived? What was his motive in asking her for a drink? Could it be purely the spark that had passed between them at the Goebbels' home? That teasing smile, as though they had shared some private joke. As she relived that moment she felt a jolt of sexual energy pass through her, but instantly reproved herself. Sommers was an attractive man, but not only was he a good ten years older than her, more importantly she could never have the slightest romantic interest in any fellow traveller of Oswald Mosley. This evening would most certainly be business, not pleasure.

Once dressed, she drew on her warm, fur-collared coat and looked for a hat. She had several to choose between: a purple velvet cloche with a white band, her soft and flattering brown cloche or her new, tip-tilted pillbox hat, draped with a fashionable few inches of veil. Veils were increasing popular just then. That was the genius of fashion, the way it suited itself to the times. Nothing could be more frivolous than the little scrap of netting that made a hat's veil, yet nothing could be more profoundly useful at a time when keeping one's eyes covered was a significant part of daily existence.

The Einstein Café on Kurfürstenstrasse, just a few blocks south of the Tiergarten, was a Berlin institution. Since the nineteenth century it had been the favoured spot for writers and artists, its walls hung with photographs of the great and celebrated, lit by great globe lights hanging from a ceiling of gilt and pistachio green. The villa itself belonged to the actress Henny Porten, a star of the silent era, whose career had taken a sharp downwards curve when she refused to divorce her Jewish husband. Clara had seen her around the studios a few times, in the early days, a mournful figure with silver-white skin and inky hair, but since Goebbels had banished her from the screen she spent the days upstairs, haunting the villa like a beautiful, brooding ghost.

Eyes swivelled towards Clara as she made her way through the marble-topped tables to where Ralph Sommers was sitting on a leather banquette with his back to the wall and a good view of the room. He wore a tweed jacket with a crimson silk handkerchief tucked in the top pocket. He stood up and smiled playfully.

'I was half wondering if you would turn up after that little dance you led me last night.'

'Well, I'm here.'

'I'm not used to beautiful women evading me with quite such ease.'

'Do beautiful women often try to evade you?'

He laughed. 'It's not a frequent occurrence, no. But I think you could tell I was following you. Where did you learn that?'

'I might ask you the same thing.'

'I asked you first.'

'I didn't learn anything. Maybe you're just more obtrusive than you think.'

'In that case, why didn't you stop and ask me what I wanted?'

'Perhaps I wondered how you knew where I lived.'

'Ah. That's simple. Our hostess, Magda, kindly gave me your address.'

Furnished by Goebbels himself, no doubt.

'I took the liberty of ordering some wine.'

As he thanked the waiter in flawless German, Clara stared into the mirrored walls behind him. The mirrors here were angled so that an infinitely receding image was reflected, folding in on itself, offering a thousand versions of herself and Ralph Sommers. Yet she still had no idea which image was the right one. Who was he? Had he been sent by Goebbels to keep an eye on her? She remembered what he had said about Magda showing him hospitality. He must be close to the Goebbels then. He may even know her father.

'So tell me about your career. What brought you to Berlin? Why isn't a girl like you living it up in London, the toast of Drury Lane?'

She laughed. 'I was only the toast of the Eastbourne Pavilion until I came to Berlin. I came here on the off chance, in 1933, because someone had said there might be a job for a bilingual actress at Ufa. And they were right. Since then I've been working non-stop.'

The wine he ordered was a Burgundy, rich and musty. He swilled it round his glass.

'And now you're filming with Ernst Udet? That's quite impressive. I know him a little. I should think he would be quite a card to work with.'

'I hope so. It's going to be fun. The other day I went up in a plane in preparation.'

'Ernst took you in a plane?'

'It was a friend of his. Oberst Strauss. He had a test flight to carry out at Tempelhof and offered to take me along.'

'A test flight? What was he testing?'

'Oh, I'm hopeless with names. All planes look the same to me. But it was one of the most exciting experiences of my life. Terrifying too. Though I suppose *you* don't find flying terrifying at all, given your job?'

'My job can get a little nerve-wracking at times. But I'm sure you were in good hands with Oberst Strauss.'

'I suspect he was breaking all sorts of rules taking me with him.'

'Perhaps he's a fan.'

'I shouldn't think so. He says he rarely goes to the cinema. And he never watches Udet's stunts on film because he says he is always thinking of technical details and it distracts him from the story.'

'He won't know what he's missing then, when your film is made,' said Sommers with a gallant little flourish of his glass.

'Thank you.'

'And are you planning on staying in Berlin?'

That question again. Why did people keep asking?

'The thing is, Captain Sommers, I've made my life here. I have a good apartment, I've made friends and I adore acting. Besides, my mother was German, so the language was never a problem. And as you know,' she said carefully, 'there's so much going on.'

All true.

'Exciting things,' he agreed.

'Yes. Germany is certainly changing very rapidly.'

True again.

'The new Germany,' he said. 'Germania, isn't that what the Führer calls it?'

He took a languid sip.

'Do you see much of the Goebbels?'

'Not recently, no. I've been so busy.'

'Of course.' Another sip. 'Joseph seems very impressed by you.' He gave his dazzling smile. The phrase 'matinée idol smile' popped into her head, with its connotations of a smile meant for a wider audience. 'I'm not sure, however, if impressing the Herr Doktor is such an advantage for an attractive actress.'

She shrugged, lightly. 'I can look after myself.'

'I've no doubt of that.'

'Excuse me, mein Herr.'

The waiter appeared and stood between them, replenishing their glasses. Ralph Sommers bent his head away from her to exhale a plume of smoke and when the waiter had gone the matinée idol smile had vanished. He stared at his drink for a second and then looked up and said quietly, 'So tell me, what's in it for you then?'

'What do you mean?'

She was confused at the change in his demeanour. The seductive expression had disappeared and instead he was observing her with forensic interest. He looked at her with his hooded eyes and dabbed his mouth meticulously with his napkin.

'You cosy up to them. You let them think you're a friend. And actually, you're watching them all the time, aren't you? Watching them with those sharp eyes behind that pretty veil. You're cleverer than them. You have them fooled, I suspect. But you don't fool me.'

'Really, Captain Sommers. I can't begin to know what you're talking about. Are you drunk?'

'Sober as a judge, actually. Though I may not stay that way.' He reached over and drained his glass, then poured himself another. 'You're an observer, aren't you? It was your remark about the ambassador that interested me. Where would a lovely German actress know a thing like that? How would she be intimately acquainted with the movements of a British ambassador? Unless, of course, she's more English than German. Unless she had access to some information that others don't.'

'This is madness. I'm going to leave now.'

Clara rose from the table, and attempted to brush past him, but he grasped her wrist tightly and pulled her down again.

'Don't make a spectacle of yourself. It's all right. You're not in danger.'

His eyes were intent on her as, with one hand, he extracted some bills from his wallet and folded them under the silver saucer on the table. With the other, he kept hold of Clara's hand and, pulling her gently to her feet, led her out of the café. He adopted a deprecating expression for the benefit of any interested customers, which suggested they were in the midst of a lovers' tiff.

Quietly he said, 'Shall we take a walk? I could do with some fresh air.'

He was still holding her hand tightly. The skin on his palm was hard and dry. The feel of it made her wonder what things he had done, and what things he might be capable of. He didn't let go until they had turned onto Einemstrasse.

'Sorry,' he murmured, releasing her. 'But it's not a good idea to talk seriously in a place like that. And I do, very much, want a talk with you.'

Her heart was hammering in her chest. 'About what?'

'About you. I was interested in you from the moment I saw you. Looking like a little Geisha at the Goebbels' party. Giving nothing away. I watched you talking to Goebbels and I thought if a girl like that can keep her nerve among a crowd of Nazi thugs with more decorations than a Christmas tree, she might just work in intelligence.'

'You're making a mistake.'

'I never mistake a woman taking risks.'

'You know a lot about risk, do you?'

'I know everything about risk.'

They rounded the corner of the street and turned left again. This was an exclusive area, on the fringes of the Tiergarten, a diplomatic quarter with grand houses whose lush, mature gardens pressed up against high railings. Against the felty darkness, the lamps glowed mistily in the almost empty street.

'I'm afraid, Captain Sommers, you're imagining things.'

'Don't worry, my dear. I'm like an art dealer. I'm trained to spot fakes. I'm quite sure your observation went unremarked by the others.'

The image of herself, like a piece of fine art in his hands, being turned over and closely examined, sent a curious shiver through her.

'So after I met you,' he added lightly, 'I made some enquiries.'

'Enquiries? With whom?'

'With my contacts in the Air Ministry. The British Air Ministry. That confirmed it.'

She said nothing.

'Though if you don't mind me saying, that remark about the ambassador was a damn fool mistake to make.'

Clara was mortified. But still she kept silent. Sommers paused until a man with a dog had passed, then said, 'It's getting more dangerous here by the day. It's no time for making silly slip-ups.'

He gave her a sidelong look and continued.

'On the other hand, I can see that it might be the first time you've put a foot wrong.'

Clara's mind was racing. She still had no idea who he was, but it was obvious that he knew far more about her than she did about him.

'Never attempt anything that wouldn't come naturally. Build on what you know. Didn't they tell you that in training?'

'The only training I've ever had was theatrical.'

She remembered Leo Quinn asking her how she portrayed a character on stage. Use the same technique, he told her. Imagine you are playing a role and then become that person.

Sommers craned a quizzical eye at her.

'My God. No training at all? What are they thinking of? In that case you've done remarkably well.'

'In what way?'

He gave a tight laugh. 'You're still not sure of me, are you? That's to your credit. I'm going to have to persuade you to trust me.'

Clara didn't reply. What did he know? How much could she deny?

'And I'm going to trust you too.'

Clara walked on, too angry with herself to be afraid. What had possessed her to meet a relative stranger, with no form of protection? She wondered if Sommers was leading her somewhere, or if they were going to carry on walking like this, through the night.

She began calculating how and where she would be able to give him the slip.

He said, 'I can see I'm going to have to go first. The fact is, I'm not without a little cover story of my own.'

'So you don't really run an aviation business?'

'Oh no. That part's true. In a manner of speaking. I've always been keen on aircraft, since I was a boy.'

The streetlights threw their shadows ahead of them and she watched them, his tall and broad, her own slender and shorter, leaning into his and merging with it, as though the shadows, unlike their owners, were lovers out on a stroll. He spoke softly and intently, staring straight ahead.

'I was born into an ordinary family. We lived in a village in Surrey. Chintz sofas, roses in the garden, tea at four, that was our life. What you might call an archetypal Englishness. I wasn't especially bookish but I did like planes. Model ones, of course, to start with. When the war broke out I ditched school and enlisted in the Royal Flying Corps, much against my mother's wishes, because I wanted to fly. I'm a Group Captain, as it happens. Unfortunately my plane was shot down by Goering's chaps and I was taken prisoner in 1917. I spent a year in a prison camp, down in the southwest of Germany. You can't imagine the tedium of that, stuck in a camp, playing endless games of chess. For a long time the family thought I was dead.'

'That must have been hard.'

'Yes. Great wails and gnashing of teeth all round,' he chuckled. 'I never knew what a fine fellow I was until afterwards when I read the obituary they'd printed of me in the local newspaper.'

She couldn't see his face well. Between the street lamps the darkness was thick and impenetrable, the texture of soot or oil. A harsh wind cursed in the trees. His tone turned serious again.

'There were, however, two good things about being stuck in a prison camp in the middle of nowhere. The first was that I learned perfect German. And the second was I gained a lot of respect for their air force. It was clear to me that the Germans had obviously thought much harder about air strategy than we had.'

'It didn't win them the war.'

'That's true, fortunately. Anyway, after the war was won I went back to England and lounged around with no real direction. I went up to Cambridge for a while but it was difficult. I couldn't think what I wanted to do. The idea of putting on a hat and taking my briefcase into an office every day was anathema. I didn't want to be tied down. Then, by sheer chance I met up with a friend who had flown with me in the war and he recommended I contact the air section of the Secret Intelligence Service.'

'And did you?'

'The truth was, I didn't even know they existed. At first I didn't waste much energy on it. I was off on a walking holiday in the Alps. I thought whatever it was could wait a couple of weeks. In the event, they called me.'

'And you agreed to work for them?'

'In a manner of speaking. It's a complicated situation.' For the first time he turned to face her and she saw he was sober. Perhaps he really was risking as much as her.

'I agreed to gather information on the development of military aviation in Germany. Even back then there was a serious concern in some quarters about the growth of the Luftwaffe. The idea was that I should come over in a business capacity and collect as much information as I could about the build-up of the air force and in the process recruit some friendly parties and create a network of contacts. I discovered that the Nazis were keen to cultivate high-level contacts in Britain. They seemed to believe that as we were an imperial power we would share their views on conquering other races. Perhaps, regarding certain quarters, they were right.'

Clara thought of her own father and said nothing.

'Anyway, as soon as I got here I decided to act as a channel by immersing myself fully in National Socialist circles. I got to meet everyone who mattered – Hitler, Hess, Rosenberg, General von Reichenau, General Kesselring, Erhard Milch. And I was able to patch together meetings between Nazi bigwigs and our own RAF. So far, it's worked very well.'

'That must take some nerve.'

'I'm sure that's something you know all about.'

She cast a glance about her at the deserted street.

'So you're an agent?'

'I'm what you might call a freelance. Deliberately so. It was my own idea and I'm a loner here. I don't have contact with any other agents. At least, I haven't had.'

'Why?'

'It's safer that way. Everything's in flux at the moment. Everyone has their own agenda. It's a complicated place, the intelligence world.'

Although they were talking in English, he gave a quick, instinctive look behind him.

'There are parties in the British government who resist any warnings about Germany as alarmist. The people you've been cooperating with, Dyson and his friends, have to deal with those men. My Nazi associates are full of praise for our new ambassador Mr Henderson. They tell me he's "sympathetic to rightful German aspirations". I fear some parts of the British government have turned a deaf ear to what people like us might say.'

His casual phrase '*people like us*' did not go unnoticed. Yet Clara was still uncertain how much he knew about her and how much she should reveal. Her deep, instinctive caution told her not to let down her defences. Not yet.

He continued. 'There are other factions, of course, who believe a war is just the thing that's needed to persuade the Germans to overthrow Hitler.'

'If everyone has an agenda, what's yours?' she asked.

'I want my information to get through to people with a real appreciation of the threat the Nazis pose. It's plain to me that the Germans intend to build the most powerful air force in the world.'

Though his mention of Archie Dyson had relaxed Clara slightly, she was still trying to assess Ralph Sommers. She knew never to take a story at face value. The part of his story about being captured in the war sounded credible. Sommers had the kind of upright bearing that suggested military training. Yet he had professed admiration for the German air force. And he had made quite clear he was acting outside normal boundaries. A loner.

'Why should they give you any access? Why should they trust you? What are you offering them?

He smiled at her broadly, as though she was a good student.

'All excellent questions, and ones which I assure you have run through my mind a thousand times. I think they trust me because I was lucky enough to have met some of the senior Nazis before the regime was in power. My British associates wanted me to pursue those relationships, and while my first response was revulsion, I was also genuinely excited by the possibilities of being up close.'

'You felt revulsion?'

'Is it possible to look at the face of the Nazi regime and feel any other way?'

They had come to a small park. He looked around in the gloom and saw there was no one else nearby. That was hardly a surprise. No one in their right mind would be walking in the park on a night like this. A shiver of rain drops needled her face.

'Shall we sit a moment?' Without waiting for a reply he settled on a bench, lit two cigarettes and gave her one. Clara inhaled deeply then said, 'If you feel revulsion, what do they feel about you?'

He shrugged proudly. 'I think they've taken rather a shine to me. The Nazis believe I'm a channel to the British authorities. They think they can use me to sound out British intentions and to send any kind of message they want. So I act as an intermediary.'

'And how exactly do you do that?'

'I put them on to people who have been talking or writing favourably about Germany in Britain and they invite them over. Not just politicians; industrialists, journalists and novelists too. Some of those guests at the Goebbels' house were suggestions of mine.'

Clara was glad she had worn her fur-collared coat. She drew it more closely around her in a vain attempt to shut out the biting cold. She felt the warmth of Sommers beside her, and longed to edge closer to him, but it was far too risky to abandon her guard. Sommers seemed quite happy to go on talking, there, in that freezing park, as though he had an urge to unburden himself. Which might be the case, but why had he chosen her?

'I'm not sure why you're telling me all this, Captain Sommers.'

'I'm coming to that. The fact is, I need your help.'

'My help?' She gave a short laugh. 'I really don't think—'

'Wait. Listen to me. You're working with Ernst Udet.'

'Only a few days' filming.'

'Udet's interesting. He's completely unsuited to be part of a war machine. He's a good fellow, even if he was indirectly responsible for one of the most unpleasant episodes of recent times. You know about the German activities in the Spanish civil war, I take it? The Legion Condor?'

'I've heard about it.' An image came to her of the navy armband worn by Arno Strauss, embroidered with the words *Legion Condor.*

'Udet bears some responsibility for what went on there. The dive-bombing that he pioneered was the centrepiece of the blitzkrieg, you know, the aerial bombardment. He even designed a special siren called a Jericho Trumpet which emits a wailing shriek as the planes approach, to terrify the poor beggars on the ground all the more.'

'But Udet's back here now. His time in Spain is in the past.'

'Precisely. And it's the future I'm concerned with.'

'So what is it you want from me?'

'It's to do with something new. Something that could make a great deal of difference to the way that wars are fought.'

'*If* wars are fought.'

'Your optimism does you credit, Clara. However, I'm afraid I can't share it. What I have discovered is something that could drastically change the outcome of any future European conflict. To the German advantage.'

Clara finished her cigarette and ground the stub with her shoe.

'And what makes you think you're not taking a huge risk, Captain Sommers, in telling me all this?'

'I am. As I said, I know all about risk. This is a calculated one.'

The park was utterly quiet. To the left came the dim, continuous sound of traffic. Her nerves strained for sounds of entrapment.

Quietly he said, 'Listen, we can't talk here. I don't want to put you in any danger, but everything I hear about you makes me think you might be able to help me.'

Everything he had heard about her? That remark, so casually uttered, startled her. They knew who she was, obviously, and they were aware of her work. But it was still a shock to think that she was being discussed somewhere, far away, in offices in central London, by military types in three-piece suits whom she had never met.

'You'll need to get in contact,' he continued, matter-of-factly.

'You want me to telephone you?'

A little snort. 'Of course not.' Most telephones belonging to suspect foreigners were monitored. Whenever a foreigner arrived in Berlin, telephone repairmen would arrive on the pretext of 'checking their connections'. Thereafter, making a call was like performing a two-handed play for the benefit of a large, invisible audience.

'I want you to come and see me. Flat 2, Duisberger Strasse 58. It will have to be soon. Any evening this week. Repeat that address to me.'

'Flat 2, Duisberger Strasse 58.'

She thought of Archie Dyson saying *Lie low. Do nothing*. Work and eat and sleep and do nothing else that anyone could consider suspicious.

He was still gazing out into the darkness. 'I hope you'll decide to come, Clara. It is a matter of great importance. I'd go so far as to say it could change the course of a coming war.'

He stood up and said more loudly, 'Now, I trust you'll excuse me if I leave you here.'

Clasping her hand he gave her the swift, dazzling smile, then turned on his heel. She stood and watched him walk away down the path, until the shadow of the looming trees enveloped him like a glove.

Chapter Fifteen

The policemen merely wanted a word with her, that was all.

The day before, Ilse had handed the lighter in. She had been down to the end of the garden, to the place where Anna was killed, to put a bunch of edelweiss on the spot and say a little prayer. To show she cared, even if nobody else seemed to. Far from remembering Anna, everyone here just wanted to forget. No one wanted to draw attention to the fact that a woman could go to a Reich Bride School and end up murdered, so the patch beneath the trees had been tidied up, just like everywhere else at school. The grass had been smoothed over and the leaves raked, and there was no sign of blood or scuffed earth or anything else to suggest that only a couple of days ago a woman standing there had been brutally shot.

Ilse's religion wasn't complicated. Her parents were Lutherans, but she reckoned God would not mind the absence of ceremony. She checked over her shoulder then said her simple prayer, very quickly, under her breath. '*Please God, bless Anna and welcome her into your eternal band of angels.*' And then, when she opened her eyes, she caught sight of a tiny speck of silver, glinting at her between the roots of the pine tree, deep in the grass. It was like a message, which said that her prayer had been heard. She rubbed her damp eyes and looked closer. It was Anna's silver lighter. She had bent down and put it quickly into her apron pocket. And there it had stayed all morning, burning a hole, until she had a chance to go back to the dormitory at lunchtime and slip it into one of her spare shoes.

Ilse was torn about the lighter. She didn't want to give it to the instructors because she knew it would be donated to the Winterhilfswerk campaign and she couldn't bear the thought of Anna's precious silver lighter being melted down with all the razor blades and toothpaste tubes and tin cans to be turned into aeroplanes. On the other hand, what if someone found it? Fräulein Kampfner, the dormitory supervisor, was always raking through the brides' belongings, ostensibly for 'tidiness' and 'hygiene compliance'. What if she unearthed the lighter and accused Ilse of being a thief? She would know it was Anna's because of the initials. What would Otto say? She might even be asked to leave the Bride School. After a couple of hours of these terrible thoughts thumping through her head, by the end of the day Ilse had taken the lighter down to Fräulein Kampfner and handed it over.

Then the next morning the men from the Reichskriminalpolizei, the Kripo, turned up.

They just wanted a word with her, that was all, said Fräulein Wolff, showing them into the music room. She provided coffee and a plate piled with ginger biscuits, and the men had been very nice. Inspector Hans Kuckhoff was a fat, avuncular sort with a white moustache, smelling strongly of cigars, and Inspector Ule Georg was a smiley little man who kept making jokes about finding a bride for himself here.

'These are respectable ladies, Georg,' his colleague corrected him. 'Too good for the likes of you. Besides, they're all spoken for.'

Both of them insisted there was no way on earth that Ilse was in any trouble. Inspector Kuckhoff said she had been very responsible to hand in the lighter and it was an action worthy of a Reich Bride.

'After all, it's a nice-looking object. Engraved and everything. It's probably worth a bit. Another girl might have tried to keep it for herself. But you were honest, Fräulein Henning. That's the kind of honesty the Führer wants in a German woman. It may well be rewarded.'

Ilse wondered if he was suggesting that she might have wanted to profit from it.

'I would never have sold the lighter. Anna was my friend. I just wanted to help find her killer.'

The Inspector spread his hands. 'Of course you did, Fräulein. My apologies.'

After draining his coffee and fitting several biscuits one after the other into his capacious mouth, Inspector Georg mentioned the visit from the *New York Evening Post* journalist and confided that Fräulein Wolff had tried to cover it up initially because she did not want to be blamed for authorizing an interview. He laughed.

'But if you could help us, Fräulein, we would like a few details of what happened when this journalist visited. Just for the record.'

So that was when Ilse had told them. She had to, really, and besides, they had commented on her honesty with the lighter, so she explained that she had passed on Anna's case to the lady because she said she was a friend of the family.

'What friend of the family?'

'I'm not sure. In fact, Fräulein Harker said she *knew* a friend of the family. So you'd have to ask her.'

Inspector Georg knitted his brows and brushed some crumbs off his trousers.

'This case. What did it look like?'

'It was just a little stationery case. It wasn't important or valuable. Anna used to keep her letters in it. That's all.'

After that Inspector Kuckhoff made a few notes in his book and slapped his thighs in a satisfied manner, and Inspector Georg commented on how lucky Fräulein Henning's fiancé was to have such a pretty young bride, and the two men left.

That might have been the end of it, apart from one curious thing. It was late afternoon and Ilse was in sewing class, where she was embroidering a pair of knitted gloves for Otto, with Heil on the back of one hand and Hitler on the back of the other. They were to be his Christmas present. She pictured Otto standing guard in some freezing outpost, his breath in clouds, clapping his hands together and thanking God for his fiancée and her thoughtful gift. That thought led to an extended reverie of the married life that awaited them, and how she would welcome Otto when he returned, cold and tired from service, with the stove lit and a fragrant stew bubbling, after which he would fold her into his arms and . . .

This daydream was interrupted by the crunch of gravel outside and the weighted thud of a car door slamming. Casting a glance down from the window she saw the strangest thing. She was absolutely certain of it. The sleek black Mercedes Benz 540K exiting the gates was one that no one could mistake. Not just because it was the size of a small tank, with bulletproof glass and armour plating. But also because it had a personalized number plate which identified it as the property of Joseph Goebbels, the Reich Minister for Propaganda and Enlightenment.

Chapter Sixteen

Since the extraordinary episode of Thursday night, Clara had been thinking continuously about Ralph Sommers. She couldn't get his face out of her mind. The smile, slightly mocking, and the patrician voice with its perfect command of German. The faint crinkling of skin around his eyes. And those eyes themselves, at once sensual and serious, with splinters of darker green around the edges. Why should she trust him? She had met him in the thick of the Nazi élite, after all. He had followed her with the skill of a professional, though just what sort of professional, she couldn't judge. He had described himself ambiguously as a 'freelance', whatever that meant, yet he had asked for her help. She didn't imagine that she could be any help to him. If his approach was a trap, then it was a most elaborate one. Surely, by confiding in her, he was taking as great a risk as she was. Yet altogether, she decided, it was essential that she remain on her guard.

Duisburger Strasse in Wilmersdorf was a row of solid, nineteeth-century, high-ceilinged houses with filigree wrought-iron balconies protruding like lace on a heavy bosom. The street door was open, so Clara entered and knocked several times on the door of apartment two but there was no answer. She would have left, but the faint strain of music coming from behind the dense oak door told her that someone was at home. Eventually it opened and Sommers stood there, unshaven and wearing a dark blue silk dressing gown, which gaped at the neck to reveal a line of tawny hair leading down the chest. She wondered if she had disturbed him with a woman. He stood aside.

'You'd better come in.'

He seemed entirely unsurprised to see her. And unembarrassed at being only partly dressed. He led the way into a drawing room and gestured at a sofa.

'Sit there for a moment, will you? I'll get some clothes on.'

While he went into the bedroom across the hall she looked quickly around for anything the drawing room might reveal about him. Nothing about the place, no glass ringed with lipstick, no flowers on the mantelpiece, suggested the presence of a woman. The only female to be seen, clipping roses in a wooden-framed photograph, was the age to be a mother or an aunt. There was a blue flask with the label 'Extract of Limes, Geo.F. Trumper, Curzon Street, Mayfair'. A pair of gold cufflinks on the desk, engraved with the initials R.G. S. A globe-shaped, cut-glass lighter, a heavy brass ashtray and an open bottle of Johnny Walker whisky on the table. A pair of brogues stowed neatly beside the armchair with the inscription 'Church's of Turl Street, Oxford' on the inside sole. A tweed jacket hung on the back of the door. The furniture of the room suggested a long-term tenancy, rather than a man living out of a suitcase. There was a desk, with a lamp and a leather-backed chair and an open copy of an Edgar Wallace thriller. It was almost as though someone was attempting to project an idea of utter Englishness.

There was a Bach sonata on the gramophone. The music hung in the air, the notes twisting up, delicately rippling and declining, like something infinitely sad. Sommers returned, lifted off the needle, then walked across the room and detached the telephone from the wall.

'I hoped you'd come.'

He tilted the whisky bottle towards her in enquiry, and when she shook her head he poured a finger for himself.

'The telephone's just a precaution. Don't worry. It's quite safe.'

She took the armchair closest to the door and Sommers sat opposite. Leaning back, his glance travelled involuntarily to her stockinged legs in a way that surprised her. An agent should know to keep their gaze steady. Not to give their thoughts away with telltale glances. The eyes were the first thing to betray you.

'I assume, given that you're here, you feel you might be able to help?'

'You'll need to explain a bit more,' said Clara, neutrally.

'Of course.' He stroked an eyebrow thoughtfully. 'Perhaps a bit of background might help. Earlier today two Panzer tank regiments were dispatched from Neuruppin, about an hour north of here, to Spain. Nothing unusual about that, but it's a sign that the German involvement in the Spanish war is not letting up. There are men and machines being sent out there constantly.'

'Go on.'

'Everyone should be asking themselves what the involvement in Spain actually means. And the answer is, it's a preparation. The Luftwaffe was mobilized at the start of this year and since then they've undergone a vast expansion. They have seventy military airfields around the country. They've increased aircraft production to unprecedented rates. The Germans possess the fastest bomber in the world – the Do 17. They've a production line at Heinkel's factory on the Baltic coast turning out dive bombers in enormous numbers. To date they've amassed thirty bomber squadrons, six dive-bomber squadrons and twelve fighter squadrons. Two thousand three hundred and forty aircraft in all. Your Ernst Udet's technical division is coming up with new ideas all the time. The only thing that's holding them back from producing ever more machines is the shortage of steel and aluminium. This matters because everyone accepts that air numbers are going to be vital in the coming conflict . . .'

'The coming conflict? Then you *have* made your mind up.'

'Clara, it's right in front of your eyes. They're preparing for war on a major scale. The German army is growing stronger by the month. All the munitions factories are working overtime and they won't stop until they've turned every saucepan in Germany into a dive bomber. Even before Hitler got involved in Spain, the rest of the high command assumed war was coming, though not before 1941. Now it seems we're looking at some time sooner. Maybe even as early as next year. Britain badly needs to get up to speed.'

'Is Britain not, then?'

'Sadly we've spent too long listening to the pacifists who are determined to prevent rearmament. Those people who say that there's no point defending ourselves because the next war will wipe out mankind. Or the others who say let Hitler have his way with Europe, as long as he leaves Britain alone. They're fools, the lot of them, if they think Hitler can be trusted. We need to match Germany's achievements right now. In heavy bombers for a start. Just think of what a five-hundred-pound bomb or even a thousand pounder could do if it was dropped on London.'

'No one in their wildest dreams is talking about bombing London.'

'There's no telling with the wild dreams of some people.'

She shifted in her seat. His sense of quiet alarm was contagious.

'When I met you the other day, you mentioned that many British people agreed on an alliance. Surely Hitler hasn't ruled that out?'

'You're right. And for what it's worth, I think that's still what Hitler would prefer. In the past he's favoured a grand alliance, with Britain being superior on the sea, Germany on land, and equals in the air. It makes a lot of sense. If he achieved that, he would be able to concentrate all his force eastwards, towards Russia, in search of that living space he talks about. He would absorb Poland and White Russia. In the meantime the regime has decided that a German–Italian alliance will be important, so for Mussolini's visit the other week they put on a huge display of military power. But Hitler is still listening to powerful British voices who would like to see Britain and Germany as brothers in arms.'

There was no doubt to whom he was referring. Her father, Sir Ronald Vine. The image of her father, with his craggy figure and penetrating blue eyes, tirelessly giving dinners and making speeches to serve fascism in Britain, rose up between them and Clara felt a faint, defensive stab of loyalty. She might hate everything he stood for, she might have devoted the past four years to undermining the Nazi regime in every way she could, but it still pained her to hear her father spoken of with contempt. Family loyalty was deep and instinctive and one of the toughest ties to sunder.

'Why not just say it? You're talking about my father, aren't you? Well, he's not the only one.'

'That's true, and it's what I fear. Powerful men like your father ensure that the case for an alliance is heard at the highest levels. And – this is what concerns me – any information from here which puts an alliance in doubt may get quietly suppressed by those factions in the Government who would prefer not to cross swords with Herr Hitler. People who favour appeasement ahead of action.'

Clara looked away to hide the film of tears which had suddenly misted her vision. Was it the mention of her father, or the fact that she was speaking English in the room of an archetypal Englishman, that brought a sudden, painful nostalgia for her homeland? Her home in Ponsonby Terrace, her friends, the theatre school, the parties and plays, even the BBC programmes on the wireless, all seemed so far away. Another life. For a second, her mind travelled back up the railway line through Kent, past embankments blowing with wild flowers and horses gazing peaceably over the fences, then slid into dingy, busy London, with its parks and squares and sooty spires.

'I wonder . . . what an alliance would really mean?'

It was something she had often thought about, but she had never before allowed herself to wonder out loud.

'If you want to know what Britain would look like, take a look around you. Don't imagine that England's Jews or her free press or her politicians would be safe for long in an alliance with Hitler. How could they possibly defend themselves? Anyone who imagines that the English Channel is enough to secure their freedom is a fool. The Nazis would start straight away, ensuring their placemen were in positions of power, and those men would be increasing the power of the police, banning demonstrations, unless they happened to be marches by our friend Mosley's people, curbing the trade unions, locking up the churchmen. Then it would be the turn of the social structures, schools and universities, the treatment of women. Books, plays, films, nothing cultural would escape scrutiny. Before long, a thousand years of British parliamentary democracy would be undermined. Britain would be a shadow of itself. And all the ugly, divisive passions that lie beneath the surface would be brought to the fore. That's why it matters so much, Clara. The appeasers can't know what Hitler has in store for them. It's a deal with the devil.'

He was no longer smooth and genial. The façade of bonhomie she had seen at the Goebbels' party had entirely vanished, to be replaced by something deeper, more melancholic.

'You seem to know an awful lot – about the aeroplane numbers and so on. Why do the Nazis give you so much detail?'

'They want me to know. I told you, they regard me as a useful channel. Goering wants me to relay it to the people back home because he thinks knowing the strength of the Luftwaffe will concentrate minds and make the British realize there's no point in putting up any resistance. They give me an astonishing level of performance data, reports on each aeroplane's engine, manufacturing levels. We share information with them too. Their chaps were shown round some RAF stations this month, though they were only shown outdated aircraft, of course. Just the old crocks, nothing important. But there's pressure of time. We have a deadline approaching.'

'A deadline?'

'A crucial one. Next month Lord Halifax, the Government minister, is coming to visit. What do you know of Halifax?'

Clara racked her brain for details of the cadaverous Earl, with his homburg hat and icy, aristocratic manner. 'I know he welcomed the reoccupation of the Rhineland. He said it was only Germany's backyard.'

'Halifax has been deputed to open dialogue with the Germans. Officially he's here as Master of the Middleton Hunt, to visit Goering and shoot foxes with him. Unofficially, he's sounding out German intentions. Goering is aiming to entertain him along with the new ambassador, Mr Henderson. As I said, Henderson is already predisposed to admire the Nazis. He's claims to admire all the regime leaders, even Goebbels. He's wilfully blind. He swallows everything the Nazis tell him about wanting closer ties between our two great nations. Halifax, I'm less sure about. But he has been heard to use the phrase "alterations in the European order" to refer to Hitler's plans for Lebensraum.'

'You mean he thinks any aggression will be confined to Poland and Czechoslovakia?'

'Exactly. And the Nazis sense weakness. So it's vital that before Halifax arrives I get accurate details of the extent of the Luftwaffe build-up. Halifax – and others – have to know what we're up against.'

'What are we up against?'

He took a long, slow pull on his whisky and frowned at her.

'I'd say Britain is at the most important crossroads she has faced in her history. Appease fascism, or face up to it. The future of the entire continent of Europe for years will depend on what happens in the next couple of months.'

'I can see that.' Clara braced her shoulders. 'But I still fail to see how the future of Europe can have much to do with me.'

He flipped open a packet of Senior Service and tilted it towards her.

'I'm getting to that. Your friend Oberst Strauss.'

Strauss. She thought of the ramrod figure at the Tempelhof aerodrome, with a tip of his hat, turning on his heel.

'He's not my friend.'

'That may be. But it was when you mentioned meeting Strauss that I decided I had to confront you. I was in two minds before then. Even when I asked you to the café I hadn't quite decided. I didn't want to compromise you in any way. I didn't see that you could really be useful to me. And you're Dyson's find.'

She bridled at that.

'I'm not anyone's find, Captain Sommers.'

He smiled apologetically. 'Of course not. You're independent. Like me. But you are immensely valuable. The problem with many British agents is that their accent is appalling. People can't forget they're not German. But your German is perfect.'

'Really, Captain Sommers . . .'

'Ralph. Do please call me Ralph. Anyway, Arno Strauss. How well do you know him?'

'I barely know him at all. What do you know about him?'

He chuckled. 'Arno Strauss. Born Berlin 1896, son of Hans and Eva Strauss. Twin brother now deceased. Wealthy background. Trained as a pilot and flew Fokkers in the war. Became an expert in aerial combat, was highly regarded and awarded the Cross of Merit. Shot down forty-five British planes. Among Ernst

Udet's closest friends, if not the closest, and now working alongside him in the Technical Division of the Luftwaffe.'

'Well then. You plainly know far more about him that I do. What do you want from me?'

'I want you to get close to him.'

'What do you mean by that?'

'To cultivate him.'

She gave a little choke. 'And how do you propose I do that?'

His mouth twisted into a smile. 'I think you underrate your charm.'

'Strauss doesn't look like a man who is susceptible to charm.'

'All men are susceptible to charm, Clara, believe me.'

'And why on earth should I do this?'

'In case an opportunity presents itself.'

'An opportunity for what?'

'I can't tell you that right now.'

She stared at Ralph in amazement.

'I'm sorry, Captain Sommers – Ralph. I hope you don't think me obtuse. But if you can't tell me what you want of me, then why in God's name should I agree to it?'

He continued to look at her steadily, and gave a slight shrug.

'Because of what's at stake.'

She looked around the room for a moment, considering, then scrutinized him afresh.

'OK. My turn to ask then. You said you were a freelance. What exactly does that mean?'

'It means this isn't school, or the army, or any of those places where one has to keep in line and wait for others to do the thinking. As I said, there's too much at stake. It's a time for action, and utilizing every possible asset that we have. Individuals who are in a position to help have to act now.'

'Yet you mentioned the Air Service. You said you're working for them.'

He stubbed his cigarette thoughtfully and crossed his long legs.

'That's true. I am. But they allow me a certain amount of freedom of operation. How can I explain it? Let me think.' His eyes lingered on her while he considered. 'When I was a boy I loved my biology lessons. I adored studying creatures under a microscope, analysing the way they work. And I remember looking at a butterfly's eyes close up. Have you ever seen them? They have an infinite number of parts, and they all add their perspective to create one compound eye. Well, Intelligence works the same way as a butterfly's eye. Lots of insights, wider perspective.'

'That doesn't answer my question,' said Clara crisply. 'And who exactly will my insights be going to?'

'To the right people. People in the Secret Intelligence Service.'

'Does Archie Dyson know you've approached me?'

'Nobody knows. Just you and me.'

'Then I'll think about it.'

He frowned slightly, at this hesitation.

'Of course. You're right to think it over. We can meet tomorrow and you can tell me your decision. It's really rather pressing.'

'I'm busy tomorrow. And then I'm going to Munich.'

'Munich?'

'There's someone I need to see there.'

There was a twist of annoyance in his eyes, as if he was unused to people thwarting his plans.

'I see. Well as soon as you get back then. If you would.'

His eyes seemed to be stripping her as she sat there. She sensed the fumes of whisky coming from him and realized he was slightly drunk. Though she had explained she needed to leave in the morning, he made no move to show her out. He smiled.

'I still can't get over how clever they are. Having an agent in place who is absolutely part of the furniture. Totally one of them, moving in all the right circles. Living here for the long term with every good reason. And a woman, what's more.'

Clara flashed him a look. 'Perhaps you should have paid more attention in those biology lessons of yours. You might have discovered that a woman is every bit as capable and intelligent as a man. More so, probably.'

He shook his head and shrugged.

'But of course.'

There was something infuriating about Ralph Sommers. As though age and experience gave him the right to issue her with orders and assume that his commands would be obeyed. Was it his remark about women, or his maddening assumption that Clara would drop everything to fall in unquestioningly with his plans that made her bridle beneath his gaze?

'So what about you, Ralph?' she said coolly. 'Are you in Berlin long term? Is there a wife at home worrying about you?'

He raised his eyebrows and flicked her a glance that was entirely unambiguous in its meaning.

'Too busy for that.'

He got up and stood at the mantelpiece with his hands thrust in his pockets, staring at the photographs there. 'You ask me why I am prepared to run risks myself. I have some personal knowledge of the situation in Spain. My oldest friend signed up to fight with the partisans last year. But there's been no word of him for nine months now.'

'I'm sorry.'

'Sure.'

He still had his back to her. He was rubbing the edge of his jaw thoughtfully.

'His name is Tom Roberts. I've known him all my life. We were at school together, and then Cambridge too. He was last heard of with a band of fighters outside Madrid, holed up in one of the university buildings with the windows blocked up with books of nineteenth-century German philosophy and ancient literature. That should suit him, anyway.'

'I'm sure he's all right.'

'Yet again, your optimism does you credit.'

Clara refused to be deflected by this brusque response.

'Had you considered going out there perhaps? Looking for him?'

He shrugged.

'Spain's a big place.'

'But you have Intelligence contacts. How hard would it be to find an Englishman answering his description? You could ask around.'

He gave her a sharp look. 'Do you have any idea what it's like out there?'

'I have a friend who was in Spain. She's an American journalist. Mary Harker of the *New York Evening Post*. She was with the International Brigades for some of the time. Would it be worth me asking her if she had run into him?'

He waved a hand dismissively.

'Forgive me for burdening you with my personal concerns. It was rude of me. If there's one thing I know about Tom, it's that he can look after himself.'

He turned and faced her, the charming smile back in place.

'Now then. If you're busy tomorrow, you'll need your beauty sleep. Think about what I've said, won't you? I'll be in touch in a few days.'

Clara went to the door and hesitated.

'There is something you need to know. Just so you understand . . . You mentioned Archie Dyson. The fact is, I saw him very recently and he told me that I had been talked about at Gestapo headquarters. He advised me to lie low.'

'I see.'

'Actually, he advised me to go back to Britain.'

'And are you lying low?'

'If I was going to, I wouldn't be here, would I?'

He approached and stood disconcertingly close. She smelled the faint trace of whisky and soap and the starched cotton of his shirt.

'In that case, I hope you'll be careful.'

'I'm always careful.'

His eyes lingered on her thoughtfully.

'You know, you took umbrage when I talked of you being a woman, but I happen to think the British are behind in using women for espionage work. The French are way ahead of us. The French have what they call their *femmes galantes*. Yet we Brits waste our women. You're our best assets and we're afraid to use you.'

'Why's that?'

He shrugged. 'Old-fashioned ideas. The people back in London say that women can't keep a secret. They're concerned that a woman will get emotionally involved.'

He was surveying her quizzically. For a moment, she wondered if he might reach out and touch her. She had to force herself not to flinch beneath the intensity of his gaze. Once again she felt the current of attraction that had flickered between them when they first met, at the Goebbels' party. An unspoken sexual connection that made the heat rise to the surface of her skin and her mind churn with possibilities.

'You needn't worry, Ralph. That's not going to be a problem with me.'

She turned quickly and walked out of the door.

Chapter Seventeen

There were more than six months to go before the baby was born and the gifts had already started arriving. Standing at the door of Reich Minister Goering's turreted, palatial state residence in Leipziger Platz, clutching a Steiff bear, Clara wondered if she would appear madly presumptuous in bringing her own present for the forthcoming child. In Britain it was considered bad luck to bring a gift before a baby was born, but here in Berlin ambition was always going to come before superstition, and a gift for Goering's child was likely to be one of the wisest investments anyone could make for the future. Besides, it was surely perfectly proper, given Emmy Goering's insistence on inviting Clara to several parties on the basis of a tangential acquaintance over several years and the fact that they were both actresses. All the same, Clara was half hoping that Emmy was not at home.

She was out of luck.

The butler led Clara through a high-ceilinged hall into a drawing room. Here were none of the doily-draped side tables or dried flower arrangements of the traditional Berlin home, but a spectacular hall whose walls were hung with Old Masters and windows crowned with swags of burgundy draping. An enormous mosaic swastika was worked into the marble floor. Emmy was sitting in a red plush throne more suited to a pope, with gilded pineapples at the corners. She didn't yet look as pregnant as her husband, whose vast bulk ballooned at the seams of his ministerial uniform, but she was visibly puffing up, like a zeppelin being slowly inflated. She wore a wedding cake of a dress, with voluminous cream flounces and a rivulet of frills, and her hair was coiffed girlishly around her face. She was smoking Turkish cigarettes and had a plate of cakes by her side.

'It's you, Clara. What a relief. I thought it might be another messenger from the Italian Embassy. Herr Mussolini has been so attentive since his visit last month. Have you seen what he sent me?'

She gestured at a pair of diamond-encrusted gold antlers, poking out in absurd extravagance from a side table.

'Extraordinary, aren't they? Italian taste has changed a bit since the Renaissance, hasn't it? I must say the Duce was terrifyingly tactile. I was afraid to be in the room alone with him. And in my condition!'

Emmy Goering had been a provincial stage actress in Weimar, but once she had caught the eye of Hermann Goering her career had blossomed accordingly. Their wedding, a couple of years ago, made the Duke of Windsor's ceremony look like a vicar's tea party. Thirty thousand soldiers lined the route to the cathedral and the Luftwaffe had performed a fly past. Now, although acting would not be commensurate with her status as Reich Minister's wife, Emmy liked to keep abreast of the film world and had taken to sending little notes to Clara, commenting on her performances.

'Everyone has been exhaustingly generous. Can you believe it?' She pointed to a stack of gifts ranged across two trestle tables. It included crystal vases, Meissen tea sets and a variety of other household luxuries entirely unsuited to the wants of a newborn infant. There was an ivory chess set studded with jewels – emeralds for pawns, rubies for bishops and diamonds for the King and Queen. The City of Cologne had sent a painting by Lucas

Cranach. *The Madonna and Child*. Clara peered at the gift message and wondered if it was supposed to be some form of flattery. The Madonna, beneath her velvet canopy, did indeed possess corn-coloured coils of hair uncannily similar to Emmy's, but that was where the resemblance ended. Emmy's thickened girth and pudgy face couldn't be further from the girlish maiden overwhelmed by the joys of nativity. Looking at the display, Clara's bear felt smaller and less consequential by the second. Emmy took it, smiled politely and plumped it on top of a Dresden cake stand.

'Presents are difficult, aren't they?' She sighed, fingering an especially hideous glass nude. 'The Führer has the right idea. He only gives three things – a photograph frame, a smoking set or a portrait of himself. Usually an oil painting.' She paused to chuckle. 'Wouldn't you just love to see the look on people's faces when they unwrap that?'

Clara risked a smile. 'I'm glad to find you here. I thought you might still be in Bavaria.'

'We're just back. We've bought a house at Obersalzburg now but it's a mistake, really. It means we're at everyone's beck and call.'

'Was it terribly busy?'

'Madly. Fräulein Eva Braun has a new hobby. You'll never guess what.'

Clara couldn't.

'Perfume! The Führer bought her a whole range of fragrances and she experiments, choosing a different scent for each person. She blends violet and lilac and jasmine and what have you. Or she chooses a perfume you've never heard of. You'll never guess what she chose for me . . . Schiaparelli's *Shocking*.' She raised her eyebrows. 'I can't imagine what that's supposed to imply.'

'She sounds happier, then.' A few years previously, Eva Braun had attempted suicide.

'Oh, one never gets the impression little Eva's really happy. When we were there she was moaning because Hitler won't let her ride horses. He says it's unladylike. And she was nagging him endlessly about the way he dresses. She says, "Mussolini looks so dashing in his uniform, and you sit beside him in your little cap looking like a postman!" The senior men can hardly help themselves laughing.'

'Who else was there?'

'Let me think. The Himmlers, of course. I can't really get on with her. Lina Heydrich calls Marga Himmler "Size Fifty".'

'Size Fifty?'

'That's the size of her undergarments. She does love her cream cakes.' Emmy suppressed a giggle.

'And did you see the Mitfords?' Clara asked. 'I met Unity and her sister the other day. They mentioned they were just back from the Berghof.'

'Unity Mitford!' Emmy Goering grimaced. 'That girl with her staring saucer eyes and the Party badge on her heaving bosom. The men call her *Mitfahrt* – the travelling companion – because she's always there. She absolutely dogged Hitler's heels at the rally. She spends every lunchtime at the Osteria Bavaria in the hope of catching Hitler's eye. She's dreadfully jealous of Eva Braun, of course, terrified that Eva comes first in Hitler's affections. I've told her, it's a bit late to worry about that. Eva has her own room in the Reich Chancellery, doesn't she?'

'So Unity's not popular then?'

'No one can understand why the Führer likes her. Apparently he loves the fact that her middle name is Valkyrie. Eva says, well, she looks the part, especially the legs. Himmler hates her too. He thinks she might be a spy. He has a tame SS man follow her around, posing as a photographer. But I said to Heinrich, spies don't go around dressed in a home-made storm trooper's uniform, do they? They'd wear something a little more subtle. Mind you, this SS chap did catch Unity with a gun. Though when he asked her what it was for she said she was practising killing Jews.'

'Do you think the Führer will marry Fräulein Braun?'

'Ach, who has ever been able to fathom the Führer's taste in women?' Emmy drew even closer. 'Hermann says the only way he will marry Fräulein Braun is if someone puts a gun to his head. And besides, he gets twelve thousand love letters a year so he's not short of choice. Though they say . . .' she lowered her voice, 'he never recovered from the death of Geli. His niece, you know, who shot herself in his apartment. Hermann says Hitler used to treat Geli like a gardener with an exotic bloom.'

'So why did she shoot herself?'

'If we knew that, my dear . . .' Emmy Goering gave her a significant look, but did not continue.

'What about Diana Mitford? Does the Führer like her too?'

'I think he's really fond of her. He took a whole day off when she married in the Goebbels' place, and for him, that's quite unheard of. And he agreed to ban the von Ribbentrops from the wedding because Diana hates them. Annelies was furious when she heard because they'd already invited themselves, but frankly, Diana's right. The Führer should never have made von Ribbentrop ambassador. He told Hermann that von Ribbentrop would be good because he knew absolutely everyone in England but Hermann said the problem was, everyone in England knew von Ribbentrop.' For a moment, her husband's wit caused a fond chuckle. 'Still, it's no good trying to fathom what you English think. You keep us all guessing.'

There was a knock on the door and the butler showed in the immaculate figure of the photographer Heinrich Hoffmann. As he greeted them, his gaze flickered over Clara curiously. He had seen her with the Goebbels only recently, and now she was here in the Goerings' home. He was wondering what brought her here, Clara recognized, and attempting to assess her social standing.

It transpired that Hoffmann had been sent to photograph the presents. While he busied himself with unfolding the legs of his tripod and positioning lights, Emmy bore off the golden antlers imperiously.

'I'm hiding these. They might lead to awkward questions. Hitler censors anything he doesn't like, so why shouldn't we?'

Hoffmann laughed. 'Of course, Frau Reich Minister.' Beneath his air of unctuous jollity was a steeliness common to professional photographers who are obliged to perform their job in a social setting.

'What does Hitler censor?' asked Clara casually as they walked to the other side of the room.

'Oh, everything, darling! He won't have any photograph of himself in spectacles, for a start. It suggests he might have the same human frailties as the rest of us. He will never bathe in public, in case anyone photographs him in a costume, and he can't ever be seen in Lederhosen. I don't know why because Hermann finds them perfectly manly.'

She regarded Hoffmann with a beady eye as he snapped and repositioned, and snapped again.

'I'm surprised Hoffmann still needs the work, he's so rich now,' she murmured. 'I mean, his pictures have sold round the world, haven't they? Stamps, postcards, a book every week, it seems like. He keeps all the royalties. But then the Führer trusts Hoffmann with his life.'

'Why is that?'

'They go back a long way. They've been together since the beginning, since the Munich Putsch. When Hitler went to prison in 1924 Hoffmann smuggled his camera in and took some lovely shots. Then he gave Hitler his Munich studio in Schellingstrasse for the first Party headquarters and now Hoffmann has offices all round Europe. They call him Hitler's shadow. I say the Führer has been his golden goose.'

She called across the room, 'Where will these pictures be appearing, Heini?'

'We shall circulate them to the news magazines,' said Hoffmann. 'The whole country shares the excitement about your news, Frau Goering.'

'Hmm. Let's wait and see,' said Emmy, then more softly, 'I'll be surprised. Goebbels can't stand any good news about us getting out. When we had a ball last January at the Opera House, we had the entire place redecorated in white satin and it looked stunning, but Goebbels refused to allow a single picture to be published. Not one.'

The rivalry between the Goerings and the Goebbels was long-standing. Both couples vied for closeness to the Führer. The main beneficiaries were the Nazi élite, who were invited to spectacular parties, each man striving to outdo the other in lavish and inventive entertaining. Goebbels' Olympic party for two thousand guests at Peacock Island last year was a failed attempt to outdo Goering's evening, as everyone present agreed.

The Reich Minister's wife shrugged. 'But then I suppose Joseph is a past master at censoring things. Remember all the antics with the film actresses who got drunk at his party last year? No one got to hear about that, did they? He's absurdly prickly about public opinion. Quite the opposite of my husband. Hermann really has a sense of humour. Do you know he pays people three marks if they'll tell him a joke about himself and he writes down the best ones in his leather book? He has hundreds!'

Emmy lowered her voice further.

'While we're on the subject of Goebbels. His wife . . .'

Clara had long realized that Emmy Goering, like Magda, needed to keep abreast of the gossip, the squabbles and the divisions that existed among the Nazi élite. Understanding the private tensions that lay beneath the surfaces of men's lives was the first rule of politics. Clara knew that she was a valuable conduit between the two women. They were rivals, after all, for the status of First Lady of the Reich, and each was avid for details of the other's progress.

'. . . you've just seen her. How is she?'

So Emmy knew that Clara had attended the Goebbels' reception. She couldn't think how.

'She seems well.'

'That poor woman. She is thoroughly fed up, apparently. She's compiled a list of thirty women who've been intimate with her husband. He's always been one for actresses. As far as he's concerned the sluttier the better. But now it's just that little Slav Lída Baarová. You'll have heard all about it, I suppose? I imagine it's the talk of the studios.'

'I've heard the odd thing.'

It was never good to give an impression of being loose-tongued.

Emmy Goering sighed, shifted her pregnant belly and rubbed the small of her back.

'He's out every evening, I hear. He can't bear to go home to Schwanenwerder and spend the evening sitting with Magda. He's become so secretive about his movements, he even keeps his officials at the Ministry in the dark. He doesn't want her to find out where he's going. They say Magda tunes into Radio Moscow to hear what he's up to.'

Clara laughed, as she was meant to.

'Joseph's getting very sensitive about it. Yet he's the one who just proposed a ten-year sentence for adultery if the wronged husband demands it. Honestly! It's the women I feel sorry for.'

She gave Clara a beady look, whose subtext Clara tried to ignore.

'So? What about your love life, then?' Emmy was always voracious about the details of other people's private lives. 'Any handsome Obersturmbannführers on the horizon? Any romances I should know about?'

Modestly Clara averted her eyes.

'Well . . .'

'There is? Go on! Tell me at once!'

'It's not a romance, but I did meet an interesting man. A Luftwaffe Oberst.'

'Called?'

'Arno Strauss. A friend of Ernst Udet.'

With almost comical speed the excitement on Frau Goering's face turned to dismay.

'Not the one with . . .?' She performed a little mime, as though drawing a zip up one side of her face. 'The scar?'

Clara nodded.

'I don't think Strauss likes women. I've never seen him with one.' She frowned dubiously. 'Not that I'm suggesting he's . . . you know . . . I just thought he was a man's man. But I daresay he's perfectly pleasant underneath . . . well, underneath the skin. In fact, I've had a thought.'

'What's that?' asked Clara, hoping it was the right thought.

Emmy Goering hesitated a moment. 'We're having a reception at Carinhall next weekend. For the Duke and Duchess of Windsor. I think Oberst Strauss will be there. Would you like to come?'

Clara remembered Archie Dyson's warning. The instruction, almost an order, he had issued just a few evenings ago. The insistence that she avoid danger at all costs. *Lie low. Don't do anything.* Then Ralph Sommers' request. *I want you to cultivate him.*

She smiled. 'I would love to come, thank you.'

Chapter Eighteen

The cleaver glinted in the morning sun as the man, a bloodstained apron straining over his enormous belly, held it aloft. Then he brought it down with a thwack on the flesh below, causing the blood to gush and spurt from the glutinous flesh, then slide into a glassy pool. Ilse felt herself gag.

Saturday generally offered a more relaxed regime at the Bride School. The lessons were replaced by simple household tasks and there was more time allotted to cultural pursuits. That morning, after her chores, which were laying the fire and bringing in the baskets of chopped wood, Ilse had gone to the kitchen to hear the talk about how to get the most out of a cheap cut of meat. The butcher showed them how to slice through a chunk of pork, swiftly and decisively, splitting it up into chops and smaller scraps for mincing. The blood leaching from the pale flesh coagulated into a dense crimson puddle on the table and the metallic smell made Ilse want to vomit. She had never been so sensitive before Anna was killed.

Afterwards, the pork was borne off by the brides on cooking rota to make lunch and the others took their cups of coffee in the garden. Some of them played with the Bride School's newly arrived puppies, two squirming German Shepherds with baby teeth and claws, jumping at shadows on the dappled lawn.

Everyone wanted German Shepherds now, mainly because the Führer liked them, yet the arrival of Prinz and Wolf at the Reich Bride School was more likely an unspoken response to the recent crime. A couple of lively guard dogs would be just the thing to help the girls feel safer.

Anyhow, Ilse recalled, it was in all respects a perfectly ordinary, normal weekend morning, which made everything that followed all the more unpleasant.

They were different men, this time, standing in the hall wanting to speak to her. The fact that they were wearing leather coats and full SS uniform meant it didn't take Ilse long to work out that they were not the ordinary criminal police, the Kripo. These men were Gestapo. The secret police. The thought of it made her feel sick inside. Ilse had never even met a policeman before and now she had been interviewed by four of them in a couple of days.

Once they had been ushered into the supervisor's office, the Gestapo men introduced themselves and told her that they had taken over the investigation from the Kripo, so there were a few questions they needed to go over. Kriminal Inspektor Wiedemann was a short, bald man, wearing glasses with a thin steel frame, behind which his lashless eyes had a reptilian appearance, like an iguana Ilse had seen at the zoo. Kriminal Kommissar Decker was older and tired, a chain smoker with a face grey as a wrecked battleship, craggy with frowns and angles. He had a moustache which sloped down his mournful face as if trying to leave it. There was no coffee and biscuits this time, no gentle joshing, no comments about Otto being lucky to have a pretty bride.

Wiedemann took the chair behind the supervisor's desk as though he owned it and steepled his tight little hands into a sharp point. They had some more questions in connection with Anna's killing, he said. Perhaps Ilse could help them. This time the tone was far less soothing. What did she know, Wiedemann enquired. Why was she covering up? What could she tell them? Anna had smuggled in her own lighter, despite the anti-smoking rule. What other secrets did Anna have?

Ilse gave a panicky glance around her. Through the window she could see a bride in the yard outside, beating a carpet as though she wanted to beat the truth out of it, the dust flying off into the air. Ilse felt abandoned. There was no supervisor around to help her, not even Fräulein Wolff. The staff here seemed determined to leave her to her fate.

Stutteringly, she said, 'Anna didn't have secrets.'

'Come now. Everyone has secrets, don't they?'

'I don't know,' Ilse muttered dumbly, twisting her apron between her hands into a damp little rope.

'Did she confide in you?'

'I can't remember.'

Wiedemann picked up a photograph of Gertrud Scholtz-Klink which the supervisor especially treasured, and stared at it with distaste before replacing it. 'Then perhaps we need to think of a way to jog your memory,' he said, levelly.

Decker leaned towards her, as if offering some friendly advice. 'You must try harder, my dear.'

Ilse steadied her trembling hands against the back of a chair. Through her tears, the sight of Wiedemann licking his dry lips triggered a thought. Anna's lipstick. Anna had found the rule against make-up at the Bride School especially hard. The other girls made do with biting their lips, or applying a slick of Vaseline. One girl had resourcefully turned to the red food colouring that was kept expressly for creating the swastika designs on wedding cakes. But Anna had smuggled in her own lipstick and used it daily.

'I know one secret she had, sir! She kept her lipstick. Guerlain. She used make-up even though it's forbidden here.'

Wiedemann's face purpled, as though she had deliberately insulted him.

'Are you trying to play me, girl? Lipstick? Don't give me this nonsense.'

Decker interceded.

'Fräulein Henning, perhaps I could explain more clearly. All we want to know is what Anna told you about her life. You were friends, you say. You must have talked. All women talk, don't they? I know my wife never stops.' He cast a weary glance at Wiedemann. 'Anyone tries to bug my telephone, they'll regret it.'

Then he turned back to Ilse. 'Just tell us everything she told you about her life.'

Haltingly Ilse stumbled through Anna's story, or what she knew of it. Anna was a dancer. She had been performing in a revue at the Wintergarten – the kind of revue where you didn't keep many clothes on. She met Johann afterwards in a bar. It was love at first sight. (Ilse had always fervently believed in love at first sight, although Otto said it was rubbish, and she had been pleased when Anna revealed it was a genuine phenomenon.) Then Johann had been sent to Spain. Anna wrote to him at least once a week and he wrote even more than she did. Anna was always getting letters from Johann.

'They were going to have a Christmas wedding. Johann's family were organizing it. The Peters were a little starchy, she said, and rather old-fashioned, but Anna was so charming, she could make anyone love her. We had already started making her wedding dress. It was going to be embroidered with scarlet swastikas on the hem and—'

'These letters,' interrupted Wiedemann, 'the ones from the fiancé. She kept them in a letter case, I hear. The one you gave the journalist. What other secrets did you say she had?'

'I never said she kept secrets! All she had was love letters, I suppose.'

Decker stroked his moustache soothingly, like a pet. 'This is not helping us, Ilse. I'm sorry that you don't feel you can help us.'

There was an impasse. Kriminal Inspektor Wiedemann was accustomed to interrogating cowering men in badly disinfected cells at Gestapo headquarters. He was used to getting what he wanted, and he had a variety of techniques for the purpose. It may be that he would need to select something else from his toolbox, because right now he was getting nowhere with the idiot woman before him, who almost certainly knew something crucial without realizing that it was important. And orders had come down from the highest level to get this matter sorted out. That annoyed Wiedemann. He was an egalitarian in matters of crime. He suspected the top brass were outraged that a murder should despoil their little idyll. He had taken a good look at Schwanenwerder's fancy cars and gated villas when he arrived, and he guessed the residents regarded the place as their own private island, immune from the murders and violence that permeated the rest of Berlin. Well frankly, they needed to open their eyes.

'Perhaps,' he suggested to Decker, as though it had just occurred to him, 'Fräulein Henning might be more inclined to help if we interviewed her in another setting.' He nodded his head in the direction of the car outside.

Horror-struck, Ilse looked from one to the other.

'No! I'm trying to think. I'm trying to remember everything I can!'

But Wiedemann was bored with her now. He behaved as though she had already been dismissed. He shifted bodily to address Decker.

'I'm beginning to think Fräulein Henning is not the right kind of woman to be training at a Reich Bride School,' he mused. 'Perhaps she will not be able to stay here, and then she won't be able to marry and what will happen to her then, eh? Maybe she will have to make a living out on Friedrichstrasse in green laced boots.'

Ilse burst into a torrent of sobs and buried her face in her apron. She could not believe this was happening to her. She had been brought up to think of policemen as good men who looked after the interests of decent, God-fearing people like herself and her family. It was true that she had seen them shouting at troublemakers in the street, hitting men with sticks or arresting Jews who had caused trouble, but that was other people. Ilse had always assumed that the law existed for her protection. This was not the kind of thing that happened to a girl like her.

Fortunately, the Gestapo men seemed to have suspended the interrogation.

'We'll be coming back.'

Wiedemann rose to leave and brushed roughly past her. As he left the room, Decker looked back and pointed a finger at her like a gun.

'Keep thinking, eh?'

Much later, when all the brides had gone to bed and Ilse was still issuing great, shuddering sobs into her pillow, she remembered something she should have told them. That builder, the one who was constructing the model house. She had seen him talking to Anna. Perhaps he was the one who killed her. She should have told them that.

Chapter Nineteen

'Fräulein! Fräulein! Wachen Sie auf!'

Clara had fallen asleep on the train somewhere outside Nuremberg. She had been enjoying the beauty of the Bavarian countryside, the tiny mediaeval villages with their fairy-tale spires, timbered gables and winding cobbled streets. The flat farming land interspersed with massive blocks of forest. But her early start, and the rhythm of the train which rocked her like a baby, had lulled her asleep for a few minutes and made her vulnerable. She was dreaming she was back in England, in a performance of *The Merry Widow* on stage at the Haymarket Theatre, and she had completely forgotten her lines.

'Fräulein! Wachen Sie auf!'

Now the man opposite her was giving a gentle nudge and she saw the curious eyes of his wife upon her as she snapped back into full consciousness. A guard in a green uniform stood stolidly before her, waiting to check her papers.

After the guard had left, slamming the steel door behind him, she looked at her reflection in the window, imprinted against the fields flashing past. The image of a young woman with dark hair floated before her, observing her soberly. In some ways, Clara was always accompanied by a ghostly image of herself, not just the heightened self-awareness that a woman in public has, but a picture of herself, a constant consciousness of her appearance to others.

She thought back to the time she arrived in Germany four years ago. How much had changed since then. She looked at her reflection and thought of the Clara Vine who arrived, full of hopes for a screen career, escaping a bad love affair, nervous and more than a little naïve. That Clara Vine no longer existed.

And yet, it was strange how suited she was to this life. As a child she had not seemed especially suited to anything. She was shy beside her gregarious elder sister, one of those quiet, watchful children who notice everything but tend to be overlooked. Even when she developed a passion for acting, it was less about self-promotion and more about self-effacement. To be anyone, and no one, at the same time. She had gained in confidence, of course, since childhood, yet this was something she was strangely good at. Perhaps she was like one of those characters Leo Quinn had told her about in Ovid's *Metamorphoses.* Those mythic women with the power to transform themselves, blending into their surroundings at mysterious speed.

She thought of Ralph Sommers' proposal. It was one thing to be gathering gossip from the wives and girlfriends of the Nazi élite. Some of them, like Emmy Goering, could barely be silenced. She only had to open the door to open her mouth. Whenever they met, Emmy Goering would unleash a torrent of anecdotes about the rivalries of the top brass, their rows, their differences of opinion, their private doubts. And it was not just the men who had feuds. The women were just the same. If only the men knew what anger and passion lay beneath those floral silk dresses, bodices and embroidered blouses! If they thought they could contain a woman's emotions by constricting her in a dirndl they were badly mistaken. Women like Emmy, with a strong propensity to gossip, found Clara an ideal companion. They trusted her because of her father's political inclinations and being half-English she seemed not entirely of their world. Yet the idea of cultivating Arno Strauss was something else entirely. Even though Clara had secured an invitation to Goering's party, she was still not sure what she planned to do.

She looked around the carriage. The man opposite was sleeping, his head nodding on his chest with the motion of the train. Automatically she wondered if he was genuinely asleep or watching her from close quarters. Apart from him there was only the elderly couple who had woken her, the man in leather shorts and green loden hunting jacket, his wife in a jaunty Tyrolean hat. They kept sending eager glances in her direction as if keen for some conversation. Sure enough, they took little encouragement to start chatting. They were travelling to Munich to visit the Führer's Grosse Deutscher Kunstausstellung at the House of German Art. Had she heard of it?

'I have. It sounds fascinating.'

That summer Hitler had opened an art exhibition to showcase what he called the New German Art. Fifteen thousand exhibits had been submitted and Hitler helped to select the final choice, seizing on Nordic nudes, gentle landscapes and genre painting, weeding out anything obscure or difficult, even kicking holes in some of them. He had his own peculiar standards, which included a ban on any colour that could not be seen 'in nature' and any scenes that depicted anguish or eroticism. Displays of extreme emotion, it seemed, were reserved for the Führer himself.

And why was Clara visiting Munich? the old couple wanted to know.

Why? Because Bruno Weiss was a dear friend, who needed to know that he had been reported to the authorities? Or because if Bruno was arrested, there was a chance he would give her name under interrogation? Perhaps it was both.

'I'm visiting my sister.'

Clara chatted about her fictitious sister, and said she hoped she might get a chance to see the Führer's exhibition too. The old couple talked excitedly and a trifle nervously about all the sights they intended to cram into a weekend. The Opera. King Ludwig's Residenz. The Chinese Tower teahouse in the Englischer Garten. For that moment, Clara poignantly wished she was exactly the person they thought she was, looking forward to nothing more demanding than a leisurely few days sampling the food and the famous Munich Gemütlichkeit.

She disembarked at the Hauptbahnhof and consulted the map she had brought with her. From what she could see, she needed to walk eastwards to Prinzregentenstrasse to reach the Haus der Kunst. The Entartete Kunst, the exhibition of Degenerate Art, was only a short distance away, in the Archaeology Institute. She had a small leather bag in which Anna Hansen's stationery case was packed, as well as a change of clothes for an overnight stay.

Munich was sparkling in the afternoon sun. Immediately she could see the appeal of the place, compared to the sober Prussian cityscape of Berlin. Munich was prettier, cleaner, less frenetic. Clara walked slowly along the broad boulevards, flanked by handsome white buildings with russet roofs, clanging with blue and white trams, until she reached the town square of Marienplatz, with its craggy, neogothic Neues Rathaus, stained with soot and encrusted with more gargoyles than Hitler's cabinet. The town was busy with shoppers, the crowds swollen by tourists attending the annual Oktoberfest, with their knapsacks, leather braces and green hats. She began to relax a little, dallying along the parades, looking into the shop windows at the displays, thinking about buying some late lunch from a bakery, or at least a cup of good coffee. The sense she had in Berlin of being continually observed had gone. There seemed little chance that she was being followed here.

As she walked she looked curiously around her. Munich was where it had all begun. The birthplace of National Socialism and still its spiritual capital, where back in 1923 Hitler and his gang of associates had led a putsch in a beer hall and ended up in jail. Since then, Bavaria had become Hitler's stronghold. In Berlin he was always on duty, always formal, in his bomb-proof marble-lined Chancellery. Munich was his playground. Here he could relax, attend the opera, eat at the Osteria Bavaria restaurant or take Orange Pekoe tea in the Hofgarten with the thuggish group of ex-storm troopers that Goebbels referred to sarcastically as his 'Munich clique' – Rudolf Hess, Putzi Hanfstaengl and, until he was executed a few years ago, the brutal SA leader Ernst Röhm.

Clara had no trouble finding the Haus der Kunst. It was unmistakeable. A spectacular neoclassical temple whose pale stone columns rippled with the blood and black of Nazi banners. It looked like a railway station might look, if it had been built by ancient Greeks. Designed by Hitler's architect, Paul Ludwig Troost, it had taken four years to construct and had been opened in a grand ceremony that July. A sweep of steps promised gleaming halls and immense vistas of blood-red marble. Clara had no interest in seeing it at all.

Instead she turned to another building a short walk away, where a banner above the door read *Degenerate Art, Entry Free.*

A long queue snaked up a narrow, wooden staircase, skirted round the first sculpture, a menacing evocation of Christ on the cross, and funnelled into a series of gloomy, low-ceilinged rooms crammed with exhibits, chaotically assembled. Everything was deliberately jumbled together, pictures hung askew and unframed on the walls, suspended by string or rope. Cubists, Fauvists, Impressionists and Expressionists were side by side. Beside each work was the price that a museum had paid for it, and some of the paintings were daubed with Nazi epitaphs. The walls, too, had slogans scrawled all over them. *A Threat to the German Nation! Purification and Extermination! We Despise the Optical Illusions of the Jews!* A couple of SS guards presided like the opposite of museum guides, contemptuous backs to the exhibits, casting bored glances over the throng. Clara scanned the crowd rapidly. Could Bruno possibly be here?

The place was crammed. Clara fell in step with a tour guide shepherding a goggle-eyed group of Munich matrons around the room. They passed a series of Kandinsky watercolours, hung in chaotic series beneath a slogan reading *Crazy At Any Price*. Despite the dim lighting the colours burst like fireworks from their frames. The guide pointed a disdainful baton and explained: 'The Führer tells us that degenerate artists cannot see colours or forms as they are in Nature. That is a sign of racial inferiority.'

It was at that moment that Clara sensed again the feeling she had had in Berlin. The distinct yet irrational impression that someone was following her. The invisible brush of eyes on the back of her neck. She waited until the group was moving on and turned suddenly to see, at the far corner of her vision, the whisk of something rounding a corner. Then a large-bosomed woman in a flowery hat sailed into view and when she looked again, it was gone.

Could that be a tail? Or was Clara merely being stalked by her own overheated imagination? Was it a person, or some figment knitted from the interplay of light and shadow? The room was so ill-lit it was hard to tell. Shaken, she tried to focus again on the paintings themselves. How shocking and energizing they were. Bodies which looked less like people than the raw carcass of some animal's kill, yet were still electrifying in their impact. She stared up at them, marvelling at the alchemy by which base pigment was transformed into the very living substance of flesh.

The next room was entirely devoted to the depravity of women and the first painting she saw gave her a jolt of recognition. *The Devil's Bacchanal* by Bruno Weiss. She had last seen it propped in the corner of his room in Pankow and now it was here, a vast six by six-foot canvas, cheek by jowl with Van Gogh and Emil Nolde.

The scene was surreal, the composition had the garish texture of a nightmare. In the foreground the earth seemed convulsed and malign, as if it had engendered the evils perpetrated on its surface. Above it a naked woman was surrounded by licentious scenes of men cavorting with each other, including, in the background, one who closely resembled Ernst Röhm. The woman herself, who had been modelled by Anna, her white flesh gleaming like a piece of meat on a butcher's block, appeared both beautiful and inhuman. Above the painting a Nazi curator had scrawled, *An insult to German womanhood*.

So this was where Bruno had stood, admiring his own work. Clara had to smile. He was right to be proud, and no wonder he was gratified to be exhibited in the company of artists he admired so much, even if the presentation left a little to be desired.

She stayed in front of the picture for several minutes, allowing the tour group to move on and hoping against hope that Bruno would materialize. Yet as the minutes passed, the sheer futility of her search became apparent. Even if Bruno had been here, even if the Luftwaffe officer Fleischer had seen him, what on earth would persuade him to return? No Jew in his right mind could feel comfortable in this place, or anywhere in Munich for that matter. Bruno must have been aware he was a living target. As a Jewish Communist agitator, who had already been arrested in 1933 on suspicion of pamphleteering, he would surely feel as relaxed in Munich as a deer in a forest full of wolves.

Suddenly some sixth sense, prickling on the surface of her skin, caused her to look round. It was a flicker at the far edge of her vision, as slight as a tree's leaves frisked by a passing wind, and as she wheeled around she glimpsed something. A man with his back towards her, his face obscured by the tilt of a hat's brim. About five foot eight with a suitcase in one hand. He was on the far side of the room, observing Otto Dix's *War Cripples*, a vista of hideous, skeletal veterans selling matches in the street. There was something familiar about the man. But even as Clara tried to scrutinize him, he stepped briskly round the corner and was gone.

Quickly she followed, turning left into a vaulted corridor lined with glass cases and then into the next room, a cramped, low-ceilinged space, where people stood three deep to view the exhibits. As she pushed through the crowds, she received several angry reprimands but the man had disappeared. Threading as fast as she could through the rest of the rooms she clattered down the wooden stairway and looked right and left along the street. A bus crawled into view, blocking her line of sight to the other side of the street. She dashed across the road, narrowly missing a truck whose driver craned his head, mouthing invisible imprecations behind the window. There was no sign of him. Either he had vanished into thin air, or he could perform optical illusions as well as any degenerate artist.

Retracing her steps along the broad thoroughfare of Prinzregentenstrasse, she tried to analyse her suspicions. She had learned to trust her instincts over the years and her instincts told her that something about the man in the gallery was familiar. Yet she could not for the sake of her think why. Added to which, nobody, except for Mary and Ralph Sommers, knew she was here. And even if the Gestapo were observing her in Berlin, what was the chance they would have tailed her all the way to Munich? On the other hand, if the man had been a genuine visitor, why would he simply vanish?

She crossed town, wandering up Leopoldstrasse, flanked by stately baroque buildings of cream and soft ochre. Lost in thought, she barely noticed that a crowd had formed ahead of her, until a forest of right arms rose around her and a supercharged twelve-cylinder Mercedes, followed by a three-car escort full of armed guards, sped past. The cavalcade stopped at the corner of Schellingstrasse and Schraudolphstrasse, in front of a dark, low-timbered restaurant, with a sign above the door reading

Osteria Bavaria. A posse of black-uniformed guards ran out of the escort cars like beetles from under a stone.

An Alsatian bounded onto the pavement, tail wagging. The Führer was in town. And lunching at his favourite restaurant.

Turning sharply away Clara was almost knocked over by a gaggle of girls on bicycles, eager, unlike her, to catch a glimpse of the Führer as he headed towards his favourite table, tucked safely away at the back. She half wondered if she might see Unity Mitford, in her black shirt, among them. *Mitfahrt*, as Emmy Goering said she was called, because she followed Hitler everywhere. Then she remembered that the Mitford sisters were in Berlin, preparing to attend the Goerings' reception.

Despite Clara's avoidance tactics, it was impossible to escape the Führer. A little way down Schellingstrasse she passed a glass-fronted shop, adorned with photographs of him. Hitler speaking, Hitler gazing into the distance, Hitler reading. He stared at the audience without breaking his gaze, in a way that speakers usually avoided – a tactic, Clara had heard, that was designed to arouse fear and awe. The Hitler gallery seemed excessive, even by the enthusiastic standards of Third Reich shop displays, until she looked up and saw the name – Heinrich Hoffmann.

Of course. This must be the shop where Hitler's court photographer first introduced the Führer to the seventeen-year-old Eva Braun, then working as his assistant. Their first date, apparently, came when Hitler had spare tickets to the opera. Eva didn't hesitate. Even then she had a sense of her own worth. She had been to a fortune-teller once who told her she would one day be 'world famous'. Clara wondered how she squared that with her current total invisibility. Hardly anyone knew that the Führer's girlfriend even existed.

Consulting her map, Clara walked rapidly southwards, past baroque, four-storey blocks painted in pastel shades, threading her way through the cobbled streets of the city centre and glancing into gloomy beer cellars, whose lamps in heavy iron sconces might have hung unchanged since medieval times, their ceilings painted with colourful flowers, entwined with the obligatory swastikas. There was one more place she wanted to see, before she delivered the case to Katia Hansen.

Past the Viktualienmarkt, heady with the smells of sausage, pretzels and crispy roast chicken, she found herself in Gärtnerplatz, a pleasant square where five roads converged. The centre boasted a patch of grass and trees, and what might be called a riot of geraniums, had anything so unruly as a riot ever been permitted in the Bavarian capital. On the far side was an elegant grey colonnaded building, surrounded by scaffolding. Between the scaffolding she saw a sign saying Theater am Gärtnerplatz. The place Anna Hansen had performed.

Clara went into a café directly across the square and, contrary to her usual custom, sat in the window looking out. Next to her were a trio of women ordering hot chocolate and cake with whipped cream, talking about the problem of finding servants.

The waitress brought Clara an apfelstrudel with rich, flaky pastry. She was plump and jolly-looking, with a frill of dirndl barely constraining a full bosom.

'What's happening to the theatre?' Clara asked.

'It's being remodelled. The Führer has decided it should become the official home of comic opera.'

'Does he come here a lot?'

'A lot! He's always here! But he's so modest. He doesn't want anyone making any fuss. He slips into the royal box just before the curtain rises. No one knows anything about it until his special flag is unfurled over the balcony. He was here just the other day for *The Merry Widow.*'

'Again. Do they perform that a lot?'

'All the time. It's the Führer's favourite.'

Clara had heard how Hitler adored Franz Lehár's operetta, with its sentimental tunes, its plot about women, money and love. Even the fact that its authors, Leo Stein and Viktor Léon, were Jewish didn't seem to perturb him.

'And afterwards they have the most wonderful parties at the Künstlerhaus.'

'What's the Künstlerhaus?'

'The artists' club? On Lenbachplatz? It's an amazing place. All gold paint everywhere and astrological signs painted on the ceiling in the hall. My man helped with the decoration. He's a builder.'

'And what are these parties like?'

'As if I'd know! They're not going to invite the likes of me, are they? I'm happy enough to see the Führer go in and out. You get a great view from here. If you sit there until this evening you might see him tonight, you never know.'

The drab apartment block where Katia Hansen lived was on the corner of Frauenstrasse and Zwingerstrasse, only a few minutes' walk from Gärtnerplatz. After several minutes the door was opened by an old woman who Clara assumed was the landlady, in a stained apron, her hair tied in a rough turban. She had apple cheeks, only the apples had grown creased and withered and her little eyes were sharp with suspicion. Everything about her was a direct contradiction of the mat beneath her feet which said 'Welcome'. When Clara asked for Katia Hansen, her expression hardened from flint to steel.

'She's not here.'

'But she lives here, right?'

'Not any more. She used to but she's gone away.'

'Where has she gone?'

'A long way away.'

Clara had not been expecting this. It had not even occurred to her that Katia Hansen might have moved. Yet now, with Bruno nowhere to be seen and Katia Hansen gone, it was plain she had travelled all this way for nothing. Suddenly, fatigue and futility combined to dispirit her. She felt moored to the spot.

'The thing is, I have something to give her. Perhaps I could leave it here.'

The landlady looked askance at the case Clara was carrying.

'Certainly not.'

'You see, Fräulein Hansen's sister has died.'

The old woman blanched slightly, but was not giving an inch.

'I'm sorry. But that's not my business.'

'This case belonged to her sister. It's of sentimental value. I've come all the way from Berlin to deliver it. Perhaps if I left it here then she would be able to come and fetch it.'

If Clara had hoped the mention of Anna's death might affect the old woman, she was disappointed. Instead the woman leaned forward and hissed, her breath rank through mottled brown teeth.

'How many times do I need to tell you? She's gone. You people need to leave us alone. We don't want anything of hers.'

'Then I don't suppose you have a forwarding address? As I have come such a long way.'

From the bowels of the building came the shout of children squabbling. The scent of boiled flesh wafted down the hall. The woman was clearly torn between slamming the door shut and the thought that her visitor might create more fuss by returning. She cast a glance over Clara's shoulder into the street.

'Wait a minute.'

When she returned, she thrust a piece of paper gracelessly into Clara's hand.

'It's the best place for her,' she commented. 'If you see her, tell her not to bother coming back.' With that she shut the door in Clara's face.

Clara looked at the scrap of paper in her hand.

Katia Hansen
Heim Kurmark
Klosterheide
Lindow in der Mark

Heim Kurmark? she thought. What's that?

Her feet sore from walking round the city and her entire body taut with the strain of heightened alertness, Clara decided to find somewhere to stay the night. It was six o'clock already, and having rejected the idea of taking the night train back to Berlin, she found a room in a Gasthaus near the station. She should have been more discriminating – the place was cold and unfriendly, the front door had a cracked pane of glass, and she noticed only too late a card propped in the hallway saying *Juden Sind Nicht Hier Erwünscht.* The owner's cook had managed to pull off the unlikely combination of overboiled cabbage and underboiled potatoes which Clara ate beneath the monocled eye of the only other guest, a parched, whiskery man who stared shamelessly at her figure as though she might later be offering it to him. Coffee was served in the gloom of the parlour, where every quarter hour a piercing clock's chime shattered the musty air.

By nine o'clock she was sitting on a bed as hard as a new Reich autobahn, reflecting on a wasted journey. No Bruno, no Katia Hansen, and to make matters worse, her back ached because she had lugged the stationery case all around the city in a cumbersome shoulder bag. Pulling the case out she opened it again and spread its contents on the bed, fanning out the sweet, schoolboyish letters from Johann that she had read so many times, she almost knew them by heart. She wondered what Anna had written back. From everything she knew of Anna Hansen, marriage to an SS officer was wildly out of character and as for a stint at Bride School . . . it was hard to imagine anything less likely. Was it simply love that drew Anna and Johann together? Or was Anna seeking something else from the arrangement? A refuge, perhaps, or a fortune? Or an escape?

She rifled idly through the papers. The only thing she hadn't properly examined was the letter addressed to Katia, and now she opened it, and read the scant couple of lines.

Darling Katia, I know you're angry with me, but I will explain everything, I promise. When you get this, please write back. Don't believe what anyone says to you about me. It will be all right, you'll see. Your loving sister, Anna

So the Hansen sisters had quarrelled. And now Katia had moved to the other end of the country and probably didn't know that her sister had been murdered and that they would never be reconciled. How long might it be before she found out?

She shook her head and folded Anna's letter back into its envelope, then bundled the papers up and shut the case again. After she had done that she undressed, lay between the chilly sheets and stared up at the ceiling, riddled with damp like a map of Africa, turning the day's events over in her head. There was one thing that puzzled her. The remark the old woman had made.

You people need to leave us alone.

Evidently Clara wasn't the first person to come looking for Katia Hansen. Someone else had been to visit Anna's sister. It might be the authorities, seeking to contact the family over Anna's death. Though if that was so, surely the visitor would have explained to the landlady that Anna had died? Yet it was clear from the old woman's reaction that she knew nothing about it. So why had someone tried to locate Katia, and more importantly, who?

The next morning she skipped breakfast in her hurry to leave but then found herself with half an hour to wait for the train. Idling in the street that led to the station, she saw a shop front containing a display of Hitler Youth knives. There, in the forefront, was exactly the one Erich had told her about. The latest model. She sighed to herself as she realized she was going to have to buy it. When she went in and asked to see it, the shopkeeper, a huge man with a barrel chest and a moustache, put it straight in her hand and it fitted her palm perfectly, as if it was made for her. It was a curiously pleasurable sensation. It lay there, heavy and smooth, with its black checkered grip and gleaming silver blade engraved with the HJ motto *Blut und Ehre* in antiquated Gothic script. Blood and Honour. Two perfectly ordinary words whose meaning the Nazis had managed to pervert. Frankly, she thought as she paid for the knife, it was hard to think of a phrase she hated more.

'Heil Hitler!' said the shopkeeper.

Clara nodded.

Except for that one, of course.

Chapter Twenty

The white, eighteenth-century palace that contained the Ministry for Public Enlightenment and Propaganda was far less imposing than Goering's Air Ministry, just a grenade's throw away down Wilhelmstrasse, yet it embodied its master's character just as well. While the Air Ministry intimidated with its sheer size, Goebbels' ministry was a far more subtle affair. The original building had been extended in clean, modernist style with a mellow stone façade and modish torch lamps to allow more Lebensraum for the Reich's propaganda empire. Inside, a viewing theatre and pine-panelled conference rooms had been added, giving the general impression of a sleek, state-of-the-art machine, producing an unending stream of rebuttals and manufactured news to feed the ravenous world media.

As she waited for Hauptsturmführer Huber, Mary watched a bustling stream of journalists filing out of the conference room behind her. Every morning a bulletin would be posted in the lobby with details of the daily press conferences, to be delivered either by Reich Press Chief Otto Dietrich or Goebbels himself. The subjects were generally attacks on the Church, the Jews, the Czechs, or the Bolsheviks. No one was left in any doubt what to write. In Nazi Germany the production of news was just as serious and precise a business as the manufacture of tanks and guns, and journalists were kept under as strict a control as possible. Officially that was achieved through minutely itemized permits and visas, and unofficially through wiretaps, threats and surveillance. It couldn't be more different from Spain, Mary thought, where plenty of the soldiers in charge couldn't read, and any old bit of paper you flourished, even an ancient love letter, would be accepted as official documentation.

Everything about Madrid had been noisy, vibrant chaos. Each day was dominated by the wail of sirens, street speakers denouncing fascism, yellow trams clanging down the street, and loud bars full of soldiers smelling of sweat and tobacco. Nights were punctuated by the distant rumble of artillery and the thunder of trench mortars as they thudded into their targets. There were queues everywhere for beans and bread, and getting anywhere meant negotiating a way around giant craters in the pavements and ad hoc barricades erected in the street to keep what the locals called 'los facciosos' out.

The largest hotels, the Ritz and the Palace, had been turned into hospitals, with local prostitutes dragooned into service as nurses, so Mary had installed herself in a smaller place, containing a strange assortment of foreigners, all with their own agenda. There were journalists, entrepreneurs and agents provocateurs, and other men whose roles seemed even less precise. It didn't matter though, because no one actually discussed their business. Their conversation focused solely on the progress of the Fascist advance and the availability of food. Which shop had potatoes, which had apples, where sausage could be found. Between forays into the city they would congregate in the ground-floor bar. Someone would commandeer the piano, or another guest with a gramophone would play Beethoven at top volume, while someone else opened a suitcase full of chocolate to be traded for coffee or bread or eggs. One day, as Franco's forces began their regular morning bombardment, Mary was sitting there listening to the waitress grumble about losing her blonde highlights now all the peroxide in the city had been confiscated by the hospitals. As a nearby shell hit its target, Mary looked out to see a telephone pole crash down, its wires draped like a clothes line across the road. The building opposite was pocked with shrapnel holes.

'Admiring General Franco's art?'

It was a pair of men eating at the next table. They asked her to join them and poured a stream of bitter coffee for her as more shells crashed around them.

'You don't need to look so worried,' said one. He was an Englishman, wiry and muscular, with high cheekbones and a sculpted face. He wore khaki fatigues and a red scarf round his neck. 'You can tell how far away a shell is by the sound of the whistle.'

His companion was a fleshy, self-assured Austrian with thick, wavy hair and dark, suspicious eyes. He had a handgun in a leather holster round his waist. To Mary's astonishment he was introduced as Emilio Kléber, the military advisor to the International Brigades in Madrid and the man popularly held to have saved the city so far from Nationalist forces. He was eating, messily, a portion of stew, but hearing her accent he paused.

'You're American. I lived in New York for a while. Down in Greenwich Village. There was a hot-dog cart outside my apartment and every morning I woke up to the smell of those hot dogs. Best sausage in the world.'

'And who are you?' she asked the Englishman.

'You can call me Pericles,' he said. That didn't seem so strange to her. Half the men out in the war had taken fighting names, for one reason or another. The men asked her about her journalism, and her career, and then began to talk with penetrating seriousness about Communism and how it was the only solution to injustice and the way to prevent war engulfing the continent. The barbarity of the Fascists knew no bounds, they argued. The fires they lit in Spain would ignite the whole of Europe if they got the chance.

'You've been to Germany, you say?' said Kléber. 'Well, that's how it will end here, if Franco gets his way. He wants a state like Hitler's.'

'I'm hoping to get a pass to go out to the Fascist lines. I'd like to interview some of their leaders.'

Kléber's face darkened. 'Beware of the Fascists. They are full of propaganda. They will tell you anything. They claim the Republicans are feeding prisoners to the zoo animals.' He gave a savage, guttural laugh. 'I say they might want to, but they wouldn't get the chance. There are no animals left alive in Madrid Zoo.'

When the bombardment finished Kléber departed and Mary went for a walk down the Gran Via with Pericles. He had a slight limp, from a bullet hole in his leg that had not properly healed, yet he walked with rapid purpose, like a man who has discovered his role in life.

'What will you do next?' she asked him.

He shrugged. 'There is so much to do.'

'If you're so interested in Communism, why don't you go out to Russia?'

He looked at her as if she was mad. 'What would be the point of that, Miss Harker? Russia's had her revolution already. My work is to create the next one.'

They parted soon afterwards and she didn't see him in the hotel again, or for that matter anywhere in Madrid.

Hauptsturmführer Huber returned, wrenching Mary's thoughts back to the present. He was fatter than she remembered and a bulge of white flesh peeped beneath the straining buttons of his tunic, like filling from a burned, overstuffed pie. The iron filings on his scalp had been shaved again, rendering his head a prickly potato. She was relieved to see he bore a sheaf of papers containing her details and stamped with the indigo National Socialist eagle, but before he handed it over, Huber flicked through with his sausage fingers and read aloud the conditions of the permit. No images depicting the Nazi government in a negative manner would be permitted. No degrading pictures of German citizens. No photographs of any prohibited site. Any violation of the conditions of the permit would be punished with immediate expulsion, by order of the Führer Adolf Hitler himself.

'Sign here.'

As Mary made to sign, he snatched the paper away again and pretended to read a further item.

'One further condition. Any Fräulein wanting a photography permit will accompany SS Hauptsturmführer Karl Huber for an evening at the Metropol theatre. So what's it to be?'

Huber gave a hearty laugh, displaying his gold front tooth to full advantage, and waved the permit in his chubby hands. The thought of what those fingers might try, sitting next to her at the Metropol theatre, made Mary shudder.

Chapter Twenty-one

This time when Clara got back to her apartment on Winterfeldstrasse there was no need to examine the powder on the doorknob to see if she had intruders. An entire crater of splintered wood had been punched around the lock, and the door gaped open.

Clara fumbled for the light, and gasped as she saw the desecration within. The place had been ransacked. The kitchen shelves had been clumsily rifled and the cupboard doors opened. In the drawing room, books had been pulled and flung from the shelves and her desk was open, papers scattered. In the bedroom the chest had been pulled away from the wall and its drawers hung out drunkenly, trailing clothing. The mattress was askew where someone had searched beneath it, and the painting by Bruno Weiss tilted on the wall. In the bathroom, the tops of the jars were open, and lavender bath salts carelessly spilled. It was as though some giant child had had a tantrum and thrown everything around like toys.

With a sudden thought, she moved towards the opened desk in the sitting room and gave one of the ornate legs a sharp tap with the side of her hand. It snapped outward, revealing a hollowed space inside. Pushing her fingers down into the narrow space she connected with the cold metal of a gun barrel. Her Beretta. A present from a friend.

At that moment she heard the heavy tread of Rudi, who had wheezed up the stairs and stood goggling at the door. He had seen no intruders, he protested, pasting a lank strip of hair back across his skull in bewilderment. He had been up the previous evening, just to put some letters through the door, and seen nothing amiss, so this must have happened earlier today. A Sunday!

'I'll call the police,' he said. 'They'll be here in no time.'

That was the sole advantage of living in a Nazi state. The police were never far away.

'No. Don't do that.'

'Why not, Fräulein?'

'I don't want police tramping around before I've checked what's missing.'

'But we'll need to get this door mended.'

'It looks worse than it is. The lock still functions. No need to call a workman out on a Sunday.'

'If you're sure,' he said distrustfully.

'Let's deal with it later, when I've cleared up,' she said firmly, as he edged reluctantly away.

Clara's first thought was of the men who had been mending the lift. Might they have been watching out for residents who had left their apartments empty? Or had someone known already that she would be away? She realized that the intruders had picked the one time of the week when Rudi could be guaranteed not to notice them. Sunday morning was when he slept off the hangover of Saturday night with his storm-trooper friends.

Moving swiftly from room to room she made a rapid inventory of her possessions. The strange thing was, despite the scale of the devastation, nothing appeared to be missing. Though her pearls were flung across the bedroom floor, her brooches scattered and her diamond clips emptied out on the dressing table, once she had collected them up she found her jewellery was all there. In the top drawer a wallet with fifty marks inside sat undisturbed, alongside a book with a speckled cover of bird's-egg blue entitled *Poems of Rilke*. Copies of *The Times*, which like other foreign newspapers were hard to obtain, lay piled on the floor. A bundle of letters from her family, and one from Leo she had never been able to throw away, had been scattered across her desk, but none was missing. What kind of burglar was this to break into an apartment with such determination, through the front door, and leave empty-handed? To take such a risk and escape with nothing to show for it?

Her mind was working frantically. She had lived here for four years without being burgled. And now this. If it was the Gestapo, then she had to assume her apartment was no longer the sanctuary it had been. There was every chance that along with reading her mail they would have installed listening devices. At the very least they would have read every single letter in her desk.

She moved about feverishly, tidying and straightening,

There wasn't time for this. It was already lunchtime and she had an appointment to keep. Today was Erich's fourteenth birthday. His present was nestling at the bottom of her bag, along with a bar of his favourite Trumpf chocolate and a pen inscribed with the logo of the Ufa studios which she knew would gain him plenty of kudos at school.

Mercifully, the front door still closed and as for locking it, what was the point of that? Grabbing her coat and hat, she headed out to meet Erich.

Even for a Sunday, the Anhalter Bahnhof was busy, full of little huddles. All railway stations were places of departure, yet there was a particular atmosphere among the Anhalter Bahnhof travellers. You could always tell them, the departing Jews, from the way the nervous mothers silenced their children, clustered around a pitiful collection of luggage, the wives in their best furs, the husbands' faces taut with anxiety, clutching passports, nervously checking and rechecking documents and tickets. Emigrating, without funds, to an uncertain future. To a land that might not be outrightly hostile to them, as Germany was, but would still be cold and unwelcoming, resentful at the influx of refugees lapping over their borders in an increasingly unstoppable tide.

Erich was waiting in their usual place, beneath the clock. At the sight of him the anxiety Clara had suppressed over the break-in suddenly rose and she found herself blinking back tears. Briskly she wiped them away. She was determined not to mention the burglary to Erich. She didn't want to worry him and, besides, it was his birthday.

'Herzlichen Glückwunsch zum Geburtstag, sweetheart!'

She enveloped him in an unusually heartfelt hug and felt his body stiffen at her public demonstration of affection.

'Thank you.' He pulled away. 'You're late.'

'Sorry, darling. I got caught up.'

'I haven't got long. There's a meeting of the HJ.' He pointed at his knapsack. 'We're practising for a big march through Berlin. I've brought my uniform to change into, seeing as you don't seem to like me wearing it.'

'But it's your birthday! We were going to go for a meal!'

He looked impatient and annoyed. The little boy who got excited every October was now at odds with the older boy who knew that birthdays were babyish beside the privilege of serving the Fatherland. His hair had been shaved savagely to the scalp and he had polished his Haferl shoes to a high shine.

'Birthdays aren't important at my age,' he shrugged.

'Just wait till you get to my age then,' she joked, but it fell flat, and instead of a special celebration they headed for a dingy café in the corner of the station, where they sat at the busy bar with travellers jostling alongside them, hurrying their drinks. Clara ordered buttered eggs and rolls, and for Erich, Käsewurst sausage with a delicious stuffing of cheese. She watched him closely as he ate. He was poised so exactly between man and boy that in one light she could still see the shy, underconfident lad who had been eager to please her, while in another the swagger of a grown man was already visible.

She tried a bit harder.

'So who's this march in favour of?'

'Some foreign dignatory.' Keen to conceal the fact that he had no idea, he added, 'We're not supposed to say. For security reasons.'

'I see.'

'We march from Kemperplatz all the way up the Siegesallee past the Reichstag, round the Victory Column and up Unter den Linden. And look at this!' He pulled out of his knapsack a grey collecting box, unmistakeably shaped like a bomb. 'Some of us have been chosen to march on the outside with the collection boxes. That's an honour.'

'You're raising money for bombs?'

'No, Clara. That's an enemy bomb. Germany needs to raise money to defend herself.'

'But no one is threatening Germany.'

'Of course they are.' Her obduracy annoyed him. Increasingly now Erich found himself correcting Clara politically. He didn't like it, but they had been told in the HJ they were quite right to do it. Young people no longer needed to feel subservient to their elders. They were the spirit of the new Germany and should feel confident in their role.

'The Communists want to overrun us. They've already overrun Spain. They are anti-Christian. They murdered all the priests.'

'There's bad on both sides in Spain, Erich.'

He shrugged. 'I hate Communists. I hope they all die. Or at least . . .' he frowned, a concession to Clara whom he knew disapproved of sweeping generalizations, 'I hope they get sent to camps so they can be educated.'

The birthday treat had got off on the wrong note, Clara

realized. How Erich had changed from the boy last summer who had laughingly learned to row in the Havel, taking the oars alongside her and glowing with pride at how quickly he became skilled. Seeing him only at weekends was like time-lapse photography, where he appeared to grow and develop at an alarming rate. And his political views were changing at an equally rapid pace.

Normally nothing was more relaxing and absorbing to Clara than being with Erich, but the burglary had distracted her and she found her mind wandering as he talked. He mentioned a speech they had received at the HJ last week. The Germans in the Rhineland were grateful for their liberation and the next people desiring liberation were the Czechs.

'Who do the Czechs want liberation from? Themselves?'

'There are three million Germans in Czechoslovakia.'

'And how many non-Germans?'

Clara cursed herself for avoiding her own iron rule never to discuss politics with Erich. He gave her a fierce look.

'England should watch out. Germany will take England's colonies. England is decaying and decadent.'

'Oh Erich, for God's sake be quiet! You don't know anything about England.'

'Why should I be quiet? Why shouldn't I tell everyone what you're like? You don't love the Führer. You'd do anything to avoid the salute.'

'That's not true!'

'You don't think I notice, but I do. And you're not even German!'

'Don't be silly. You're far too young to understand.'

'I have to go.' His eyes glinted with tears. 'If that's how you feel about our country, perhaps I don't want to see you again.'

He slipped off the stool and darted out of the café. Helplessly Clara watched his dark head bobbing in the crowd until it was lost in a sea of grey coats and trudging figures. She remembered another speech Hitler had made: '*When an opponent says I will not come over to your side, I calmly say, your child belongs to us already.*'

It was a teenage tantrum and he would be regretting it already, she knew, yet arguing was never going to be the way she won Erich's heart. How was it, when in every other area of her life she managed to remain composed, that she lost her cool with the person she most cared about? The shock of the day and her tiredness came together. She groaned out loud as she stared after him into the crowd.

Beside her at the bar an old woman eyed her sympathetically and smiled.

'Trouble with men?'

'You could say that.'

'Same old story.'

'I suppose.'

Clara realized she had not even given Erich the knife. It lay at the bottom of her handbag, a red ribbon tied incongruously around its leather sheath.

Chapter Twenty-two

Despite its prestigious address on Unter den Linden, the offices of the *New York Evening Post* were far from impressive. Even the word 'office' was a generous description for the sixth-floor room behind a frosted-glass door, containing a couple of desks ringed with coffee stains, on which stood several black telephones, ash-trays melted with cigarette burns and towers of old newspapers. Mary reached for the brown paper bag containing a carton of bockwurst and some rye bread she had brought for lunch and chewed an absent mouthful. As if there wasn't enough to report, now it looked like she needed to become a photographer too.

'Get yourself a camera!' Frank Nussbaum had suggested, when she called him with her proposal for a piece on the Bride School. 'Get some snaps of these ladies in the kitchen, or taking lessons on Führerworship or whatever it is they do.'

'Whatever happened to the art of telling a story with words?'

'Words aren't enough now, Mary. It's pictures with everything now. Have you seen the circulation of *Life* Magazine? It's shifting a million copies a week.'

'But I'm a journalist, Frank.'

'If you can take pictures too, it'll make all the more impact. Pictures put more emotion in it. Tug at the heartstrings. Look at Robert Capa out in Spain.'

Mary had met Robert Capa once in a bar in Madrid, a sinewy young Hungarian who had changed his name and reinvented himself, reinventing war journalism too, in the process. His pictures were stunning. There was no possibility she could ever produce something like that.

'Photography's an art, Frank, for God's sake. It's not like taking family snaps on Coney Island.'

'So be an artist!'

'You need to be a chemist too! You need to know about, oh I don't know, fixer and developer and darkrooms. That kind of thing. I'm not good with those.'

'The office can help you with that. Let them do the chemicals. You do the shooting. It's called photojournalism. I have faith in you, woman. You can do it.'

'And I'd need to register,' she moaned. 'Goebbels says all photographers must wear a special armband now, to identify them as press. It was tough enough to get this visa in the first place. I'm not sure they'll appreciate the idea of me with a camera too. I'm hardly Leni Riefenstahl.'

'Leave it to me.'

So Mary had gone out and fixed herself up with a Zeiss Ikon Ikoflex, a sturdy black box with a twin lens and a smart little case, and practised focusing with the knob on the left side and loading the film. Sneakily she liked it, though she resented the implication that the truth of her stories wasn't enough, and you needed the proof in black and white. But Mary had always been one to look on the bright side and the fact was, there were so many illustrated newspapers and magazines in Germany, if she had to turn herself into a photojournalist, Berlin wasn't a bad place to start. Just so long as she never had to learn the technical details of focal lengths and lenses and how to turn her negatives into front-page splashes.

And, she had to admit, Frank had a point. Mary wished she

had had the camera back in Spain. Sometimes, when she was there, she reckoned her words might be written on the air for all the good they did. If she had had a photograph of what she had seen, of the pitiful victims of that savage conflict, how much more attention might she have grabbed. How much better she could have reached the people back home who liked to dismiss the Spanish war as just another wrangle in Europe's dismal history. Sometimes it was hard to find the words to describe what she saw but a camera would have done the job.

So from now on her Zeiss was going everywhere with her. Starting with the Propaganda Ministry where she would apply for a permit and armband with a tin badge marking her out as a registered press photographer. Despite what Frank said, that would not be easy. Her old contact there, Putzi Hanfstaengl, the former head of foreign press who was half American himself, had fled the country in February fearing a plan to assassinate him. He had been summoned to Goebbels' ministry and issued with orders to fly to Spain, but Hanfstaengl suspected the idea was to push him out of the plane and he had instead taken the first train to Switzerland. Since then Goebbels had said the whole assassination idea was a joke, but that was hardly reassuring. As everyone knew, Goebbels' sense of humour was not to be trusted.

All of which meant Mary would need to be extra persuasive. She might even have to approach Hauptsturmführer Huber, the fat official in the Press department who was always leering at her during Doktor Goebbels' interminable press conferences. She groaned at the thought. The only man to have asked her out since she arrived in Berlin, and it had to be a Nazi oaf with a face like a prize fighter who was no longer winning any prizes.

Mary banished the image from her mind and licked the oniony grease from her fingers. She had better get around to it straight away. Once she had the permit, she would be able to return to the

Bride School and tell that godawful Fräulein Wolff that she was officially permitted to take any photographs she liked. At the same time she could see if there had been any developments in the case of the murdered bride.

Chapter Twenty-three

The Residenz-Casino on Blumenstrasse, known as the Resi to its clientele, was the place all of Berlin went to drown its sorrows. It had a dance floor that could hold a thousand people, and the air was alive with music, laughter and the clash of cheap perfume. Shards of light splintered from the mirrored globes fixed to the ceiling's reflective glass, showering everyone below with dappled brilliance. The special attraction of the Resi, however, was the telephones. The dance floor was surrounded by a series of cubicles fitted with Bakelite receivers which could be called from any other of the cubicles. There was even a system of pneumatic tubes suspended above the tables, along which gifts could be sent.

Wearing a black satin dress and a slender string of pearls, Clara sat in her cubicle and stared out at the dance floor below. She had spent the entire day clearing the mess of her apartment, folding clothes which had been torn out of the cupboards systematically back into drawers, and rehanging her dresses, putting away the fragments of smashed crockery in the sink, working out what, if anything, had been taken. The answer still, it seemed, was nothing. Once she had established that, the other question was whether anything had been left behind. She had made a thorough inspection of the hidden places in the apartment, behind the radiators and the panels in the bathroom. She had unscrewed the light fittings and the telephone receiver and checked the underside of the bedside table. But there was nothing. In one way the burglary bore the hallmarks of a Gestapo raid. They could be heavy-handed in their operations and were never too concerned with tidying up afterwards because they knew no one was going to file a complaint. Yet if it was the Gestapo, the sheer chaos in her apartment told her that this was no ordinary search. It was sufficiently unsubtle to be a message to her. A warning almost. But a warning of what? Once more, Archie Dyson's words rang in her ears. *Lie low. Do nothing.* But it was clear to her now that doing nothing wasn't working.

Rudi, who had come up a second time, ostensibly to pass her a letter, surveyed the scene of the crime avidly. No one had come past his cubicle on Saturday, he repeated. He would have seen them. Perhaps they came in the window on the stairwell. Clara examined it. Outside was a tiny ledge with a railing which could easily be accessed by a determined burglar but the fitting was clogged with verdigris which showed no sign of having been disturbed. They must have come in from the ground floor. Had they dressed up as maintenance men and pretended to mend the lift while planning how to gain entry later? Had they arrived on Saturday might when Rudi was always out or waited until Sunday morning when he was still in a drunken stupor?

'What did they take?' Rudi asked.

'Nothing important,' Clara replied coolly. She knew better than to give Rudi any additional information.

'Perhaps you had nothing they wanted,' he shrugged, his little eyes darting pruriently around the apartment for evidence of female immorality. His eyes lit on a bra which had been left dangling over the back of a chair. He left reluctantly, saying the handyman was coming to fix the door that afternoon. As soon as he had gone, Clara had ripped open the letter he had brought to find a short note from Ralph, inviting her for a discussion on her 'latest role'.

The telephone on her table cut through her thoughts and she picked it up.

'Devilishly good fun these things, aren't they? I think all bars should have them. Then old married couples would never need to sit next to each other in silence. They could just pick up the receiver and say "Mine's a gin and tonic".'

Ralph's jocular tones were unmistakeable. He could be any Englishman, out for a night on the town, determined to enjoy every minute of it. The sound of his voice cheered her instantly.

'Where are you?'

'Look to your right.'

He was sitting several tables away, his arm flung over the back of the chair, a bottle of champagne and two glasses in front of him. He was wearing evening dress, his thick hair trained back with brilliantine and tie loosened. He was a tourist, determined to have the time of his life in Berlin, and hang the politics.

'Care to join me? To tell the truth, I've an aversion to speaking on the telephone.'

She moved over to his table and he kissed her on the cheek, a swift, masculine brush of warm skin and cologne, then poured the champagne. He took a sip and gave a little shudder.

'Filthy stuff they serve here.' She noticed his eyes roving across the room as he talked, lingering on an exceptionally lovely woman in a low-cut dress propping up the bar. 'How was Munich? Pretty place, isn't it?'

'Very. They have some fascinating art down there. Have you been busy yourself?'

'Non-stop. The Luftwaffe was holding some manoeuvres near Frankfurt to show off their new planes. They invited a handful of foreign air attachés and I went along too. They do have some impressive machines. Particularly the Messerschmitt fighters and the Dornier bombers. There must have been thirteen hundred aircraft there at least. They're very proud of them.'

'And they want everyone to know it?'

'The Luftwaffe has decided it's time to flex its wings in public. They were hoping to get the Duke of Windsor along too, but the poor wretch was down a mine in Düsseldorf or somewhere.'

'Seems like everyone feels sorry for the Duke.'

'Rightly so,' Ralph smoothed his moustache insouciantly. 'It's incredible how much fuss the British press are still making about his private life. To think we're on the brink of an international crisis that could threaten thousands of lives and all the British public seem to care about is the state of their ex-king's morals.'

'Do morals not matter then?'

He caught her eye and frowned.

'I'm talking about sexual morality. What two people do in bed with each other is a matter for themselves only, I always think. Don't you?'

For some reason, his remark stirred something in her and she shifted in her seat. At that moment her body felt ripe, ready and perfectly alive, as though it was responding to him on a purely animal level. She amazed herself. How could she possibly feel this way, given Ralph Sommers' infuriating manner, not to mention the trauma of the break-in? The burglary had left her feeling more vulnerable than ever before. She couldn't walk down the street without a fear of being followed. Perhaps it was like what people said about pilots or soldiers, that they never felt so alive, as when they were under threat. She only hoped he didn't notice her blush.

'Mind you,' he continued, 'the British newspapers are only making up for lost time. They didn't mention Wallis for years, when the whole of Europe knew. Now they're taking the same approach to rearmament. There's a wall of silence. The press derides Churchill when he talks about the dangers of German militarism because they don't dare tell the truth. It's as though they think the public can't take it. Well they'll have to, soon enough.'

At that moment there was a shout from across the room and Ralph broke into a warm grin. He gave a wave to a table of men a few feet away who were laughing in his direction and gesticulating that he should join them. Instantly he was transformed again into the genial man about town, a socialite enjoying the high life in Berlin with a pretty actress beside him in crimson lipstick and a tight satin dress. Anyone looking at them would think they were an attractive couple, out for an evening on the town. Turning back to Clara he leaned towards her, patted her hand and said, 'This is no good. We can't talk here.'

'Why did you ask me here then? It has to be the least private place in Berlin.'

'Precisely for that reason. You mentioned you might be watched and I wanted to see if you were.'

'And was I?'

'Only by me.'

Leaving the Resi, he flagged down a taxi and they drove to Duisberger Strasse. The apartment was cold and dark. He snapped on the lamp and helped her off with her coat.

'Sorry. You were probably expecting a lovely dinner. Instead of which you get an old bachelor's flat with nothing in the kitchen but half a bottle of bourbon.' He poured a generous slug into a glass, placed it on the coffee table, then rooted around in the cupboard and came up with some biscuits which he laid before her, like a trophy.

'So. Any progress with our Oberst Strauss?'

She delivered her triumph coolly. 'Frau Goering has invited me to a reception for the Duke and Duchess at their hunting lodge. Strauss will be there too.'

He nodded. 'I'm impressed. All the Luftwaffe chaps in Frankfurt were talking about Goering's little party. It turns out to have some strategic significance. Apparently Hitler is to put some important proposal to the Duke later when he travels down to Berchtesgaden. Goering's reception is a buttering-up exercise.'

She sat down and crossed her legs.

'I do hope you're going to tell me what this is all about.'

'All in good time. You mentioned Strauss took you in a plane the other day, but you said you were hopeless with names. I assume that was the opposite of the truth.'

'It was a Henschel Hs 126. A two-seater. It's the third prototype and one of ten being tested.'

He raised an eyebrow. 'Excellent. Just as I thought.'

'What do you mean by that?'

'It's my understanding that Strauss reports to a new division of the Luftwaffe called the Squadron for Special Purposes. It's allied to the Intelligence service. A special operations unit run by a man called Theodor Rowehl. He's been recruiting pilots and developing aircraft with the aim of developing aerial reconnaissance.'

Ralph prised a Senior Service out of its packet and sent it across the coffee table.

'You do understand what I mean by aerial reconnaissance?'

'You could try explaining,' she said, helping herself to a cigarette.

'The Germans first tried it in the war. They fitted miniature cameras to the breasts of pigeons and flew them over the battlefield.'

'Pigeons!' Clara couldn't help laughing, but he was serious.

'It's true. It was ingenious but pretty rudimentary. Things have got a lot more sophisticated since then. You see, Clara, the blitzkrieg strategy which our friend Udet pioneered requires detailed knowledge of the terrain. If you're going to swoop down with a payload of bombs, you need to know beforehand exactly what you're going to attack. You need detailed aerial photographs.'

'I see.'

'So they need to experiment with aerial photography. But until now German military intelligence has had a problem. They can't make flights with standard Luftwaffe aircraft because this would be a violation of other countries' airspace, not to mention a pretty clear warning sign of their intentions, so they've been using cameras hidden in passenger and commercial aircraft. Already they've taken pictures of Poland, Belgium, France and Russia, mapping out factories, power stations, railways, reservoirs and ports.'

'But why?'

'Why do you think?' he continued briskly. 'The plan is to select targets in case of war.'

He craned a quizzical eye at her to check that she was following.

'So this is serious?'

'It's deadly serious. And if it comes to war, General von Fritsch, the Army commander, says the side with the best photographic reconnaissance will win. It's a race, and at the moment the Germans are streets ahead. Our Air Service recognizes how desperately important it is that we develop our own photographic reconnaissance. We need to keep track of the German military preparations, where troops are being deployed, ships prepared, where aircraft are being assembled. We need the ability to look right into factories and see what machines they are building. To be able to tell whether a building on the ground is a military installation or simply a factory. Do you follow me?'

She nodded. The bourbon and cigarettes were making her head swim slightly. She had eaten almost nothing all day.

'You said the Germans had a problem?'

'That's right. The Luftwaffe want to develop their own aircraft for aerial reconnaissance, but they're limited by two things – the performance and range of the aircraft and the scope of the camera. So they're busy on two counts. They're intent on developing the right aircraft for the job, and they're working on camera lenses that can see positions with pinpoint accuracy. That's the hardest thing, because above eight thousand feet most camera lenses become fogged with condensation. At lower altitude the plane is all too visible.'

'And what exactly does Arno Strauss have to do with all this?'

'Strauss is in charge of developing and testing the cameras on the new aircraft. Recently I've had word that he's masterminding something far more exciting. An advanced aerial reconnaissance camera with a lens more powerful than anything we've seen before, fitted into a camera the size of a lady's handbag. German cameras are the best in the world. You've heard of Zeiss? Along with Leica they make the most sophisticated lenses. Anyhow, it's taken years for the Zeiss photographic division to develop this. It also uses infrared film, so they can take pictures at night. It's a whole new way of seeing, apparently, and it's going to be of massive assistance to them.'

He leaned closer to her, cradling his whisky in his hands.

'What we need, what I would really like, is to find out more about that camera.'

'You seem to have plenty of access. You were just telling me how the Luftwaffe show you all their new fighter planes.'

'This is top secret, Clara. For Nazi eyes only.'

'Then I don't see how I could help.'

'Let me explain. This camera sits in a bay behind the back seat of the aircraft, right next to where the machine gun is placed in a bomber. My man says that Strauss is due to trial the camera within the next two weeks, probably in a Henschel 126, like the one he took for your joyride. What I would really like is to get some more details of this camera. To understand what it's capable of. Depth of resolution, focal length and so on. It could make all the difference.'

'To a war?'

'I'd go that far, yes. If we can rival the Nazis' aerial reconnaissance it will be like . . . oh, seeing properly. Having a whole new perspective. What does that chap in the Bible say? Not through a glass darkly . . .'

'Now I see as through a glass darkly, then we shall see face-to-face.'

'That's it.'

'I still don't see how I could help.'

He frowned and tapped his fingers on the arm of the chair.

'Nor do I just yet. It's a question of waiting for an opportunity to arise. But you do understand, don't you, that Arno Strauss is the lynchpin? The man at the centre of it all. Which is why, at this party of Goering's . . .' he looked at her eagerly, 'it's essential that you are friendly, or more particularly that you—'

'I understand.' She cut him off tersely. 'I know what to do. I'll cultivate Strauss.' She ground the cigarette stub, ringed with her lipstick, in the ashtray, and then said, 'Sorry. I didn't mean to snap. It's been a long day.'

His eyes roved over her, taking in the shadows beneath the eyes, the pallor of her skin. She knew he was trying to read her. He would certainly have registered the ceases in her dress caused when it had been torn carelessly from its hanger during the break-in. Perhaps he was wondering why a woman like Clara would come out looking less than her best. He must have noted her abstraction and realized there was something on her mind. Clara desperately wanted to tell him about the burglary, even about the row with Erich, but she stayed silent. She needed to find out the truth for herself first.

'Why are you here, Clara? Why are you doing this?'

'I might ask the same of you.'

'You could give it all up tomorrow. Go back to Britain. Resume your stage career. Become the toast of the Eastbourne Pavilion again.'

'Perhaps I prefer the pictures.'

He seemed to ignore her answer. The intensity of his gaze seemed set on penetrating her defences.

'You must know that there is a whole apparatus of horror out there that would have no compunction in locking you up or sending you to a camp so you would never see the light of day again. You haven't seen those camps – I have. Do you know the penalty for espionage?'

'You can't seriously be asking me that.'

Every day the newspapers carried reports of people arrested for treason against the Fatherland, complete with the verdicts and the sentences spelt out in aggressive detail. When she came across them Clara read them with secret horror, but mostly she tried to avoid them. She turned a blind eye.

'If something happened, there's not much anyone could do to protect you. Despite all your family contacts. In fact the Gestapo take a dim view of spying by those closest to the élite.'

'I know that.'

'So why do you stay?'

She resented the tone he had taken. This was not some job they were talking about. He was not some chap in a pinstriped suit grilling her about an opening in the Civil Service.

'I can be useful.'

'But you have no emotional ties? No boyfriend? No lover?'

'There is someone actually. Someone I care for very much. He's called Erich.'

Like a chess player watching her opponent, she noted the involuntary flicker of his eyes.

'Oh. I see.'

She paused a while, deliberately, then added, 'He's a boy. A godson, sort of. He's the son of a friend who died. I take care of him. At least, he lives with his grandmother in Neukölln, but I see him often and help a little with money. He has no father either and I don't ever want him to think he's alone in the world. Before she died my friend Helga asked me to look after him. Those were her last words.'

Ralph leaned back and ran a hand through his hair. 'Poor chap, losing his parents. I think I know how he must feel. My parents were pretty much missing in action. I was packed off to boarding school at seven.'

'Did you not like it?'

'It was a place down in Sussex, Hardingly Hall, it's called, and perfectly typical of its kind. Not brutal, and not kind either, though I was terrified when I first saw it. All those gothic crenellations and turrets put the fear of God into a little kid. A list of alumni as long as your arm in Government and the Church, all of whom spent their formative years singing *I Vow To Thee My Country* and building an invisible armour around themselves so no one would ever know if they were lonely or unhappy. Emotional discipline is the highest virtue of a place like Hardingly. It's a perfect machine for manufacturing men to run the Empire. It takes them in at seven, homesick and crying for mother, runs them through a production line which toughens them like anodized steel and your end product is a chap adaptable to any situation, anywhere in the world. Good at a cocktail party, excellent behind a desk, useful at cricket. Great at deciphering Latin on tombstones. Utterly self-sufficient, able to be alone, without the need of anyone else. The only trouble is, some find it impossible to be any other way.'

'Was that where you met your friend? Tom Roberts?'

'Tom was the best thing about Hardingly. Funny thing was, I didn't like him at first. His family was Welsh and they were pretty humble. In fact he was on a scholarship and the other boys never let him forget it.'

'How did you come to be friends?'

He reflected a moment. 'I suppose the thing that drew us

together was that both of our fathers were vicars. It meant I understood the make-up of his mind. After a while, when both his parents died, he would come and stay with us in the holidays. Tom was the most argumentative person I ever knew. The only time we weren't arguing about politics, we were rowing about cricket, but he was also the closest thing I had to a brother.'

This moment of reminiscence had changed the atmosphere between them. He pulled off his jacket, and removed his bow tie, loosening his shirt collar.

'What about you, Clara? I'm guessing you had an idyllic childhood in the Home Counties.'

Clara paused. His suspicion was right, but only half right. Her childhood was like a tapestry with a rent through the middle of it, happiness followed by awfulness. When she thought about the past, a series of disconnected images flashed before her. Angela teaching her to pick out *Für Elise* on the piano. Their old home with its mossy stone covered in blowsy roses, its alley of espaliered fruit trees and topiary through which the children would play hide and seek. Her mother gardening in a straw hat and linen apron. Chilly holidays on British beaches where the sand got into their picnics and their father organized games.

'It was pretty idyllic, I suppose, up to the point that my mother died. It changed a lot after that.'

It had changed, and grown sadder and more constrained. The family navigated their wounds warily, as if afraid of reopening them. The sisters talked less frequently to each other and Kenneth immersed himself in sport. Their father retreated to a world of his own and everyone trod on eggshells around him. When she first came to Berlin, Clara had experienced a sudden rush of liberty, as though she was at last free of her family and her social status and all her past. As it turned out, she couldn't have been more wrong.

Ralph was leaning forward, gazing at her intently, waiting for her to go on and suddenly Clara longed to reveal more. She had an urge to reach beneath her carefully constructed surface to the self that she always concealed. Telling him was a risk, but she had already gone too far to worry about that.

'When I came here I discovered something else. I'm a quarter Jewish. My grandmother Hannah was a Jew, but my mother had always hidden it from us. I think my father was ashamed.'

He cocked his head, curiously.

'You're a quarter Jewish? So how did you get to work at Ufa then? Aren't quarter Jews excluded from the Reich Chamber of Culture? I know there are still some who've managed to hang on there, but only through forging their documents.'

Clara thought back to the day Leo Quinn left. The final envelope he had left for her, hand delivered and simply addressed with her name. It was a gift. The work of a master craftsman, as expertly created and exquisitely precise as any necklace or precious ring. Only it wasn't jewellery, but a complete set of ancestry documents, the kind you bought at stationery shops, tracing your genealogy back three generations. It was filled out in her name, yet her grandmother had been transformed into an Ayran. Clara's Jewish blood had been diverted into different channels. The document had been stamped by the official race office – or rather a contact of Leo's whose expert forgeries were much treasured by the British Secret Service.

'Someone got me the right papers.'

'Someone must have thought very highly of you.'

'I suppose he did.'

Ralph rose and stood before her, then reached down to her hand, turning it over to reveal the bluish white, unsunned flesh of her wrist as if examining the newly christened blood in her veins. His touch was electrifying. She felt exposed, as if he was peeling back her skin.

'I can understand why.'

He pulled her to her feet and moved his hand upwards to the

pearls at her throat, feeling their warmth, then he reached over to the shoulder of her dress and pushed it a fraction, exposing the strap of her pale pink crêpe de Chine slip. She edged towards him so that they were separated only by inches of trembling air. Her body quickened and, lifting her face, she saw his eyes cloud with desire. The image of him kissing her, smoothing his hands over the tight satin of her dress, the weight of his body pulling her to him in a tight embrace, was already running through her mind. Her senses filled with the warm scent of limes and tobacco, mixed with the starched cotton of his shirt. Every particle of her flesh was attuned to him like a physical force. But despite the current of attraction between them, she sensed resistance too. Ralph reached down and touched the tips of her fingers, then his fingers pushed hers gently away.

'Forgive me. That was unacceptable.'

'There's nothing to forgive.'

'I should have stopped myself.'

'Did you see me object?'

'All the same. That mustn't happen.'

'Why do you say that?'

'It's not something I can easily explain.'

She remained as she was, her blood racing, her breath caught in her throat. She felt dazed, all the atoms inside her still vibrating for his touch. He had stirred an ache in her that clamoured to be fulfilled.

He turned away, thrusting his hands in his pockets.

'So . . . do you want me to leave?'

He kept his back turned, his shoulder blades tensed.

'I think it would be for the best.'

'All right then. I'll go.'

Summoning a strength she did not know she possessed, she turned, picked up her coat, and walked out of the door.

Chapter Twenty-four

Dr Theo Morell was the doctor to the stars. A stout, balding dermatologist with an expensive practice on the Ku'damm, his marriage to the actress Hanni Moller had opened the doors to a long list of actors who wanted moles and warts removed and other unphotogenic blemishes remedied. As a sideline he specialized in 'vitamin injections' which were said to promote instant vitality, perhaps because their principle ingredient was amphetamines. One of Morell's early patients was Heinrich Hoffmann and it was through him that Morell had been taken up by Hitler as his personal physician and had somehow managed to cure the stomach cramps that plagued the Führer. As a result of this triumph, Morell's waiting room was now crowded with senior Nazis. He was the most famous doctor in the Third Reich and that day he was attending Ufa to administer a course of injections to Doktor Goebbels, who was, for all purposes, in perfectly robust health.

Clara sat outside Goebbels' office, disguising her trepidation by flipping through the latest edition of *Filmwoche*. There was a photograph of a rising actress, one of the many who Goebbels had put through nose surgery to correct an over-Semitic appearance. Cosmetic surgery was one of several perks Goebbels was known to offer his protégées, and most of them found the offer impossible to refuse. 'Be careful,' Albert had quipped as Clara left for the meeting that morning. 'Don't let Joey get his hands on your lovely face.' Yet in the case of the girl in the magazine the surgery had paid off. She had just won a leading role in a prestigious new biopic of Frederick the Great.

That morning a scrap of chilling news had fluttered along the Babelsberg corridors like a newspaper in the breeze. The actress Gisela Wessel, following her arrest, had been sent to the Moringen concentration camp, the women's camp in Lower Saxony. She had been taken from Prinz Albrecht Strasse where she apparently confessed to making a drop into the letter box of the Soviet trade envoy on the evidence of two secret policemen who had observed her passing information. Clara shuddered to think how Gisela's confession had been obtained. She thought again of Ralph's comments the previous night.

'*Don't you know that there is a whole apparatus of horror out there that would have no compunction in locking you up or sending you to a camp so you would never see the light of day again?*'

It had taken all her strength to walk away from Ralph the previous evening, and the ache that he instilled in her had lingered through a long night. Their contact was fleeting, but the exhilarating shiver that his touch had stirred surprised her and left her longing to see him again.

The unexpected call from Goebbels' office at seven o'clock that morning, however, had succeeded in banishing Ralph entirely from her mind. The Propaganda Minister was visiting Babelsberg that day, a cool secretarial voice informed her, and he hoped Fräulein Vine would be able to see him at eleven o'clock. Hastily Clara went to her drawer and unearthed a diamond swastika. Goebbels himself had given it to her, because he trusted her to supply him with the gossip she heard from Nazi women. She stabbed it into her lapel.

Dr Morell emerged from the door and Goebbels followed him,

rubbing his hands vigorously, as though washing off invisible blood.

'Morell was just telling me he's up to his eyes in work. He was saying that most of our top men now require his services. My God, what an unhealthy bunch they are!'

Goebbels himself looked sleek, despite his deformity, and full of health. He was wearing a beautifully tailored dove-grey suit and bespoke patent-leather shoes. He moved with a malign vigour in his trim frame, trailing a miasma of Scherk's Tarr aftershave.

'Come in, Fräulein Vine.' He waved her to a chair and pointed to the smoking set of matching silver cigarette box and lighter on the desk. 'The Führer sent me such a lovely gift for my birthday, I've been hard put to think how I can repay him. But I've decided to give him a set of Mickey Mouse cartoons for Christmas. What do you think? I know he loves Mickey Mouse.'

Was this a joke? Did Goebbels know that his nickname was Mickey Mouse? Clara decided that it was probably not. Goebbels' jokes were rarely self-referential.

'It's an inspired idea.'

'Thank you.' He folded himself into a chair and crossed his legs in a way that concealed the deformed right foot. Goebbels enjoyed being at the studios. It enabled him to adopt the persona of the cultured arbiter, the one he had longed for since he first began writing his interminable novels back in his home town of Rheydt, submitting them endlessly to publishing houses and receiving repeated barbs of rejection. Invariably they had been Jewish publishing firms, who had since been made to pay for the error of their literary judgements.

Clara glanced around her. Amongst a number of framed posters for Ufa movies like *The Blue Light*, *Hitler Youth Quex* and *Black Roses*, was a poster for *Patriots*, the latest big-budget film to star Lída Baarová. It was a thriller about a brave German soldier shot down by the French and befriended by a rebel French girl.

The poster featured Baarová in a clinch with the heroic soldier played by the handsome Mathias Wieman. What kind of masochism did it require, to spend all day looking at the girl you loved being kissed by another man? But there was no accounting for the strange tastes of Nazi men. Alongside the posters were the usual selection of Reich-approved art – dull Teutonic nudes covered in appropriately gauzy veils and robust peasants gathering in the corn. Goebbels could not possibly have chosen them himself. He had been a connoisseur of the Expressionist Emil Nolde until it was decided that Nolde must qualify as degenerate.

Goebbels followed Clara's gaze. 'I know what you're thinking. I should get Herr Speer to redesign this place, but he's very busy right now. As a matter of fact I've just commissioned him to make a film about the racial aspects of architecture. You probably didn't realize architecture had a racial aspect, did you?' He smiled to show that his question was rhetorical. 'Anyhow, Fräulein, I wanted to tell you, I've been asked to send a selection of films to Obersalzberg. The Führer enjoys seeing all the latest movies in a relaxed setting and I've decided to include *Madame Bovary*.'

'Thank you, Herr Reich Minister.' Clara was surprised because rumours were already starting to surface about the film's star, Pola Negri. She had only reluctantly returned from America because she lost a fortune in the Wall Street Crash, but now there was gossip about her Jewish blood. It wouldn't be long before she left again, people said.

'I like *Madame Bovary*. It's an interesting story, I think, and morally sound. Unfaithfulness in women is never attractive. I'm sure the Führer will enjoy it. He has a weakness for love stories. Just look at all those operettas he sees.'

'They're a slightly different thing.'

Goebbels laughed, as though she had made a daring joke. 'I share your distaste, Fräulein, of course. Operetta has never been an art form I enjoy. But the fact is, where you see naked girls flaunting themselves at the Wintergarten as vulgar Jewish sensuality, I see it as healthy exuberance likely to stimulate the birth rate! It's all a question of perspective.'

She knew Goebbels was deliberately entrusting her with this display of cynicism, getting her to relax her guard. To make comments which may tell against her at a later date.

'Anyhow, it's not the Führer's taste in operettas that concerns me this morning. It was another matter.'

The main matter.

'I wanted to ask you about our friends the Mitfords. Fräulein Mitford and Frau Mosley, I should say. Delightful girls, but I wonder . . .' he waved a cigarette in the air, as if contemplating how to frame his question, 'I wonder myself if they really spring from the soul of the English people. What do you think?'

'Undoubtedly.'

Clara knew the Mitford girls' father was a cousin of Winston Churchill's wife. Hitler must be aware of that connection too and no doubt assumed that the women had the power to sway opinion in the upper echelons of the English establishment. Goebbels, however, was more astute.

'Unity is unusual, isn't she? She has sent me a copy of an English magazine, *The Tatler*, with circles round the photographs of people who might be sympathetic to our cause.'

'How efficient of her.'

'Magda says she keeps a live rat in her handbag.'

'The English are great animal lovers,' said Clara blandly. 'Unity used to take her pet sheep in the second-class carriage from Oxford to London. She has a snake too, I believe. It's called Enid.'

'A snake?' he winced. 'I hope she keeps it locked up. We've known her for some years, of course, and my wife is much closer to her than I am, but she appears a most . . . emotional . . . young woman. Her attachment to the Führer is as passionate as any German's.'

'More so, if possible. Unity said the greatest moment of her life was sitting at the Führer's feet, having him stroke her hair.'

Goebbels seemed startled.

'Did she really?'

There was a small triumph in being party to information that had escaped Goebbels' all-encompassing net. But Clara knew she needed to tread carefully. Goebbels trusted her to supply gossip that he might miss, but it had to be innocuous gossip. Nothing that really mattered.

'She's intensely enthusiastic. Back in England she gives the Hitler salute to shopkeepers.'

'That shows an unusual degree of loyalty.'

'The shopkeepers certainly think so. Unity says following the Führer is her destiny because she was conceived in Swastika, Ontario.'

Goebbels raised his eyebrows. 'Well, I must admit the Führer is much taken with her. He ferries her around all over the place, wherever she wants to go. He has provided her with a personal driver in Berlin and he takes her to Munich on his own train. More importantly they discuss England frequently, he tells me. Fräulein Mitford has given him to understand that the British are foursquare behind an alliance with Germany against the Bolshevik threat. She insists that Britain will never take up arms against Germany.'

Goebbels paused here, thoughtfully. Was he waiting for Clara to confirm Unity's assessment, or was he asking her to point out the truth – that Germany had access to a huge range of newspapers, Embassy staff and contacts and transcripts of political speeches, not to mention an intelligence agency, that could keep the Führer better informed of British attitudes than a twenty-three-year-old girl with distinctly eccentric habits?

'I think Unity's opinions are as individual as her choice of pet.'

He smiled. 'The Führer spends much time with Frau Mosley

too. He confided in me that he finds Diana tremendously intelligent. She has told him there are only three anti-aircraft guns in Britain. Does she know, do you think?'

'You mean, does she know how many guns the British have, or does she know what an anti-aircraft gun actually is?'

His smile dropped like an iron shutter.

'My thoughts exactly.'

Plainly Goebbels felt reassured in his own assessment of the Mitfords. They were eccentric young women whose opinions were no more serious than their party games. Yet still, he must be concerned at their influence on Hitler. Hitler was more susceptible to the charms of the aristocracy than Goebbels, more prone to assuming that their opinions were representative.

'Now, Fräulein Vine, I understand you are attending the reception for the Duke of Windsor at Reich Minister Goering's lodge.'

'Yes, Herr Minister.'

'I unfortunately will be unable to attend. I have business elsewhere, but I shall be most interested to hear about it.'

'Of course.'

'In particular . . . I believe our friends the Mitfords will also be attending.' He gave her a smile which didn't meet his eyes. 'I will be interested to hear more of their views. I think we should have another chat when you return.'

'I'll see what I can do, Herr Doktor.'

Clara couldn't help reflecting on the irony of the situation. How extraordinary it was that having offered to observe the Mitfords for British Intelligence and been rebuffed, she should be asked to perform the same service for Goebbels himself. He sprang up, signalling the meeting was over.

'I myself am planning something a little more stimulating than a bunch of tipsy Luftwaffe officers to entertain the Duke, delightful though that sort of thing may be. I have a cultural treat in store that I think he will appreciate. The Duke's an intelligent man, I would go so far as to say a great man. He's far-sighted, modern, clever. Perhaps he was too clever, too sophisticated to remain in Britain.' He limped swiftly across the room and opened the door. 'I daresay you sympathize with him in that regard.'

Clara walked away, wondering how Goebbels had known that she would be attending the Goerings' reception. The rivalry between the two men would ensure that the Goerings did not discuss their guest lists with him. Then she realized an event like that was simply too important for Goebbels not to find out.

It was a relief to find Albert and throw herself into his leather chair. The news about Gisela Wessel and the network of Communists who had been arrested with her had made him unusually concerned. He rose quickly when she came through the door and went to fetch a glass.

'How was your visit to the Doktor?' He would never ask what Goebbels wanted with her. Nor could she possibly confide in Albert that the Propaganda Minister had effectively asked her to spy on her own compatriots.

'Let's just say I'm glad it's over.'

'You'll need this,' he said, passing her the gin and tonic that he had mixed in preparation.

She sighed. 'This is the kind of medicine Dr Morell never provides.'

'Unless it comes in one of his injections. Perhaps that's his secret. A dose of neat gin straight into the vein. No wonder they come back for more.'

'I'm looking forward to getting back to filming, Albert. Rehearsals start next week, don't they? Thank God for work.'

'We all need work,' smiled Albert. 'It takes our minds off life.'

Chapter Twenty-five

Anyone wanting to stage a Wagnerian opera could do no better than Goering's vast hunting lodge, Carinhall, which emerged at the end of a long winding track in the deep forest of Schorfheide, north of Berlin. The forest, bisected only by the occasional path, was oppressive. It was not the deciduous tumult of an English forest but a strict, regulated wall of impenetrable gloom, the pines erect and uniform like ranks of soldiers. They made Clara think of the ranks of the Wehrmacht, expanding relentlessly into Spain and Europe, and perhaps eastwards too, an indomitable forest of grey-green soldiers.

Carinhall, a white stone, baronial hall decorated with turrets and a steep, thatched roof, was named after Goering's adored first wife Carin. Even though he now occupied it with his second, Goering had ensured that the eponymous Carin would always be with them, and not just in spirit, by digging up her body from her native Sweden and reinterring it in an elaborate underground mausoleum beneath the lodge itself. If that was not enough, the first thing visitors saw on entering was a solid gold bust of the first Frau Goering which had pride of place in the lobby.

That night the great hall was filled with the scent of pine and candlewax and the ceiling glittered with chandeliers. The walls were hung with antlers and the heads of numerous other creatures, but that was nothing to the number of living animals kept in cages and stables in the grounds. As well as bears, wolves, lions and a species of bison specially bred in his attempt to recreate the Germanic ice age, the Reich Minister had assembled an exotic collection of wild creatures in his private zoo. Goering loved keeping animals, almost as much as he loved shooting them.

Though he was Minister of Aviation, Chief of the Luftwaffe, head of the Four Year Plan, and second in command in the Third Reich, Goering was, for the purposes of this weekend, Reichsjägermeister, Master of Hunting. That evening he was entering fully into the role and appeared like something out of a mediaeval fairy story in his leather breeches and Tyrolean hunting hat, with buttons on his olive suede jacket made from silver-mounted deer's teeth. His bloated fingers glinted with emerald, sapphire and ruby rings and his nails were varnished. The Führer was absent that evening, but Rudolf Hess with his beetle-browed glower, Heinrich Himmler with his banal, bank clerk's demeanour and the alcoholic Labour Front leader Robert Ley were there in black SS dress uniform. Around them other Nazi men strutted like peacocks in full display, their sashes and decorations pinned to their chests and their hearty cries resounding round the room.

The women, by contrast, were one heaving mass of fur: ocelot, ermine, silver fox, mink, and sable stoles above creamy shoulders, so closely packed that they resembled a single hybrid animal, moving and rippling through the hall. And it was as one, too, that they stared at the Queen of England manquée, the slender figure of Wallis Simpson.

Clara, with her own fox fur swathing her bare shoulders, stared too. The photographs gave no real clue of how tiny Wallis was, in her crepe satin evening gown of greyish blue and jacket fastened by three mirror buttons. Her voice was a slow, Southern drawl and her severe classical clothes complemented the angular lines of her figure. A sapphire choker closely encircled her throat and a white parting ran dead centre through the gleaming hair. She resembled some exquisitely engineered, streamlined machine, as hard and shining as the jewels she wore, as steely as an aeroplane. Her pencil thinness seemed to accentuate the flesh of the Nazi women around her and though her wide-jawed face was an impassive expanse of ivory, her chest was rising and falling swiftly as a bird's as she was led through the throng. As Robert Ley introduced Wallis and kissed hands, his wet lips glistening, some women, flummoxed by her exact standing, even curtseyed. Emmy Goering brought up the rear, shuffling her guests around, like pawns on a chessboard, to gain a better view of the almost-queen. Clara recalled the ivory chess set given to the forthcoming Goering child and thought how appropriate it was. The incessant political manoeuvrings of the Nazi court were just as complex a game, and far more vicious.

As she watched, a familiar figure bore down on her. In comparison with the woman her husband admired, Annelies von Ribbentrop was the size of a tank, swagged in cream satin like a coffin lining. Heavy emeralds tugged at her lobes. Her face, with its slash of garish lipstick, had the predatory menace of a Venus flytrap.

'Fräulein Vine. What a surprise to see *you* here.'

She gave Clara a quick assessment, taking in the violet sheath dress she had been sent from House of Horn and the pearl drop earrings. With her strong nose and hawk eyes, Annelies von Ribbentrop might have been a bird of prey poised to peck away the jewels of the other guests. She nodded over at Goering who had approached the Duchess and was extending his peculiar, duck-like smile. Beside his towering bulk Wallis looked even tinier. She could probably fit into his trouser leg.

'They're talking diets. The Reich Minister's on a new one.

And he's just installed an exercise bicycle because Elizabeth Arden told him he was overweight. She's always nagging him about his size, but it won't make the slightest difference. He already has an entire gym here in the basement with weights and a massage machine and an electric exercise horse.'

'He has an electric horse?'

Frau von Ribbentrop smiled glassily at an acquaintance across the room and murmured, 'It's probably the only kind of horse that doesn't groan when he sits on it.'

'I can't imagine the Duchess needs a diet,' said Clara, watching Wallis's hands fluttering over Goering's sleeve like flirtatious white doves.

'Oh, the Duke and Duchess are always on diets. Didn't you know? Their diets are the talk of London. We had to make special arrangements when we entertained them at the Embassy. They are both so particular. It all has to be American food. The Duchess sacked the Duke's butler for refusing to put ice in drinks in the American manner. I saw it happen.'

Clara didn't doubt it. Frau von Ribbentrop had eyes like a sniper. She never missed a thing.

'But then we're all in favour of Americans right now. My husband tells me that they've finally shuffled off Ambassador Dodd to make way for a new man who is much more clear-sighted. He came to the Parteitag. Adored it.'

Clara had heard about that. Mary said the decent old American ambassador, William Dodd, had grown so aghast at the Nazi regime he refused to attend any more functions. He would be leaving next month and his successor, Hugh Wilson, was said to take a far softer line.

The royal couple were coming closer. 'We love the Duke, of course,' continued Frau von Ribbentrop. 'My husband thinks of him as a kind of English National Socialist. He is a man after the Führer's own heart. The Duchess, on the other hand . . .' She left the assessment of her rival hanging, scrutinizing Wallis with the cold detachment of a snake watching a mouse.

A maid wearing peasant dress with pleated skirt and smocked blouse approached to refill their crystal goblets, enabling Clara to pivot away and escape. The hall was full of well-fed Nazis, as if all the calories that the rest of the population were missing had ended up inside these SS uniforms. Clara threaded through the crowd listening to the talk, switching between German and English, tuning in and out of conversations. The chat was of art, fashion, cinema, film stars and as always in Nazi circles, the latest doings of the Führer. The Führer had been regaling everyone with Mussolini's faux pas on his recent visit. When the Duce was presented with the ceremonial sword, he drew it from the scabbard and waved it in the air, prompting Hitler's SS bodyguards to rush him in fear of an assassination attempt. The Führer, however, had kept his cool. He needed to, what with all these foreign guests, Mussolini and the ex-King of England, flocking to meet him.

Clara heard Heinrich Hoffmann's jovial Bavarian accent rising above the chatter, and from time to time the distinctive laughter of Diana Mosley rang on the air. Unity Mitford was holding forth animatedly to a group of officers, including Ernst Udet, who was regarding her with frank fascination. She was lecturing them in her heavily accented German on the state of the movie industry.

'All these war films now. The Führer doesn't really enjoy them, you know. He told me. He says Goebbels is far too heavy-handed. He thinks the public need an escape from all that sort of thing.'

'Oh yes? So what does he prefer?' asked Udet, choosing not to point out that he was the star of innumerable war movies himself.

'Something light and pleasant. That's what he likes to watch. Preferably a love story. He adored *Black Roses* with Lilian Harvey. It was so romantic. He screened it for us at the Chancellery.'

'Well, we're all in favour of love,' said Emmy Goering, sinuously. 'Indeed we're hoping the sight of the Duke so happy will encourage the Führer to take a wife. He has long thought that the King's search for love was like his own.'

Unity hesitated, uncertain whether this reference was intended for her, or was a direct dig at her infatuation. Clara remembered Emmy's remark: *We have never been able to fathom the Führer's taste in women.* Before Unity could respond, the royal progress was upon them, and Ernst Udet bowed deeply to kiss Wallis's tiny, starved hand.

'I've seen your stunts, General Major Udet. I was married to a pilot once,' came her languid American drawl. 'He was called Win. He used to take a flask of Jack Daniels with him when he went up and by the time he came back he'd be blind drunk. He gave me a lifelong fear of flying.'

'Yet the Duke is a qualified pilot, I think,' Udet countered.

'Yes, God help us! Perhaps I'm destined to marry only pilots. David loves airplanes. The King, his father, was terribly disapproving when he learned to fly. He said David had dangerous passions.' She laughed, a gravelly, worldly laugh. 'Dangerous passions! You can say that again.'

The assembled company joined warily in the joke.

'I share the Duke's passions in many ways then, your Royal Highness,' said Udet gallantly.

Despite her joking, there was a vapour of anxiety around Wallis. Her dark eyes darted constantly to the Duke in his parallel pilgrimage on the other side of the hall, but the phalanx of Nazis around her was too great for her to escape. The pair was being paraded like the latest additions to Goering's collection of exotic creatures. No wonder Hitler thought they could be moulded to his will.

Clara looked around for Arno Strauss. He was the reason, after all, that she was here. Ralph's instructions had been to cultivate him. Exactly what that would involve she wasn't herself sure, but the first step, surely, would be to strike up a conversation. And yet there was no sign of him. Emmy Goering, observant as ever, approached and murmured, 'If you're looking for your Oberst Strauss, I saw him just a moment ago. He doesn't enjoy parties, I fear.'

But before Clara could look further, the gong had been sounded for dinner.

The food was characteristically extravagant, an entire roast boar revolving in the fire place, nearly raw beef darkly oozing, mountains of trembling jellies, wine as red as arterial blood. Bowls of creamy roses were placed on the tables and beside each dinner plate the cutlery branched out in pairs, dwindling in order of size like an extensive German family. What with the smell of the roasting flesh, the waiters in leggings and jerkins, the candlelight and the gloom of the forest outside, they might have been back in mediaeval times.

Clara had often noticed this Germanic craving to escape to the past. As fast as the Nazis were rebuilding a new Germany, a yearning for the old Germany lay just below the surface. She had heard that the Brothers Grimm, compiling their tales at the birth of modern Germany, had pretended to find their tales from old women in the woods, as though to create an oral history for Germany that never really existed. An ancient, mythic country, with deep mediaeval roots. In terms of brutality, of course, the Nazis were finding no difficulty in returning the entire country to the Middle Ages.

She found herself seated in a clutch of Luftwaffe officers, opposite Diana Mosley, with Unity two places to her left. The convention of talking to one's neighbour in strict rotation didn't seem to occur to Unity, who leaned across the silent General between them and bellowed in English, 'Hello, Clara! Are you having fun? I'm not. I didn't want to be here tonight at all. Diana made me. I'd much rather be with the darling Führer, but he absolutely refused to come.'

'Why?'

'It's because of the hunt tomorrow. He simply loathes blood sports. He detests cruelty to animals. He decided to spend the night at the Wintergarten.'

'Again?'

'The Führer adores opera. He can never see too much of it. He often sits up at night designing stage sets and lift mechanisms and lighting. If he hadn't been Führer he would have been an opera designer, he says. And it's not all gloomy Wagner. He would never miss *Die Fledermaus* or *The Merry Widow*. He's seen *The Merry Widow* six times already this year!'

'He must love it.'

Unity seemed entirely unconcerned by the stares of the other guests. It was almost as if they didn't exist. She had the kind of loud, upper-class confidence which meant she said whatever came into her head.

'He does. I'll ask him to take you with us to the Wintergarten if you like.'

'Oh, I really don't think . . .'

'Honestly. You'll love it, Clara. As long as you don't go making eyes at him. Are you coming hunting tomorrow?'

'Afraid not. I have to leave before lunch.'

'Bad luck. I simply adore hunting. When we were children, our father used to have a child hunt. We were the foxes and he used to track us cross country with bloodhounds. We'd run like merry hell. I learned an awful lot about being the prey. You've got to avoid sudden movement. That always draws the eye. You learn to blend in with the scenery. I was frightfully good at it, I never stuck out.'

So unlike real life. The same thought must have occurred to the rest of the guests, who by now had dropped all pretence of conversation and were eavesdropping shamelessly. Even the moulting stag's head behind Unity was slack-jawed, as if with astonishment.

'Have you seen the Führer recently?' Clara asked.

'Last night actually. He had us over to the Chancellery for supper. It was nothing special, but the thing about Hitler is, his company is so thrilling, it always feels like a party, even when it's just a quiet evening in. Haven't you noticed how people simply adore being with him? We had cauliflower cheese, which is his absolute favourite, and then he had a screen put up in the Music Salon and we watched cartoons.'

Plainly Goebbels' gift would go down well.

'He loves cartoons. He has a terribly good sense of humour. But do you know what makes me sad?' Unity frowned, as though contemplating some insoluble puzzle. 'The English always get the wrong idea about our dear Führer. I wanted cousin Winston to come and meet him but he's a dreadful stick-in-the-mud. He just said no, rather rudely.'

It was clear what Unity felt about Hitler – it was pure, unadulterated infatuation. But what did the Führer see in Unity? He was supposed to have summed up a woman's ideal occupations as Kinder, Küche, and Kirche, yet Unity Mitford didn't look as if she would waste five minutes on any of those occupations. Clara realized that Goebbels must be preoccupied by the same question. Did the Führer see in Unity and Diana a true reflection of British opinion, or did he understand them for the eccentrics they were?

Clara looked around for the man whom Emmy Goering had said was tailing Unity at Himmler's request, disguised as a photographer. In theory that was an inspired idea. If you needed a disguise, posing as a photographer was ideal. The only props you needed were a camera and an observant air. Despite that she spotted him at once, a few places along, a giveaway with his ill-fitting evening wear and Leica to hand. He had a pasty face, a shock of dark hair and eyes fixed obediently on his charge.

At the head of the table, Goering stood up and began delivering a speech about the need to safeguard the purity of the

Nazi soul. The Duke of Windsor stifled a yawn. On his other side the Duchess sat rapt, gazing up at her host, seemingly oblivious to the fact that all other eyes were trained on her. It seemed an ideal moment for Clara to excuse herself and escape.

She made her way up a flight of wooden stairs and through the winding corridors of Carinhall. Here, again, was the blend of Renaissance kitsch that Goering adored and Goebbels so disdained. The walls were decked with tapestries, paintings and sculptures, the rooms stacked with treasures like a pharaoh's tomb. She peered into one room to see an enormous model railway extending across the entire floor, with splendidly decorated trains and tenders snaking through tunnels, past perfect Bavarian villages and towns with miniature S-Bahn elevations. A few doors later she came to the library, which boasted as many dead animals as there were books, the walls hung with the skulls of deer and the pelts of a couple of bears lying prostrate on the floor. A large map of the Reich was painted on one wall, illustrated with mediaeval-style pictures. When she looked closer she noticed that Germany was coloured in green, but curiously Austria seemed to be depicted as part of the Reich, with no sign of a border. Presumably, the 'territorial readjustment' she had heard the Nazis talking about had already happened as far as Goering's mapmakers were concerned. How rapidly they were changing the world.

Turning left, she mounted another flight of oak carved stairs and wandered further along the corridors. The guest bedrooms had porcelain plaques on the doors, with cards attached, presumably for the assistance of the servants. The first floor was devoted to the female guests. She glanced into one and saw a dressing table strewn with jars and perfumes like a sacrificial altar to some cosmetic god. Another floor up she found the corridor for male guests, and when she came to the name of Ernst Udet she saw that the door next to it bore a card saying Oberst Arno Strauss. On impulse she knocked, and when there was no reply, she slipped inside.

The room was draped in shadow. It was decorated in the same Bavarian hunting style as the rest of the house, with the ubiquitous stag's head mounted ominously above the bed, the bone of its skull gleaming in the moonlight. The room was empty, thankfully – she had half expected to find Strauss skulking here, or perhaps even asleep. As she looked around, she wondered what she was even looking for. Her mission was to 'cultivate' Arno Strauss, because he was involved in testing an advanced aerial reconnaissance camera. Yet she could, at that moment, see no way that she could be any use at all.

Gradually her eyes became accustomed to the darkness and she saw a desk, on which were a couple of papers. Her pulse quickened. No doubt he had brought some work with him, as an excuse to escape the dinner early. Perhaps the papers related to the details of the aerial reconnaissance programme. If only she had a camera of her own, she would be able to photograph them right here. As it was, she would have to read and memorize any significant details. She was making her way over to the desk when she heard a step behind her and froze.

'What a delightful surprise to see you, Fräulein Vine. At this reception, I mean, just as much as in my bedroom.'

He stood with his back to the wedge of light from the landing. His face was in shadow, so it was hard to read Strauss's expression, yet she sensed his habitual twisted grimace.

She could not suppress a nervous laugh. 'I was exploring.'

'That can be a dangerous business here. There's a room across the corridor where the Reichsminister keeps his lion cubs. You wouldn't want to step in there by mistake.'

He closed the door behind him without switching on the light and crossed his arms.

'Did you have other business here?'

'No. I just . . .'

'You just thought you would have a good look through my papers?'

There was nothing else for it. She smiled up at him.

'I was looking for *you*, since you ask. Frau Goering said you were here but I couldn't see you anywhere. I was longing for a friendly face.'

For a moment, he continued to scrutinize her stonily, then he gave a harsh laugh.

'Of all the things people have said about my face, no one has ever called it friendly.'

His levity encouraged her. There was nothing for it now, but to continue with the flirtatious pretence that she had deliberately sought out an assignation.

'Do you mind telling me how it happened?'

'This?' He brushed a hand over it. 'Many women would think it was bad form to ask a pilot how he sustained an injury. It might imply he was not quite as excellent at his job as he would like to think.'

'I don't care about that. I've flown with you after all, remember. I know you're excellent at your job. So you can tell me. Was it an accident?'

'I prefer to call it a lucky escape.' He gave a wry smirk. 'Like the lucky escape I made from that dinner. I was treated to an audience with your Duke. He was complaining about how poor he is. He wants to buy a yacht but his stingy brother won't give him the money. Not much brotherly love lost there.'

'I can't believe the former King of England has no money.'

'He claims he's penniless. The brother won't hand over a thing. Even on this trip, the Reich's paying for everything. All I can say is, they're certainly getting their money's worth out of him. There's a week of dinners and lunches and then they've lined up factory visits in Dresden, Stuttgart, Nuremberg and Munich.'

'Royalty are used to touring. Someone said they believe everywhere smells of fresh paint because they spend their life making visits.'

'I think a little more will be required of your Duke than shaking hands with a few factory workers.'

'What do you mean?'

Even though they were alone, Strauss lowered his voice. 'The talk is that the Duke has said, if necessary, he will serve as president of an English republic.'

'If necessary?'

'If circumstances came about. A war perhaps. They're going to hold him to it. A document has been prepared promising a permanent alliance with Germany and pledging the return of German colonies and the gift of northern Australia. Two copies of the document have been drawn up for the Duke to sign. They've been brought here, for Goering's perusal.'

Could it be true? If the Nazis achieved that it would be an astonishing coup. At once a vision of England came to her, a republic ruled over by the Duke of Windsor and other Nazi placemen, even perhaps her father. It would be the same England, but shabbier, robbed of its authority, under the Nazi thumb. Then she remembered what Ralph had told her. That certain people in the Foreign Office deliberately suppressed fears about German militarism because they craved an alliance with Hitler. They ignored the warnings of men in the Air Service that Germany would turn on Britain. Might Clara have been warned to lie low because of what she might find, rather than because she was under observation?

There was no going back now. She smiled at Strauss, keeping her eyes from straying to the damaged half of his face, trying not to look at the curve of the scar which sliced like a scimitar through the soft flesh.

'I enjoyed our flight the other day.'

'Did you? You did a very good impression of being scared out of your wits. But then I suppose you are an actress.'

'I wasn't acting. It was exhilarating. In fact I felt a kind of euphoria.'

'Euphoria, eh?'

'I'd do it again in a flash.'

He regarded her thoughtfully for a moment, rubbing a hand along the line of his scar.

'All right then. I'm going out to the countryside the day after tomorrow. I have another test to do. You could come, if you've developed a taste for it.'

She felt a little pulse of success. Testing an aeroplane. Could that mean he was trying out the new camera?

'We could fly out to a field close to a little restaurant I know, eat and then fly back again.'

'Sounds dreadfully illicit.'

'It is. But a lot of us do it. It's good to get a break and this place serves the best schnitzel you'll find in the country. The only thing is, we'd not get back until dusk. Does flying in the dark frighten you?'

'Not being able to see how far up we are might be an advantage, I suppose.'

'It would save you having to look at me.'

Startled by this comment, she said, 'It's very kind of you to do this for me, Oberst Leutnant Strauss.'

'Not so much of the Oberst Leutnant. Call me Arno.'

'Thank you, Arno. I appreciate it, when there's nothing in it for you.'

'And what would you imagine I want?'

He remained staring down at her intently, as if he was about to say more, and suddenly she couldn't take it. It was as though he was seeing right through her. She edged towards the door and, sensing her move, his relaxation evaporated and the stiff formality returned.

'Good. Well unless you have any other business in my room, I'll see you at Tempelhof. Friday at ten.'

The next morning, before the wild boar hunt, Strauss, like all the men, was obliged to attend an open-air breakfast in the woods, where coffee was heated over a wood fire and taken with schnapps and hunter's black bread. The guests were driven off in open-topped carriages, complete with bearskin rugs over their knees. Goering took the first carriage, attired in a white silk blouse and yellow soft leather jerkin, his official uniform as Reichsforstmeister, topped off with leather thigh boots and a tuft of chamois tail sprouting from his hat. The Duke of Windsor sat captive beside him, peering without enthusiasm at the gloomy forest around. Not far behind them came Udet and Strauss, who had secured a carriage to themselves and were conferring with frequent laughter, no doubt inspired by the absurdity of their boss. Clara, who had been watching this parade from her window, had breakfast brought to her room. The tray was laid with orange juice and coffee, crusty rolls, silver pine-cone jars filled with jam and scrolls of sweet butter. She tucked in hungrily. Plainly the idea of 'Guns Not Butter' had yet to reach Carinhall.

Chapter Twenty-six

In normal times, when a crime was committed, everyone had an opinion about it. Everyone wanted to say what they saw, to speculate on the perpetrators, the modus operandi, the getaway and the likelihood that anyone would be caught. But these were not normal times, and it turned out nobody could remember anything much about the murder of Anna Hansen. No one saw it take place, no one heard anything, no one recalled anything unusual and no one had any idea why the thing they had already forgotten could possibly have happened in the first place. That, at least, was Mary Harker's summation of the situation after a few minutes' conversation with the inhabitants of the Schwanenwerder Bride School.

She could have broken into Alcatraz more easily. They had flatly refused her first request to return with a camera and photograph the brides. Mary had already been granted a morning at the Bride School, and that was surely enough. Now she had finally persuaded the Press Office of the need for pictures to show off the happiness and healthiness of the Reich brides, she was struck by how normal everything seemed. Fräulein Wolff glared at her from the office, but did not intervene. A few brides looked up incuriously from stitching tablecloths as she passed, the reek of herring floated from the kitchen where a cookery lesson was in progress, and out in the gardens a bevy of brides with sun-burnished skin were engaging in energetic athletic kicks. Mary aimed her new Ikon at them, and was rewarded with a symmetrical row of beaming smiles and a shot she knew Frank Nussbaum would adore.

As she stood there, watching the women exercise in the pine-scented breeze, a couple of puppies tussling in a play fight on the lawn, and beyond, the sailing boats bobbing on the lake, Mary almost understood the appeal of the place. Who was to say this was not a good way of living, in this idyllic setting, with the friendly smiles and the vigorous bodies, glowing with health and optimism? Who was Mary to criticize the idea of teaching women how to care for children, or to cook wholesome food? Yet no sooner had this thought crossed her mind than she shook herself. Life in Germany was like those papier-mâché cakes they displayed in bakery windows now, since the food shortages hit. A wooden circle, plastered with fake icing. Take a bite and you were likely to break your teeth.

The first sign that everything was not utterly normal came when Ilse Henning, who had been assigned to chaperone Mary's photography session, hurried across the lawn. Only a few weeks ago Ilse had been a plump, apple-cheeked girl with a shiny forehead and a generous bosom stuffed into a dirndl too small for her. Now she had visibly lost weight, her face was a hollow oval of anxiety and her fingers clutched repetitively at her apron hem. She shook hands tentatively.

'Fräulein Harker? So nice to see you again. Fräulein Frankl suggested I accompany you, as I had met you before. Is there anything I can help you with? A cup of coffee perhaps?'

Mary noticed that she was trembling. She took her hand and patted it.

'Ilse, it's great to see you again. Don't worry about the coffee. What I'd really like is to take some pictures of the garden.'

That was partly true. Mary wanted a picture of the place where Anna Hansen had been shot.

'Could you carry this for me?'

She had no need of a tripod whatsoever, but had guessed, accurately, that it might prove a useful piece of equipment in other ways. It looked professional, and conveyed a certain artistic seriousness. In this case, it provided Ilse with something to carry, making her look needed. Mary proceeded down the path to the end of the garden, intending to take a long shot of the house, and Ilse followed, grappling awkwardly with the tripod legs.

'Are you OK, Ilse?' she said quietly. 'You're the only person in this place who looks like they've been losing any sleep.'

Ilse glanced at her uncertainly. She liked the American Fräulein. Though her German was execrable, she had a kind face and a motherly air which reminded Ilse just how badly she longed for her own dear Mutti back in Wuppertal with her braids and her pancake-flat face and worried eyes. When her only daughter went away to Bride School Mutti missed her a lot, but she had tried to understand that it was for the good of Germany that Ilse learned how to become a new German wife with the right attitudes and education. Ilse couldn't tell Mutti about the murder – she would be horrified – and having no one to confide in made Ilse feel all the more lonely. Fräulein Harker was the sole person who had enquired after her feelings since Anna's death. It hadn't occurred to anyone else here that Ilse might be mourning her friend or that being interrogated both by the criminal police and by the Gestapo might have been horribly traumatic.

'It has been very difficult. The pressure has been quite hard for me. First poor Anna, and then the Kripo came and wanted to talk to me.'

'The Kripo?'

'The criminal police. I gave them Anna's lighter. I found it in the grass where she was killed, and then, after that, the G . . . the Gestapo.'

The word trembled on her lips.

Why would the investigation be turned over to the secret police, Mary wondered. The Gestapo was in charge of matters relating to security and crimes against the state. But this was just a murder investigation, wasn't it?

'They were not nice men.' Instinctively Ilse lowered her voice. 'They said I didn't deserve to be at the Bride School. I'm terrified they will drag Otto into this. That it could somehow damage his career. I only have two weeks left here but if Otto's superiors hear that his fiancée has been investigated by the Gestapo . . .'

She was biting her lip, trying valiantly not to cry.

'Hey, Ilse,' Mary took hold of her arm. 'That's not going to happen. You were helping them, not being investigated. It's to your credit that they came and talked to you. They obviously saw you as trustworthy.'

Mary was making this up as she went along and privately her brain was whirring. The Gestapo were never going to win any cups for courtesy but why should they threaten a girl like Ilse who was patently innocent of any involvement in the murder? Someone must want to solve this case very badly.

'I don't know, Fräulein. They seemed so angry. They made some nasty threats.'

It was hard for Ilse to explain the terror that those men had raised in her. That remark they made about her having to work in Friedrichstrasse. She knew what they meant by that. It was Anna who told her, in fact. Ilse had had a sheltered upbringing, just Church and the Bund Deutscher Mädel and a few vague guidelines on married love from her mother who was a devout Lutheran, but Anna had explained that in Berlin there were women who sold their bodies for money. And what was more they defined their sexual speciality according to the colour of their high-laced boots. Ilse had been so shocked she had not asked any more, so she never got to know what obscenity the green boots were supposed to promise.

Yet the more she thought about it, the more Ilse realized that there was something she could have told the Gestapo. There was one person whom the police had not considered. Someone who might well have been responsible for Anna's death. She decided to tell Fräulein Harker about it. Perhaps *she* would be able to sort it out.

'There is something I would have told the policemen but I only thought of it later.' She corrected herself. 'I mean I will tell them. I promise.'

'Take your time.' Mary instinctively disliked the idea of the Gestapo knowing anything before she did. 'There's no need to rush into anything. Perhaps I could give you an idea of whether it's important. I mean policemen don't like to be disturbed with irrelevant details, do they?'

Ilse recalled Kriminal Inspektor Wiedemann's face when she had mentioned Anna's secret lipstick. His enraged question, '*Are you trying to play me, girl?*' spat out like a curse. She shuddered.

'No. You're right. I wouldn't want to waste their time.'

In truth Ilse wouldn't want to speak to another policeman ever again. Not even a traffic policeman.

'So what is this thing that occurred to you?' prompted Mary, gently.

'They asked me if Anna had any secrets. Had I seen anything unusual. Well, I thought about it, and I realized, I had. I saw her speaking to a man.'

'Which man? Do you know who he was?'

'Yes, I do.'

Ilse looked in the direction of the model house, which was now almost completed. It was a pretty, Bavarian-style cottage with petunias in the window boxes and a picket fence.

'He's over there.'

Mary followed her gaze and saw the man. He was bearded and cadaverously thin, a row of ribs sticking from his skin and biceps standing out on the sunburned arms. He was bent over, mixing a heap of concrete, blending the dry materials and the water with repeated scoops of the spade with artisanal precision. Over and over the spade churned the concrete with a satisfying slap, blending the grainy gloop like the mixture for a giant grey cake. The builder's face was pearled with sweat as he worked and he kept his eyes trained rigorously on the job in hand. But he could sense them watching him, Mary knew, because he looked up momentarily with black, piercing eyes, which although he was a stranger, seemed to take in everything about her in a single glance.

Chapter Twenty-seven

The plane shuddered like a living thing and the bolts strained in its aluminium sides. Peering out of the window with relief Clara saw the grass shiver and flatten as the wheels hit the ground with a bump and juddered over the muddy ruts. The vibration penetrated her to the core, making her bones rattle and the teeth shake in her head. Finally, Strauss doused the engine and removed his goggles. She looked out at a field clotted with thistles and weeds, and the remains of a concrete hut.

'Is this it then?'

'The place we like to eat is through that wood. This disused airfield is quite convenient for us. We pilots think of it as our little secret. Come on.'

They climbed out and headed across the airfield to a fringe of trees, through which led a chalk-stoned path. It was a beautiful afternoon, and the trees were at the height of their autumn colours, creating a vivid tapestry of russet, amber, yellow and gold. Inside the wood the sun penetrated the birch leaves to make a mosaic of light and shade, and above them in the boughs the birds were calling to each other. Clara and Strauss walked side by side, the ground beneath them springy with pine needles, the air tinged with woodsmoke. Clara was just thinking how exquisitely lovely the place was when they passed a sign saying *Jews are not wanted in these German woods.*

The path petered out into a track that led to the village and, just around the bend, a white-painted, timbered inn with green shutters, leaded glass and heavy wooden doors, the kind of place you might find in the Tyrolean section of the Haus Vaterland. Inside, a row of steins stood above the fireplace and a landlord in traditional red waistcoat and white apron was pouring beers with a frothy head. A couple of locals leaned against the bar, and a few elderly men holding cards gathered in a corner around a game of skat. Clara sat in an oak inglenook while Strauss went to the bar. He returned balancing three glasses.

'Is someone else joining us?'

'No. Two are for me.'

He downed the first quickly, and she noticed a slight tremble in his hand. He surveyed her wryly.

'So how did you like the flight?'

'It was a different plane this time, wasn't it?'

'A Heinkel He III, if that means anything to you.'

She laughed.

'Not a thing.'

'It's probably better that way. There's a security scare in the Air Ministry right now.'

'What's happened?'

'Some top secret information leaking out where it shouldn't. They suspect a Luftwaffe staff officer. It's tiresome, but we're having to go through all sorts of new procedures and security checks. The Gestapo tried poking their nose in, but Goering told them the Luftwaffe can handle its own internal affairs. That showed them. I tell you, the affair between Germany and France has nothing on the rivalry between the Gestapo and Goering.'

Clara placed her cigarette in the ashtray and watched the slight string of smoke blowing in the breeze, its delicate skein tugged each way by divergent currents. This was what she was here for.

She recalled what Strauss had said when he took her for the first time in the plane. *Officially, you don't exist.* He couldn't know how accurate that was.

She paused while the waiter brought them their food: schnitzel for Strauss; for Clara, trout which had been caught in the nearby lake, with creamed potatoes. After she had given the pink-fleshed fish and rich buttery sauce her full attention, she said, 'Don't tell me a thing about the plane then. I positively don't want to hear. But what on earth were you doing with that camera?'

'That's technical stuff. You don't want to know about that.'

'But I do. I'm interested. I'm a film actress, remember. I work with cameras myself.'

He cast her a quizzical glance.

'All right then. I was using the camera to map the terrain beneath us. It uses special thirty-five-millimetre film with a perforated edge, which allows motors to turn the film automatically behind the lens and get a precise exposure. It can also be used for night photography.'

'So you're taking pictures of the ground beneath you? Why would you do that?'

'To examine the lie of the land.'

'The lie of the land? What's that?'

'It's everything.' He leaned towards her eagerly. His enthusiasm for the subject had overtaken his normal reserve. 'You see, it's not just a question of taking pictures of the terrain. It's a question of working out their meaning. You've got to know what you're looking for. What information a photograph may contain.'

She cocked her head and frowned. 'Information?'

'Exactly. There is so much more than meets the eye. You need to be a geologist, a mathematician, an archaeologist and, I don't know, a botanist, to work out everything a picture means.'

She laughed. 'A botanist? As in plants and flowers? Surely not. When did flowers ever reveal anything?'

'Oh, you underestimate flowers. They're not just pretty little innocents. The type of plants reveal crucial details about the terrain. Is it swampy or marshy? That would mean it would be too soft for landing. Is the ground hard, does the earth shift? Botany can tell you a lot. Have you ever read Goethe's *Metamorphosis of Plants*? It's a wonderful combination of botany and poetry. You'd like it.'

'So you're saying, a pilot has to read the land . . .'

'Exactly. And you would be surprised what you can make out once you get the photographs back. Sometimes you see the remains of an ancient settlement, a fort, or a castle, that literally doesn't exist any more. All that's left is a grey smudge on the map. And you think, long ago people lived there, and loved and fought, but now they're nothing. Just shadows on the ground.'

Clara thought of people, long dead, leaving their ghostly shadows for those who knew where to look.

'Of course we're more interested in what's there now,' Strauss continued. 'These photographs reveal all kinds of secrets. Some of the most important things are hidden in plain sight.'

'What kind of secrets?' She glanced at him closely, uncertain of his meaning.

He laughed warmly and leaned back, signalling to the waiter.

'Now then, they wouldn't be secrets if I told you, would they?'

She waited until the waiter had deposited another couple of drinks on the table then said, 'Do you know, I don't think I've ever seen you smile before? Not properly.'

'Perhaps I don't have much to smile about.'

'When did you first think about flying?'

'Oh, that's dull.'

'I wouldn't ask if I wasn't interested.'

'You really want to know all this? My life story?'

'Of course.'

As she watched him his face softened and the habitual sour

demeanour relaxed into something gentler. 'Well then. Where shall I start? Our parents were wealthy. My mother was descended from a banking family, the von Eckdorffs, who came from just outside Potsdam. My father was a professor of law, who wrote books about the German legal system and so on. They were highly cultivated, sensitive people with great ambitions for their children. Not that we thought much about that. It was a good childhood. In the summer we went to our villa on the Wannsee. It was a lovely house, full of light, with a beautiful view of the lake. Deer would come into the gardens from the wood. We had endless picnics there, and barbeques, and we went boating. I loved that time. Whenever I smell grass crushed beneath my feet it brings it right back to me. I remember lying on the sunlit lawn talking about our plans. Guests coming in and out of the house for our parents' parties. Playing with my brothers. I had a twin called Harro. We were identical, but he was the older. We were both crazy about flying. A neighbour of ours had a glider and he taught us to fly.'

It was all too easy to picture the sunlit lawns, the expensive villa, the pre-war elegance, but far harder to imagine the young Strauss, happy and unscarred.

'Anyhow, we turned out to be very good at it. We joined a flying club. We had great plans to become professional pilots and make a name for ourselves. We competed against each other all the time, though to tell the truth he was a little better at it than me. Harro was fearless, you see. He was not reckless, but he was lacking in fear, whereas I still had a sliver of fear inside me.'

'You mean you were cautious.'

'No. It was not caution, it was fear. Genuine fear.'

'Perhaps you need fear to be good at your job. Fear makes you careful. It stops you making silly mistakes.'

That was certainly true for everything Clara did. The razor's edge of fear sharpened her. It kept her watchful, and wary.

Strauss considered her point for a moment.

'I think it's fear that separates the great pilots from the lesser ones. Ernst, for example, has no fear. Not one iota. Fear means you haven't accepted what might happen. You haven't looked it in the face and embraced it before you start. It's only when you acknowledge the worst that could happen and accept it, that you can proceed without fear.'

'Do you still have that fear?'

'It's fading. But I would be a liar if I said it had left me completely.'

Pensively, he traced the silver scar that bisected his melted cheek.

'Anyhow, one day it all went wrong. We went up together in a two-seater, Harro at the controls. The conditions were perfect. Nothing should have happened, but the plane came down and we were thrown. We were lucky, of course, to be alive. My face was badly crushed, just a mass of blood and flesh, but Harro had hardly a mark on him. At first I thought he was just knocked out, so I lay down beside him and told him I was going for help. It took hours to get him home. It turned out he had broken his back. He was paralysed.'

Strauss's gaze passed hers, trained on the elaborately carved inglenook beside them bulging with wooden fruit and leaves.

'He lived for months. You can't imagine how it felt to see my twin, this handsome, lively young man, reduced to nothing, just a suffering body, marooned in a bed. He shrivelled up in front of our eyes. It wasn't just his back broken, he had brain damage, apparently, at least that was what my mother said. She spent all day with him, but my father could hardly bear to look at him. I had to carry on, of course. They patched up my face and I went to school, though I skipped every other engagement outside the house because I only wanted to be at home with Harro. I felt very guilty, you see. Every time I came back there were just his eyes looking up at me, mute with pain, and he was mumbling. The doctor said he would never walk again. We would never achieve all those things we had dreamed of. Eventually, I decided I would stop flying completely. If Harro couldn't go, then I wouldn't either. I stayed in and read to him, and brought work home from school for him, though we were fooling ourselves to think he might have a decent life. Pretty soon, he caught pneumonia and died. And the moment our father came and told me, I felt relieved. That was actually my first emotion. I was relieved because it meant I could go out flying again without feeling guilty. That only lasted for a second of course. Then came the grief. It destroyed my mother. She never got over it. Occasionally I wonder how it has affected me, too. Sometimes, in my daily life, I have a feeling that I've lost something, and it's a moment before I realize what it is.'

He pursed his lips.

'We buried him in the churchyard next to the villa at Wannsee. People find it strange, but we put no headstone to mark his grave. My father said Harro was a free spirit and should have nothing above him but the patter of deers' hooves.'

He blinked, and took another gulp of his drink.

'There. Now you have my sad story. Make of it what you will.'

Clara focused on her drink as a familiar, sick feeling rose in her gullet. It was a conflict that tore at the heart of her, and threatened to overwhelm her with self-loathing. She knew she was a honeytrap. A *femme galante*, as the French called them. A Mata Hari. However shadowy and double-dealing the life of a male spy, the female spy's life involved an extra layer of deception. Eking out confidences like this, faking closeness, pretending intimacy, coaxing a man to strip the layers off himself. Somehow it seemed even more deceptive than stripping off his clothes. Whenever this feeling threatened to engulf her she reminded herself what was at stake. The information she could get from Arno Strauss was valuable. Thousands of lives might depend on it. If deceiving him was the price, it was well worth paying.

'Some people might be surprised, Arno, that you never stopped flying.'

'Quite the reverse. You have two choices when it happens. Either your nerve gives out, or you get back in the cockpit. I joined up in the war.'

'And you went to Spain.'

His head rose sharply, detecting an undercurrent in her voice.

'Yes, I volunteered for Spain. And I'm glad of it. I was motivated by the chance to prevent the spread of Bolshevism. It's a rot that's spreading through Europe. A cancer. What's happening in Spain will soon be happening in Germany if we don't help stop it. Germany will never recognize a red Spain.'

'Who says Spain would go red?'

He snorted. 'You haven't seen it. The country is packed with agents of Moscow. They're not just sending arms and aid. They're sending spies. The Soviets exert huge control over the Republicans. They have secret prisons around Madrid where they torture and kill Nationalists and Catholics. The spies aren't easy to spot. They're not always Russian, they're German and Spanish too. Nearly all Jews of course. There's a Ukrainian Jew called General Kléber – at least that's his nom de guerre – who advises the International Brigades. In reality he's a senior member of the NKVD, hotfoot from Moscow, real name Manfred Stern. Some of them are English too. You should take heed. It's the declared aim of Bolsheviks to overthrow the leadership of Great Britain too. If the British aren't careful the hammer and sickle will soon be flying over Buckingham Palace.'

'The way you speak about them, it's like they're not human.'

He shrugged. 'Bolsheviks, Jews. They're different from us. It's not that I think they're dull-witted animals. Quite the contrary. I think they're dangerous. They stand for the destruction of everything we believe in. Have you heard what's going on in Moscow right now? Stalin's purges?'

Clara said nothing. It was astonishing to hear Strauss talking about the terror being perpetrated by Stalin when illegal executions, show trials and arbitrary arrests at dawn were a fact of daily life in Hitler's Germany.

'But what about you, Arno? What did you do in Spain?'

'Are you asking me what goes on in a war?'

'Just generally.'

'I flew with the Legion Condor. My commander was Lieutenant Colonel Wolfram von Richthofen. A relation of the Red Baron, you know? The overall commander was a man called Hugo Sperrle. Perhaps you've heard of him?'

Clara had seen the pictures of Generalmajor Sperrle in the newspapers. A human bulldog, with a monocle and a savage, downturned mouth.

'I think so.'

'We flew on missions against the Communists.'

'So all the people you bombed, then, were Communists?'

Strauss's voice turned to ice.

'What's this about Clara?'

'It's not about anything. I'm interested in the war.'

'You're interested, are you? That's why you're asking all these questions. Are you going to ask me what I've seen? What I've done? Do you expect me to recount it here, over a pleasant meal, for your entertainment? Are you one of those women who like to hear how many we killed and what they looked like when we bombed them? Do you want to know whether they were burned or buried alive in rubble?'

There was a silence as he finished his drink, slammed down the glass and rose to pay the bill. Bitterly Clara chided herself. God knows why but she had introduced politics, which was the last subject she should have risked, and ruined the confidential mood between them. She had probably aroused Strauss's suspicions about her own motives, but even if she hadn't, it was almost certainly too late to retrieve the situation. Great work, Clara. Mission unaccomplished.

They walked in silence back through the village. A slanting, late-afternoon sun burnished the red roofs and lit up orange and gold chrysanthemums leaning over the garden walls. Above them, a flock of migrating geese formed a hooting black arrow across the sky and beneath, on the grass, a scatter of hens pecked. Gradually the beauty of the countryside must have had its effect on Strauss, because he relaxed, the lowering frown left his face and she sensed his previous anger dissipate.

They entered the cool, verdant light of the wood, where there was no sound but the shift of branches and the rush of a distant stream. After a while Strauss stopped, obliging her to come to a halt beside him, and pressed her against the trunk of a tree that was peeling with lichen like an ancient plaster statue. The light filtered down through the leaves above them, sifting sun and shadow.

'Why did you come here today?'

'I told you. It's useful for my research. It helps me understand the character I'm playing, Gretchen. I'm supposed to know how she would be without having to think about it. So I can inhabit her.'

'What does this Gretchen do?'

'She flies into enemy territory to rescue her husband.'

'And the husband is Ernst?'

'Yes.'

'He's a lucky man.'

She realized the drink had had its effect. She laughed lightly.

'I'm seeing him this week. We're doing the publicity shots for the film.'

'Is that so? I would like to have one of those pictures. My walls are pretty bare.'

'I'll get them to send you one.'

'And what about me? Am I part of your research?'

His hand reached down to hers and grasped her fingers with his. She tried hard to prevent herself withdrawing her hand.

'You know, Clara, I find you fascinating.'

He ran his fingers lightly over her face, as though he were a blind man, or a lover. Feeling out her features, his fingers gliding over her skin, as though searching for something her features might say, across the temples, then down the cheekbones, stroking the planes of her face.

'We have something in common, you and me. I don't show my feelings because I can't. This thing on my face prevents me. You conceal your thoughts behind a façade. Which is why I wonder at your interest in me. There are not a lot of pretty actresses who throw themselves at me. What are you hiding?'

'Who says I have anything to hide?'

'Sunlight and cloud. That's what I see in your eyes.'

The arch of trees above threw shifting patterns on his face as he smiled down at her. For a moment she thought, if Strauss was not a National Socialist, if he didn't believe what he believed, could she possibly become involved with him? In some ways he was not so different from Ralph. Ralph's easy charm was a deterrent just as effective as Strauss's damaged face. But then she reminded herself: Strauss was a senior officer of the Luftwaffe. He kept company with thugs like Goering and Himmler, ruthless, violent men who regarded anyone who disagreed with them as degenerate or Bolshevik or in some other way undeserving of walking in German woods or breathing the fresh, green German air. Strauss might lack the sadism of his masters and their more vicious beliefs, yet he had chosen, hadn't he, to serve the regime? Like them, he despised Jews. He had elected to work in Goering's ministry, and fly his bomber under the Nazi flag.

Strauss reached his crumpled face down and made to kiss her.

Instinctively she ducked away. His mouth hardened into a thin line.

'You find me repulsive. Well, it's not a surprise. I should be used to it by now.'

His face was stiff with anger and annoyance. 'Women always avoid me. They don't want to get too close to this monstrosity. They give the boys in the Arbeitsdienst a teaspoon of bicarbonate of soda every day for that problem. Perhaps I should take their advice.'

'Your face has nothing to do with it.'

A flash of his bitter, grey eyes. 'You don't need to say any more, Fräulein. Thank you for your candour.'

'I mean it.'

'I spent years training in the boxing ring, so that men would hesitate before they said anything they would regret, but it doesn't work with women. I disgust them. They can't see beyond this thing, and who can blame them. No girl wants to be seen out with a freak show. When I march in parades and the BDM girls come to give flowers, they always shy away from me.'

'Oh, for God's sake!'

How could Clara make him understand? His face might be scarred but the scars in his mind were so much deeper. Those scars had silvered over and lay flat until someone touched them, and then they rose savage and scarlet, as painful as the day they were made. How could she tell Strauss she didn't recoil from him because of his face, but because she didn't want to deceive him any more than strictly necessary? Rapidly she cast around for a credible explanation.

'It's not what you think.'

'Is that so?' His expression was disgusted.

'My response had nothing to do with your face.'

'And what else could it be?'

'You said I had a secret and you're right. I do. You see, Arno, you have been consorting with a Jew.'

He stared at her for a moment then she felt the stiffening of his recoil. He took a step backwards, his voice flat with shock. 'You should visit the anthropologist. I can't believe there is any Jewish blood in you.'

She had regretted the words as soon as they had left her mouth. Her heart was hammering against her ribs. What had possessed her to tell a Nazi officer that kind of secret? The secret she hid every day. That had been so carefully covered by Leo's false documents, made and printed by men who ran enormous personal risks. What right did she have in an unforgivable moment of emotion, to risk all that? Not just to risk herself, but to risk the lives of all those brave men, throughout Berlin, who would undoubtedly be traced and rounded up if her false identity came to light? Just because she wanted to stop Strauss from kissing her. She would have to pretend it was a joke.

'Not that kind of Jew. I meant, because I'm half English. That SS newspaper, *Das Schwarz Kopf*, says we are white Jews.'

He gave a bark of laughter. 'You should have said. There's nothing wrong with that. Nothing at all.'

Nonetheless, he did not repeat his attempt to kiss her. As they walked on through the wood he appeared entirely detached, almost as if she was not there at all. When they came to a tangle of ferns and mossy stones he held out an arm momentarily to support her, then removed it again. Clara's comments about the beauty of their surroundings went unanswered. His face had frozen over again, the currents of emotion beneath it icily suppressed. At one point he reached into a pocket and withdrew a silver hipflask which he tipped, swiftly, to his mouth. It wasn't until they reached the airfield and made their way to the plane that he looked at her and said, briefly, 'Perhaps we could meet on Thursday. If you're free.'

'I'm so sorry, Arno. I have to be at the studio that day.'

He slid open the cockpit door and reached for the jackets.

'Well then. There's a lunch at Horcher's in a few days' time to celebrate the retirement of Sperrle from the Condor Legion. He's been promoted to General der Flieger. I'll send you the details. I think you should come. It would be interesting for you to see Sperrle at close quarters. Consider it part of your research.'

'Thank you. I will.'

The answer seemed to satisfy him.

Chapter Twenty-eight

It was dark by the time they had landed at Tempelhof and she made her way back to Winterfeldstrasse. A thin rain had polished the tarmac and emptied the street. Albert's red Opel was still parked where she left it outside the apartment and as she passed she caught a flash of something pale on the windscreen. It was probably a flyer distributed by a National Socialist organization exhorting her to save crusts or mend socks. Picking it up, she saw it was a plain envelope, with no address. That was unusual. Propaganda leaflets were generally brightly and garishly decorated. Opening it, she peered in and saw a photograph. It was a picture of a little boy smiling, in uniform, aged about six. Her hand trembled as she took it out. Erich. The photograph that used to sit on her mantelpiece. She had never even noticed it was gone.

She glanced rapidly up and down the street but there was no one. The envelope was slightly damp, which suggested that its sender had been caught in the rain. The person who left it could only recently have gone. If they had gone at all.

Clara felt her breath coming in fast, jagged gasps. The photograph was a threat, a direct threat by whoever it was who was stalking her. Without the need for words, the threat said that Erich would come to harm. Erich, whom she had last seen storming off from his ill-fated birthday outing. Panicky images crowded her mind. Erich's body lying in the road, his thin chest barely fluttering with life, or falling out of a window, like his mother. The young boy whose life had become intertwined so unexpectedly with her own, was now at risk. Erich, whom she had grown to love, who at times was the only thing keeping her here in Berlin. Instead of keeping him safe she had put him in danger.

At that moment Clara felt as though she was only a bit player in a story she couldn't understand. A story devised by someone who was directing the action, pulling the strings, and moving events towards an end only he could see. Who was he, this person behind the scenes? What did he want? And what did he have in store for her?

Back in the apartment, she forced herself to think calmly about where and when she might have been followed. She had been told, by Archie Dyson, that the Gestapo had its eye on her. For weeks she had sensed there was someone on her tail, even in Munich. She had been burgled; that must have been when the photograph was taken. She cursed herself for having failed to notice that it was missing. Whoever took the picture knew enough about her to understand how much she cared for Erich. And now, that same person must have known she was away from the apartment. They knew where she lived. They knew the car she drove. The message was pretty clear. They had threatened something that Clara held dear because she knew about something that they held dear. She just didn't know what it was.

The apartment in Neukölln was not on the telephone and she resisted the temptation to jump on the U-Bahn straight away. Instead, she called Erich's Gymnasium where the gruff headmaster, who was working late, answered the telephone himself and assured her that Erich Schmidt had been in as usual that day. Then she sat in her silent apartment, a cup of black coffee in her hands, and forced herself to think. She had gone to Munich to find the sister of Anna Hansen. Somehow, though she could not see why,

Anna Hansen's life had become linked to her own. The unexplained death of a rackety model turned Reich bride was now casting a shadow over her own life. She needed to discover what happened to Anna Hansen and soon.

That night she had to will herself to sleep. At last, as her breathing slowed and sleep approached, she saw a figure beckoning to her and in the dark spaces of her thoughts, where images swam before dreams descended, she felt something on the edge of her perception. It was trying to force its way out from the pictures in her mind, to separate itself and come to the fore, but it had no face or voice and it moved like a memory might, shifting in and out of the shadows in her mind.

Chapter Twenty-nine

The Heim Kurmark was in Klosterheide, a small village five kilometres north of Lindow and an hour and a half's drive north of Berlin. It was a stately, high-gabled building of rose-coloured stone which sat on the ridge of a hill, its slate roof topped by a cupola with a bell inside, sounding the hour with a gloomy, metallic toll. The austere façade hinted at its origins. It had been a monastery originally and there remained an odour of piety about it, competing with the strong scent of ammonia and cleaning polish. Earlier that year the place had been taken over by the officials of the SS, given a deep clean, and rechristened as a Lebensborn home – part of a string of institutions throughout the Reich funded by the Well of Life Foundation and devoted to the care of unmarried pregnant women who wanted to escape the moralizing of priests and family members. Here, in a programme devised by Heinrich Himmler, they could bear children with the choice of keeping them, or donating them to an SS family keen to meet the officially sanctioned target of four children. Above the heavy oak door a black SS flag twitched in the brisk autumnal breeze.

Clara climbed out of the car and waited at the door. So Katia Hansen was unmarried and pregnant, then. That might explain the contempt of the landlady back in Munich. But it did not explain why she had chosen to travel halfway across the country, trusting to the tender mercies of the SS when she was at her most vulnerable. Unless that had to do with the fact, as the landlady also mentioned, that other people were looking for her too. Clara had no idea whether her journey here would be any more fruitful than the one to Munich, but this time she was spurred by more urgent considerations. Someone wanted to find Katia Hansen and, it appeared, Katia Hansen didn't want to be found.

There was no bell, so after a while Clara pushed the door and ventured inside. It seemed strangely quiet for a place devoted to babies and young children. She saw linoleum faded by repeated scrubbing, drab mustard walls and a scuffed wooden floor. Even the light slanting through the cloudy windows was wan and drained of radiance, as though promising the babies that the world outside would be no less drear than the place in which they were born.

Before she had taken more than a couple of steps a nurse, dressed in a white headdress, bustled out to meet her.

'Katia Hansen, you say? Was this visit arranged?'

'I'm a friend of the family. I have some sad news for her,' said Clara, sidestepping the enquiry and summoning a tone of grave solemnity. 'Her sister has died.'

The nurse flinched, as though Clara had uttered an obscenity. Perhaps, in a way, death was an obscenity in this place of birth.

'Her sister, you say. She has died?' Clara watched the nurse analysing this information, pondering whether Katia Hansen had illegally concealed some familial flaw, some health defect which ran in families, a tendency to early death.

'She was murdered,' Clara clarified. Surely being murdered couldn't run in families.

'Murdered! Really? How shocking! Then I shall have to go and find her. I think she's in the lecture room. But I would ask, please, be gentle. A girl in her condition should not have to take a shock.'

Clara was shown into a waiting room, featuring a battered array of cane furniture and a poster promoting porridge and brown bread as a wholesome diet for pregnant women. A window at the side gave onto the garden where more nurses swathed in white, their caps bearing a red cross, were sitting in a circle with a baby on each lap. There was something peculiar about those babies, Clara thought, and it was not just that they were uniformly blonde and dressed in identically knitted suits and bootees. Then she realized the peculiarity was that they looked so much better fed than the babies one saw in Berlin. They had round, apple cheeks beneath their bonnets and chubby little arms, braceleted with fat. On the terrace immediately below the window stood a line of cribs, done out with lace covers and flowery blankets, and a little further down the lawn was a round table where ten children were eating a meal from steel bowls.

Katia Hansen was a slight girl of around twenty whose voluminous smock suggested a pregnancy of at least seven months. Her hair was dark brown, probably the same as Anna's before it was bleached, and her delicate features reminded Clara instantly of Katia's older sister. She shrugged off the nurse's arm and looked at Clara in amazement.

'Is it true? What Krankenschwester Flick told me about Anna? What happened?'

'Sit down, dear,' said the nurse, with a glimmer of kindliness. 'This lady has come to explain everything.'

'It is true, I'm afraid,' said Clara. 'I'm sure the Reich Bride School has been trying to trace you. And the rest of the family.'

'There is no rest of the family,' said Katia, sitting down. 'It's just me. And they can't have tried very hard. Who are you, anyway?'

'I knew Anna in Berlin.' Clara took a deep breath and explained. About meeting Anna through Bruno Weiss. About the Bride School and the shooting. She tried to keep the details of the murder vague, but she thought she should add that the police had already released the gardener who had first been arrested.

'So who do they suspect now?'

'I don't know.'

'Poor Anna.' A tear fattened on Katia's cheek and she swiped it away with a forefinger. 'Whatever else, she didn't deserve that.'

Whatever else?

Out of the corner of her eye, Clara noticed a car draw up in the drive and a group of SS officers slamming the door and stamping on the gravel. One of them carried a bouquet.

'They've come for the ceremony,' explained Katia, matter-of-factly.

'What ceremony?'

'There's a baby being dedicated to the Fatherland today. The mother doesn't want to do it, but she can't see much alternative. She knows it'll have a good future as a child of the Reich. There are always plenty of takers.'

'Why's that?' When times were hard it seemed strange anyone should want more mouths to feed.

Katia shrugged. 'SS families need a minimum of four children. Himmler says they have to be "kinderreich". If you get a child from the Lebensborn it's guaranteed to be racially pure. Oh, here's Eva now.'

A large girl with a frizz of red hair entered the room, and settled nervously in a chair. She was formally dressed in a hat and coat and clutching a baby draped in a white shawl. The child began to grizzle, and the girl hushed it urgently, rocking it back and forth in her arms. The crying only grew louder and eventually, looking quickly around, the mother undid her blouse to breastfeed. Clara watched as the baby's navy, unfocused eyes swivelled towards the distended, blue-veined breasts and seized the nipple, causing the mother to flinch. Eva sat and stared directly ahead of her as the child suckled, a look of desolation on her face.

'Eva had her little girl a month ago.' Katia smiled across at her, then lowered her voice. 'It's being adopted by a childless couple. We're all supposed to attend the dedication ceremonies, only I can't stand them . . .'

She glanced outside. 'Is that your car? Do you think we could go for a drive? We'd have to be quick but I'm dying for a cigarette.'

They walked swiftly down the corridor. As they passed, Clara glanced into the dining room where the SS officers had congregated. It was set with a couple of rows of chairs, and a table made up like an altar at the front, covered with a white linen cloth and dressed with a vase of flowers and a portrait of the Führer. A crimson banner was hung behind on the wall and next to it the black banner of the SS with its jagged lightning strokes. Beside the table, a couple stood, a grizzled Sturmbannführer and a woman in a flowered hat with a grim expression that suggested she would cope with whatever life threw at her. Even if it was a baby.

Katia walked smartly towards the car and lowered herself effortfully into the front seat. She had the same bold, no-nonsense manner Clara remembered from Anna. Though she had only just heard about her sister's death, she had barely shed a tear. Catching Clara's eyes on her, Katia said, 'In case you're wondering, it was an accident, so what was I supposed to do? The doctors can't give contraceptive advice. If they do, it's off to a camp for them, and the contraceptives you can find are all duds. Deliberately so. More kids for the Fatherland. And as for an abortion, forget it.'

'Of course,' said Clara. Abortions were banned in the Third Reich. The punishment for assisting an abortion was death. Except for Jews, for whom terminations were actively encouraged.

'Not that I'd have considered that,' Katia continued as they headed off up the drive. 'Anyway, it's supposed to be an honour to be here. You have to apply, and they only accept half the applications. They prefer the father to be SS, and you have to prove you're hereditarily healthy. Thankfully my boyfriend wasn't racially inferior. Just inferior in every other way.'

'Who was he?'

'A chauffeur. He was in the SA and he drove the SS, back home in Munich. Drove off into the sunset in the end. Still, it turns out I'm well rid of him.'

'The home seems like a very restful place.'

'Restful? You're joking. We're run off our feet. There's no end of lessons on diet, and babycare, obviously, and lectures and films. This morning we had a talk on a foolproof way to ensure our next child was a boy. Information straight from Herr Himmler, apparently. Make sure the man drinks no alcohol for a week and takes a lot of exercise.' She laughed bitterly. 'So not much chance of that then. Himmler had better think of another way of creating more soldiers for the Führer.'

'What happens after the baby's born?'

'Oh, they're very good with them. They take this scientific approach, which means the nurses weigh all the food and give them two baths a day and everything is sterilized. They feed the mothers up too. Whole milk, fresh vegetables and second helpings. That's one of the few advantages of a place like this.'

'I meant, what happens to the child afterwards?'

'If you are not in a position to look after it, it's given out to an SS family. No matter how many children they already have. They're always telling you large families are good. We've had lectures on great Germans who have come from large families – you know, if there hadn't been such a large family, certain geniuses would not exist. Mozart and people.'

'Is that what will happen to your baby?' asked Clara gently. 'Will you give it up for adoption?'

Katia's face clouded. 'I don't know. The others don't mind it. Some of them have older kids already. I've got a friend here who says, "I'm proud to give the Führer a baby. I hope it will be a boy who can die for him." But I hope mine's a girl and I don't want some old SS hag taking my kid.'

Clara noticed that tears were once again sloping down Katia's cheeks.

'This isn't how I imagined having a baby, you know. I wanted to do everything properly, nice husband, nice house, nice wedding, and then this happens.' She sniffed. 'Didn't you say you had cigarettes?'

The road passed into a copse of trees and Clara drew up. They got out and lit up. Katia inhaled greedily, then leaned back against the car. In the dappled light of the leaves, she looked exhausted. Lines of bitterness were already carved on her face.

'I'm sorry you had to come and tell me about Anna. You probably think I'm very unfeeling, seeing as she was my only sister and everything. It's probably that I can't take it in quite yet. The joke is, I was always the good girl in the family. Anna was the black sheep. Right from early on, she was the one who had rows with our parents, getting drunk, staying out late. Not wanting to join the Bund Deutscher Mädel. Having unsuitable boyfriends. Deciding she wanted to be a dancer, which our father said was no better than being a prostitute. And I was the clever one, top of the class at school, never put a foot wrong. Yet here I am now, pregnant without a man, while Anna was attending a Bride School and about to get married to an SS officer.'

She shook her head, as though still amazed at the turn of events.

'Why did Anna leave Munich?' asked Clara.

'She wanted to escape, probably. She'd got in with a pretty bad crowd at home. Not that we expected her to meet a better class of person in Berlin.' Katia corrected herself: 'Nothing personal, of course, Fräulein, but Anna wasn't the sort who enjoyed drinking tea and knitting. Once I heard she'd joined the chorus at the Wintergarten, I guessed she'd be hanging around with the same types she knew at home. At least our parents weren't around anymore to be embarrassed.'

She crossed her arms protectively over her bump. 'Probably good that they weren't around to be embarrassed by me either. You know, I almost choked when she wrote and told me she'd met a handsome blond SS officer called Johann. Anna being an SS wife! And good little Katia getting herself into trouble and then being dumped by a rat of an SA chauffeur.'

'Do you know why anyone would want to kill your sister?'

A car passed them and Katia jerked like a startled deer. The girl was on edge, Clara thought. Terrified.

'How should I know? I don't know why anyone should kill anyone!' She burst into a fit of sobbing and, to distract her, Clara hauled out the case.

'Anna left this at the Bride School. There's a letter for you inside. I'm sorry, but I opened it. I didn't think I was ever going to find you.'

Katia blew her nose. 'Don't worry. I can guess what it says.'

She opened the letter and read it, taking far longer than anyone might need to scan its short, pleading message. Eventually she folded it away.

'Well, it doesn't matter now, anyway.'

'What had you rowed about?'

'Money, among other things. She was always on the scrounge.' She glanced away with filmy eyes. 'Whatever I've said, she was still my big sister. I did love her, and now she'll never know.'

'Of course she knew.' Clara put an arm round her. 'Only Katia, there's one thing that's puzzling me. Why did you come here?'

'I told you. It seemed like the right thing to do. I didn't have much choice.'

'I mean here. Klosterheide. It's a long way from Munich.'

She ducked away from Clara's arm. 'I needed a break.'

Katia was hiding something. There was a Lebensborn home

outside Munich, Clara knew. Why did she need to come so far, unless there was something she needed to escape? Was it the 'other people' the old woman had complained about?

'When I went to Munich, to your old apartment in Frauenstrasse, the landlady said that someone had come looking for you. Do you know who it could be?'

Katya's cheeks were flushed and her lower lip stuck out in a pout. If she did know, she was not about to tell Clara.

'Could have been anyone, couldn't it? Thanks for the cigarette. I'd better be getting back now.'

She flicked the stub into the grass and climbed back in the car, giving Clara no option but to follow.

'The thing is, Katia, the person who was following Anna might well have been following you. And now, I think they're after me.'

From the corner of her eye Katia gave a swift startled glance.

'Why do you say that?'

'Someone has made threats against my godson.'

'Why would they do that?'

'That's just the problem. I don't know. I hoped you might.'

They drew up outside the home as the SS group were emerging, at their centre the new mother in the flowery hat, carrying Eva's child in an awkward clutch, the way a farmer might carry a pig. Katia's face, already mottled with tears, flushed further at the sight. As she made to get out, Clara handed her the stationery case.

'Don't forget this.'

'Keep it. I don't want it. They don't encourage personal possessions here.'

Katia leaned through the window and placed a hand on Clara's arm. 'It was decent of you to come all this way and tell me, and I'm sorry about your godson. I can't really help you. I don't know what happened to Anna and I hope they catch the bastard who did it, but the way she lived, something bad was always going to happen. She attracted trouble.' She sniffed. 'Though I suppose, if anyone's able to help, it would be Heidi Kastner.'

'Who's Heidi Kastner?'

'Anna's best friend. As much as she had a best friend. Her companion in crime, more like. They were as thick as thieves. They'd known each other since they were ten and Heidi was behind every problem Anna had. I blame Heidi for most of what happened to Anna.'

'Where could I find her?'

'The last I heard of her, she was dancing at the Wintergarten.'

Katia slammed the car door and disappeared inside.

It was an hour's drive before Clara reached the outskirts of the Grunewald. She suddenly felt desperately tired. Every part of her body ached. The Opel's heater had packed up and an icy wind ran through the car. In her head she heard Mary's voice saying, *Just come home and get warm. You're no good to anyone if you exhaust yourself.* She wondered if Mary had gone back to the Bride School and if she had found out any more about Anna's death.

Alongside these thoughts, another concern arose. The sight of the babies at the Lebensborn home had revived that craving which came increasingly often now, a sensation that was visceral in its intensity, tugging at something deep within her. The longing for a child. She recalled the unfocused eyes of the baby in its mother's arms, the fragile skull with its feathering of hair, the petal-soft flesh and the foot that stretched out of its blankets, flexing itself like a kitten. Clara wondered what it was like to feel the weight of a baby in your arms, to feel the curl of its fist around your finger, or the fix of its eyes in yours. Would she ever know that feeling herself? Would she ever have a child of her own to cherish? And would that child grow up loving and needing her, only later to push her away?

Clara allowed herself to dwell on this for only a few minutes before putting a firm mental lid on her thoughts. No time could be worse to have a baby and there was no place worse to have one than the Third Reich. Added to which, there was the little matter of needing a man to have it with. None of the reasons convinced her, of course, but she found that repeating them often enough really did succeed in drowning out deeper thoughts. Just like Goebbels said.

By the time she reached the outskirts of Berlin, she wanted nothing more than to go to sleep. Her mind was running ahead of her, back through the streets, under the arches of Nollendorfplatz, to Winterfeldstrasse, through the door, up the stairs, into the apartment and her bed. She drew up in the street, parked across from the door, and stepped out of the car. Out of the corner of her eye she saw it, a fraction of a second before she felt the savage thud as the wall of shining steel hit her, swerved back into the road and she fell.

There was a blur of sky and a face, then the earth came up to meet her and she felt herself crumpling, the back of her head exploding in pain.

Chapter Thirty

Clara had been dreaming about her parents. Long ago, when life was still normal. Briefly she woke, to find herself somewhere cool. The pain was beating against the inside of her skull, crashing in waves against the bone. Dim memories crowded her mind. Lying in the street in Winterfeldstrasse, people around her, her head pounding. Being picked up and travelling in a taxi. She shifted and a sharp ache shot through her ribs.

The threat to Erich. Bruno. Arno Strauss. The dead girl and the visit to Katia Hansen. She could not make sense of any of it. In the past few weeks her entire life seemed to have become unhinged from its normal path. It was like the moment in a cinema when the film speeds up and slips from its projector, spooling crazily away with all its images, leaving only a flickering darkness. She fell asleep again.

It must have been some hours later when she woke. Fatigue pressed down on her like a great weight, making it difficult even to stretch out. The bed she was in felt luxuriously deep and soft, the sheets deliciously chill against her hot limbs. Gradually the room came into focus. The curtains were drawn but she could tell it was morning because the sun pressed urgently at the edges, lighting up the damask roses of the fabric with a vivid blue flame. The light stung her eyes so she shut them again. Footsteps came towards her across the floor. Burnished black brogues from Church's of Turl Street, Oxford, fitted with a steel tip in the heel. The characteristically languid tread.

'Hello.' It was Ralph, stroking her head. His face was ashen. His shirt collar was unbuttoned and a bow tie hung, untied. His hand cupped her chin and lay soft against her flushed cheek.

'Your fingers are freezing, Ralph.'

He laughed. 'You're better than I thought. No harm done. Just a lump the size of an egg where you hit the back of your head and a few scratches.'

She noticed a porcelain bowl on a table to one side, and a wad of cotton wool beside it. A flower of blood bloomed up beneath the water's surface.

'Is that my blood?'

'It's just a graze on your temple. I patched you up as best I could. Tried to remember what I learned about first aid in the boy scouts. Here.' He propped her up on the pillows. 'Not a conventional way to get an attractive woman into my bed, but . . .' Seeing her look he laughed and said, 'Don't worry. I slept on the sofa. You've been out for hours.'

He picked up another piece of cotton wool, wetted it with disinfectant, and dabbed her forehead tenderly.

Looking down, she realized she was wearing a man's white cotton shirt. Ralph's shirt, it must be, and beneath it, she was entirely naked. A blush rose to her face. He glanced politely away.

'How's the head?'

'It hurts.'

'Wait a minute, I'll fetch you some aspirin and a cup of tea.'

From her position propped up on the pillow she looked through to the drawing room, with its Persian carpet and the desk in the corner. She could hear him moving around the apartment, boiling the kettle, making tea, and waiting for it to brew, lighting a cigarette and blowing the smoke away as he stared into the distance. She found her handbag at her side and reached down for her Max Factor compact to reveal her face, milk white, and highlighted with a gash on the temple.

He returned with a tray, bearing aspirin, two tea glasses and toast.

'Careful. It's hot.'

The tea was sweet and malty. Assam.

'What happened to me?'

'Looks like some idiot ran into you. Car came out of nowhere and knocked you out cold, momentarily, without stopping. Lucky for you I was there. Otherwise you'd be mouldering in some hospital this morning.'

He spoke as if she had been negligent in getting run down.

'Why were you there?'

'Pure chance.'

'You can't expect me to believe that.'

'Good luck, then. By the way, I collected your bag, and you had this with you.'

He gestured to the case stowed at the side of the bed.

'Thank you.'

'I'm afraid your clothes were a little dirty.' He pointed to her stockings, bra and underclothes neatly folded across the back of a chair. 'I've washed them as best I can, but it's not my forte.'

Clara wriggled down further in the bed and drew the sheet more tightly around her. The thought of Ralph undressing her like a sleepy child, then wrapping her in his own shirt and putting her to bed caused a wave of conflicting emotions. Embarrassment first, then annoyance and, underlying that, excitement. What had he felt when he pulled her clothes off and saw her naked? Had he reacted like a nursemaid, or a man?

'Why can't I remember anything? I remember coming here with you . . .' The images were beginning to knit together again in her brain. The taxi, the firm arm beneath hers, guiding her up the stone steps. 'But I don't remember a thing about being knocked down.'

'It's normal to be a little groggy after a concussion. Nothing to worry about. You can remember what you were doing yesterday, I take it?'

The visit to Katia Hansen.

'Yes.'

'And the day before?'

'Arno Strauss took me for another test flight. We landed near a restaurant he knows and had lunch.'

The day with Strauss came back to her. The desolation in his eyes. The twist of vulnerability and contempt when she refused his kiss.

'Very nice. Did you learn anything?'

'A lot. He explained all about the camera.'

'Do you think he suspects anything?'

'Nothing I can't cope with.'

'Did you part on good terms?'

'I suppose.'

'That's good. You should rest now because I'm going to need to know everything you can tell me about Strauss. Take those aspirin and drink your tea. I'll be in the next room if you need me.'

She drank, and felt the energy flooding back to her. The anxiety that she had felt since discovering Erich's photograph on the car ebbed away here. The distant sounds of Ralph moving around the drawing room, a muffled cough, the soft thump of books, imparted a sense of security she had not known in all her years in the city. It was as though nothing could penetrate the cocoon of this apartment.

An hour later he put his head round the door to find her looking curiously around the room, running a hand through her disordered hair. He came and sat on a chair by the bed, stretching out his long legs.

'Do you feel up to talking?'

'Just about.'

'Good girl. Tell me about Strauss then. You saw him at Goering's reception?'

'Yes. And he told me what they're proposing for the Duke of Windsor. The suggestion is that in the event of a Grand Alliance between Britain and Germany the Duke would return to the English throne, with Lloyd George as Prime Minister. Alternatively, if a war was needed first, then Edward would serve as a president of an English republic. And they're going to hold him to it. A document has been prepared promising Germany the return of her former colonies and the gift of northern Australia. Two copies have been drawn up for the Duke to sign. They had just been delivered for Goering's approval.'

His eyes widened. 'I'd give a lot to see that document. Presumably the deal will be done when the Duke visits Hitler at Berchtesgaden.'

'If it happened . . . I mean if war came and then an alliance was formed, what would happen to the new King and his family?'

Clara thought of shy King George who had taken over from his older brother, with his pretty, plump bride, Elizabeth. They had two little girls – eleven-year-old Princess Elizabeth and her younger sister Margaret Rose. Elizabeth, or Lilibet as she was called, was the serious, dutiful one and Margaret was lively and spirited. Already, the British public seemed to love them.

'Who knows? Either they'd fade away into the background again, or they might emigrate, to Canada say, along with all those politicians who backed Edward's abdication. Baldwin and Churchill.'

'And do you think the Duke would sign such a document?'

He shrugged. 'I couldn't say, but I'm certain of this: the only way the British public would have Edward back would be if they lost a war. Which is exactly why we need to cultivate our friend

Strauss. Now he took you to lunch and you had a glimpse of the camera. What did you learn?'

'He talked about what aerial photographs can reveal. I memorized what he told me about the camera. It uses special thirty-five-millimetre film with a perforated edge, which allows motors to turn the film automatically behind the lens and get a precise exposure. It can also be used at night, too.'

'You obviously got on well with him. Sounds like he was quite forthcoming.'

She grimaced.

'What is it?'

'He was, very talkative. Over lunch he told me all about his childhood.' She paused. 'Oh, I don't know, Ralph. I wanted him to be more savage, then it would have been easy. But there's something so sad about him. Desolate almost.'

'Desolate?' Beneath the genial demeanour, a flash of anger rose in Ralph's eyes. 'Who cares what happens in that cold Nazi heart of his? Perhaps next time you start feeling sorry for Strauss, you should remember all those civilians mown down by his bombs in Spain.'

Almost as quickly as it had erupted, his anger was suppressed. He became brisk and businesslike.

'Anyway, I'm glad you found him approachable. It makes our next step easier.'

'What's the next step?'

'We need to encourage him to come over to us. Everyone's getting their Intelligence ducks in a row and there's no time to lose. We had a report earlier this month that Udet had advised a friend to get the hell out of Germany and added that he would be doing the same were it not for his position. Udet believes it won't be long before he falls out of favour with the regime and I'd wager Strauss feels the same. And seeing as he has bent the rules by taking an attractive actress on an unauthorized joyride, our job might be a little easier.'

Despite herself she was aghast. 'You're not going to blackmail him!'

'Don't be foolish, Clara. You know that's what this is about. There's a lot riding on Strauss. Given his closeness to Udet we think he might be open to persuasion anyhow. But if he isn't, there are other ways.'

She sank back against the pillow. She felt a lurch of despair. She knew, of course, that Strauss's information was valuable, but she had not thought he would learn so soon of her deception. The thought of Strauss's ravaged face when he learned of her betrayal made her quail. She was glad that he had been horrified at the idea of kissing a Jew.

'Strauss is going to be very valuable to us,' said Ralph, with satisfaction.

'Don't talk about him like that!'

He looked at her strangely.

'I thought I'd made this clear.' His voice acquired an edge of steel. 'This isn't about making friends. It's not about having charming little lunches and getting pally with the chaps in the Luftwaffe. I see these people every night of the week, and I never doubt that they would put me up against a firing squad, or that I'd do the same to them, if needs be.'

Clara stared at the ceiling, her hands clenched beneath the sheets. 'I understand that.'

'If you're not capable of basic emotional discipline . . .'

'Emotional discipline!' A wave of pain and weariness flooded over her. 'Isn't that what they taught you at that boarding school of yours? Never feel anything. Never get involved. Damp down any remotely human emotions because they're going to get in the way? Forget anything like friendship, or basic human decency. *I Vow To Thee My Country*. Build an invisible armour around you that nothing can penetrate? Well, I'm sorry, but I can't be like that. I get affected by the people I associate with.'

There was a moment of silence. Then he said, 'Have you finished?'

She looked away.

'It's part of the job, Clara, I thought you understood that. You led me to believe it wasn't going to be a problem for you. You said there was no chance you would get emotionally involved. But if you're going to start falling for every Oberst Leutnant who makes friendly overtures . . .'

'I haven't fallen for him,' she said, through gritted teeth.

'Feeling sorry for him.'

'I don't feel sorry for him.'

'I'm afraid I don't see the problem then.'

Clara's head was throbbing badly. She wanted to stop thinking about Arno Strauss, to stop imagining the moment when he was confronted with the evidence of her double-dealing. That look, both aggressive and vulnerable, in his hard grey eyes.

Ralph got up. 'You're probably still affected by the accident. Perhaps we should talk later. When you're feeling more yourself.'

She turned her head away so he should not see the tears pricking at her eyes. This time he shut the door behind him.

Some time later he returned with two glasses of schnapps and a determined smile.

'Let's talk about something else.'

She gave a faint shrug.

'Tell me about you, Clara.'

'What do you want to know?'

'When I first met you, I tried to find out as much as possible about you. It wasn't prying. I was just being professional. I was told there had been a chap who was madly in love with you, but that it hadn't worked out.'

'His name was Leo Quinn and he worked at Passport Control.

He was busy getting visas for Jews who wanted to escape Germany.'

'Sounds like a brave man. The Foreign Office disapproved of that, I hear. They refused to give Passport Control officials diplomatic status. So he was risking a lot. Where is he now?'

'He went back to England in '33.' She met his eyes frankly. 'He's probably married to someone else by now. There's been no one serious since.'

'Was it Leo Quinn who recruited you?'

'He realized I had useful access.'

'Perhaps that's not all he realized.'

'What do you mean?'

He smiled. 'When you first came here, I noticed you looking around. I saw you look at the photograph on the mantelpiece and work out that it was my mother. You're naturally observant. You probably always have been.'

'I suppose so.'

'You're secretive, too.'

'I think anyone is, who has brothers and sisters. You're always trying to preserve your privacy, not to have your secrets held up for the public amusement of others.'

'So you had secrets?'

'Only the normal things. I kept a diary, hidden in drawers and behind beds and cushions. I tended to hide things.'

Emotions too. From the age of twelve she had perfected the art of keeping her confidences deep within herself, buried beneath layers of caution and circumspection. It wasn't hard. In her family, emotions had always been rigorously concealed. Falling out of a tree and ripping the skin off her knee meant a severe dabbing with iodine but no tears. Kisses were a rare gift. Any passions, whether grief, joy or hilarity, were allowed only decorous display, like the collection of antique Chinese porcelain her parents kept behind glass-door cabinets. When Kenneth left for boarding school at the age of eight, he had shaken hands with their father, who would no more have told his son he loved him than fly to the moon.

Ralph was still gazing at her, scrutinizing her.

'Perhaps it would help if you told me a few of those secrets now.'

So she began to talk, and as she did she found herself telling him everything that had happened, right from the beginning, as though she was thinking out loud. About Bruno and the trip to Munich and her conviction that someone there had been following her. The burglary. Coming back from the flight with Strauss to find the photograph of Erich on the windscreen of the car.

'I realized that whoever is threatening me knew all about me. He knew about Erich and he was prepared to make a threat against him, too. I called the school right away and the principal told me he was fine, but just knowing that someone has threatened Erich, and knows how much I care about him, makes me . . . what I mean is, if anything happened to Erich, I couldn't bear it.'

'It won't.'

'Perhaps not. But I'm responsible for him.'

Gently he said, 'You're fond of the lad, aren't you? Do you like children? All that combing hair and scrubbing knees and teaching them to keep their nails clean?'

'I never used to. I suppose being with Erich has changed how I feel.'

'Perhaps you should be having children yourself. Don't you want them?'

She tried not to flinch beneath his steady gaze.

'Now's not a good time to be having babies.'

While they were talking he had edged nearer and taken her hand. He was rubbing it with his finger in soothing concentric circles, and when she paused, he suddenly dipped his head towards her and kissed her, his lips soft at first then insistent.

Without realizing how much she wanted to, she wrapped her arms round his neck and drew him down to her, responding with a deep, lingering embrace. He moved onto the bed and she shifted beneath him, her fingers brushing the fine golden stubble of his face. Heat blossomed through her as his hands moved over her breasts and travelled the length of her body, but after a few moments he drew back.

'I'm sorry.'

'Don't be.'

'No. I am.' He moved sharply away, his face set. 'This wasn't supposed to happen. It's not what I intended.'

He made to get up, but Clara couldn't bear to let the moment go. She had forgotten everything that had gone before. Desire was coursing through her in waves. She wanted nothing more than for him to make love to her. She was sure it was true for him too.

'I'm half naked in your bed, Ralph. You brought me here and took my clothes off and then you kissed me. What the hell were your intentions?'

'I don't want to give you the wrong idea.'

Quietly, she said, 'When I came here before you said there were all sorts of reasons why you shouldn't get involved with me. What are they?'

'I'm too old for you.'

'You're what, ten years older than me?'

'I'm in my forties,' he said gruffly. 'Set in my ways. Used to my own company. Accustomed to pleasing myself.'

'You asked me about my love life, so what about you? You must have known plenty of women. You joke about them.'

'They come and go. No permanent fixtures. I don't think they see me as a good bet.'

'I'm not a betting girl.'

Still his eyes avoided her. He knitted his hands together and leaned forward, frowning at his feet.

'Do we have to go through this? I've told you, I've always needed to be alone. All my life.'

'That's not the reason.'

'Spare me the inquisition, Clara, would you?' he said tersely. 'I'm too old for all this. I plainly overstepped the mark and I've apologized. It was irresponsible of me. Particularly in your condition. I'm going to leave you now.' He stood up.

She felt herself flushing. 'Leave then, Ralph, but at least be honest with me.'

For a moment he stood, hands rammed in his pockets, face grim and sulky, as though he might refuse to speak. Then reluctantly he said, 'All right then. If you insist. I won't get involved with you because it's risky.'

'So is everything we do.'

'This is doubly so. We would be a risk to each other. There's enough risk out there without multiplying it. If either of us were ever arrested we would have to disown the other. You know that, don't you? I would deny all knowledge of you.'

She didn't doubt it.

He leaned down, took her face in his hands and his eyes burned into hers. 'And I would loathe myself for that. Don't you see? I could never forgive myself. And then, if they were certain that I did know you, it could be worse . . .'

'You could betray me?'

He didn't answer. But she knew that was his deepest fear. To seduce and deceive and betray, these were the tools of espionage and every spy learned to live with them. To deny a friendship was one thing, but to betray something precious to you, something you treasured, whether it be your country or your lover, that was a deeper fear.

He turned away and occupied himself fixing a cigarette into his ebony holder.

'So it's best we stay as we are.'

'Don't you ever get tired of it, Ralph? All the lying? The subterfuge?'

His eyes clouded. She knew this was something he didn't want to discuss.

'Lying is like learning another language. For a long time you have the translation, which is the truth, running continuously through your head. But once you're fluent, it comes naturally, and then you're in a different state. The trick is to make it as much like your real life as possible. I'm used to this life now. I can hardly remember it any other way. I'm used to being watched and observed and one step away from arrest. I have responsibilities to other people and I appreciate the immense need for self-control. We both do. To put two people like us together . . . it would be combustible. We'd risk losing control. And that's a risk I can't take.'

He reached down to the brogues stowed under the chair, picked one up, and turning it over with a sudden twist, swivelled its heel to reveal a compartment the size of a penny, containing a twist of newspaper. Inside was a brown, rubber-coated pill the size of a pea. It looked innocuous, as he held it up to her. Dull, even.

'I take it seriously, you see. Part of the uniform.'

She took a quick look, gasped and looked away. She knew about cyanide capsules, though she had never seen one before and hoped she never would again. The thought of carrying death with you everywhere you went was sobering. Yet she persisted.

'I'm just as controlled as you, Ralph. That experience is the same for me. I understand everything about the need to avoid risks. Dissembling is part of my nature too. But I'm here in your apartment, aren't I? You expressly brought me here.'

'I had to,' he replied, curtly. 'It was unavoidable.'

Finally, his rejection had its effect. He was speaking as though she were a parcel, delivered to the wrong address. Flinging off the sheets she swung her feet round and rose from the bed.

'Thanks for your hospitality then.' Her head was light as the blood rushed to her legs and tears stung her eyes. Frustration and annoyance mingled in her. 'Do you know what I think? I suspect you believe you're the only person who has a sense of independence and that any woman you meet will try to entrap you. Don't worry, Ralph, that's not going to happen with me. I'm perfectly happy as I am. I haven't the remotest interest in trying to snare you. I'm leaving now.'

She snatched up her bra and was pulling on her clothes when he reached out behind her and imprisoned her in his arms.

'Wait.'

She struggled out of his arms and continued buttoning her blouse.

'Please, Clara! Let me explain. I shouldn't have kissed you.'

Her fingers were trembling, but she had her back to him and she persisted with the buttons, furiously.

'I don't see why.'

'It would be a crazy idea.'

'You've already made that quite plain, thank you.'

'I'm a good deal older than you.'

'You're not particularly old. And I'm not some young girl who doesn't know her own mind.'

'Calm down.'

'Stop talking like you're my father or something.'

He reached out a hand. 'You're being unreasonable.'

'Leave me alone, Ralph! I understand.'

'You understand nothing!' He looked exasperated. 'Just . . . don't speak.' Taking her by the shoulders he forced her to face him, then with deft deliberation unbuttoned the blouse she had just buttoned, slipped it off, and took her in his arms and onto the bed.

His body was a revelation. His chest, carved with muscle, was lithe and taut. Though he had made play of his age, his body was as hard as a man half his age with only a slight fold of flesh at the stomach. There was a reddish line of hair running down the centre of his chest to his belly. Softly he kissed her eyes, nose, shoulders and breasts, then ducked his head down and his lips grazed her belly. As she arched beneath him, he turned, fumbled in a drawer beside the bed and she heard the rip of foil, before he turned back to her with a hunger that amazed her.

After everything he had said about self-control, it was a joy to abandon herself entirely to sensation, to feel the pleasure flooding her body as he towered above her. She revelled in the sense of his skin against hers, breathing his breath, the intimacy of his face a few inches from her own. After so long on her own, just the touch of a man, his fingers searching her out and his limbs entwining hers, was startling and new. She felt delicate and precious beneath his hands, like the piece of fine art he had once compared her to. Yet his touch was firm too, turning her over deftly beneath him, controlling himself, spicing his urgency with a deliberation that prolonged her pleasure, gripping her hips hard to steady her beneath him. At the edge of Clara's mind the thought of death, that he carried with him wherever he went, only made her surrender more complete.

When he had finished, he lay with his arm flung beneath her and soon fell asleep, his breathing growing deep and slow. But Clara couldn't sleep. For a long time, she lay thinking, then she propped herself up on one elbow to look at him.

As she watched, she saw his body shudder, the twitch of movement rippling across his tanned skin. At one point he muttered something, and she craned towards him but couldn't make it out. She wondered what was going on in that dark undertow of thought; what private dreams he had that left him quivering in his sleep.

They spent the whole of the next day together, in bed and out of it. Clara lay soaking in his deep porcelain bath, feeling her bruised limbs relax, using his Pears soap, whose translucent amber with its familiar carbolic tang reminded her powerfully of the nursery bathroom of her childhood, with its clanking pipes and towels like stippled cardboard. She stood at the mirror and explored the bump at the back of her head, trying to conceal the gash on her temple with make-up. The smell of onions and mushrooms rose tantalizingly from the narrow kitchen where Ralph was making lunch with what he had in the cupboard. She craned her neck and saw him cut a square of butter from its waxy wrapping and send it sizzling in the pan.

'So tell me about Babelsberg,' he called from the kitchen. 'Is it everything you imagined?'

'I never imagined it, because I'd never acted on film before I came to Berlin. It was a whole new art for me. Coming here was a step into the unknown.'

His voice had lost its wariness and was full of unguarded enthusiasm. He had thrown a white cloth over his small dining table and lit a candle, but offset the romantic touch with a small, ironic bow, offering her a glass of Hock.

'German wines are much better than we give them credit for, but no one much drinks them back in Britain.'

The lunch he had prepared was surprisingly good. Though the onion soup was canned, the mushroom omelettes were springy and glistening with butter. He had made a salad of cabbage and apple. She ate ravenously, realizing how hungry she was. It was as though all her senses had been starved up to this moment. His eyes searched her face anxiously as she ate.

'I hoped you might have an appetite. I'm not much of a cook, but I can knock up the basics.' There was something endearing about this admission. It was like a chink in his armour. Clara savoured every mouthful, realizing that it was years since anyone had cooked specifically for her.

When they were sated, she lay on his cracked leather sofa with her head on his lap as he talked, smoothing her brow with deft, hypnotic strokes.

'My father was vicar of St Anselm's in Brooklands. It was a standard, redbrick, Victorian place with a standard Victorian congregation to match. I think Dad had ambitions to be a bishop, but he didn't have quite the right connections and by the time I was aware of it, he seemed always to have a lingering resentment about him. Not that he'd ever express it, of course, he was far too buttoned-up for that, but it was clear he intended to fulfil his ambitions through me. He always wanted me to follow him into the Church; unfortunately he was disappointed.'

'You're not a believer then?'

He gave a dry laugh. 'When I was younger I was perfectly happy to pay lip service to God. The kind of childhood God you say grace to, or pray to when your dog is ill. But the war changed everything. After what I saw there the idea of God meant nothing any more. How could a God of love preside over such desolation and misery?'

'Did you tell your father that?'

'He would have seen it as weakness. My father didn't have much patience with human weakness.'

'And you do?'

'That depends entirely on the human.'

His fingers traced her hair tenderly as he spoke. 'The only person I discussed it with was Tom. We'd always talked about everything, especially politics, even if we didn't always see eye to eye. Tom was an intellectual. He was the kind of person who sees things entirely in black and white. Ideologies mattered very much to him, more than people, I sometimes thought, and yet after the war he lost interest entirely. He said all politicians were a load of frauds and none of them were any better than the others. I suppose the war affected everyone in different ways. That's why it surprised me when I heard he'd gone out to Spain. I got a letter from him at Christmas, saying that the place he was holed up in had come under heavy bombardment and he didn't rate his chances of coming out of it alive. Since then I've heard nothing.'

'Surely there are people you could ask? I mean you have so many connections?'

'Spain doesn't work like that, Clara. It's not orderly like Germany. People don't keep records of every prisoner taken, or every body found. Whatever the moral chaos of the Nazis, their filing skills are second to none. But Spain is, well, it's a maelstrom. I . . .' He looked away, unwilling to finish the sentence, as if by uttering the words he was making them true. 'I rather suspect that Tom's dead.'

Then he smiled, a little too brightly.

'Still. There's no point discussing it.'

He fell silent so Clara began to talk about her arrival in Berlin, about meeting Leo Quinn and agreeing to spy on the Nazi women for him. Her discovery that her maternal grandmother Hannah Neumann had been Jewish, a fact which Clara's own mother had never told her. Her determination to do everything she could to bedevil the Nazi regime. Ralph was a good listener. He absorbed her story without interruption, just the occasional nod, or raised eyebrow. The intimacy between them felt so complete it was as though they had not just stripped off their clothes, but entire layers of their being.

'What you said before, that I understand nothing. What don't I understand?'

He sighed, and kept stroking her hair. 'The thing about me is, I've always needed to maintain control. I've become used to keeping other people at arm's length. That's the job, isn't it? Control. Distance. Self-discipline. What you said about learning to build an invisible wall around oneself, well it's true. It's essential, in fact, if you're going to do what I do. Nothing should breach it.'

'And now you've let me breach it?'

'Perhaps I was crazy to think I could avoid it. Or that I wanted to.'

Later, she watched him as he shaved, the blade flashing smoothly backwards and forwards as he scraped against his face, the splash of the hot water as he rinsed his razor, the intense concentration as he stared into the clouded mirror. Seeing her watching him, he kissed her and she ran her fingers through his damp hair where it was threaded with grey at the temples. For the first time in years she was free of the caution that waited at the edge of her mind, the need to keep part of herself secret. She hoped it was the same for him.

At one point he left the apartment to fetch milk and food and out of habit she had a quick look around the bedroom. There was the Harris Tweed jacket with leather on the elbows hanging in the wardrobe, and clothes neatly folded in the drawers with an orderliness that spoke of a boarding school training. When she felt beneath them she found nothing but a torch. She unearthed a photograph of a couple she took to be his parents in old-fashioned clothes standing in front of a wisteria-framed oak door, and another of Ralph standing next to a young man in cricket whites whom she guessed to be Tom. He was shorter than Ralph and a handsome man, though there was a severity in the set of the jaw and a hardness in his chiselled cheekbones that suggested a certain arrogant self-assurance.

When she heard his key in the door she resumed her place on the sofa and picked up *The Times*, trying to focus on the crossword. Her eyes glazed over the clues. *A prize for exhaustion, 7 letters*. But almost immediately she put the paper down again. Her mind was so full of Ralph, she didn't require any distraction. He came up behind her and kissed her.

'Atrophy.'

She frowned.

'Seven letters, prize for exhaustion. A trophy.'

'Oh, of course.'

'On which subject,' he said, reaching down to pull her towards him, 'how exhausted are you?'

She kissed him back, and they went to bed again.

Afterwards, she saw him looking at her, his eyes glazed with thought, and she questioned him.

'To be honest with you, generally after I've slept with a woman I want nothing more than for her to leave as fast as possible.'

She laughed. 'I suppose I did ask you to be honest with me.'

'I feel differently now. It's like . . . I don't know, like jumping into some damn Scottish loch and feeling the water so bracing that the blood rushes to your heart. Being with you reminds me I'm alive.'

The following morning when she woke he was not in bed beside her. She slipped quickly into her clothes, brushed her hair and came into the kitchen where he was standing at the window, wearing his dark silk dressing gown, staring sightlessly out at another leaden Berlin sky. He acknowledged her with a slight hunch of the shoulders.

'Ralph.'

She approached and touched him, tentatively. He faced her, once again brisk and businesslike, with the inbuilt rigidity of the military man.

'I need to be out today. I have a meeting with Rosenberg. We're driving out to the Staaken airfield where he's going to show me the Messerschmitt Bf 109. They've refined it in Spain, apparently. It's much improved. Then we're on to inspect the new Heinkel factory at Oranienburg and after that there's a dinner. It means I'll be out pretty much all day. I can't see myself getting back much before eleven.'

'That's fine.'

'And there's a lot going on in the next few days. You've heard of Charles Lindbergh, the American aviator?'

'Of course.' Wasn't it Lindbergh who had helped Mary with her visa?

'He's coming over. It's supposed to be an unofficial visit but all the air force top brass are turning out to meet him. There's a reception at the Adlon.'

'I'll get my things together.'

'No. Wait.'

He turned to her, took her in his arms and brushed the hair out of her eyes.

'There's something I need to tell you. I didn't want to worry you until absolutely necessary. It was selfish of me, I know, but I just wanted a little time alone with you before . . .'

'Before what?'

'When I went to your apartment the other day I saw a tail. A standard-issue Gestapo shadow. You're being watched.'

'I knew that.'

'But then you were knocked down, and it was quite deliberate.'

'I thought it was an accident.'

'I saw it, Clara. That was no accident. The car drove straight at you. I couldn't see his face but the man who knocked you down was not Gestapo. The shadow was already there. And besides, why watch you, if the order is to kill you? If the Gestapo wanted to get rid of you it would have happened already. It's clear there's someone else on your tail.'

She saw anxiety etched in his face, his brain rapidly calculating, his mind running through the possibilities.

'Someone is after you, Clara. But why? Who are they?'

She shook her head.

Ralph drew himself up. 'I've been thinking about it over the last two days and I've changed my mind. Archie Dyson was right. You're going to have to lie low.'

'You can't mean that.'

'I do. It's the safest thing. It's imperative. You need to stop everything you're doing with Arno Strauss. You need to go back to being an actress whose only concerns are her wardrobe and the affections of her leading man.'

'I won't do that.' She frowned.

'You must. Don't use the telephone, except for business calls. Don't fraternize with American journalists. Don't talk in bars.'

'Give me credit for knowing the basics.'

'Look at me, Clara.' He took her shoulders. 'You asked me why I didn't want to get involved with you. Perhaps it was because of what's happened to Tom. I've lost one person already. I wouldn't want to lose another.'

He tipped her chin towards him.

'The most important thing is, you mustn't go home. There's someone out there who wants to kill you. I don't know who they are, or who they represent, but it's essential you don't give them the chance. You need to stay here. For your own safety. Promise me.'

She glanced away, but his fingers dug into her arms and he gave her a little shake. 'Don't look away! This is important, Clara. You could be jeopardizing far more than just yourself. If we were at war then this would be an order. Treat it like that. Promise me.'

'I promise.'

Chapter Thirty-one

That Friday Ilse had been assigned the linen change. It was one of the better jobs at school, right up there with baking, and she wondered briefly if perhaps the staff recognized this and were making allowances for her, until she realized that it was just the rota. She loved the sweet, starchy smell of the fresh linen as she unfolded it stiff from the washing line, then took it to the ironing room, bright with clouds of scented steam. After ironing, the linen had to be taken to the cavernous airing cupboard, tucked away up in the eaves of the house, which meant you could disappear for a while with no one watching, and relax in the dim space with your eyes shut, leaning against the fragrant linen and feeling the warmth enter your bones. Ilse enjoyed everything about the linen change. She even loved the idea of it, rendering something fresh and clean and new.

But the last couple of times she had gone to unpeg the washing, she had a bad feeling. A prickle on the back of her neck which said someone was watching her. She could not see, smell or hear anything, but she felt it, at the limit of her senses. She whipped round several times, and caught nothing more than a few last leaves abandoning their branches and whirling down to a damp mulch below. One time she caught a flash of something white from the corner of her eye, but it could have been the tail of a bird, or the flick of the sheets in the breeze.

After lunch she had gone out again to feed the geese, which were being fattened for Christmas. The birds were confined in wooden boxes with just their long necks and heads protruding, so that they grew as big as possible before being killed. Ilse had grown up on a farm, so she wasn't sentimental, but she felt sorry for the geese all the same. Most of the time they were quiet but whenever they sensed anyone approach they would crane their necks as much as they could, cackling for grain. As she stuffed the corn down their throats she looked around constantly, but there was nothing.

All afternoon she tried to focus on her household accounts, sorting everything into neat columns, Coffee, Tea, Milk, Sugar, with the amounts required and the cost, and then totting up everything at the bottom, stretching her terrible arithmetic to the limit. During all this time she cast glances out into the darkening garden, trying to probe the mass of shadow at the end of the lawn.

She had thought about calling the American lady, but she couldn't find the card with her number on it. She must have dropped it somewhere. And how on earth would she go about telling Fraülein Harker she had a bad feeling in her bones?

After supper there was a short period before lights out which the brides used to write letters, read and chat or listen to the wireless. Ilse took the opportunity to slip down to the kitchen. The place was completely empty. Everything had been cleaned, the pots were washed and the pans hung in their places above the range. The kitchen smelled comfortingly of baking and faint wafts of that night's chicken dinner. The dough for the next day's bread was rising on the stove, swelling like a great bloated skull, and outside trails of woodsmoke curled through the evening air. Everything in Schwanenwerder was tranquil and Ilse was scared.

She wasn't going to make Anna's mistake and wander into the garden. She would only venture a couple of steps out from the kitchen door to the yard at the back of the house and see if she had the same feeling. Keeping the door open she edged a couple of steps forward. She couldn't switch the kitchen light on, because she was out of bounds, so there were only the dancing flames of the woodburning stove to go by. The air was as cold as a knife, edged with moss and pine and the soft lapping of the lake. The distant sound of dance music on the wireless rippled from the drawing room. Ilse peered blindly into the dim garden, past the tall daisies beginning to crumple from the first frost, through the shrubs and the flowerpots lining the gravel of the path.

And that was when she saw it. Or rather him, because it was a man, she was sure of it, fifty metres away from her at the other side of the garden, emerging from the mass of trees towards the house itself. Ilse's throat clenched with fear, preventing any scream she might have emitted, but her legs buckled beneath her and she took a step backwards. At the sound of her staggering the figure froze like a fox, stared at her, then hurried on, moving swiftly across the grass until his dark shape merged with the shadow of a wall, like a piece of the night itself.

Chapter Thirty-two

Clara waited until Ralph had left and then another fifteen minutes before she slipped out of the apartment and walked swiftly along Duisberger Strasse. She could keep her promise about not using the telephone and not fraternizing with American journalists, but she couldn't stay with him. However much she liked the idea, it would compromise him. Ralph was right to be afraid, but for the wrong reason. If someone was pursuing her, it would draw the danger to him, too. But at the same time, if the Gestapo really were watching her apartment, there was no sense in going straight home either.

The day was dingy and overcast. She walked deep in thought, barely seeing what surrounded her. Berlin was a city of straight lines, the perspective was in every way rectilinear, from the flatness of its terrain to the long avenues, even ascending to the rigid right arms of its people. Yet beneath those lines, everything was devious and twisted. Berlin was like a crossword – an apparently straightforward grid filled with puzzles and enigmas.

Who was on her tail? The Gestapo, almost certainly, but an assassin too? Was he a professional hitman, hired to kill? The idea seemed too ludicrous for words and yet, Ralph told her, she had been deliberately knocked down. He had seen it himself. What did she know, that someone needed so badly to obliterate it? What danger could she possibly pose to anyone? All around her the familiar streets were coated in a sheen of invisible danger. Everything ordinary glinted with threat, like rain on the cobblestones.

Eventually the cold overtook her. Her fingers were freezing because her gloves were at home, her coat was a little torn from where she had fallen and the clothes she was wearing were too flimsy to keep out the penetrating breeze. She crossed Wittenbergplatz and entered KaDeWe.

Ever since Clara had arrived in Berlin, she had loved that department store. Beyond the brass doors, within the warm, glistening, scented interior, it was almost a world of its own. The store had thought of everything its customers could wish for, from the special room at the side of the entrance, where a uniformed assistant would look after your dog, to the racks where gentlemen could rest unfinished cigars while they perused the shop. Just stepping through the doors caused you to relax, as the wall-length mirrors reflected your image back to you, replete with a patina of glamour and luxury. You could happily pass half a day immersed in the book department, or sipping coffee among the potted palms in the sixth-floor café.

In the past Clara had always enjoyed lingering in the clothes department, or trying out the perfumes, but that day she found it impossible to distract herself with hats or cosmetics. She had intended to keep herself surrounded by people, and yet she felt utterly alone. She dallied aimlessly, feeling the warmth enter her bones but unable to relax. There was a competition in the lobby to guess the total of Winter Relief collected by the city of Berlin in the last six months. The winner could choose between the prize of a vacuum cleaner or a portrait of the Führer, and both of these cherished objects were displayed side by side. The portrait was one of Hoffmann's photographs, which had been badly colourized, with Hitler's low, sloping forehead and prominent nose rose-tinted in a way that defied irony. Hitler was striking the commanding, hands-on-hips pose that he had developed over the years to look intimidating, and his famously piercing blue eyes seemed to follow the observer like the Mona Lisa. It was a frightful thing. All the same, Clara wondered if anyone would be brave enough to choose the vacuum cleaner.

In the afternoon she went to a cinema. The air was thick with cigarette smoke and the smell of damp clothes. The newsreel was full of the recent Party rally and it moved on to images of the Duke of Windsor meeting workers. He was touring a factory, with a rictus smile on his face, mechanically shaking hands. The workers returned his salute and shouted 'Heil Windsor!' The Duchess was emptying her entire purse into the hands of an SA man for the Strength Through Joy fund. Clara dropped off to sleep momentarily, an uneasy doze from which she jerked and looked around her. Never relax, she told herself. *Never relax*. The place on her temple ached where she had hit the road and her head was throbbing again.

She reached into the pocket of her coat and found a handkerchief. It was a large, white man's handkerchief, stained brown with blood. The blood was hers, she knew, but the initials on the corner belonged to Ralph. He must have stuffed it into her pocket when he picked her off the road. She pressed it against her face, inhaling a faint trace of him. It was consoling to carry a little piece of him around with her.

After the film she walked further down the Ku'damm and sat in the companionable fug of Kranzler's, oily steam pressing against the misted windows, the ceiling stained nicotine yellow by decades of cigarettes, and a man beside her with a newspaper full of the victories in Spain. She glanced at the headlines and thought of the way Ralph talked about the imminence of war. How similar his language was to the way Arno Strauss talked. Mapping the terrain. Noticing every little change in the environment.

Watching which way the wind was blowing. Studying the lie of the land. But Strauss was talking about flying, and Ralph was talking about war. She imagined German bombers like a great flock of migrating birds darkening the European lands beneath them, and Strauss in the cockpit, losing the last traces of his fear.

Since Ralph had told her about the Gestapo shadow outside her apartment, every person she passed looked as though they might be the one. Was there anything about the man beside her that could mark him out as a tail? He was middle-aged, with calloused hands suggesting some form of manual work, and a worn heel to his shoes, which meant either that he did a lot of walking, or that he was short of cash, or both. He had a rash of spots on his neck and the faintest whiff of wurst about him. The man sensed her scrutiny and glanced indifferently in her direction before returning to his paper. Was he looking at her without interest because she was just one of a thousand suspects to be watched and followed, dehumanized? Or was he merely bored? She had lost all powers of discrimination.

Then, Clara thought, there was the other one. The man who had tried to kill her. Perhaps he was watching her even now, as she sat here finishing a cup of hot chocolate, gazing out of the café window. Maybe he was waiting for his second chance. What did he want from her? What did she know that was so important he would kill to keep it quiet?

She left Kranzler's and carried on. As the rain intensified she slipped into a Catholic church and sat in the flickering light, noting how the shrine to Our Lady now had a picture of Hitler above it, sharing the same lighted candle. The Virgin gazed frigidly into the distance, as if offended by this forced proximity. Clara had a sense of sanctuary in the church and perversely, in that dim, holy place, infused with the smell of incense and damp stone, her mind began to brim with the memory of sensual pleasure. She relived every moment she and Ralph had spent in bed together.

Ralph's hands caressing her, and his face, as his desire overcame the jealousy of Strauss and the mental barriers he had erected. His tousled hair and the fuzz of golden stubble rasping against her skin. His innate military posture, shoulders back, head straight, chin up. *If we were at war then this would be an order.* Then the way he bent to take her in his arms, ceding to the insubordination of desire. She yearned to be back in bed with him. She had not felt this way about a man since Leo.

She had felt safe there, in the circle of his arms. Whatever Ralph said about doubling the risk, the fact was, it was also shared, and it had been so long since she had someone to share it with. Clara wasn't cowardly. She had endured a long separation from her family and turned her face against feelings like this, but perhaps she had been wrong to think it was possible, or that she should even try.

She stayed in the church for a long time as the rain slackened, until checking her watch she saw that it was time to go.

Chapter Thirty-three

Heidi Kastner, a chorus girl at the Wintergarten Theatre, consoled herself that although her job was both tedious and repetitive, at least the setting was glamorous and the pay regular. The show required her and twenty-four other girls to switch from geisha costumes to schoolgirls, from sombreros to tiaras in the space of two and a half hours. At one point they had to arrive on stage on bicycles, and then, immediately after, dash back to change for the finale which involved wearing a cumbersome plume of ostrich feathers, that were a devil to fix on the hair, and a frilly strip of gauze across the body which covered barely anything.

When she came offstage that night Hedwig, the old woman who looked after the girls and their costumes and managed to perform repairs of infinite skill with a cigarette perched permanently at the corner of her mouth, signalled with a tilt of her head that a visitor awaited Heidi at the stage door.

'A Fräulein wants to see you.'

'What Fräulein?'

'How should I know?' Hedwig was stitching a froth of pink feathers to a bustier. 'She's been there a while.'

Outside in the corridor Heidi found a slender woman in a navy suit with soft brown hair and an anxious expression. Not the usual type of fan at all.

She offered her hand.

'Heidi Kastner? I'm Clara Vine. I wondered if we could have a quick word about someone you used to know – Anna Hansen?'

Half an hour later they were sitting round the corner in a smoke-filled bar, where most conversation was drowned by a piano thumping out old dance tunes. A woman in a French maid's outfit was gyrating on a dance floor, her every move shadowed by pairs of eager male eyes. After a while an old, fat waiter came onto the floor, dressed in a dinner jacket and carrying a feather duster. As the girl danced around he made a feint of whacking her short-skirted bottom to a chorus of encouraging shrieks.

'Do you like the job?' Clara asked.

Heidi tossed her frazzled blonde hair. 'At least it's varied. We have trapeze artists, acrobats, magicians, singers. There's a performing horse on tomorrow night. A real one, you know? It dances. Then it's all change. We're doing *The Merry Widow*. Again.' She narrowed her eyes and helped herself to another of Clara's cigarettes. 'So you want to know about Anna?'

'She used to work here with you at the Wintergarten? And before that in Munich?'

'We were dancers together in Munich. We worked the chorus in the Theater am Gärtnerplatz. Everyone worked there. There were up to two hundred girls in some productions. You could get ten costume changes in a performance. There was always loads of work.'

'So why did you come to Berlin?'

'Ach. There was no money in Munich. You could get better money cleaning houses, and you were risking your neck on those props. The place was always freezing too. Several of the girls died of pneumonia while I was there. I mean it! I've been here more than ten years now. Though it's just as cold.'

'But it's better money in Berlin?'

Heidi gave an instinctive glance around the bar, then crossed her arms and stared at Clara meaningfully.

'As I say, money matters.'

'Of course.' Clara took the hint. 'Here's something for your expenses.'

She slid some folded notes across the table, and Heidi swiftly placed them in her purse.

'So tell me about Anna.'

'What can I say? I've known Anna since I was ten. We grew up together. We used to talk at school about being dancers, even though her old man was dead against it. For a while she fooled around doing some dull secretarial job in a laboratory, but when I got my first job she was so jealous, she joined me in the theatre. We had a wild time.'

Heidi inhaled deeply and regarded Clara out of the corner of her eye.

'That was until Hitler appeared.'

From across the room there was a roar of approval as the waiter seized the French maid by the hips and pressed himself against her with repeated lascivious thrusts. The dancer feigned outrage as the audience egged the man on. Clara glanced away then leaned closer.

'He was always there. He loved variety shows and operetta. He liked something a bit daring, you know? A chance to let his hair down. The theatre manager was all over him. Everything for Herr Hitler. Nothing could be good enough. He wasn't even the Führer then, but we had a routine where we danced the can-can and ended with a Heil Hitler salute using our legs instead of our arms. He loved that. Anyhow, after the show we would all climb into chartered buses and stay in costume for the after-party at the Künstlerhaus. Everyone went there. They had this special room. The Astrological Hall, they call it, because the ceiling is covered in gold astrology signs, and there are rugs and cushions on the floor. You would be asked to do another performance in there which had to be even more risqué than the one you'd already done. There was an American girl, a dancer called Dorothy van

Bruck – that was her stage name anyway – who the men adored. She used to dance naked and when things started to droop she got herself plastic surgery. Sometimes she'd wear these transparent butterfly wings but mostly gentlemen didn't need their opera glasses, if you know what I mean.'

'Sounds pretty wild.'

'You have no idea. The Nazi Artists' Guild had files on all the girls with their statistics and personal details. And it wasn't just the ladies. There were plenty of young men there for those who liked that sort of thing. This is going back some time now, you understand.'

She sighed, and unconsciously stroked her neck in an upwards direction, as if smoothing out a decade of wrinkles.

'You were saying Anna met Hitler there.'

'Oh yes. She was all over Herr Hitler. As soon as they were introduced she flirted like mad with him. And he liked her. He must have done, because he gave her presents and flowers. But at the same time I could tell there was nothing in it. Hitler was never alone with her. He always had a group of people around him. That photographer, you know, Hoffmann. And his adjutant. Hoffmann was always taking pictures. It used to get on my nerves. And Hitler would bring along his old pal Ernst Röhm. The one who got himself executed a few years ago for sleeping with the choicer young lads of the SA.'

'So he and Anna weren't. . .?'

'Lovers? Not at all. Besides, Anna wouldn't have dared. She had a boyfriend already.'

'A boyfriend? Who was he?'

'Just a local lad. But he was the jealous type. No, I'm sure there was nothing in it.'

'In that case, what difference did it make? Anna meeting Hitler?'

'It's hard to explain, but quite soon after they were introduced,

Anna changed. She got above herself, like she was something special, you know? I couldn't understand it myself. I mean, it wasn't like he was giving her money, or anything. He wasn't even that famous then, the way he is now. After a while I couldn't stand it. Even though I was her best friend, I wanted to get away from her. That was when I started thinking about coming here.'

'Where eventually she followed you?'

Heidi gave a throaty chuckle.

'That was just like Anna. She turned up one day years later at the Wintergarten as if nothing had happened, all kisses and best friends again, so I thought, why not let bygones be bygones? It was good to see a friendly face and besides, I was on the lookout for someone to share the rent. I sorted her out with a job, then Anna got herself an SS boyfriend and, well, you know the rest.'

Some of the other dancers had arrived at the bar, caught sight of them and were approaching the table. Hastily Heidi pulled her purse towards her.

'I'm sorry Fräulein, I don't know anything else. I need to go now.'

She rose and paused, casting a quizzical glance at Clara.

'Just asking, but you don't know that old boyfriend of Anna's, do you?'

She nodded at the gash on Clara's temple, which she had tried to conceal with Max Factor foundation.

'Of course not. Why?'

'Because that bruise you've got there looks like just the kind of artwork he specialized in.'

Chapter Thirty-four

Joseph Goebbels' Propaganda Ministry was probably the only place in the Reich not lying about its food supplies. Which was ironic, considering the way it lied about everything else. On a trestle table in the conference room, a veritable feast had been ferried over from the Hotel Kaiserhof. Mountains of spicy marzipan Streuselkuchen, Apfeltorte glistening with apricot jam, Windbeutel cream puffs and Viennese Sachertorte were displayed on a magnificent silver cake stand. There may have been chronic shortages everywhere else in Germany but here was a spectacular array of fine white bread, not the gritty, black variety that the rest of the population ate, and a bulging heap of cheeses. Waiters with tea towels folded over their arms darted forward to ensure that everyone's glass was filled with sparkling wine. Nazi officials and journalists alike fell on the feast with alacrity, as though, like everything that proceeded from Goebbels' department, it might turn out to be an illusion. Mary, who had not had such a good meal for months, was not stinting.

The party was in honour of the film that had just been screened in the viewing theatre to mark Joseph Goebbels' birthday. There was not much of a story in it, but Mary was discovering that if you wanted to keep in with the Nazi authorities, it was a good idea to turn up when they asked. Despite an onerous workload as the head of Propaganda and Culture for the entire Reich, Goebbels had made time to oversee every aspect of this production, simply titled *Papi's Birthday*. It was a work of exquisite, almost Expressionist simplicity. There was no plot as such, merely a tableau of the Minister's life, or at least the life he wanted people to see, with pictures of his family at Schwanenwerder, Magda on the garden swing, little Helmut leading his pony across the lawn, Helga with the toy sewing machine Hitler had given her, and Goebbels himself cruising up the drive in his new Maybach sports car, arm resting on the door, and a wide grin on his face. It was to be screened in all cinemas, after the newsreel and before the main feature.

'Isn't the film absolutely killing? The family look adorable of course, but the Doktor's risking an awful lot with all those shots of his new sports car, don't you think? The Führer has bet me that people will throw things at the screen.'

'Anyone who does that had better watch out. I dread to think what the Doktor would do if he caught them.'

The sing-song cadences of upper-class English rising above the civilized clink of glasses caused Mary to turn round. Not far away were two women with gleaming blonde hair, tweed suits and silk scarves round their necks. They wore Peter Pan collars and pearls and the taller of the two had a prestigious gold Nazi Party badge on her bosom. They were unmistakeably the Mitford sisters.

Unity paused from demolishing a large piece of chocolate cake and laughed. 'Did you hear, Lord Rothermere has offered Goebbels a job at ten times his current salary? I bet he'll have second thoughts when he sees this.'

'Poor Doktor. Perhaps he's worried there'll be competition for first family of the Reich when Goering minor comes along. But the Goerings have got an awful lot of catching up to do.'

'Exactly. I can't see Frau Goering managing four little Hermanns.'

Mary was astonished. The lobby was heaving with senior aides, press liaison officers and officials from Ufa and some of them, presumably, could understand English. Not even the top Nazi brass dared make open mockery of the Herr Doktor. He might have a taste for vicious sarcasm, but Goebbels' sense of humour ran out where his own life was concerned. Yet the Mitfords, Mary suddenly realized, could say what they chose, even in the Minister's own domain. These young women had the protection of the Führer himself. It occurred to her that this was an incredible story. Had anyone properly considered the influence of the Mitford sisters? Did Americans even have a clue who they were? Europe could be on the brink of war, and the only people who had Hitler's ear were a pair of eccentric English girls. Mary moved nearer, eavesdropping shamelessly.

'Now, Bobo,' Diana was saying, 'I want you to come across to the Kaiserhof and see the Reichswehr uniforms that the darling Führer sent for my boys. It will be wonderful to see their little faces when they wear them. And a hoot to see everyone else's faces too. It's the only way I can bear the thought of going back to England. Lucky you staying here with him.'

'Isn't he marvellous? He's taking me to *The Merry Widow* later this week and right after that he's giving me a lift down to Munich on his train. I can't wait to get back there. I'm missing my dog awfully. And my rats.'

Did she really say rats? Mary almost choked on her cream puff.

'I'm frightfully jealous,' pouted Diana. 'Everyone's so gloomy in Berlin. I can literally think of nothing nicer than sitting in the Hofgarten and forgetting all this beastly talk about war.'

'Actually,' said Unity, 'the Führer told me Lord Halifax is coming out to meet him at the Berghof next month. I think it could be good news. I'm going to keep badgering him to make a deal with England. I've decided it's my mission.'

Mary was transfixed. Her first thought was that she was longing to tell Clara about this. Her second thought was to remember that she had something else to tell Clara – something that had been at the forefront of her mind for several days. Something Clara would badly want to know.

The problem was, Clara seemed to have disappeared. There was no reply from her telephone, though that in itself didn't mean much. All foreigners were cautious about using the telephone now and Clara was always careful in that regard. The day before, Mary had walked over to the apartment and engaged in a friendly chat with her old pal Rudi the Blockwart, who readily yielded up the information that Clara had not returned home for the past couple of nights. Though Rudi attempted to place a salacious spin on this fact, it probably meant nothing. Clara was no doubt away filming. Yet Mary felt a nagging anxiety. She needed to try again.

Slipping a few sandwiches and a cake into her handbag for later, Mary left the Propaganda Ministry and made her way to Winterfeldstrasse. Clara was home, Rudi gestured, but when she had laboured her way up the stairs and knocked on the door, Mary's smile faded.

'My God, Clara! What happened.'

'This?' Clara fingered the bruise on her temple, now going yellow at the edges. 'Oh, I fell over in the street. I was going to cover it, but I wasn't expecting visitors.'

Mary was worried. She stared at her friend, her eyes brimming with concern, then bustled into the apartment, put the kettle on for tea and laid out the Ministry's sandwiches on a plate, beside the battered cream cake. She had been intending to tell Clara about the visit to Schwanenwerder and the startling discovery she had made there, but the sight of her bruised forehead banished it momentarily from her mind.

She went over and placed a hand on her arm.

'There's something wrong, Clara. What is it?'

Clara wrapped her arms tightly round her chest and looked

away. She had no make-up and was wearing a plain white blouse which emphasized her pallor.

'It's nothing, I told you. I just fell over as I was crossing the road. You don't need to worry.'

Mary brought over the tea and sat herself down opposite Clara.

'You've been away. I came to find you yesterday and Rudi said he hadn't seen you for days. Something's happened, hasn't it? I'm your friend. You can tell me.'

Clara sipped her tea gratefully. 'You're sweet to worry. I do appreciate it, but there's nothing to tell.'

'Give me credit for having eyes in my head.'

'Honestly, Mary, it's nothing.'

There was something, Mary knew, but it was going to take some time to find it out. When Clara decided to keep something private, that was how it tended to remain. She bit down the implied rejection and carried on.

'OK. You don't want to tell me, so let's start with my news. Because this you do want to hear.'

She was gratified to have Clara's immediate attention. 'I went back to the Reich Bride School to take some photographs and I talked to that girl Ilse Henning again. She told me the Gestapo has been put onto the case. They've taken the investigation away from the Kripo, which seems awfully strange. The Kripo men had been kind to her – she'd found Anna's silver lighter and handed it in.'

'A lighter?'

'Yes. Quite a valuable thing with Anna's initials on it. But the Gestapo men seemed to think Ilse was hiding something. They treated her like she was working for the Red Front Fighters' League. She was scared out of her wits.'

Clara was alert, her mind whirring. 'Poor girl. How cruel they are.'

'Exactly. I can't work out why the Gestapo should have got involved, but I've found out something else, Clara. It's something you need to know. That artist friend of yours, Bruno Weiss? He's been working as a builder at the Schwanenwerder Bride School. Ilse pointed him out, so I took him aside and got him to tell me everything that's happened. But he was holding something back, Clara, I could tell. The guy was in quite a state. And he was desperate to see you.'

Chapter Thirty-five

The Moabit area of north Berlin was a grim district of rented flats and tenements crouching under a sullen sky. Clara passed the granite walls of Moabit prison and turned into Turmstrasse, heading for a high grey block in a courtyard of peeling plane trees. She climbed a dank stone staircase to the third floor and knocked, hoping that Mary had taken the address down correctly. Her heart was in her throat.

She barely recognized the figure who peered through the crack of the door. Bruno Weiss's hair had receded further from his brow, leaving only thin wisps across the skull, and his face was bled of colour. The skin was taut over his cheekbones, and his slender frame looked not so much undernourished as starved. For a man still in his thirties, he could have passed for two decades older. Yet at the sight of Clara a grin of delight spread across his face and he grabbed her inside swiftly and held out his arms.

'Clara Vine!' He hugged her to him, then kissed her formally on both cheeks, the way he always did. There was a pungent surge of sweat and unwashed clothes as his ribs jutted against her body like sticks.

'My God, I never thought I would see you again. Except on the screen. You're looking well.'

He peered outside nervously to see if they had been observed, then ushered her along the hall. 'Forgive my precautions. I feared it was other visitors entirely.'

Bruno's room looked as though it had been abandoned by its previous occupant. The floorboards were bare and a shiver of wind blew in through the cracked window. To one side there was a stained mattress and pair of cracked suitcases stood by the door.

'I've seen all your films, you know.'

'And I've been down to Munich to see your paintings, too.'

'You went there? Magnificent exhibition, wasn't it? And free entry too. Such enlightened politicians we have.'

The old, mocking humour came into his eyes. The defiance that told her Bruno's spirit had survived. He held onto her arms and gave her a searching look, as if assessing her motives, and as he did Clara felt a rush of shame at believing Bruno would ever have denounced her under police questioning. The lines scored in his face suggested he had been interrogated, but there was nothing but honest affection in his eyes.

'It's so good to see you, Clara. Are you still keeping an eye on that lad Erich? How is he?'

She shrugged. 'Moody. Passionate. Temperamental. The last time I saw him he accused me of not loving Hitler.'

Bruno gave a wry smile.

'Perceptive boy.'

Clara winced. Since their argument and the threat against him she felt a desperate urge to see Erich, but she didn't dare. She dreaded the possibility that she might have drawn him into danger.

'He's a good boy, Bruno. He adores the HJ right now, but he'll see through them in time. He's very intelligent.'

'Like his mother then.' He shrugged. 'I think I know why you're here.'

'Don't worry. You can trust me.'

'How could I ever doubt that?' He gestured towards a table where an ashtray overflowed, as elegantly as if it were a dinner table at the Adlon, and bowed stiffly. 'Please, sit. Forgive my less than perfect housekeeping.'

He made her a glass of tea, and as he placed it on the table she noticed his hands were shaking. Bruno had an artist's hands, large and capable, with fingers which had always been stained with paint and even now were weathered and workmanlike. Except for the tremor. She wondered if he would ever be able to paint again.

Brightly, she said, 'I don't think I've ever seen you when you didn't smell of turpentine.'

He scooped away a lank wisp of hair from his face. 'A treacherous fragrance, turpentine. I keep well away from it. It's the kind of perfume that could get me locked up.'

'You think turpentine could get you noticed?'

'They notice everything. Sights, sounds, smells. If there's one thing I've learned, Clara, it's not to underestimate them. Once I was excluded from the Reich Chamber of Art, it meant I couldn't paint. I might have thought I could keep it up behind my own four walls, but I reckoned without the ways of the Gestapo. They make lightning raids to check if your brush is wet. They check up at art supply shops to see if banned artists are ordering paint. Eventually I realized I would have to abandon painting completely. Down in Munich I had no way to earn a living, and the chances of getting work as a Jew are, as you know, much harder in beautiful Bavaria.'

'So you came back to Berlin.'

He shrugged. 'It's safer here. It's easier to disappear.' He reached for a scrap of tobacco and began rolling out a cigarette, shaping it elegantly, smoothly, like a piece of origami. Hastily Clara drew from her bag the cobalt-blue tin of cigarettes with a picture of Ernst Udet on the lid.

'Take them, please.'

Bruno picked up the tin, scrutinized it and smiled. 'As a matter of fact, a cigarette was how I got back into it. One day, an old friend I had been talking to left a packet of cigarettes on the table and when I looked at them I found an address written on the inside. It was a place in Rudow, on the outskirts of Neukölln. When I went there I found a couple of guys operating a construction company. A chap called Max Grabowski, and his brother Otto. They had a shed with paint, wallpaper, supplies and equipment, that sort of thing, and hidden inside there was a printing machine. They had been producing some flyers denouncing German involvement in the Spanish war and they wanted my help.'

Clara remembered the first time she had ever seen one of Bruno's pamphlets. She had been sitting outside Kranzler's café when she found a leaflet on the seat beside her, extolling the German Communist Party, the KPD.

'That's dangerous, Bruno.'

He raised his eyebrows and gave her a frank look. 'And you think what you do isn't? But you're right, Clara. It's getting harder. The Gestapo watch everything. They even count the number of office supplies and stamps that people buy in bulk. That way they can work out if anything covert is going on. Our people have to be extremely careful. One guy gets his brother to play the violin to disguise the sound of his typewriter keys. The only problem is, his brother plays so badly he fears the neighbours will have him arrested on account of the noise.'

He laughed delightedly, and Clara wondered how he managed to retain a sense of humour in such perilous circumstances.

'So how long have you been pamphleteering?'

'A couple of months now. We've been dropping them everywhere you can think of: mailboxes, telephone booths, luggage racks on trains. One of our people is a doctor and he posts our little flyers on the pretext of making house calls.'

'And you?'

'I only go a couple of times a week. It's something to do at night when I can't sleep. I keep waking up thinking I hear the crunch of boots on concrete outside or banging on the door.'

'Bad dreams.'

'Usually, thank God. Except when it's real. When I first came to this apartment I was sharing with another man but one morning there was a knock at the door and two policemen arrived. They told me to stay in bed, while they took him. They barely gave him time to dress. When I looked, the policeman shook his pistol in my face. I asked where they were taking him, but they ignored me. I was lucky not to be taken myself. Max Grabowski found out what happened. He was guillotined at Plötzensee Prison.'

Bruno blinked and looked away. Clara focused on her tea. Silence hung heavily between them. People here were getting used to these silences in conversation. They observed them, the same way they might observe a commemoration for the dead. They were eloquently emotional, dense with memory. Yet within a few seconds, Bruno assumed a lighter tone.

'Enough of me. It's another sad story you're after today, isn't it? I take it you want to know about Anna Hansen?'

'I remember she used to model for you, didn't she? Way back?'

'Yes. You met her once, I think. Anna was quite a character. She liked to live on the wild side. I can't say I'm wholly surprised she ended up dead. Not half so surprised as I was when she turned up a Reich Bride.'

'How did you come to see her again?'

'That's the funny thing, if anything can be called funny in this story. It was pure chance. I had to eat, and there's so much construction work going on in the city that they'll hire anyone, even Jews. I was called up to a job on Schwanenwerder, building a little model cottage in the garden of the Reich Bride School. It was a pleasant job and I was enjoying myself. Out in the sunshine and fresh air, plenty of pretty girls to look at. Then one day I got the shock of my life because I saw a girl who looked the spitting image of Anna Hansen. She was attending a lesson on being an obedient bride and because it was a sunny morning they were taking the lesson in the garden. I nearly choked. It was definitely Anna. I couldn't fathom what she was doing there, but you don't spend a month painting a woman and not recognize her, even if she is disguised in an apron and a dirndl.'

'Was she pleased to see you?'

'Put it this way. I've had some luck with women in my time, but I've never seen a girl so keen to see me. She could hardly control herself. She passed me a note, asking me to come back that night and we met up at the back of the garden, behind the trees. I thought she had something else in mind until she told me her story.'

'And what was her story?'

Bruno moved over to the window and looked down at the street below, before dragging the tablecloths that were serving as curtains across the window and switching on the lamp. Unconsciously, he lowered his voice.

'Anna was a pretty girl but she had an eye on the main chance. She made sure she'd collected a whole lot of secrets that their owners would rather not have publicized. That was just how she operated. She didn't have a lot of morals. Back in Munich she'd been surviving by withdrawing money from the account of an elderly Jew who had been obliged to emigrate. She said he owed her money as his housekeeper. When that money ran out and she needed a new source of funds so she decided she would have to rely on her artistic talents. She'd been a dancer.'

'At the Theater am Gärtnerplatz?'

'You know it? Back in the day that place was famous for the after-parties they'd throw. Decadent parties, to borrow the Nazis' favourite phrase. Girls dancing naked, men and girls together, men and men, girls and girls. Anything went. I did some paintings based on what Anna told me. You might have seen them if you went to Joey Goebbels' art exhibition.'

Clara recalled *The Devil's Bacchanal*, the contorted bodies and their naked writhings.

'What did Anna tell you about the parties?'

'Hitler and his gang used to attend. Anna claimed she got to sit on his lap and he told her she was a special favourite. But that was as far as the decadence went, she said. She was already sleeping with the darkroom assistant at Heinrich Hoffmann's photographic shop. He was a nasty piece of work, Anna said. It made sense that he worked with chemicals because his face was as bitter as a bottle of acid.'

'What was his name?'

'She never said. But she reckoned he was her ticket to a better life. The thing was, Hoffmann used to take pictures at these parties. At that time, Hoffmann went everywhere Hitler went and he took photographs of just about everything. He would snap Hitler in the mirror, making gestures and funny faces. Practising for his speeches. Whatever Hitler did, wherever he went, Heinrich Hoffmann would be in the background, snapping away. The deal was, Hitler would let Hoffmann have exclusive access to his private life and make him his official photographer, provided that Hitler would get to see every single picture he took. That way, he could keep absolute control over his image.

'Did it work?'

'Like a charm. Hoffmann and Hitler used to spend hours poring over every frame, and any picture Hitler didn't like, the negative would be smashed. They were working with the old glass negatives then, so they were easy to destroy. They smashed thousands and thousands of them. It was important, you see, that the right image should be portrayed. Hitler was clever. He was always aware of that. You don't want a picture of your Führer looking absurd, though some of us would say he can't help it. Anything unflattering, wearing the wrong clothes, or with his mouth open, or his eyes half shut, or with undesirable characters – which to me would be everyone he knows – those negatives all got destroyed. The trouble was, there were so many that Hoffmann couldn't manage to destroy them all. So he would give this guy, Anna's boyfriend, the job of smashing up some of the negatives, and Anna came too. Well, you can imagine what she did. She took a couple for herself, without his knowledge. Just for a rainy day.'

'What were these pictures of?'

'Anna didn't say. Years later, long after they'd split up, she was in a fix and needed the money, so she went looking for him. By this time she had moved to Berlin and was doing a bit of dancing at the Wintergarten and this guy had also left Munich and got himself a job up here. It was a good job, lots of money, so Anna reckoned it was payback time. She told him what she had and asked him how much he was going to give her for the negatives. If he didn't pay up she was going to sell them to an American newspaper. That was a big mistake.'

Bruno looked around and lowered his voice to a whisper.

'The guy went crazy when she told him. Threatened her and everything. She said she realized he might even kill her, only she didn't have the negatives with her right then, and he badly wanted them back. Not so much because they might cause a problem for his beloved Führer, though they would, but because it would point the finger at him. He'd been the one entrusted with disposing of those things. It would be his fault if they came to light emblazoned across the front page of some foreign newspaper.'

'So Anna didn't give him the negatives?'

'Precisely. The guy changed tack, went all sensitive and told her to meet him and bring the negatives with her, but Anna was scared. She was a tough girl and it was hard to fool her. She realized she might be signing her own death warrant if she actually turned up like he said. She knew she needed to escape. She had to disappear, and the best way she could think of doing that was to get married. Where could be safer than an SS Bride School?'

'You usually need an SS officer for that.'

'Anna did say meeting Johann was a stroke of luck. And to her credit, she seemed genuinely fond of the poor boy, but still she was scared. She felt certain the old boyfriend was going to track her down. The day I saw her she was terrified because there had been a photograph that morning in the women's pages of *Der Angriff*. It showed the Bride School girls doing gymnastics right there in the garden and Fräulein Anna Hansen was standing in the front row. She was certain he'd see it, and work out where she was.'

'So he did?'

Bruno shrugged. 'I guess so.'

'What will you do now?'

'I can't go back to Schwanenwerder. Not now that girl has told the police about her suspicions. The place is crawling with secret policemen. I would be arrested in an instant. I shall need to find some more papers. And another place to live, of course.' He gestured towards the suitcases in the corner.

'I was packing when you arrived. I should have gone already but after I saw your friend Fräulein Harker and gave her this address, I thought I would hang on. Just in case.'

Clara leaned over and placed her hand on his arm. 'You must come and stay with me, Bruno.'

'You know that's not possible.' He smiled wistfully. 'I have often thought of the time when Herr Quinn offered me a visa for England, and I have wondered if I should have accepted it. That will have to remain in the realm of conjecture. I have friends. You mustn't worry.'

'What will you do now?'

'What I always do. Daytimes I spend waiting, planning paintings in my head. Drawing with pencil on the back of paper bags, and pages torn from books. I plan to study the frieze at the Pergamon Museum. I thought I might make a sculpture myself, something about a struggling people oppressed, when all this is over.'

As he showed her to the door a brilliant smile lit up his gaunt face and he spread his arms expansively. 'Don't worry, dear girl. This barbarity won't last. A nation that has produced Goethe and Rilke and Caspar David Friedrich couldn't endure this state of affairs for long.'

It was raining again when Clara left, sharp little razor blades of rain. She pulled her collar up and made her way back to Winterfeldstrasse, oblivious to the traffic and the people around her, so lost in thought that she was almost at her front door before she noticed the hulking black Mercedes with its engine running, waiting outside.

Chapter Thirty-six

Dressed in her long-serving duffel coat because of the penetrating cold, Mary was perched in her habitual pose – nose six inches from her Remington typewriter and eyes squinting in concentration. She was trying to write about the Bride School murder, but it was no good relying on the local press for details. Unlike the journalists at home, who would have pounced on a murder with delight and spent days eviscerating the case in ghoulish detail, newspapers here preferred to focus on the miraculous achievements of the Reich. Mary had flipped through them in vain and found nothing but the record harvest and the triumph of Mussolini's visit. The premiere of a new film to be attended by Goebbels. Good news from abroad. In Spain the Fascists had encircled Madrid and a Republican destroyer, *Ciscar*, had been sunk by Nationalist aircraft.

Spain. For a moment, Mary took off her glasses and rubbed her tired eyes. The thought of Spain brought troubling memories. Something had happened there which she could still not properly work out.

When spring came she had moved up from Madrid to the north of the country and a small village in the Basque stronghold of Bilbao. At that point this area of the country, including Santander, was still in Republican control but the Nationalists were launching new offensives all the time. That evening the International Brigade fighters were playing guitars and singing revolutionary songs out in the dusty square and Mary was in a bar, watching the bartender flicking dead flies off the counter and moping over the collapse of another love affair. Alfonso had been dark-eyed and charming and utterly useless. His hands smelled of guns and he spent every evening sodden with drink. He told Mary she was too independent for a man. Men were scared of her, Alfonso explained. At least he had tried to explain, in a very unromantic drunken monologue, until the sheer intellectual effort exceeded him and he collapsed in a puddle of Rioja and self-pity. Eventually Mary decided she might as well join him in alcoholic oblivion. She was on her second carafe of rough local wine, mopping the occasional tear, when a young man walked through the door.

'Pericles!'

It was the Englishman from the hotel in Madrid. He didn't seem at all surprised to see her.

'Hello, Mary. Why are you crying into your glass when you should be filing reports?'

He slid onto a chair next to her. His curly hair had been bleached in the sun and he had the beginnings of a beard. He wore a beret and an old blue jacket on top of a collarless shirt.

'There was another successful counter-attack today . . .'

Mary lifted a hand to forestall him. 'Stop right there. I don't want to talk about the war. I'm sick of it. I'm sick of all politics,' she slurred.

'Fine.' He offered her a Gauloise and she accepted it quickly. Tobacco was in short supply at that time and packets were ten pesetas apiece. 'Let's talk about you then. But before that, let's find you something to eat.'

He took her off to another bar and magicked up a hot meal of salami, rice and olives which she ate as though famished. Pericles watched her intensely as sobriety descended and eventually he had coaxed the whole sorry tale out of her.

'I never meet a suitable man. The interesting ones are either married or mad. The uninteresting ones want me to live in New Jersey and wash socks. I'm no good with men. I don't think I'll ever get married!' she had wailed.

'Why would you want to?' he asked, in all seriousness. 'Who wants to be hobbled in some eternal three-legged race? You're better as you are, Mary. You're free.'

She looked at him wet-eyed with gratitude. It seemed, in the lingering haze of drunkenness, as if he had just shown her an entirely new way to live.

'You're right. Marriage would ruin everything, wouldn't it?'

She sniffed and tilted her glass at him.

'How would I continue my magnificent career?'

She was half joking but he chose to take her seriously. 'Exactly. And on that subject I have a tip for you. There's something happening later today, not far from here. It's something you'll want to cover. A scoop. The Germans have been holding a military conference in Burgos under Wolfram von Richthofen, the commander of the Condor Legion. You know who I mean?'

'Of course.'

'Good. The thing is, they're planning to target Republican troops at Guernica.'

'I've not heard of it.'

'No reason you should have. It's a market town about thirty-five kilometres away. Why not head out and take a look? I guarantee it will be worth your while.'

The flames were still burning when she arrived on the outskirts of Guernica at dawn the next morning with a couple of local fighters in a ramshackle van. The glow lit up the sky from miles away and as they approached they met civilians struggling along in ox-drawn carts and tractors, all their possessions piled high. Out in the parched fields bodies were splayed and blackened corpses leaned out of burned cars, half incinerated. Once they reached the town itself the scenes were worse than she could imagine.

Until Mary had arrived in Spain she had never seen a dead body apart from her father's, turning slowly yellow in his mahogany bed back home. She might have said she knew what death looked like, but she knew it wasn't true. Guernica was a different dimension of death altogether. These bodies had been wrenched out of life in the middle of it, eyes open and mouths agape. Some were buried in ash and others burned alive. Then there were the living, who moved as though the soul had been sucked out of them, scrabbling through the smoking ruins with their bare hands, searching for their loved ones. Basque soldiers were lining up the bodies outside the church of Santa Maria, which was the only building still standing. And everywhere the rank smell of burned flesh caught in the throat. Standing in the marketplace where bombs had rained from the sky, Mary was aware of an eerie stillness, a kind of outraged silence, broken only by cries and shouts as another charred corpse emerged from the decimated buildings and the frantic barking of dogs.

She wandered around the market square stunned, robotically clutching her notebook like a doctor with a stethoscope. Houses were still collapsing around her into heaps of glowing debris, sending out showers of sparks and bricks bouncing like tennis balls. She knelt down beside a farmer who was cradling a boy of about fourteen and moaning repetitively. 'My son needs some air! Just let him have some air and sun on his face.' The man snatched at the feathers that were whirling like snow out of a split pillow and grabbed handfuls to prop up the boy's head. His cries were harsh and jagged, like an animal's. Mary took one look at the boy and saw he had plainly been dead for hours.

She met a priest coming out of the church who told her a third of the inhabitants had been killed. All the men and women he had ushered into bomb shelters at the beginning of the raid had been burned alive. He told her he had trained his binoculars on the sky and seen a squadron of planes coming in close, circling high, and by the drone of their engines he knew they were German planes – the Legion Condor.

It turned out that Mary was one of the first journalists on the scene. She filed yards of copy, which Nussbaum ran on the front page.

It was clear at once that Guernica marked a change in warfare. Something grave and terrible was written on the faces of those people in the market square. Though there were Republican forces in the area, the village had never been involved in any fighting. A place like Guernica had no air defences. What Mary had seen was sheer terror bombing, the strafing of people with no defences, to intimidate and terrify. Children weren't a military target. They weren't an industry or a vital infrastructure. The true target of Guernica was the people's morale. What sort of men would do this kind of thing?

Mary wrote that in the next war, when it came along, air attack was going to be the prime weapon of terror. The idea of wiping whole towns, perhaps even entire cities off the map, was now a reality.

Yet when she thought about it, there was one thing she could not puzzle out. If it hadn't been for Pericles, Mary would not have been there. He had known for certain that the Germans were planning an attack. But at the time she had never asked herself where he got his information from. He was English, not German. So how had he known? What's more, how had he known that Mary would be sitting in that bar, on that evening, ready to witness it?

Pericles knew Guernica was going to be important. He guessed it would be the attack that drew the attention of the world.

But if he had advance warning, why didn't he try to stop it? Why didn't he alert the townspeople to what was coming? Unless, of course, he thought it needed to happen.

The shock of Guernica had faded quickly. For Mary, writing about Spain presented the same problem she now faced when covering Germany's troubles. Nobody at home much wanted to know. Americans were preoccupied by their own concerns. Apparently thousands of people were starving in Cleveland, Ohio. A United Airlines plane had crashed in Utah. The New York Yankees had beaten the New York Giants in the World Series. No matter how hatefully the Jews were persecuted in Germany, too many people back in America actually agreed with the Nazis. Mary got the feeling that people back home preferred foreign affairs to stay just that – foreign.

The death of Anna Hansen, on the other hand, was just what the American public liked, according to Frank Nussbaum. A murder story with plenty of photographs of pretty girls. All Mary needed to do was deliver it. But that was where the problem lay. When she called up the bureau of criminal investigations the police could not be less interested. They admitted, grudgingly, that Hartmann, the gardener, had been released, but would not reveal if anyone else was under suspicion. Judging by the sleepy tone of the officer in charge, the death of the Reich Bride mattered about as much as a bicycle collision and a little less than the theft of a bratwurst from a market stall. Yet Ilse Henning had told her the Gestapo was involved. Which meant that somehow, Anna Hansen's murder mattered very much indeed.

That was why Mary was impatient to hear what Bruno Weiss had to say. She did not believe for a second that the artist could have had a hand in Anna's murder, yet he had been distinctly reluctant to talk to her, all the same. When she approached him on that day in the Bride School garden, it was terror, nothing less, that leapt into his eyes. Even when he had established that she was a friend of Clara Vine's and had ushered her away somewhere private, behind the tall pines at the back, he would barely speak to her. He kept looking about him, wide-eyed, as if the very trees and shrubs concealed devices which might overhear and report him. Bruno Weiss had about him the terrible, feral caution of the hunted animal. Mary recognized that look. She had seen it before. It was the fear of approaching death, and it needed no translation.

Chapter Thirty-seven

Memories flickered through Clara's traumatized brain. She thought of her mother, and tried to remember what it was like to be embraced by her, but she couldn't recall her face. For a long time she only had a photograph to remember her by and photographs never really told the truth, did they?

Clara wondered if she would ever have a daughter herself, and if she did whether she would fold her in her arms the way her own mother must have done. She couldn't forget the face of the tiny baby at the Lebensborn home. More images floated through her mind. Angela with her cool, combative elegance. Her strawberry-blonde hair and wry half smile that always implied Clara was doing something slightly offbeat, bohemian or plain crazy. Erich, the tears smarting in his eyes as he accused Clara of not loving the Führer. Mary's anguished face. *'I'm your friend Clara. You can tell me!'*

She regretted not telling Mary the truth, but friendship these days meant not telling anything. Confidences were dangerous. To love someone, it was necessary to deceive them. How had it come to this, that the true measure of closeness came in what you concealed? You could know everything about a person, how they brushed their teeth, what perfume they wore, whether they preferred Arabica or Java, even what position they favoured in lovemaking, but you could not know their deepest secrets. Not if they loved you. To love someone was to lie. And Clara was good at lying. It was her skill.

She thought of herself with Ralph, their bodies rolling and turning in the tumbled linen, the sheets between their hot limbs like heaped clouds. His hands mapping the contours of her body, her fingers running through his damp hair and along the deep cleft of his back. His lips, moving towards hers. The days they had spent in his apartment had been like a world apart. Only two days, yet she treasured that time, in case it never came again. She relived it in her head, hour by hour, as though just by thinking she could block out everything around her.

Clara was in a small white-tiled room, measuring barely six feet across, with a wooden plank bed which was let down from the wall. There was a bare bulb which swung every time the steel doors along the corridor clanged, throwing wild shadows across the walls. Although there was no natural light, she guessed it must be dawn. She wondered how long she could hold out before needing to use the bucket in the corner. Her mouth was dry and she could barely swallow, but no one had offered her water. The wash of disinfectant couldn't entirely mask the stink of ammonia and the smell of fear. She remembered Bruno telling her about the night classes he had once attended in this building, when it was still an art school. They practised a different kind of art here now.

She tried not to think about what she had heard. Of the tortures, the twisted limbs, the broken fingers. Persuasive measures to jog the memory. The faltering moment when a prisoner's story changed. The faces of people who had been interrogated, pulply and swollen, unrecognizable to their own family. She wondered when they would start on her own face.

The sounds were sporadic. The slam of steel doors, the crunch of footsteps, hard and booted, the occasional yell, of fury or fear. An official voice, feigning patience but underlaid with a steely anger.

And in the distance was the clatter of traffic from Prinz Albrecht Strasse outside and the footsteps of people going through the government district towards the Anhalter Bahnhof, ordinary citizens who, though they had no interest in what happened within, still averted their eyes from the grim, neoclassical façade.

Why was she here? Did Goebbels know? Was it his idea to arrest her? She thought of him, limping down the corridor in his patent leather shoes, which everyone said concealed a cloven hoof, like the devil. Goebbels had asked her to report back on the Mitford sisters, but surely he was not intending to elicit her discoveries in this setting?

Then she thought of Gisela Wessel, arrested at the studio and brought here for interrogation. Clara knew, though she tried not to think about the lengths to which they would go to get the answers they wanted. She thought of Gisela's face plunged repeatedly into freezing water, lungs tearing for air, gloved hands grasping her hair. What other methods would they resort to? There must be special horrors reserved for female prisoners. Those sadists were as attentive as a lover to the sensations their hands could provoke. Like seducers they took pains to get a woman to surrender.

Even though she had no clue why she was arrested, it was still essential for her to work out what the Gestapo believed. If there was a suspicion that she might be passing information to the British, then there was no hope for her. She wondered how long it would be before anyone realized she was missing. Would Mary start to ask questions, even though she had assured her there was nothing to worry about? Would Albert report her absence from the studio? And Ralph? Clara remembered what Ralph had said about disowning her if she was apprehended. She hoped for his sake that was true.

There was the sound of boots coming down the corridor. She knew they were coming for her.

Fear ran through her like a steel blade. Terror settled right in the marrow of her bones. She had never pretended to anyone that she was courageous. Not even to herself. She was not abnormally brave. She was terrified at the prospect of pain and was calculating wildly who, if anyone, could save her from it. She would not even have hesitated to ask her father to intercede, though how she would get a message to him wasn't clear. She wondered, perhaps, if the mention of the Mitford sisters might work the same charm on the Gestapo as it had on Adolf Hitler, but the idea would have been laughable, if she was capable of laughing.

Her flesh felt defencelessly soft, like a child's. Bruises were appearing on her upper arms, like photographic negatives against the white of her skin, recording the brutality of the previous night. Her ear was ringing and painful from where the back of a hand had lashed her. She knew there would be several interviews, going over and over the same ground. So far, she had only survived the first.

Hauptsturmführer Oskar Wengen's face was cadaverous. It reminded her of an ancient preserved mummy, found in some distant Teutonic swamp. The skin clung to the skull beneath, perfectly delineating the bones, folding down the throat in ropey sinews. Only the eyes were alive and watchful, like a snake, with the same fathomless depth.

The room smelled of human fear. When Clara was brought in, he had gestured at a wooden chair opposite his desk and with a jolt she saw a manila file bearing her name and the stencilled numbers 6732. What could it possibly contain?

She decided to take the initiative.

'On what charge have I been arrested?'

Wengen smiled grimly, his thin lips pressed as though they had been stitched together. 'You have not been arrested, Fraülein Vine. You have been invited here for questioning.'

'There's no point questioning me. I don't know anything.'

'I hope you're not suggesting that we would have brought you in here for no reason. That might be an arrestable offence in itself. Do you know why you are being questioned?'

'Of course I don't know. Why don't you tell me?'

'I'm waiting for you to consider why you might have been brought here.'

'I told you. I haven't the faintest idea.'

'It might be good for you if you began to have some ideas.'

He didn't ask her about the burglary. Perhaps they didn't know about it. She hoped against hope that they had not tailed her all the way from Moabit, because if they had it would mean discovering Bruno, and perhaps through him a whole circle of brave people manning the printing works. Yet to start with, Hauptsturmführer Wengen seemed more interested in her work at Babelsberg.

'We are checking some disturbing information from one of your friends.'

In her pocket her fingers encountered the handkerchief that Ralph had given her. The thought of it was a fresh cause for alarm. God forbid that they should find it, or ask questions about the person with the initials RS.

'None of my friends would supply you with disturbing information about me because it would be false.'

'That's for us to decide. Who do you associate with at the studio?'

'Let me think. I see Herr Doktor Goebbels frequently.' The quip earned her a savage look.

'Names, please.'

'I see hundreds of people. It might be easier just to check the cast list of my films, Herr Hauptsturmführer.'

'I assume you don't spend your time drinking with a cast of hundreds.'

'I rarely spend time drinking at all.'

She racked her brains to think who might have denounced her. Gisela Wessel had probably been in this same interrogation cell.

Might she have mentioned Clara? It seemed unlikely, they barely knew each other. It couldn't be Mary, could it? The Gestapo regularly visited foreign correspondents to question them about their informants. Might someone have seen the two of them together in the Press Club and jumped to conclusions? To stop the shudder of nerves, she braced her shoulders in a semblance of calm resolve. The calmer she appeared, the more furious Wengen grew.

'You must have friends there, surely?'

There was only Albert. And she couldn't mention Albert. Albert's preference for young men would be enough to have him sacked and in a concentration camp before his feet touched the ground.

'I try to be friendly to everyone.'

'Everyone? It's difficult, surely, to be friends with everyone, Fräulein?'

'You forget I'm an actress, Herr Hauptsturmführer.'

He cast her a frosty glance, but there was something else troubling her. A thought that had flickered in and out of the depths of her mind, like a hideous fish in deep water. It might have been anyone who had informed on her, so why did she have the feeling that it was someone close to her, someone who might know where she was and when? At that moment when Hauptsturmführer Oskar Wengen asked her about her friends, the answer came. His kind, crinkled eyes. His careful avoidance of direct questions, which she had taken for tact. His dangerous secret that made him vulnerable to any kind of blackmail. *Albert.* He could not be trusted. Albert must have informed on her.

It should have hurt to think that she had been betrayed by someone so close, who had laughed with her and cared for her and followed every step of her career since she first arrived in Berlin. The skinny young man who had grown stylish and self-assured, apart from the big secret that made him vulnerable. Was that why he was so loathe to ask her too many questions? Because he didn't want to implicate her any more than necessary? Yet he had insisted she keep the red Opel, which meant that her movements were easy to track. Being denounced by Albert should have hurt far more, but at that moment all she felt was a rush of relief. That she had not betrayed Ralph. Indeed, that they had not even asked about him.

Wengen tried a fresh tack. His voice took on a conciliatory tone.

'We cannot always be aware of the secrets of our associates. Sometimes we mingle with undesirable people without knowing it.'

She felt his gaze raking her face, looking for the spark of desperation that said she was ready to break in exchange for handing over some information. That suggested she might implicate others in the hope of going free herself.

'The activities of those people stain our good name and land us in all kinds of trouble.'

'What kind of trouble am I in then, Herr Hauptsturmführer?'

The conciliatory tone evaporated as suddenly as it had appeared.

'A lot of trouble if you don't start answering my questions. I want the names of everyone you associate with, Fräulein Vine. You must have some special friends in that crew of Jews and Communists up at Babelsberg. A pretty woman like you.'

She forced herself to stare unflinchingly into the black pits of his eyes.

'The German woman finds her truest friends within the Party. Isn't that what Gertrud Scholtz-Klink says?'

Wengen laughed, a jagged laugh that cut through the air like a saw. And that was the first time he hit her.

That was yesterday. Now, at dawn, the clanking boots were coming for her again. She could feel the pressure rising in her skull. She tried to summon again the energy for the great effort of dissembling but she began to tremble, involuntarily, and felt her bowels clench within her. This was her second interview, when they would go over the ground they had already covered. Whom did she associate with? Who might she be passing information to? Which of her friends were secret Communists or Jews? And with each question there would be fresh blows, until she gave them some different answers. How long would she be able to hold out? Hours, or even days? There was no lawyer to help her, and no one knew where she might be. She had left Ralph's apartment despite her promise to him and, angry though he would be, he must assume she was staying safe somewhere, far away from her own home. No one in Berlin was worrying about Clara, or checking their watch for when she got back, or calling the police to report her missing. She wished it was over already, that time had jumped forward and she was in a truck on her way to a camp. That way she might still have her secrets safe with her.

The guard unlocked the door, and handed her the case and her bag.

'You are free to go, Fräulein.'

'What do you mean?'

'Unless you choose to avail yourself of our hospitality a little longer.'

Clara stumbled out into the cool Berlin air and looked around her. Everywhere she saw people walking to their jobs, to the station on Stresemannstrasse, to meet friends, to catch trains, as though they were on a different planet, as if the grotesquerie of the building behind her simply didn't exist. She gathered herself up and headed away as fast as she could. She felt a giddy mixture of excitement and fear. Like the sensation she had when Strauss's plane had pulled out of its dive. Relief at disaster averted. Euphoria at still being alive.

But the euphoria only lasted a moment, before it was replaced by bewilderment. If Albert had informed on her, then he would have entrusted his suspicions to the head of the studios. The man responsible for all cultural activity in the Third Reich. Joseph Goebbels. Goebbels must be the reason she had been tailed and arrested. He had decided that if Albert was right, and Clara was hiding anything, the political police would find it out. But if Goebbels was the reason she was arrested, what, or who, was the reason she had been released?

Chapter Thirty-eight

At the corner of Friedrichstrasse and Unter den Linden, which had once been the top gathering spot for the city's prostitutes, a model torpedo rocket with glinting silver fins had been erected. It was positioned as though poised to smash into the very pavement beneath it, and alongside was displayed a colourful map of Europe showing all the countries which bordered Germany with cartoon bomber squadrons pointing ominously at the Fatherland. Above the map was the slogan: *Air Defence For Every German*. Two sentries in steel helmets bearing collecting tins shuffled their massive boots alongside. Mary noticed that most people ignored the map and quickened their step as they passed. No one wanted to take geography lessons from the National Socialists.

Mary had been looking forward to seeing Charles Lindbergh again. As far as she knew, she was the only journalist to be invited to the reception, which had to mean Lindbergh himself had requested her name be included. The very idea of it sent a ripple of pleasure through her. Lindbergh had asked for her! Not only would anything the great aviator said be a scoop, but more than that, she would get an opportunity to thank him personally for fixing her return to Berlin. Camera at the ready, she had arrived at the Adlon with high hopes.

The Adlon was, as ever, a warm oasis of luxury, where

chandeliers glinted above a marble floor. It seemed to exist in another universe from the real Berlin, with tantalizing smells wafting from the grill room and bowls of freshly cut hothouse roses on every table. Mary spotted Lindbergh at once, towering above a sea of Nazi officialdom. Flashbulbs exploded around him as he pumped hands with men in uniform. At the age of thirty-five, with rumpled fair hair and a keen blue gaze, he cut a striking figure. Already that day he had toured Tempelhof and piloted a bomber, visited a couple of airfields and lunched at the Berlin Air Club. Now he was surrounded by an impermeable wall of Lufthansa executives and military attachés, all anxious to hear his views on the build-up of the German air force.

Mary, it went without saying, could not tell one end of a plane from another, and after half an hour she realized if she had to listen to one more Nazi talking about the performance characteristics of the ME 109 or the superiority of the Junkers Ju 88, she was going to scream. It took a while to elbow her way through the uniformed scrum, but eventually she managed to battle her way through to Lindbergh's side, just as he was off to be presented with a ceremonial sword as an honoured guest of Germany.

He seemed delighted to see her and shook her hand vigorously. 'Miss Harker! I've gotta run, but I'm glad to find you here.'

'Well it's down to you, Colonel, that I am here. I wanted to thank you for your help with the visa.'

'Quite all right. I'm pleased you made it. I think it's important we get as many good American journalists as possible here. We need to tell the world about the true strength of Germany.'

'So from what you've seen today, what do you think?'

'It's very impressive,' he said warmly. 'In fact, from what I've seen of the air forces, I'd say Germany now has the means of destroying London, Paris and Prague if she wishes to do so. And you can quote me on that.'

Mary was taken aback. It may be that Lindbergh was speaking

for the benefit of his Nazi hosts, who were beaming and nodding all around him, yet he gave no impression of dissembling. He was all smiles. Lindbergh seemed entirely sanguine about the idea that the Nazi regime had amassed enough air power to achieve supremacy in Europe. How could he talk of London, Paris and Prague being destroyed? Hitler had just announced that he would not allow the Sudeten Germans to become 'defenceless and deserted' like the Arabs in Palestine. Could Lindbergh, the all-American hero, not understand what the Germans had in store for Czechoslovakia? Or did he simply not care?

'Colonel, surely you don't think . . .?'

'What I think, Miss Harker,' said Lindbergh with the zeal of the convert, 'is that we Americans have a valuable role to play in spreading the word about the new Germany. That's why I was so certain that it was right for you to come back.'

'You thought that I . . .?'

He bent towards her, radiating sincerity. 'I thought that you would be able to give a fair and accurate picture of the kind of society that Herr Hitler is producing. And I told them so.'

Well that much was true. Mary was increasingly determined to give a fair and accurate picture of the society around her. But not in the way that Lindbergh seemed to expect. He was the second high-profile American visitor to Berlin right now, after Wallis Simpson, and both of them seemed to have something in common. A wilful refusal to see what was right in front of their eyes. How was it they could see the window displays and the construction works, but not the posters on the walls, or the opponents in camps, or the refugees flooding the borders?

Mary left the hotel in a daze. She had a vision of German planes in mass formation, the drone of bombers and the whine of fighters, blackening the sky. Anti-aircraft guns on the roof of the Adlon and armies mobilizing for the front. Lindbergh had confirmed what she already feared, that Hitler had the ability to do as he pleased and no one, especially not America, was going to stand in his way.

She was yards down the street when she felt a touch on her arm.

'Excuse me. Mary Harker? I wonder if I might have a word?'

It was a well-dressed Englishman, with tawny hair and a suave, cultivated accent. She had caught sight of him across the room at the Adlon, downing vodka Martinis like they were going out of fashion.

'I hope you don't mind my mentioning, but I read your reports from Guernica. I found them tremendously affecting. Would you mind if I asked you a little about them?'

He seemed entirely in earnest. Mary looked at him curiously.

'Not at all. Do you have a special interest in Spain?'

'You could say that. It's about a friend of mine.'

'Would I know him?'

'I'm not sure. But I wonder if we could talk somewhere, out of the cold?'

One of the sentries approached, rattling his collecting box meaningfully in their direction and the man turned fractionally away.

'And I rather think, now that Colonel Lindbergh has assured us of the formidable strength of the Luftwaffe, that one is perfectly justified in devoting one's funds to buying dinner instead.'

Chapter Thirty-nine

Horcher's restaurant on Lutherstrasse was the chosen place in the city for the Luftwaffe top brass. The owner, Otto Horcher, had known Goering in the war, and always made a huge fuss of his honoured guest, cooking him his favourite game and providing other special customers with their own set of monogrammed wine glasses. With the same punctilious attention to detail, Herr Horcher had also ensured that carefully concealed microphones were built into the fabric of each table, with the help of which the waiters were able to compile their reports to the authorities. The interior was lined with dark oak panelling and plush leather banquettes, where officers lolled, bowls of scarlet tulips at each table. That lunchtime there was a sprinkling of Wehrmacht in field grey and the rest were mainly Luftwaffe. As Clara arrived Arno Strauss approached and kissed hands, his manner, as ever, deadpan.

'I'm glad you could make it. I know you've been busy.'

Suddenly she understood. 'It was you who rescued me.'

'The Blockwart at your apartment informed me that you had moved to less desirable premises and I didn't want you to miss this luncheon. You agreed, on our little outing, that it would be valuable for your research to see General Sperrle, and I had, of course, been looking forward to seeing you. I mentioned your circumstances to Ernst and he pursued it with Goering. At least, he approached Frau Goering and she took it up with her husband.'

Clara was staggered. So Hermann Goering himself had authorized her release.

'As I mentioned, there's been a little difference of opinion going on. Air Intelligence is concerned about a leak. The Gestapo were very keen to investigate but Air Intelligence said they were perfectly able to mount their own investigation. These interdepartmental squabbles go on all the time. Just turf wars, really, but it means that the Air Ministry are especially keen to pursue their own ends, as they see it.'

Strauss's eyes flicked over the bruise running down Clara's arm, a trace of consternation in his face. 'I hope you're feeling well. You received the flowers, I take it?'

The flowers had been waiting for her when she returned to Winterfeldstrasse. A tight bunch of creamy roses, bright against the black tissue paper like starbursts against a night sky. Pinned on the side of the bouquet was a note from Strauss, with the time and venue for the lunch.

'They were lovely, thank you.'

He studied her a moment, his look impenetrable, then he took her arm.

'You must be hungry. Come and eat.'

The lunch was lavish. Meat was piled upon the table, rabbit, hare, venison, pork and beef, as though there was no end to the animals which had died to feed the Luftwaffe's guests. The creatures' flesh and their internal organs, liver, kidneys and tripe, were offered up in an unending range of dishes, served by waiters in black knee breeches, white stockings and red waistcoats. But the events of the past twenty-four hours had left Clara unable to swallow a thing. It was incredible to her that just a short time earlier she had been sitting in a cell at Prinz Albrecht Strasse, awaiting a beating or worse, as investigators tried to determine if she was an informer. Yet now she sat in the midst of the Nazi élite, plied with food, celebrating the achievements of their bombers in Spain. Though she had not eaten for a day, it was impossible that she would be able to consume anything now. She sat, watching the maroon hunk of meat on the plate in front of her pool in its own blood.

As the officers ate and drank, their celebrations became louder but Ernst Udet and Arno Strauss sat on either side of her, forming a protective cordon.

'How's that boy of yours?' asked Udet.

'Fine. At least, we had a bit of a tiff when we last met. He thinks I don't Heil Hitler enough. He gets all these ideas from the HJ about correcting his elders.'

'That's the HJ for you,' smiled Udet. 'Here. Let me have his address. I've got something that will win him over.'

Instinctively Clara hesitated, reluctant to give away any snippet of information that might endanger Erich, but one glance at Udet's good-natured face and she scribbled the address in Neukölln, and passed it to him.

'Whatever it is, Ernst, he'll be thrilled.'

Udet must have sensed her preoccupation because he spent the rest of the meal in a one-sided conversation about his plans to perform a death-defying stunt at a forthcoming rally in the Lustgarten, taking a small plane all the way along Unter den Linden and right through the Brandenburg Gate. Strauss, on her other side, ate in silence, drinking heavily and glancing up occasionally with a dangerous glitter in his eyes. After the luncheon, General Sperrle rose and made a speech about the Legion Condor, paying tribute to its work and its future. His voice was a harsh baritone, the kind of voice that was used to being obeyed, and his address entirely bypassed Clara, who registered only the occasional words – 'technical excellence', 'victory', 'domination'. As Sperrle concluded, amid a spatter of applause, Strauss nodded towards the guest of honour.

'What do you think of Sperrle?' he asked, conversationally. 'Did you know the Führer called him one of his two most brutal generals? Whenever I look at him I am reminded of Hitler's comment in *Mein Kampf*. He said his generals should be like butchers' dogs who need to be restrained by their collars from setting on their enemies. General Sperrle has a look of the butcher's dog about him, don't you think?'

'I think this is the wrong place to be making that kind of comment,' said Clara quietly.

'You're right of course. You actresses are experts in saying the right thing.'

He stood up and offered her his hand. 'Shall we dance?'

A band had struck up and they moved onto the tiny dance floor, where several officers were already circling with their women. As they began to move together Clara felt dizzy. It wasn't just the fact that she had not eaten, it was that Strauss was holding her so tightly she could hardly breathe. When she struggled to move away from him, his grip tightened like iron. He leaned down and she felt his breath, hot against her cheek.

'Do you know, my dear Clara, if I didn't know better I would say you are not what you seem.'

'What on earth can you mean by that?'

'Not everyone's flaws are written on their face. It would suit a girl, wouldn't it, to befriend a senior Luftwaffe officer? If she were a spy.'

'That's a ridiculous thing to say.'

Her heart racing, she tried to turn her head, or even look him in the eye, but he had her clamped to his chest and refused to release her. His voice in her ear was soft.

'You *are* a spy, aren't you? Don't deny it.'

She squirmed against the tight wall of muscle that imprisoned her.

'That's why they were entertaining you at Prinz Albrecht

Strasse, I guess. And, my dear, I don't trust you an inch. All those questions about the plane, the photographs . . . my childhood. My brother.'

Clara shook her head. Strauss's hands were still gripping her but he continued pleasantly, conversationally, as if they were discussing the excellence of the restaurant's orchestra, or a weekend trip to the Grunewald.

'I should have guessed it from the first.'

They were playing *Küss Mich Jetzt*, a cheerful, romantic tune that could be heard on every dance floor in Berlin just then. Clara couldn't help casting a quick glance around the restaurant. This conversation was suicidally dangerous. Despite the music, everyone knew the place was bugged and on top of that there had to be listening ears everywhere. Yet Strauss seemed unconcerned. His body swayed slowly and rhythmically, keeping her folded tightly in his arms.

'To tell the truth, I hope you are a spy. I despise all those English women like your Miss Mitfords who seem so ready to forsake their own country. Can't they see what Germany will do to them? Have they no idea what is planned? Someone ought to warn them.'

With a renewed struggle Clara wrenched herself free and made to leave the floor, but deftly Strauss stopped her and pressed her lips in a quick kiss before letting her go with a grimace. His eyes were bloodshot. He smiled at her, a savage smile contorted with self-loathing.

'Forgive me, Fräulein, it's this drink. It anaethetizes me. It stops me feeling anything. It's like that for a lot of us. Look at Ernst. He's the same. Every night, drink till you drop.'

He was beginning to attract glances. Wildly Clara thought how she might silence him. She pulled him over to a quieter part of the room but there seemed no way to make him stop.

'I almost killed you in that plane, you know.'

'You mean when you lost control?'

'I wanted to die. I was planning to die. I think I took you up with me to stop myself. I thought, if I had you there, I would stop myself. But it was close. There's a saying we pilots have: Wet or dry? Do you want to die wet in a crash, or dry in a fire? I can never answer that one.'

Clara leaned towards him and murmured, 'Arno. You've got to stop talking like this.'

He held her at arms' length for a moment, studied her face, then gave a dreadful, bright smile.

'You're right again. Fine. Let's talk about other things. Why don't we talk about art, yes?'

She nodded cautiously.

'Have you seen the latest one by Picasso? The one that's all grey with the bull and the horse?'

'Guernica?'

'That's the one.' He spoke with a kind of musing menace. 'You know, with due respect to Herr Picasso, it wasn't a bit like that actually. I don't know why he chose to paint it grey. The grey of newsprint perhaps. But I tell you, it was nothing like the newspapers said. There was nothing grey about Guernica. It was red with blood and fire against a white sky. The only grey I saw was the smoke of burned flesh.'

'You were there?'

He carried on, as though she had not spoken. 'From what we were told, the idea was not to destroy the town. We were told it was the roads and the bridge to be targeted because loyalist reinforcements were arriving. The Basque front was on the point of collapse so the plan was to demolish the bridge and prevent the Republican troops escaping. Besides, they had informed us the inhabitants were away. It was a holiday that day. Only troops were left in the town. Unfortunately that was not true.'

'When we came over the mountains there was smoke

everywhere. You couldn't see what was road, or bridge or housing, so you just dropped everything in the centre. It's called bombing blind. Once you've destroyed the buildings, it makes it easier for the incendiaries to spread. The way they build their houses there – wooden porches, tiled roofs, a lot of timber, well that just makes it burn all the better. The idea was, the Messerschmitts would maintain cover and we would come in close, strafing and bombing the target. We'd fly in waves, wingtip to wingtip, with fragmentation bombs. Behind us, they had orders to machine-gun everything that moved.'

'The thing was, Monday was market day in Guernica. And once the bridges and the roads were destroyed, all the people in the town went to the centre, to the marketplace, because they couldn't get out. There were a lot of women and children who had come in from the surrounding villages. They probably thought they were safe there. They must have assumed that was the best place to be.'

'So you targeted the marketplace.'

'Indeed, as it turned out, it was the ideal spot for our new tactics. We've been experimenting with carpet bombing. That means dropping bombs from every available aircraft all at once. Teaching young pilots to destroy whole towns from the air. Sperrle was especially interested to observe the effect of burning buildings in cities. He wanted to see how it affected the civilian population.'

He rocked back on his heels and passed a hand over his eyes.

'Personally I think I have seen too much.'

'But you said you were bombing blind. Presumably you didn't see anything.'

'You can always see if you look hard enough. You can get low in those planes, you know. After the first wave, people started to come back out of the shelters. They probably thought it was over. We were flying so low we could hear the bells ringing and see the people scattering like rats. I swept over something, it looked like a flock of pigeons, until I realized it was nuns. They had children with them and they were running towards the church. Can you imagine that pathetic group of boys, crying and cowering from us? There was one nun among them who stopped right where she was, to pray with the people in the square. As I came down very close, she stood there, quite still, knowing it was the day she was going to die. I will never forget the look in her eyes. She had two boys holding her hands and they looked identical. They must have been twins, I think.'

'You couldn't have known that there were going to be civilians in the square.'

'I didn't, Clara, but that's just the thing. Our superiors knew. They knew the market square was full of children.'

'Who knew?'

'General Sperrle over there, he knew.'

'How could he know that?'

'On the morning of the raid a series of aerial photographs were taken. They had sent the reconnaissance planes over. I told you, the pictures tell you everything. Pictures don't lie. Pictures mean that you can never act without knowledge or accountability. They knew it wasn't a holiday. They knew the marketplace was full of women and children. And that was fine. Because those people were going to be guinea pigs for a new kind of war. Our commanders wanted to see if we could destroy an entire town from the air. Well, they got their answer.'

She looked up at his face. It was contorted with something more ugly than his scar. Self-hatred. He lurched closer, his voice a harsh, urgent whisper.

'But I haven't told you the worst thing. The thing that really bothers me. Do you know, Clara, I enjoyed it! It gave me a buzz. Flying in, seeing a woman with a pram darting for cover, I felt myself wanting to hit her. I wanted the feeling of flying past her and machine-gunning. When I saw that nun, I was excited because she was wearing black and white, like a perfect target. She made me want to score a bullseye.'

'You can't have enjoyed it. That's not like you. You're a good man.'

'But I did. I adored it. It was the most exciting experience of my life. Euphoria, isn't that the word you used? Dive bombing made me feel euphoric. It made my pulse race.'

He caught up her hand and put it to his chest so that she could feel the rapid beating of his heart.

'That old German mythology we studied at school, they probably had a word for that feeling.'

The thought of his schooldays seemed to impassion him further.

'I always believed I would be the Irish Airman. *Those that I fight I do not hate*. But you see, Clara, for that moment, I did hate them. I wanted them to die. I enjoyed killing them. And afterwards I could see what I would become. In fact, what I had already become.'

His fingers were digging into her wrist. It hurt, but she couldn't wrest her hand from his grip.

'Have you ever had that feeling of seeing your life from above? When you're at ground level you can't understand your life, you can't make sense of the twists and turns. But when you see it from above the pattern becomes clear.'

She grabbed her bag and coat. 'Let's go and get some fresh air.'

The idea seemed to appeal to him. He followed her mutely out of the restaurant, then stood at the door and winced at the light.

'Arno, you've got to be more careful. You shouldn't be saying these things here. I think it's time to go home.'

'Is that an invitation?'

'No.'

He laughed, a harsh scrape of a laugh.

'I thought not. Well, no matter. I have a test flight first thing tomorrow.'

'I don't think you're in any shape for that.'

'I'm in perfect shape for it, I assure you.'

He caught her in his arms again, and this time he pressed on her a hard, lingering kiss from that twisted mouth, a kiss that felt as much of an assault as a caress, as though he wanted to imprint on her all his pain and fear. Clara pulled away from him and he released her and gave a little bow as she turned and walked away into the afternoon.

Chapter Forty

The man was coming after her. That was all Ilse knew. She was going to fall with her face down in the damp grass the way Anna had, so the scent of it would be the last thing she remembered, and the stains would cover her clean apron and she would fall crying to the ground and her tears would disappear into the mossy earth. She ran through the trees, her mouth catching the air, her long hair hanging down her back wet and heavy, like a rope.

Her breath was coming harder as she threaded through the implacable Grunewald. The brambles snatched at her and the rigid trees with their uniform bark crowded out the light. It was growing dark now, the black tangle of boughs above her even darker as they framed themselves against the sky. Ilse was crashing through the undergrowth, spongy with pine needles underfoot, avoiding the snags of trailing ivy that reached and grasped at her. She thought she might reach the soft, grey sand at the edge of the lake and follow the waterline round towards its western edge. But what if he pursued her right to the lake? The water out there was deep and treacherous, rolling and plunging in darkness, flexing its muscles like something alive. There would be no chance of an escape in that direction.

She wanted to stop and catch her breath and listen for sounds that he was still behind her, but she didn't dare. The forest seemed to be growing denser now, wild and terrible. She had the strange sensation of being in a book, one she had read a long time ago in childhood, one of those tales that told of the tenebrous, Germanic forest, the kind of forest you got lost in for ever. Stories like that of Hansel and Gretel, wandering deep into the uncharted wilderness. Of Snow White being hunted like a deer by men who wanted to cut out her heart. Forests were places where the ordinary rules of human society no longer applied, and people were turned into animals.

She stumbled, and pulled herself up again. Her breathing had become ragged, and a hoarse note sounded in her throat, like a bird's cry. She should never have left the house. She shouldn't have gone out to see what was making the puppies whimper in their kennel and the geese cackle and call. She had wanted to comfort the dogs and run her hands through their soft fur, but she shouldn't have stepped out of the warmth of the kitchen, where the glimmering stove was reflecting in the copper saucepans that sat above the range and the baking spices hung in the air, only to find the door slammed shut by an unseen hand, a terror which had set her running into the night.

The sweet, pudgy face of Otto came to her. What would Otto do without her? Otto's parents would tell him they always knew he could have done better. They thought little enough of Ilse anyway, and to have her die an undignified death would be a further slur on the family name. And what about her own parents, on their farm? Poor Papi and Mutti had never wanted their only daughter to marry a man who lived so far away and now they would be left with no daughter at all.

Images flashed through her brain. Ilse thought of the American lady and felt glad that she had talked to her. She had lovely kind eyes and a laugh that made you think nothing really mattered. Ilse tried to remember the address on the card she had given her. It was Winterfeldstrasse, wasn't it? If only she could remember it she could head there, then perhaps Fräulein Harker would look after her. But that was a crazy hope. How could she possibly reach the city from here?

She ran on and on until her thoughts became a jumble, a kind of harsh music. All she had ever tried to do was obey the Führer's ideas on how to honour the Fatherland and behave the way a good German woman should behave. She had been good, hadn't she? What more could the Führer ask of a girl? She began to pray, the new kind of prayer, the Führer's prayer. 'Führer, mein Führer, bequeathed to me by the Lord. Protect and preserve me as long as I live.'

Chapter Forty-one

It was late afternoon by the time Clara got back to her apartment. She sat down, kicked off her shoes, exhausted, and lay back in her chair as the light leaked out of the sky and the yellow glow of streetlights took its place.

After some time she sat up again. She had dumped Anna's case down on the floor, but now she took it up and looked at it. Anna had her secrets. Secrets she kept even from her oldest friend. And it was those secrets which had killed her in the end. Because everything that had happened to Clara – being followed, Erich being threatened – had happened since she took care of Anna's case. Yet she had looked at it a thousand times, she had been through Johann's letters time and again. The theatre programmes, the souvenirs. If there was anything secret about this case it was either invisible, or hidden in plain sight.

She remembered what Strauss had said to her about aerial photography. *Some of the most important things are hidden in plain sight.*

Clara opened the case again and shut her eyes. Then she felt around it like a blind person, her fingertips feeling out the sleek plush of the velvet lining, the tooled edge of leather that formed the writing insert, the drawers with their little ivory knobs. She pulled them out again, but they were empty. She ran her fingers along the outside of the case and swept down to the bottom and then up again to the top.

A ledge.

Her fingers sensed a dip in the velvet. She opened her eyes and looked again but could see nothing. Her eyes said there was nothing to see, but her fingers told her it was there. A slight depression that ran along the entire upper edge of the case. She pressed experimentally, and the depression rose smoothly to her hand. So that was it! A partition. Concealed in the upright of the lap desk. She pulled it all the way out and looked at the contents.

There were four packages about six inches square, each made from four flaps of brown paper, constructed like envelopes so that the flaps overlaid each other. Opening one she saw that it contained an old-fashioned glass plate negative. You never saw them now, not since everyone worked with rolls of film.

Now we see through a glass darkly.

Holding them up to the light she squinted to see what they represented. It was hard to make out at first, but she discerned a group of people, at a party perhaps. Men in uniform, with their arms around each other. Two of them, she thought she recognized. Rudolf Hess, with his beetle brow and lantern jaw, and Ernst Röhm, the commander of the SA, an intimate of Hitler's since he was an education officer in the army, a devoted friend from the days of the Munich beer hall and the only man who was allowed to address the Führer as 'du'. She knew it was Röhm from the way the cap sat on his bullet head, the sleek outcrop of hair, centrally parted, and the dimpled fold of fat on his face. Röhm, who had been slaughtered on Hitler's orders back in 1934, when the Führer feared that the power of his storm troopers threatened the Wehrmacht. In the picture Röhm had his arm around another man and something about the composition of the group reminded her uncannily of the picture painted by Bruno Weiss in the Degenerate Art exhibition.

She spread the negatives out on the rug and scrutinized the second, then the third. More groups of people in close embraces. Squinting at the fourth, it was then that she found the most extraordinary thing. This time the man in it was unmistakeable. The intense burning eyes, the mirthless grimace which passed for a smile. It was that picture, Clara realized at once, which held the key to Anna's death.

Kneeling there on the floor, she looked at the photographs in amazement. She switched from one to another as her eye accustomed to the negatives, and adapted to seeing everything in reverse. It was the reverse, too, of what everyone believed. An astonishing opposite. As she looked a chill crept over her and the implications became clear. Anna's old boyfriend cared enough about these pictures to kill Anna. He had pursued Katia Hansen, too, so much that she had fled to the other end of Germany in fear of him, and the same man knew that Clara had these pictures now. How far would he go to get them back?

For a long time she stared in panic from one picture to another, then rocked back on her heels and put her face in her hands. She felt a throb of fear that rose within her and then a plummeting sensation, like falling from a great height. She had no idea what she could do now. Like Arno Strauss, she felt as though she had seen too much.

There was a rap on the door. Clara froze. Then she heard a woman's voice. An English voice, young and imperious.

'Come on Clara! Let me in.'

Unity Mitford was wearing a powder-blue evening dress, with a velvet cape draped across her shoulders and a fur-trimmed hat on her shining blonde head. Her complexion was powdered alabaster white and she had quite unusually applied a slick of cherry lipstick, but the elegance of her appearance was diminished by her breathlessness at climbing several flights of stairs. The swastika brooch that was, as usual, pinned to her breast, bounced up and down as she caught her breath. Her eyes were bright with nervous excitement and she clutched an evening bag, like an eager puppy holding its lead.

'Guess what, Clara. The Führer says yes!'

'Hello, Unity. What on earth are you talking about?'

Unity stared at her petulantly.

'I told you. At the Goerings' party. I said I was going to ask him to invite you to the Wintergarten to see *The Merry Widow*. And the Führer said that was fine. So hurry up. We're due at the Reich Chancellery in fifteen minutes. My man is waiting outside. What's all that on the floor?'

For the first time Unity seemed to register the negatives which Clara had pushed behind her on the rug. She poked one with her foot. 'What are all those?'

'Nothing interesting. Just some historical pictures.'

Unity approached and took one up. 'Really? I say, that looks like the Führer.'

'Don't touch them, please, Unity, they're fragile.'

Clara's request was ignored as Unity dropped to her knees and picked up the negatives, staring from one to the other. Her lower lip pushed out in a childish pout.

'And that must be . . . Ernst Röhm? But . . . what are they?' Then she turned to Clara savagely. 'Where did you get these?'

'They came from Hoffmann's studio. They were taken a long time ago. Back in the twenties. Before you knew him, Unity. It was a party in Munich. They got up to some wild things.'

'But the men. They're kissing!'

'I know.'

'It's lies. These are lies.' Unity jumped up. Her face had gone from pale to scarlet. Uncomprehendingly she waved them in the air. 'Pictures are manipulated all the time. Goebbels does it non-stop in the propaganda department. These are just shoddy. They're fakes.'

'Of course they are.'

Unity turned to Clara, anger and bewilderment warring in her face.

'So what are *you* doing with them!'

'I found them. I'm keeping them safe. You're right. No one must get hold of them.'

'You're planning to use them against him, aren't you?'

'Don't be silly. Just the opposite. I want to stop them falling into the wrong hands.'

Unity was still staring at the pictures, but now she started crying, great gulping sobs like a toddler, swiping the tears angrily away from her face. 'It's not true. They are a despicable scandal. The Führer is the finest of men.'

'Stop it, Unity!'

'He is a man of the highest emotions. He would never engage in . . . he would never . . .'

She was weeping wildly. Her nose was streaming and her milky complexion was mottled with emotion. With a sudden movement she slammed the negatives to the ground so they rebounded on the wooden floor and splintered into dancing fragments.

'They're lies. Lies should be destroyed. That's what the Führer says.'

The glass negatives lay in shards, some of the bigger slivers embedded upright into the parquet. Unity stared momentarily at the splintered glass, as though slightly stunned by what she had done, then turned to Clara, defiantly.

'I don't want you to come to the opera any more, Clara. I shall tell the Führer you're not coming. And don't worry, I'm planning to tell him everything. He's going to be very upset.'

Chapter Forty-two

As soon as the door had slammed behind her, Clara went to the window and watched Unity dash towards a large Mercedes that stood in the street with its engine running. She saw the peaked cap of the driver turn, and Unity jump into the back seat. As the car pulled away, Clara knew she had no time to lose. She didn't doubt that Unity would tell Hitler exactly what she had seen. She would inform him furiously that Clara Vine, the actress who had been so kindly invited to accompany them to the Wintergarten that evening, had a photograph in her apartment of him kissing another man. A photograph that, although it lay in shards, pieced together the dark puzzle of the Führer and presented him as he was. Like a crossword put together, complete and comprehensible. A picture that could drag him out of the shadowy glamour of celebrity and expose him to the common light of day. Truth lay around her in a litter of broken glass.

Clara looked at the wreckage of the negatives. She had no doubt that these pictures could destroy Hitler. They could slice through the Führer's reputation throughout Germany and stop his plans for domination of Europe in its tracks. Homosexuality was the vice, after all, for which Röhm and his SA associates had been executed. If Hitler, the object of adoration for millions of women, should be found to have indulged, should be seen as a sexual deviant . . . well, the Nazis had a word for behaviour like that. Degenerate.

There was no chance that Unity would stay silent. She had the deadly combination of slavish devotion to the Führer and the political instincts of a teenager. There was no doubt she would boast about how she had personally destroyed the negatives. As if that was an end of it. As if the Führer would be overcome with gratitude and perhaps give her a medal as a reward.

If Unity was making her way to the Chancellery now, Clara might have an hour before police arrived at her door. Probably less than that. Wildly, she considered her options. She longed to run straight out of the apartment and head for Duisberger Strasse, but her desire to seek refuge with Ralph was swiftly quelled; she couldn't risk drawing the police to him. There was only one person in Germany who could save her now, and she needed to find him before she herself was found.

Fighting the urge to flee immediately, she forced herself to hesitate, then went over to the cupboard and selected a navy satin dress that perfectly emphasized her curves, navy elbow gloves, pearl necklace, diamond earrings and dark glasses. She needed to use all the persuasive skills she possessed. She paused for a second to survey herself in the mirror, twisted her hair up into a chignon, then drew on the long coat with the frosted fox-fur collar. Picking up a cut-glass atomizer she sprayed a cloud of *Evening in Paris* about her and finally, with her gloves on, she carefully collected up the shards of glass from the floor and stuffed them into a beaded black and white clutch bag. Looking around her she saw something else. Erich's knife. Sheathed, with a red ribbon tied around it. She slipped it into the bag and left the apartment.

She made herself walk calmly down the stairs and nod to Rudi, who was immersed in *Der SA-Mann*. Looking up, he seemed about to comment on the young foreigner who had just slammed out of the door and insert some reprimand for Clara about visitors needing to have respect for other tenants, but she left before the words were out of his mouth and headed into the chill evening air.

She walked the length of Winterfeldstrasse, crossed Potsdamer Strasse and headed north. It was busy now. People were hurrying out to their evening's entertainment, to the cinema or a show. She tried to stick to the side streets, with her head down, keeping her pace firm and steady. After fifteen minutes' brisk walk she had reached halfway down Wilhelmstrasse, past the Aviation Ministry, to the wrought-iron gates of the Chancellery. Across the road and slightly set back from it was the Propaganda Ministry. Even at this time of the evening, most of the windows were still lit. The Ministry was never really shut. The message of the new Germany was too important to keep to office hours.

Clara pushed open the door and crossed the wide marble hall to where a uniformed guard sat at a desk, looking her up and down. He was a heavy-set bruiser with a dusting of bristles on his scalp and eyes that had been squashed too closely together in his face.

'I need to see the Minister. Please tell him Fräulein Clara Vine needs to see him urgently.'

The man regarded her insolently and made no attempt to lift the telephone.

'Can I ask what this is about?' He had a wet smirk of a mouth.

'It's personal. He'll understand.'

With another sardonic look the man rose and crossed to the opposite side of the hall where another guard sat. The two men conferred, smiling and darting glances in her direction. She forced herself to concentrate on the guard's cigarette, dwindling into the ashtray on his desk. Fear lay like a great weight on her chest. It was a risk she was taking now, probably the biggest risk she had taken since she set foot in Germany, but she had no choice. So long as Unity knew that Clara had the pictures, there was no possibility that she would keep quiet.

The guard returned across the wide marble hall with all the urgency of a man out for an evening stroll.

'So sorry, Fräulein. I regret the Minister has left for the evening.'

He smirked a little more, betraying his conviction that here was another desperate actress whose business with the Herr Doktor was strictly unofficial. 'Perhaps you could try another night?'

Clara ignored the implication. 'Can I ask where he might be?'

The guard found this hilarious. He choked his laughter down. 'The Minister does not permit us to give out details of his whereabouts to anyone who happens to turn up. Not even beautiful ladies. Is there any message?'

'No. No message.'

As swiftly as she could, with the eyes of the two men on her, Clara left the building. Where was Goebbels? He could be anywhere in Berlin. He could even be at home at Schwanenwerder, but Emmy Goering had said he never went home until late. What had she said? *He's become very secretive about his movements, apparently. He even keeps his officials at the Ministry in the dark.* Goebbels had to be somewhere in the city, but where? Berlin's ceaseless, churning nightlife, with its hundreds of bars and theatres, which usually excited Clara, now existed to taunt her. Her chances of unearthing Goebbels in the plush depths of some west-end nightclub were next to none.

She exited the courtyard and turned right into Wilhelmstrasse, heading towards Unter den Linden. She walked rapidly, intent on staying inconspicuous, trying to melt into the shadow of the hefty baroque buildings. It was then that she saw it. A flicker of movement that took on the shape of a man. He was walking about fifty yards behind her on the other side of the road, yet she knew at once that he was watching her. It was the way his attention shifted, without any outward signs, just some microscopic angling of his body towards her, that said he had her in his sights.

And there was something about him, to do with his carriage or the tilt of the shoulders, that she recognized. She had only seen him for a fraction of a second, and had not caught full sight of his face, but it was enough to tell her she had seen him before. On the night she had led Ralph Sommers on a trail through Berlin. The man with the pale fedora in Voss Strasse. He was the man who had been at the art gallery in Munich too. The man who had been following her ever since she first took possession of Anna Hansen's case. And now he had found her. He looked absolutely calm, intent and unhurried. He was a normal businessman, anxious to get home to his Frau and a couple of delightful children.

The wind whipped her hair into her eyes and when she looked again he was gone.

At once, everything Clara knew about being shadowed kicked in. There was no need to ascertain that the man was genuinely a tail, so she did not slow her pace, or vary her direction. All she needed to do was shake him off. It sounded simple, put like that, but this man was a professional, she could tell, and he had been watching her for weeks. Like a lover, he would know the shape and gait of her and could read in the mere movement of her body the workings of her mind.

She walked purposefully on to the top of Wilhelmstrasse and paused fractionally to decide her direction. To one side the doors of the Adlon Hotel spilled a golden corridor of light across the pavement, its uniformed doormen shuffling and blowing clouds in the icy air. To the other side, beneath the enormous eagle-topped pillars that marched off into the distance, the evening bustle of Unter den Linden was underway. Turning right would be the obvious choice. The theatres and restaurants that clustered around Friedrichstrasse would be the best place to disappear. Yet it was also what he would expect of her. So she dipped into the subway of the S-Bahn, rose the other side and as she reached street level swerved left, and clipped towards Pariser Platz, in the direction of the Brandenburg Gate.

Above her, Victoria, the goddess of triumph, championed her four horses in the ominous direction of Hitler's chosen Lebensraum in the East. Beside her the windows of the French embassy sent bright oblongs of light into the square. Clara kept to the shadows, calculating fiercely which route to take, longing for crowds and traffic to obscure the path between them. She could sense the man behind her, his step quickening, trying to make up the ground between them. She felt danger, thrumming in her skull, rising and jangling.

No sooner had she emerged the other side of the gate than she had another choice to make. To her right lay the Platz der Republik and the Reichstag, heading northwards to Lehrter Bahnhof. To her left was a short walk to the bustle of Potsdamer Platz, where she could disappear down the U-Bahn. But if she went into the U-Bahn she risked being trapped. On impulse she took the choice right ahead of her and headed into the darkness of the Tiergarten.

It was properly dark now. A hard moon slipped behind filigree clouds in the sky. The park was empty. No one wanted to be out on a night like this, still and bitterly cold with the taste of snow in the air.

She headed resolutely off the paths, past heavy statues of forgotten German statesmen and bronze heroes struggling with wild boar and bears, threading her way deeper between the trees. Clara zigzagged from tree to tree, halting in the pool of deeper shadow cast by each trunk. For a moment she stopped, breathless, and thought about sinking down to the earth, huddling in the darkness and waiting for her follower to abandon his search. She dared to hope she had shaken him off. There was no crunch of footsteps on the fallen leaves, no human sound apart from the distant thrum of traffic. It was as though he had vaporized.

As she stood there, motionless, she imagined for a moment that she had gone back to childhood and was in the nursery, tucked up in the eaves of the house. Night after night, as she curled in her warm bed trying to sleep, she would see shadows in the corner of the room rise up and form themselves into menacing shapes. Her fears would grasp her by the shoulders and shake her as she lay. Eventually her father would appear, sternly dismissive and almost as frightening as the shadows themselves. The experience was just night terrors, he would explain when he found her sobbing figure on the stairs. It was merely her own imaginings stepping outside of her mind and taking a shape of their own.

'Your fears are nonsensical, Clara. You have always had an overactive imagination.'

But this was no night terror. The man following her had a most deadly agenda.

Clara wouldn't have seen him if he hadn't made a mistake. He was about a hundred yards away from her, still on the path, and he passed a lamp. For a split second his shadow twisted up under the light, revealing the brim of his hat, even though his face remained obscured. A moment later darkness swallowed him as he veered off the path in the direction of the trees. He was coming towards her. She remembered what Unity Mitford said to her about hunting. *I learned an awful lot about being the prey. You've got to avoid sudden movement. That always draws the eye.*

If she was being hunted, she needed to remain where she was, completely still. Looking behind her she was sure she heard his step, but when she glanced, he was nowhere to be seen. She forced herself to be calm. She would stand completely motionless in the deep shadow. She bitterly regretted choosing the coat with the white fox collar. The fur gleamed in the moonlight and made her far easier to spot.

Even while she tried her hardest not to move, Clara was cursing herself for choosing the route into the Tiergarten. The place was deceptively large. If you strayed off the paths, getting lost was a real possibility. The Tiergarten was no tame English park. There was something wild and impenetrable about it. It seemed incredible that in the heart of the city – and such an orderly, monumental city as Berlin – this wildness should be enclosed. Perhaps, Clara thought, it stood for something in the city's soul.

Her thoughts were interrupted by a crunch of twigs a few yards away and instantly she knew that he was perilously close. She needed to make a decision. Abandoning her stillness she lurched forward and ran. She ran, though her heels hobbled her and the darkness was so solid it stunted her movement, as though she was running through sand. She ran until her lungs were screaming for air and fear dragged her backwards like a tide, pulling her down into the sweet surrender of oblivion. All the time she ran, she strained for the pitch of his footsteps behind her confirming that he was gaining ground.

She was terribly afraid. Fear rose in her gullet like acid, but in the midst of her fear she found anger, hard and cold as a stone. This was the man who had threatened Erich. Who had murdered Anna Hansen. If she slowed, if she surrendered to a man like this who thought he could dominate and destroy women, she would give up her life. She would give up her life, so hard achieved, to someone who wanted to save his own. The thought of Unity, who would even now be passionately regaling the Führer with the story of the photographs Clara possessed, spurred her further on.

Ahead of her, the trees thinned and she saw a glistening blank stretch of water she recognized as the Neuer See, a favourite weekend spot for Berliners who loved to drink beer under the pine trees or hire boats to sail on the lake. Bobbing darkly at the water's edge, moored to a post, there was, she could just make out, the dim shape of a rowing boat. A pair of oars were lying along its bottom. Clara thanked God that Erich had persuaded her that summer to learn to row. She knelt down and fumbled with the rope, but the knot which tied the boat to its mooring post might have been devised by an entire brigade of Hitler Youth. It was fiendishly complex and tightly coiled. Her fingers slipped helplessly as she grappled in the darkness with the damp and muddy strands. She sank back on her heels in desperation. A chance of escape was in front of her, but a single rope prevented her from taking it. Then she remembered Erich's knife at the bottom of her bag and, unsheathing it, she marvelled at its sharpness in slicing through the rope in one blow.

On the edge of her vision she saw something, a flick of shadow on the water, but it was only a heron, lifting off from its nest in the reeds. The boat rocked as she stepped into it, and reaching for the oars she fixed them into the rowlocks and pushed off into the night.

Despite the cold, she was damp with sweat and hair clung to her face. Her head felt dizzy with the effort as she pulled faster through the black water that was heavy as cement. There was no sound but the splash of the oars as the water dragged against the blades. She had no idea where she was rowing to, but she felt sure that if she could only remain in the boat, on the water in darkness, then she would be safe. For a few minutes she let the oars drop and allowed the boat to drift free and undirected on the ripple of the lake.

The crack of a shot changed her mind.

Instinctively, she ducked down. Crouching against the wet bottom of the boat, she thought of the Beretta that remained, uselessly, in the hollowed-out leg of her desk. If only she had listened to Leo Quinn when he gave her that gun, together with the smooth leather holster that slid over the left shoulder. She had shrunk at that time from carrying death around with her, but now she realized that, like the cyanide tablet in Ralph's heel, death and danger were constant companions. There was no virtue in being unprepared.

Ralph might well know by now that she had vanished. Perhaps he would be searching for her. He might even have been to Winterfeldstrasse and discovered her hasty exit. Yet no matter how hard he was looking, his searches would never lead him to a lake at the heart of the Tiergarten. There was no one to save her now but herself. Around her was shifting darkness, and beneath her was bottomless black. The man who was pursuing her wanted her dead and would surely shoot again until he caught her. She thought of herself sinking beneath the choking weeds, sodden clothes weighing her down like chains, blood spiralling upwards towards the closing surface of the lake.

The sound of the gun had, however, unleashed something else. An unearthly screech, followed by a cacophony of bird and animal calls rising up into the night, to be joined by the melancholy, plangent roar of some caged creature, yearning for its jungle home. Clara glimpsed a tangle of lights stretching beyond the trees that she recognized as the western end of the Tiergarten, and realized just what she had heard. She was approaching the zoo, from whose walls the strange, night calls of animals would often startle Berliners out for an evening stroll, reminding them of the captives in their midst.

The zoo. It was then that it came to her. The Ufa Palast am Zoo. Of course! That evening the Ufa Palast am Zoo was hosting the premiere of Lída Baarová's new film, *Patriots*. The story of a brave German soldier captured by the French in the war, and befriended by a rebel French girl. The story was all part of Germany's harsher policy towards France, and it must have seemed an ideal film to show to the city's most prestigious visitors – the Duke and Duchess of Windsor. Goebbels had mentioned that he planned a special evening for the royal couple. What had he said? *I have a cultural treat in store that I think they will appreciate.* If Goering could give them dinner at his hunting lodge then Goebbels could go one further, with an evening at the city's plushest movie theatre, in front of an audience two thousand strong. It would be adequate recompense for the humiliation of the Olympics party, when Goebbels' attempt to outshine his rival had descended into debauchery and farce. Hitler would not be there, but almost certainly Goebbels would have assembled as many top-ranking Nazis as he could muster to showcase his latest film triumph, plus, of course, his latest girlfriend.

Clara sat up and began to row frantically, until the blades struck the shallows of the lake, and reaching the other side she jumped out onto the jetty. She ran along the sandy path to the park exit and, breath tearing her lungs, slowed to a jog, as she made her way across the Cornelius bridge. It wasn't until she reached the safety of the streetlights that she paused and found a lipstick and comb in her bag. She peeled off the muddy elbow gloves and discarded them. The fur-collared coat, sodden and flecked with dirt, went over a nearby wall. Her shoes were soaked too, but less visible beneath the evening gown. Tidying herself as much as possible, she headed for Joseph Goebbels' night of the stars.

Ahead of her a phosphorescent glare lit up the sky. SS guards flanked the door. The name of the Ufa Palast am Zoo was picked out in lights over the turreted entrance. Giant posters of the film's stars, Baarová and Mathias Wieman, towered over the excited crowd. Clara wondered if it would be possible after all to pull this off. Her dress was damp with sweat and water from the lake. She felt entirely wan, as though pain and fear had seeped into her pores and bleached all colour from her face. She slowed to a walk and as she approached the red carpet, an SS guard moved to bar her entrance but at that moment, cameras began to flash and she caught sight of Mimi Reiter, an actress she had worked with, who came up and kissed her.

'Clara darling!'

'Fräulein Vine! Could you smile for us, please?'

The guard, bewildered for a moment, waved her through the velvet rope.

Another shout came. 'Fräulein Vine, look this way, please!'

Clara posed automatically as the glare of a camera flash momentarily blinded her. Then, as another burst of flashlight lit up the faces of the crowd around, she saw him. He must have lost his hat at some point because he was bare-headed now and she could see his bullet skull and crop of silvered hair. The slit of a mouth and the eyes as pale as slivers of ice. It was the first time she had seen him in plain view, and the moment she did, she knew where she had seen him before. It was the man she had met at Ernst Udet's party. The Luftwaffe officer who had seen Bruno at the Degenerate Art exhibition and reported him to the police. His name, what was his name? Rudolf Fleischer.

So Fleischer was the man who had gone from an assistant to Heinrich Hoffmann to a big-paying job in Berlin. It made perfect sense. It must have been Fleischer's expertize from Hoffmann's laboratory which secured him a job in the Luftwaffe's Technical Division. Yet no sooner had he secured this prestigious position than his past had risen up and threatened to engulf him. His old girlfriend Anna had stolen compromising photographs, which he should have ensured were destroyed. His solution had been to kill Anna. Only the photographs were still there, and he knew it was Clara who had them.

Clasping Mimi's arm, Clara progressed through the doors into the hall.

The foyer of the Ufa Palast was given over to an immense party space. The walls had been hung with billowing lengths of rose damask and extravagant displays of pink hothouse camellias were unfurling in the heat. Waiters with silver trays of champagne slid through the crowd, and from above gilt chandeliers sent their sparkling light over the cream of the National Socialist regime.

Germany's new aristocracy had turned out to greet the English royals in full, glittering regalia.

Rudolf Hess was there, a mad glint in his heavy-browed face, alongside his matronly wife Ilse, and Heinrich Himmler, his glasses a sinister glitter in the lights, was standing with his wife Marga. No amount of velvet and Russian lynx could prevent Marga Himmler from looking like the broad-beamed farmer's wife that she was. Her hair was in Brunhilde braids and her face was as scrubbed as a scullery floor. Magda Goebbels had told Clara she always avoided Marga Himmler because she was very dull and talked only about pig-keeping. The only SS wife who could stand her was Annelies von Ribbentrop, who Clara could also see, eyes raking the outfits of the prestigious guests, like a general on guard inspection.

In the absence of the Führer, the women had ignored his stipulations about dressing in Germanic clothing and had given free rein to their collections of haute couture. Shimmering Balenciaga gowns competed with dresses by Patou, Lanvin, Ricci and Chanel, capes edged with white mink and jackets with chinchilla cuffs. The jewellery on display might have been ransacked from a treasure chest compiled exclusively by Cartier and Van Cleef. Annelies von Ribbentrop was in a damson gown, with a sable stole. Inge Ley, the wife of Robert Ley and an actress herself, effortlessly outshone the other wives in a dress of wine-coloured chiffon, with a diamanté clip at the breast, her blonde hair polished to a shine. Among the politicians threaded the Babelsberg élite: Gustav Fröhlich beaming and toasting with his glass, Zarah Leander in a dramatically low-cut sheath, Brigitte Horney and Olga Chekhova with her sultry, Russian glamour. And in the midst of this sea of splendour the royal honeymooners stood, keeping close like a pair of orphans in a Nazi forest. They looked as though they would rather be anywhere than here.

As Clara hesitated, Karl Ritter strolled past, the man who had risen from a captain in the Imperial Air Force to become Ufa's top director, and beside him, laughing obsequiously at some joke, was Albert. Albert caught Clara's glance out of the tail of his eye and gave a quick wave. It took all her strength to smile back, hoping that he didn't see anything amiss with her damp dress, and that his eagle eye did not catch the splashes of mud on the hem.

Yet there was no sign of Goebbels at all.

Mimi squeezed her arm. 'We're late, damn it. The champagne's running out and the film is starting. Are you coming in with me, darling?'

The guests were being shepherded towards the doors of the auditorium but the more important people were hanging back, still drinking and talking, lingering until the last moment before taking their seats. The royal couple were cordoned by a sea of black uniforms, Wallis's wide-jawed face drooping wryly in some private joke, her grim-faced husband at her side.

Clara walked as swiftly as she could up the sweeping staircase. She needed to reach the circle because that was where Goebbels must be, ready to show himself off alongside the Windsors in the place of honour. In the royal circle, mahogany doors led to private boxes, each with eight gilt armchairs and a tray of refreshments laid out. The central box was reserved for the guests of honour.

Clara tapped and opened the door. It was empty, save for a single figure.

'Frau Doktor?'

'Fräulein Vine. What a surprise.'

Magda Goebbels was seated alone on a little gilt chair, her hands folded in fists on her lap. Her face was expressionless.

'I was looking for the Herr Doktor . . .'

Magda remained impassive. Her powdered skin was pallid. She wore her humiliation proudly, like pearls.

'Perhaps you should try looking a few doors down.'

Clara edged out of the box. Of course, it was clear to her now. Goebbels would be sitting with Lída. Even though Lída's own husband was in the audience, the Propaganda Minister was exercising his *droit de seigneur*. His right to the attentions of the leading lady would go unchallenged.

She hurried wildly along the corridor, knocking on every mahogany door and apologizing to startled faces until she reached the right one. It was at the far end of the corridor, and Clara's knock was answered by the actress herself, looking flushed, in an ivory silk halter-neck dress that caressed every inch of her curves, a dazzle of diamonds at her throat. Beyond her, Goebbels jumped up, his features distorted with rage, his jacket in one hand, the very image of the adulterer uncovered. Within a split second he had resumed his professional smile, but fury still burned behind his eyes.

'Fräulein Vine?'

'Herr Doktor, I wouldn't interrupt, but this is of the utmost importance.'

For a moment she thought he would scream at her, but instead, frowning, Goebbels dismissed Lída with a wave. She flounced past Clara, her Slavic eyes flashing, leaving the box with a glare.

'So what's this about?'

She proffered the evening bag full of shards.

'I've found these negatives. I think they may be pictures of the Führer. I've no idea whether they are genuine. I was going to hand them over to the police but unfortunately, before I could, Unity Mitford found them in my apartment and destroyed them.'

'Unity Mitford destroyed them?'

'She smashed them to pieces. She is, as you said, an emotional woman. She felt if they fell into the wrong hands, they could do the Führer some harm.'

'The Führer? Why?'

'Because of . . . the scenes they represent.'

'And how did they come into your hands, Fräulein?'

'They were in a lap case that belonged to Anna Hansen. The bride who was murdered. The case was passed to me because they thought I knew her family.'

Goebbels held the larger of the shards up to the light, squinted curiously upwards, then put it quickly down. Instantly he understood.

'No doubt the wretched bride intended some blackmail. Have you discussed this with anyone?'

'Not a soul.'

There was something strange about Goebbels' reaction. Why was he not more surprised? Clara had presented him with the solution to Anna's murder and yet he was as phlegmatic as ever. He looked her up and down, noting the splashes of mud on her dress and the locks of hair that had fallen from her chignon.

'It seems you arrived in a hurry. Perhaps you would like to sit down for a moment.'

He held out a chair for her, leaned forward and lit her a cigarette. As he thumbed the lighter she noticed that the silver polished rectangle was inscribed with the initials A.H. It was the Führer's birthday present, she recalled. Part of the set that Goebbels had shown her that day at the studio when he asked her about the Mitford sisters. Suddenly, something came into focus. That remark Heidi had made about Anna. She said Hitler had given Anna presents. But Hitler only gave three presents, didn't he? One of them was an oil painting, wasn't that what Emmy Goering had told her? That, or a photograph frame. Or a smoking set (a cigarette box and a lighter). Anna Hansen had a lighter with her own initials on, but what if the AH didn't stand for Anna Hansen, but Adolf Hitler? If Goebbels had found out about Anna's lighter, if he had been shown it, he would have recognized it at once as one of the Führer's special gifts. Just the same as his own. And he would have understood that Anna was a special bride indeed. A bride with a past.

The Nazis were fond of blaming violent crimes on convenient halfwits – they had managed, after all, to find a simple Dutch boy to take the rap for burning down the Reichstag. But when Goebbels saw the lighter, he would have realized that it was no soft-headed gardener who killed Anna. He must, at the very least, have suspected that Anna was killed for a reason. That was why he sent the Gestapo to interrogate that poor girl at the Bride School.

'Now I wonder how this blackmailing bride came by these photographs.'

'She had a boyfriend back in Munich. A Rudolf Fleischer.'

'Fleischer, you say?' He pulled out a card from his inside pocket and made a note.

'Oberst Leutnant Fleischer now, I believe. He's employed in the Technical Division of the Reichsluftfahrtministerium. He met Anna Hansen when he worked as an assistant to Heinrich Hoffmann.'

Goebbels' eyes widened.

'I see. Then I think this is best dealt with quietly. Thank you, Fräulein. It seems I am yet again in your debt.'

'I'm very anxious that you will be able to explain to the Führer—'

'I will assure the Führer of your good intentions. Rest assured he will hear of your service.'

He rose and gave her a swift, assessing glance, noting the silver and diamond swastika that he himself had given her.

'I would suggest, of course, that you stay on for the film, but I suspect, Fräulein, you might prefer to return home.'

'I am rather tired. And filming begins tomorrow.'

'Then you must let my driver take you back to your apartment.'

As she was driven through the streets in the ministerial Mercedes, Clara wondered where Fleischer was now, and how long it would be before Goebbels' men found him. How those pictures must have haunted him. What rage he must have felt when the past rose up and threatened to overtake him. Yet in the end even murder had not been enough to save him.

In the hall at Winterfeldstrasse, Rudi's collection point was brimming. There were tins, balls of aluminium foil, cutlery, even a frying pan in the mix, all destined to be melted down and turned into aeroplanes. Junkers and Henschels and Stuka bombers which might one day cross Europe and drop their bombs on England.

Clara thought for a second, then tossed Erich's knife on top of the pile.

Chapter Forty-three

'Your publicity shots, Fräulein.'

The studio boy put his head round the dressing-room door and smiled politely, handing Clara a thick cardboard envelope. Both she and Udet would that day be signing publicity photographs to be sent out to all Germany's film magazines and newspapers. This honour was new for Clara because Gretchen was her first title role. They had taken photographs of her scanning the skies, presumably in search of her lost husband, and another, which would be the film's poster, featuring herself in the arms of Ernst Udet, gazing rapturously into his eyes. It had been hard, shooting that one, because Ernst kept making her laugh.

Automatically she reached in her bag for a mark to tip the boy, but when she looked up, he had gone. That was unusual, Clara thought. The studio runners were generally keen to collect as many tips as possible. It occurred to her that she had not seen this particular runner before.

She opened the envelope and found a scrap of notepaper with a single line of sharp handwriting, uncoiling like barbed wire across the page. As she read the words, she saw the brief, twisted smile behind them.

'In belated thanks for the photograph you sent me, my dear Clara. Here are some in return.'

There was another envelope within. She pulled out a sheaf of prints. They weren't publicity pictures at all, in fact they looked like nothing she had ever seen. Bewildered, she shuffled through them, trying to make sense of the grey and white blotches until she realized that they were pictures of terrain from above, crisscrossed fields, dull masses of buildings and soft blocks of forest. She sifted the pictures through her hands, squinting at one and then another, as aerial views of ports, factories, railway lines and bridges came into view. There were coastlines and hills, all rendered with astonishing attention to detail. They seemed at once alien and familiar. It took her several minutes until she realized: the photographs were not of Germany but of England. She was seeing the land of her birth.

Gradually the images came to life and she saw Essex, Kent, Surrey, Sussex, and further west, Devon, Cornwall and Somerset. Hills, valleys, oil refineries, churches and power stations. Aerial shots of factories, railways, reservoirs and ports. There was London, with St Paul's and Big Ben and the Tate Gallery, and further out the woods and fields, villages and market towns. The docks at Plymouth and Portishead, Croydon airport, the Firth of Forth. Sissinghurst in Kent and Wimbledon Lawn Tennis Club leapt out at her. They seemed so real to Clara it was as though she could touch the grass in the fields, see the drifting fog over the Thames, and smell the tang of petrol in the London streets.

She let the pictures fall to her lap while she worked out what they meant. Together, these photographs made a meticulous map of the whole of Britain, but what had Britain been mapped for? Was it destruction or invasion? Or simply accommodation, when the Duke of Windsor returned as President with Hitler's blessing?

Jumping to her feet, she looked down the corridor for any sign of the delivery boy but he had vanished. She shut the door and leaned against it, the pictures pressed to her chest. Arno Strauss had not put his name to these photographs, but he might as well have done.

Strauss knew that Clara was deceiving him, yet in a way he had collaborated. Perhaps deception, like love, needed to have two willing partners. He had been assigned a part, and he had agreed to play it. So where was he now? She remembered his face as she left Horcher's restaurant. A test flight, wasn't that what he had said?

Realization dawned in a rush of dread. *I know that I shall meet my death.* She thought about him circling in the sky. Diving to the earth without a passenger to think of. She thought of him dead, his name pasted on the long list of those who had died in the glorious service of the Fatherland. His eyes glazed over, matching the blankness of the clouds. His body in the earth, with nothing above it but the patter of deers' hooves.

Strauss had never said goodbye, but this, she suspected, was a farewell of sorts.

Chapter Forty-four

Like Roman emperors displaying their foreign captives, the march past to showcase the Duke and Duchess of Windsor, who were taking the train down south to meet the Führer, was subject to the full pomp of the Reich. So far the Duke had attended Wagner's *Lohengrin* performed by the Berlin Labour Front, visited the training school of the Death's Head division of the SS and a luxury hotel development on the Baltic for the Nazi Youth. The Duchess, meanwhile, had been shopping. Now they were approaching the finale of their visit, tea with Hitler, and their car was swallowed up in a sea of swastika flags, jackboots, and the proud, bobbing caps of the Hitler Youth.

Clara and Ralph were walking through the trees towards the Avenue of the Dolls, the wide boulevard that ran north to south through the Tiergarten. It got its nickname from the thirty-two marble statues commemorating Hohenzollern princes that were lined pompously to each side. When they were installed, the statues had been designed for posterity, but no one in Berlin cared about the Hohenzollerns now that a new kind of aristocracy held sway.

It was a sparkling morning, as though, just for a while, winter was holding its breath. The grass was seeded with glittering frost and the linden trees throbbed with vivid autumnal red. In the distance a tumult of church bells challenged the tramping feet of the Nazi parade.

As the centrepiece of the march passed them, Clara caught a glimpse of the Duke and Duchess, performing that peculiar English royal wave which gave the unfortunate impression of brushing an annoying insect away. Wallis was wearing a tailored suit in teal wool with a matching cape, clutching a bouquet of orchids and white lilac. Around her neck was a mink stole, its sharp claws glinting in the sun. Her husband was in a light grey double-breasted suit, with a red carnation.

'If Hitler gets his way, they'll be travelling down the Mall before long,' said Ralph.

Clara tried to imagine the royal pair driving down the Mall before a subdued crowd, the Duke of York and his wife relegated to a latter horse-drawn carriage, perhaps followed by some of Edward's German associates, their black SS dress uniform towering over the eighteenth-century leather seats.

'That document you told me about. The one they've drawn up for the Duke to sign,' said Ralph quietly. 'We've been given a copy of it.'

'So it's true?'

'Yes, and we have Strauss to thank for it.'

She stared at him.

'Strauss gave you the document?

'So it seems.'

'As well as the photographs.' She bit her lip. 'That was brave of him. He said he had to be careful. There was a leak in Luftwaffe intelligence.'

'Did he say that?' Ralph gave a dry laugh. 'That leak was himself.'

'But?'

'Strauss had been passing small pieces of information for some time. The Air Ministry had their suspicions but they hadn't yet pinned him down. Nothing he gave us, though, was as valuable as his gift to you. Those reconnaissance maps are intended for a new Luftwaffe intelligence operation under Oberst Beppo Schmidt. It's been formed to monitor the capabilities of foreign air forces and to select targets in case of war. The photographs you received show all England's key factories, railway stations and power stations. Anything strategic has been marked out for bombing.'

'So they would bomb London.'

'Apparently Hitler was heard to say he was pleased that there are so few baroque buildings in Britain. Baroque is his favourite style and he hates having to destroy it. Those maps are an open rebuke to anyone who says the Germans have no thought of warfare.'

Above them a plane passed and its vapour cut the sky like a knife. The image of Strauss's face came forcefully back to Clara and she tried to block out the thought of that final sortie, which had ended in a forest south of Berlin in a heap of fused metal and twisted limbs, a plume of black smoke rising into the sky. Whatever she suspected, it was still a shock when she passed the newspaper stand at Nollendorfplatz on her way home from the studio and saw a grainy photograph of Strauss on the lower section of the evening paper. She had taken it home and wept so hard she could barely read the platitudes which accompanied the cursory report. *An unavoidable mistake at high altitude. A tragic loss for the Fatherland.* She had stared at the photograph until it grew damp with tears, trying to read some motive in his ruined demeanour. What had Arno Strauss thought before he embarked on that final flight? Had he looked the future in the face and found it overwhelming?

'How exactly was Rudolf Fleischer involved?'

'Ah, Fleischer.' Ralph's mouth narrowed at the thought of the man who had so nearly managed to take Clara's life. 'Fleischer had all the qualifications to work in the new operation. He was not only an ardent Nazi, but he had an extraordinary technical ability with cameras. Hoffmann had recognized it years ago back in Munich, where he first employed the man in his laboratory. When the Technical Division was looking for experts to develop a camera that could function at high altitude, Hoffmann recommended Fleischer to Udet and . . . you know the rest.'

'What do you think will happen to him now?'

'He's already been arrested. Goebbels is no doubt delighted to have one of Goering's boys behind bars.'

They had reached the road, and threaded through the crowd to watch the march trundle on. A battalion of cyclists passed, swastika pennants fluttering, followed by a cadre of Hitler Youth. Periodically a forest of right arms would rise, as though hoisted by an invisible magnet. Suddenly, through the mêlée of marching boys, Clara caught sight of Erich, carrying his bomb collecting box, his face shining with pride and concentration. She jolted Ralph's arm.

'There he is! Erich!'

She waved, and was gratified to see Erich, still facing rigidly ahead, give her a sideways grin. She had met him from school the day before and taken him for a meal, answering his shame-faced apology with the promise of a chance to meet Ernst Udet. If she seemed unusually sombre, he didn't detect it. His enthusiasm was infectious. He launched into a disquisition on which planes he intended to fly when he was a pilot, all memories of the unfortunate birthday outing forgotten. Clara had a sudden craving to introduce Erich to Ralph – to join together the two halves of her life – but she realized immediately how impossible that would be. Would it be years or even decades before she could live her life without secrets? Would it ever happen?

Once Erich had passed, Ralph drew her away again to walk across the frozen grass.

'I'm leaving for London this afternoon. The sooner these pictures are seen by the men who matter, the better. I'm taking them personally, in my own briefcase. I suppose there's no chance of you coming over with me?'

She shook her head. 'I can't. We've already started filming *The Pilot's Bride*. Udet came to Babelsberg yesterday and we have a day out at Tempelhof tomorrow.'

Udet had stopped her in the studio corridor and started to talk about Arno Str[illegible] had turned away, his face contorted with grief, and for the rest of the day, as if by mutual consent, they had not spoken of Strauss at all. Udet seemed hunched with sorrow, and the smell of schnapps on him was stronger than ever. Clara wondered how much he suspected about Strauss's motives, or what he knew.

'Udet can't devote more than a couple of days to filming. And after this one, I get the impression I'll be busy. Goebbels has already sent down some other scripts for me to consider.'

They were walking closely, hands brushing lightly, deliberately projecting the impression of casual acquaintances, out for a stroll. But the feeling of his skin against hers made her nerves tingle and suddenly she couldn't keep the urgency from her voice.

'Promise me you're coming back.'

'How can you doubt it?' He gripped her hand briefly, then drew away. 'But it might not be soon. I'm going to return through Spain.'

'Spain?'

'Yes.' He hesitated. 'There's something I didn't tell you. I met that American friend of yours, Mary Harker, at the reception for Colonel Lindbergh. Jolly girl, isn't she? She told me all about her time in Spain and she mentioned that she'd come across an Englishman by the name of Pericles. I was immediately interested.'

'Pericles?'

'Did I say Tom was a classicist? Pericles was his great hero. That would be just like him.'

'So Tom Roberts might be alive? That's great news, isn't it?'

'It is. Only . . .' Ralph's jaw tightened. 'There's more I need to find out. It was something Mary said. This chap Pericles had information about German movements. He was aware of all the details of the impending attack on Guernica before it took place.'

'How is that possible?'

'One of the pieces of information Strauss gave us was that the Germans believe their high command in Spain was compromised. They think they were infiltrated by spies working for the People's Commissariat for Internal Affairs. Better known as the NKVD.'

'NKVD. You mean Stalin's people?'

'That's right. Stalin's people. Though not always Russians.'

'Are you saying . . . Ralph, are you suggesting Tom Roberts is an NKVD spy? I thought you said he lost interest in politics.'

His face was solemn. He avoided her eye.

'Tom was always a passionate man. He saw things in black and white. I thought I knew him well, but how well do we know anyone? Communism is a faith, Clara. It can be a kind of fanaticism that blinds you to injustice or cruelty. Tom always feared that our ruling class would find common cause with Fascism, so he must have concluded there was only one way to fight them.'

'All those victims in Guernica, though. Those innocent people.'

'The Russians wanted the world to know the extent of German involvement in Spain. Guernica did that job.'

'So it wasn't just the Germans who knew the civilians would be there. The Russians knew too.'

'If I'm right, yes.'

'But if Tom knew the German planes were coming, he could still have warned people. The women and children.'

'Some people believe that death is relative. A few deaths are worthwhile, if it means the right ideology prevails. I don't happen to agree with them. Indeed I've devoted my life to proving them wrong.'

He stiffened his shoulders as though bracing himself for what might lie ahead and Clara had an urge to hurry back to Duisberger Strasse, up the steps to his apartment and close the door behind them. She wanted to make the most of what time there was left; to lie, just for a short while, in the safety of his bed, with nothing between them but their own warm flesh. To bury her face in his shoulder and feel his hands running down the curves of her body, pulling her towards him, the roughness of his chest against her own, stretching her body along his, face-to-face, her toes pressing down on his feet. To feel his arms enclose her, his mouth on her mouth and her legs wrapped around him.

They came to a small rose garden where a fountain splashed, its iridescence shimmering in the sunlit air. A gardener moved among the bushes, culling the dead, brown heads of flowers, tossing the withered offcuts into an ever-growing heap, yet even this late in the year a few roses remained, pushing palely out of the dark leaves. Something Arno Strauss had said went through her head. *Have you ever had that feeling of seeing your life from above?* And for a transitory moment she understood what he meant. In that moment life seemed to bloom in intensity, the colours and sounds around her sharpened, the fragrance of the grass and the earth rose up and the foliage flamed against the sky. All thoughts of the past and the future fell away and for a while it was just the two of them, walking beneath the trees, as behind them the music of the parade diminished and the surging crowds moved on.

Epilogue

An intense cold had gripped the city, almost paralysing it. Puddles were covered with a brittle skin and cracked like a million broken mirrors when you stepped on them. A weak sun hauled itself up in a bone-white sky. Winter was no longer hiding behind the veil of autumn but had finally shown its face. The previous night the sky had been clogged with snow like whirling ash and by morning Berlin was black and bridal white, a city in chiaroscuro.

In Köllnischer Park in Kreuzberg the snow lay inches deep, blanketing the divisions and softening sharp edges. Little avalanches slid from nearby roofs with cracks like a gunshot. Statues of dead statesmen stood awkwardly in the small square, covered with dustsheets of snow. Snow picked out the detail of tree branches and made the world simple again.

The three of them, Clara, Mary and Erich, were amongst a gaggle of people who had gathered to witness the unveiling of Berlin's latest attraction. A bear pit containing four brown bears to commemorate the seven hundredth anniversary of the city's founding. The pit was far smaller than one might expect – just a patch of grass sunk deep into the ground on which a few rocks had been scattered in a passing reference to the animals' mountain habitat. The crowd were craning their heads over the railings, but the bears were disappointingly publicity-shy. All four had taken shelter in the invisible depths of their den.

Mary had brought her camera and was angling for an artistic shot of the children's faces framed by the bars. She had wholeheartedly embraced her new existence as a photojournalist. The photographs she had taken of the Bride School had made a double-page spread in the *New York Evening Post,* alongside the scandalous story of the murders of Anna Hansen and Ilse Henning. Ilse had been shot in the head while running through woods to escape Anna's former boyfriend, Rudolf Fleischer. The death of a second Reich Bride was too much even for the domestic papers to ignore and the Bride School had been besieged. Fräulein Wolff had been put in charge of handling journalistic enquiries, a task she accomplished by locking the school gates, barring brides from leaving the premises and slamming down the telephone whenever it rang. As for Fleischer, Goebbels had acted quickly. He had been arrested at dawn, the day after the gala performance of *Patriots*. His Walther 6.35-calibre pistol matched the bullets that killed the two girls.

Clara shivered and rubbed her arms with her gloved hands. Of Fleischer's other secret, the photographs of the Führer, there was no word. Goebbels was the custodian of those splintered fragments now, and although they had not seen the light of day, the negatives remained a dark bond between Clara and him. Her decision to hand the pictures over might be enough for now to still his suspicions about her, but there was no telling how long that would last. The Minister of Propaganda and Enlightenment was good at keeping secrets, she knew, and he must assume the same of her. This particular dangerous secret would stay buried, deep, until it was needed. Her enemy was, for the moment, also her protector.

She looked down at the frozen puddles, peering through the panes of ice as if she might divine something stirring beneath them, and thought of Bruno Weiss. He had vanished from the Moabit apartment and disappeared into the great underground network that spread through Berlin, an underground that was not just symbolic but actual, made up of brewery cellars and U-Bahn tunnels, subterranean walkways and a maze of bunkers being built for war. She wondered how many people there were like Bruno, frozen beneath the surface of normal life until the time came for them to stir. Let alone how many others like herself.

As she stared into the puddles, Erich stamped on them, turning them into great shards of glassy ice, and grinned. The snow bounced light into his face.

'Here, Clara. You haven't looked at it properly yet.'

He held out the gift that Ernst Udet had sent him. It was a model aeroplane, complete with a tiny tin figure of Ernst Udet himself that could be removed from the cockpit. Erich had been slightly embarrassed at receiving a toy at his advanced age. Clara had given him plenty of lead soldiers over the years – smart little Wehrmacht figures in field grey with impressive rifles, and some indeterminate enemy troops that looked suspiciously French – but Erich had donated them all to the HJ's metal collection. Yet this was different. The Stuka was an artistic object, not a toy, he rationalized, and any embarrassment was overwhelmed by his pride at receiving a gift from General Udet himself, along with a personally signed letter wishing him well in his future as a pilot.

'Are you looking forward to seeing your sister, Clara?' he asked.

Mary and Clara exchanged a quick glance. 'Of course.'

'Does she look like you?'

'Far more glamorous.'

'No one could be more glamorous than you,' he said, with a quick, loyal stroke of her lapel to show that everything was fine again between them.

'You'd be surprised. Even though she's my sister, she's not a bit like me. She's nothing like me at all.'

Which was true, and yet they were well matched. Angela was clever and curious and she knew Clara better than anyone on earth. Clara braced, as though tightening a buckle inside her, readying herself. She would show Angela the sights of Berlin with all the insouciance of an actress only interested in her own career. She would let slip the names of leading men who she might, conceivably, have an eye on. If Clara could deceive her own sister, she could deceive anyone.

'Will I like her?'

'I hope so.'

Angela and Sir Ronald Vine were flying in that afternoon. Angela had sent her usual, peremptory letter, requesting that Clara be at Tempelhof at two o'clock and accompany them to the hotel. Unfortunately, Angela wrote, it looked as though she would be missing the Mitfords. Diana Mosley had returned to England and Unity was back in Munich. But the Goebbels had kindly offered to throw a dinner for them at the Kaiserhof later in the week and Clara would be pleased to hear they had tickets for that evening's production of *The Merry Widow* at the Wintergarten. Would she like to come too? Angela had heard that it was the Führer's favourite operetta. Clara thought she might as well go and see it. When war came there would be no more Merry Widows in Germany. No one would dare.

'Hey, look!' said Erich.

One of the bears had emerged. Tentatively at first, the huge beast prowled the pit, peering up at the civilized citizens staring down at it, protected by a tangle of iron and barbed wire. The bear's breath hung in a cloud as it sniffed the air of its new captivity. The pit was ten foot deep at least, made of musty bricks the colour of dried blood.

'Do you know, there hasn't been a bear pit in Berlin since the Middle Ages,' said Erich, solemnly.

The animal began to pace out the confines of its den, round

and round, barging its dull, matted pelt against the walls, poking its long snout and tiny black eyes into the crevices, as if to find some escape from its predicament. Children leaned over the railings, thrilling to the spectacle of such strength and vitality contained, recoiling in delighted terror as the bear reared up on its great hind legs, pawing the walls with ugly, curving claws. They shrieked. Someone threw a pretzel. The bear dropped down again to resume its pacing, round and round the circle of the pit, issuing small grunts from the narrow, crimson cave of its mouth. A ripple of laughs ran through the crowd.

'Do you reckon it could escape?' wondered Erich.

'Of course not.'

But the more she watched, the more Clara wished it could. She had a vision of the bear leaping over the railings of its prison and disappearing into the city, running on its ugly, clawed paws through the streets of Berlin, past the granite, Wilhelmine façades bristling with scarlet banners, disrupting the soldiers' marches, scattering pedestrians, ripping down flags with its dirty, yellow teeth and knocking over newspaper stands as it went. Up past Potsdamer Platz, the wind flattening its fur, skidding over tramlines, trampling the postcard racks with their pictures of the Führer and sending the pretzel carts flying. Causing chaos in the Ku'damm and shocking the affluent shoppers in the west end. Then slowing, its clumsy bulk lumbering out west through the leafy streets of Charlottenburg, before disappearing for ever in the grey-green depths of the Grunewald.

Erich linked his arm through hers. As he grew older such physical gestures between them had become increasingly rare and she felt a surge of love for him. She turned and smiled.

'Don't worry. We're completely safe.'

And anyone watching would swear that she believed it.

Author's Note

In 1937, two versions of the Heinkel He III were fitted with hidden cameras and flown from Germany to begin the secret aerial reconnaissance of Britain. They were soon joined by other aircraft and the resulting photographs were used to identify airfields, dockyards, factories, military installations and any other sites considered valid bombing targets in case of war. Together they made up the first ever aerial survey of Britain.

One of the most important figures in assessing the secret build-up of the Luftwaffe, and understanding the importance of aerial reconnaissance, was Group Captain Frederick Winterbotham, who joined the Secret Intelligence Service in 1929, and travelled widely in Germany between 1934 and 1938, when his cover was blown. His book, *The Nazi Connection*, details his meetings with Hitler, Goering, Rosenberg, Hess, General von Reichenau and General Kesselring, all of whom believed he was sympathetic to their aims.

Ernst Udet continued in the Luftwaffe until after war broke out. He was blamed for the Luftwaffe's defeat in the Battle of Britain and further despaired of the direction of the war when Hitler attacked the Soviet Union. Increasingly unhappy, he committed suicide in November 1941, but the Party announced that he had died testing a new weapon.

In October 1937, the Duke and Duchess of Windsor toured Nazi Germany as personal guests of Hitler. There is a curious addendum to this episode. In 1945 the spy Anthony Blunt was sent on a secret mission on behalf of the royal family to Schloss Friedrichshof, the home of Edward VIII's cousin Philip of Hesse. Blunt's mission was to retrieve certain letters and it has been speculated, though never proved, that these included letters between the Duke of Windsor and the Nazi hierarchy. Some have suggested that this intimate knowledge of royal secrets delayed Blunt's unveiling as a traitor.

Unity Mitford remained a devoted follower of Hitler. In 1939, following the declaration of war between Britain and Germany, she went into Munich's English Garden, took out a pearl-handled pistol which had been a gift from Hitler and shot herself. Her attempt at suicide failed, however, and she was transported back to England with Hitler's help, lingering on as an invalid until 1948.

Berlin's bear pit still exists, at time of writing, in Köllnischer Park.

Once again my heartfelt thanks go to Suzanne Baboneau, Clare Hey and Hannah Corbett at Simon & Schuster and to Caradoc King.

Read on . . .

For an exclusive extract from *A War of Flowers,* the new novel by Jane Thynne

Prologue

August, 1938

Another fine, summer's day and the MS *Wilhelm Gustloff* cruise liner was making its leisurely way across the Atlantic Ocean. The 25,000 ton ship rose like a sheer white cliff from the water, eight storeys high, gracefully transporting a cargo of more than a thousand citizens of the German Reich. The sun was already dazzling, bouncing back from a sea of hammered cobalt as the liner's prow carved a confident line past the spectacular coastline of Madeira. The island, with its black volcanic sand, its coves fringed with laurel trees and red-roofed houses clambering up the mountain slopes, glittered in the sapphire morning light. Birds with iridescent necks and little dashes of blood at their throats fluttered through the wooded mountains, which were swathed at their peaks with a light garland of cloud. A fine spray, thick with the tang of salt, pearled the faces of the people watching from the deck, many of whom had never set foot outside the Reich and had mostly never seen the sea. The liner was the first tailor-made ship of the National Socialist Strength Through Joy movement, the Kraft durch Freude, organized by the German Labour Front, and it was the only way an ordinary German was able to leave the country now. The fact that they were getting a glimpse of the world that lay beyond the borders of the Reich – for now at any rate – and they were seeing it on a two-week cruise costing less than a fortnight's wages, was yet another reason to be grateful for the Führer's reforms.

Ada Freitag had never seen the sea before either, but that didn't mean she wanted to hang over the deck, waving a swastika flag at it. Smearing a little more Elizabeth Arden suncream on her freckles and over the skin on her shoulders, already turning a rich caramel, she anchored her bag more firmly beneath one arm, lay back in her deckchair and tried unsuccessfully to relax.

Relaxing was not, Ada had quickly realized, a priority on a Strength Through Joy holiday. Even when at sea, any citizen enjoying a KdF tour had a packed schedule of daily activity, requiring daunting levels of enthusiasm and stamina. The day began in the main dining room with a ceremony of dedication to the Führer (compulsory), presided over by a portrait of the man himself, regulation scowl in place, tar-black hair slicing diagonally across his brow. The ship had originally been named the *Adolf Hitler*, until the assassination of Gustloff, Party leader in Switzerland, by a Jewish upstart provided a Nazi martyr tailor-made for the bow of a ship. But even without his name on the side, Hitler's image was still everywhere; in the cocktail lounge, above the swimming pool, even glowering out at passengers when they took a bath. There was no such thing as a holiday from the Führer.

The morning's dedication ceremony was followed by a strenuous series of PE workouts on deck, gym sessions, fencing, table tennis, dancing lessons, piano recitals, swimming galas and bridge parties, all of which were not so much obligatory as strongly recommended by the ship's holiday reps who didn't leave you alone until you gave in.

Just walking round the ship was a major expedition. There was the Führer suite on B deck, kept for VIPs, the walnut-panelled Folk Costume lounge, and the Winter Garden. The German hall, the Music salon, the Ballroom and seven different bars. There was an indoor swimming pool, bouncing with echoes from excited Bund Deutscher Mädel girls bathed in dazzling, refracted light. And then there were meals, meals and more meals that you had to dress up for and were served with napkins folded into swastika shapes, beneath banners sewn with the KdF slogan '*Enjoy Your Lives!*'. The coffee tables had ashtrays with pictures of the ship on their plastic bases, and matchbooks, with *Wilhelm Gustloff* printed in gold lettering alongside them. Someone had put the Hitler Jugend in charge of the ship radio, which meant that in between the dance music and regular broadcasts from Joseph Goebbels, random exhortations were bellowed over the Tannoy, mostly concerning military excitements. The most recent one had come when the *Wilhelm Gustloff* passed a couple of German warships idling off the coast of France, and passengers were urged to 'think of the man who had given the German people their reputation and their position of power in the world: our Führer'. The HJ boys had also instituted a daily quiz – sample question 'What is Adolf Hitler's favourite flower?' – to which the passengers roared the answers in unison.

In her deckchair on the sun deck, a silk scarf round her head, Ada kept her eyes shut and sighed. Looking at the sea made her feel sick, what with the glare of the sun off its writhing currents and the smell of fish. The vast expanse of water only reminded her how far from home she was, and the proximity of so many others made her feel nervous. Far better to lie back and pretend to be asleep, even if there was no chance of relaxing.

Yesterday, to break the tedium, she had taken a trip ashore, but even on dry land the pace did not relent. It was an outing to Funchal to view the flora. The group wended their way past jacarandas thrusting fiery purple blossom in their faces, giant ferns and dragon trees, yellow frangipani and tremulous orchids. Above them the mountain slopes were tumbling with verdant growth and in the market old women in shawls attempted to sell them lace, wicker baskets and painted gourds. One woman had a fruit Ada had never seen, pomegranate it was called, a fruit like a cup full of jewels, but as she stretched out her hand, the tour guide leapt forward and advised her not to touch it on account of disease. The guides were exactly like schoolteachers. While everyone was marvelling at the banana trees and the birds of paradise and flamingo flowers, the tour guide kept pointing out the poverty of the local inhabitants, their ramshackle homes and gutters flowing with waste, saying it proved how other cultures were inferior to the Germans. It was lucky the locals didn't understand. The peasant women kept on smiling their toothless smiles while the group ignored them and hurried on. Bringing up the rear were a couple of SS surveillance staff, employed to prevent the women striking up holiday romances with foreign men. The guards were a burly pair, who saw everything and wouldn't hesitate to rough up any locals who tried as much as a friendly greeting.

Avoiding men had become a full time occupation for Ada. She couldn't help having good legs, a nice dress and a suntan, but the ship was full of lads who had qualified for their tickets in groups from the factories where they worked and were delighted to find any unattached women, let alone a pretty twenty-three-year-old with a voluptuous figure, a snub nose, full lips and eyes of bright Aryan blue. Ada's creamy blonde plaits framed a face as delicate as a porcelain doll and her red and yellow halter-neck sundress emphasized her generous curves. They hung around her like wasps, offering to buy her a beer and asking for a dance. Even when she picked up one of her stack of film magazines they didn't let up, making idiotic comments about movie stars or suggesting, predictably, she should be on screen herself.

But Ada had not the slightest interest in men just then, or Madeira and its flowers. She was far too nervous for that. Her entire attention was fixed on the ship's next stop, Lisbon, where the

Wilhelm Gustloff would dock and she would complete the business she had come for. Then there would be plenty of time to enjoy herself and she might even take one of the young men up on his offer. In the meantime, to stop being bothered, she had come up with a pretty good deterrent.

At first, when the teenager from the neighbouring cabin had begun stealing glances at her, she sighed inwardly. He couldn't have been more than fifteen, with a wiry boy's frame just beginning to fill out and the faintest dusting of hair on his upper lip. Actually his lean, dark-eyed face reminded Ada of her little brother. The lad was on holiday with his grandmother, who had qualified for the tickets through her job at Berlin's Charité hospital, and they had been assigned to Ada's table at breakfast. As she tried to eat her eggs, Ada found herself machine-gunned with questions. Where did she come from? Berlin? Them too! Weren't they lucky to have tickets on the best ship of the fleet? And only its second cruise. How had she qualified for hers? Then the boy noticed the film magazines and an album of movie star cards she had – the kind you sent off for with coupons from your cigarette packet – and he became even more excited. Did she know his own godmother was a film actress? Her name was Clara Vine and she featured on a cigarette card herself. Perhaps Ada had her picture?

Enboldened at this shared enthusiasm, the boy had skipped his post-breakfast gym session and offered to carry Ada's coffee up to the sun deck. She groaned inwardly, until she suddenly realized the boy might actually be an advantage. His name was Erich Schmidt, and he wanted to tell her all about his plans to join the Luftwaffe. That was fine by Ada. She closed her eyes and instructed Erich to keep talking.

The fact was, it wasn't just the factory workers who had set Ada's nerves on edge. Yesterday, she had been lying in the same spot on her lounger when she caught a brief snatch of scent that made her sit up in alarm. She couldn't understand why she had reacted the way she did. It was inexplicable. But there was some prickle of danger in that harsh, citrus-edged cologne, some quality in its musky base notes that left an ominous imprint on the air. It was the kind of perfume that hung on a person, like garlic on the breath. For a second the perfume formed itself into something mistily substantial – a wraith with an arrogant face, eyes black as olive pits and a smile sharp as a knife – but the image was gone as soon as it had come, like a puff of breath misting a mirror, wiped away to reveal nothing. Ada tried to conceal her alarm, yet she must have looked worried because a girl in a deckchair near to hers, with pasty skin, lank braids and thick spectacles, noticed her distraction.

'Is anything the matter?'

Ada was tempted to ask whether the girl herself had seen anyone, but realized instinctively that this was a matter she needed to keep to herself, so she turned a dismissive, suntanned shoulder and said rudely,

'No. Why should it be?'

That morning, after Erich had gone off to fetch the coffee, Ada caught a trace of the cologne again. There was definitely a memory floating there, amid the mix of lemon, amber and moss. Though the day was perfectly warm, a chill crept over her and she clutched her cardigan to her and sat up, her filmy scarf snapping in the breeze. She looked around at the women, wedged in their deckchairs with their copies of *Stern* and *Die Dame,* and their husbands with their trousers rolled up, but she could see nothing to account for it. Yet like an animal hearing a note much higher than human ears can hear, Ada detected in that perfume a note of danger, a high, ringing register of alarm with a bass undertone of fear. Attempting to rationalize the feeling, she reminded herself how many different thousands of people used the same scent. Kölnwasser, Eau de Cologne, for instance, Germany's oldest scent, was used by millions. It was said to be the Führer's favourite. There was no reason why this one particular scent should mean anything at all. It reminded her of something though, and it was something that made her afraid. It was a male scent, so it must be a man she was reminded of, but which man?

Was it someone back home? She frowned and chewed her lip as she tried to place it, but all she knew was that the scent made her heart race and the hairs rise on the back of her neck. She needed to know where that perfume came from, if only for her peace of mind.

Thank goodness for the boy, who was just coming back at that moment, balancing two cups on a tray and two pastries which he must have bought with his own cash.

'What a darling you are, Erich! Now I have to go somewhere, just for a minute. Could you look after my things? Make sure you keep an eye on them. And don't let anyone take this deckchair.'

The boy looked dismayed at having his coffee spurned and she felt a pang of guilt, but there was nothing for it.

Decisively Ada put down her magazine, rose from the deckchair and strode off.

Erich waited an hour watching Ada's coffee grow cold and ate both pastries himself, before he realized that she did not have an important appointment at all. She had just been trying to get rid of him. A humiliated flush spread across his cheeks as he imagined all the fat women – friends of his grandmother's sitting around in their deckchairs – secretly laughing at him while they pretended to read their magazines. They must assume he had an adolescent crush. He felt a twist of anger. He had never wanted to take a summer holiday with his grandmother, what boy would? Oma kept going on about what a privilege it was to go on a KdF trip and how the ship would be luxurious beyond their wildest dreams. There was even a library on board. But what boy in his right mind wanted a library on holiday?

A little after four o'clock that afternoon a squall blew in from the east, pitting the watered silk of the sea and driving everyone from the sun decks inside to play Skat or table tennis and watch the spray lashing the portholes from the warmth of the recreation areas. Only one hardy passenger, shivering in the spitting rain, remained on deck to witness what followed.

The first thing she noticed was a commotion at the port side of the ship, where a gaggle of sailors were shouting and hauling an object onto the rain-lashed deck. She thought at first it was a fish, a shark perhaps, or a porpoise, but looking closer she saw it was a young woman's body, beached like a delicate, exotic mermaid from some child's fairy story. The dead girl lay on her back, curly hair plastered across her face like seaweed and skin as white as a fish, her flesh already turning to ice. Water gushed from her mouth and nostrils and ran in rivulets down her face, pooling around her body as it lay defencelessly still. For a second the sailors stood staring at her until the youngest of them, the one who had first glimpsed the white shape rolling on the waves and raised the alarm, felt sick and grabbed a tarpaulin to wrap her up. So the woman watching caught only a glimpse of the girl's face, just enough to see that it was extraordinarily pretty in the conventional Germanic model, with high, arched eyebrows and blue eyes now fixed and empty, as if their colour had already been washed out by the sea. She wore a halter-necked sundress that clung to every voluptuous curve, leaving nothing to the imagination except, perhaps, the method of her death. For on the back of her head was a great bloody mess of hair and bone, the kind of wound that might have been sustained by hitting the side of the ship as she fell, or even, perhaps, a blow from a heavy instrument, if such a thing were possible.

The horrified passenger was moved swiftly away from the scene and later that day received a personal visit in her cabin from Heinrich Bertram, the ship's captain, who was most solicitous about her shock. He suggested that she try to forget it as much as possible and enjoy the rest of her holiday. It would be wrong to allow a tragedy like this to mar such a special voyage, let alone spoil the enjoyment of others by talking about it. Going further, Captain Bertram had to warn the gnädiges Fräulein that any mention of the incident anywhere else at all would have serious repercussions for her, both at home and in the workplace, and put at risk the chance of any future trips she or her family might hope to make with the KdF.

Chapter One

Paris

Paris in late August, 1938, was a city living on its nerves.

Rumours swarmed like rats around the streets, refugees from every corner of Europe brushed shoulders on the boulevards, and the cafés were a babel of foreign languages, Spanish, Italian, Czech and, of course, German, rising and falling in anxious disputation. In the city centre the clatter of cream-topped buses, the blare of taxi horns and the shouts of traffic gendarmes were overlaid with the distant sound of reservists, in hastily assembled khaki, marching along the Champs Elysées. German, Austrian, Polish and Hungarian Jews congregated in the Marais quarter in anxious exile, scraping a living by day, and drinking it by night. Morsels of foreign news were picked up and ravenously chewed on, then discarded as propaganda or lies. Refugees choked the railway stations. Native Parisians were packing up and moving their families to the country. Others spent longer than usual in the churches. A dry summer wind blew around the city, chivvying along the gutters a vortex of leaves and litter and small scraps of newspaper alarm. Hitler was claiming that the German-speaking population of Czechoslovakia's Sudetenland, just south of the German border, desired reunion with the Reich. If the Czech government did not agree then he would march in and take it. France and England seemed certain to reject Germany's demands. Hitler had set the date of 1st October for military action. The threat of war hung like a distant thunderstorm on a sunny day.

Clara Vine threw open the tall shutters, leaned over the narrow balcony, and gazed down at the Boulevard de Sébastopol below. She only had three days in Paris and the last two had been spent shooting scenes for her latest film, an adaptation of Maupassant's *Bel Ami,* but the third, today, was entirely free. A whole day ahead of her and only an engagement that evening before catching a train at the Gare du Nord early the next morning and heading back home to Berlin. She could visit the Louvre, go shopping, see a concert, or maybe just sit in a square beneath the dusty trees and drink a café crème. An entire day to herself in Paris. No lines to learn, no character to assume. No takes or retakes, no director's tiff or costume fittings. No delays or disputes. After filming almost non-stop for months, a day off in a foreign location felt like a fantasy. And despite the mood of the city, Clara was determined to make the most of it.

The Bellevue, where the cast were staying, was not everyone's idea of Parisian chic. Its forty rooms were squeezed into a narrow, five-storey building and Clara's bedroom on the top floor was sweltering. The paint on the wrought-iron balconies was flaking, the plaster decayed and the entire building was imbued with the reek of drains. But who cared about that when there was all of Paris to look at?

The city seemed impossibly beautiful, the elegant precision of its buildings and the classical uniformity of its blocks and streets complemented by a golden light that seemed to saturate the pale stone. Even now, in high summer, when most Parisians were on their August vacation, the pavements were thronged with people. Immediately below Clara's window, between the patchy trunks of the plane trees, a cart of flowers bulged with red, yellow and pink blooms, like a bright shout of colour in the morning air. Vans making deliveries and a porter hauling a crate of baguettes almost collided with a man bearing a box of oranges on his head. In the fishmonger's window a chorus line of doomed lobsters waved their limbs helplessly on a tray. Young women with crimson lips and kohl-lined eyes clipped past wearing Breton-necked tops with wide scarves slung diagonally across them, in keeping with the latest fashion, and little felt hats studded with flowers or feathers. Some wore printed summer dresses in ice-cream colours and they even managed to make their heavy wooden-soled shoes look stylish. Men in open-necked shirts and berets swaggered past. Despite the undercurrent of nerves that ran through the city, the citizens on the Boulevard de Sébastopol were doing their best impression of elegant nonchalance.

What a contrast with Berlin. In Clara's home city the daily round-up of Jews and the sporadic Gestapo cruelties had worsened throughout the year. That spring Hitler had marched into Austria and found himself greeted not with hostilities but with a carpet of roses; *Blumenkrieg*, he called it, a war of flowers. The lack of international outcry over the Anschluss had only emboldened him. Hitler was, everyone realized, more confident than ever.

Unlike Clara herself.

As an Anglo-German actress, who had grown up in England, Clara Vine had made a successful career for herself since arriving in Berlin five years earlier. She had seven films to her name, and by sheer chance had forged connections with many people in Berlin's high society. Yet despite her acquaintance with the wives of several politicians, Joseph Goebbels, the Minister for Propaganda and Public Enlightenment, had become increasingly suspicious of Clara's motives. The previous year he had even had her arrested briefly, and interrogated. For Clara, merely thinking of that day in the Gestapo headquarters, and of the tightrope she trod daily in

Berlin, brought a chill to the morning's warmth and a familiar sick twist of nerves. It was as though Goebbels was determined to prove what he suspected – that even though Clara's father was a British aristocrat and Nazi sympathizer, and she herself was working full-time in the Babelsberg film studios, Clara was an agent of British Intelligence. That she was passing snippets of information and gossip to her contacts in the British Embassy. That she purposefully mingled in Nazi society to observe the private life of the Third Reich.

It would have been absurd, if it hadn't also been true.

What made Clara's position more perilous was her discovery, when she arrived in Germany, that her own grandmother was a Jew. The document of Aryan heritage Clara carried everywhere was as much a fabrication as the russet highlights in her hair, but infinitely more significant.

Every day she asked herself why she stayed in Berlin. Every day she came up with the same answer. She would stay in Berlin as long as she could because it meant seeing her godson Erich. He was the only man in her life right now, and for his sake most of all she prayed that war could somehow be averted.

A passing barrow boy aimed an admiring whistle up at her balcony, forcing Clara's mind back to the present. Paris had always been one of those big, statement places, like a famous perfume that everyone knows, burdened with the weight of expectation. The Parisian air was a complex fragrance of baking and drains, a whisper of flowers, undercut with something acrid and rotten. The leavings of vegetables from the market stalls mingled with the enticing aroma of garlic and coffee. Berlin's own air, by contrast, carried the grey, metallic edge of wet stone and steel offset by the tang of pine from the Grunewald.

Much as she relished the prospect of a day in Paris, Clara wished she had someone to share it with. Most of the time she liked her solitude; at the age of thirty-one it was part of her identity almost, her self-sufficiency a toughened carapace against the barbs of loneliness, and safer too. But solitude seemed wrong in the city of romance. This was Paris after all, whose streets murmured with the promises of lovers through the ages, and she was alone. Leaning back against the casement, a whirlwind of memories assailed her, like leaves thrown around in a breeze.

She had not seen Ralph Sommers, the man she had met in Berlin the previous year, since the day he left for London. Since then, his work as a British agent had been exposed and now it was too dangerous for him to return to Germany. He had sent Clara a message saying that so long as she stayed there, she must do her best to forget him. It hurt, but she was trying her hardest.

Then there was Leo Quinn. Leo, who had returned to England after she turned down his proposal of marriage. In her darkest moments Clara questioned if there was something within her that destroyed her deepest relationships. Did she shy away from intimacy or deliberately reject it? Did she emit some invisible signal that said, 'Leave me alone'?

The previous evening the director, Willi Forst, had hosted a dinner at Maxim's for the cast. Maxim's, just off Place de la Concorde, was the restaurant of choice for German visitors to Paris and Willi Forst thought its Art Nouveau opulence perfectly suited to celebrating Maupassant's story. The group had the best table in the house, the one usually reserved for the Aga Khan, spread with snowy linen tablecloths and silver cutlery, and they were served platters of oysters with vinegar and shallots, *quenelles de brochet* floating in a rich cream sauce, and *crème brûlée* to finish. Ice buckets holding bottles of vintage Krug rested to one side, furred with frost. Even though they had had an early start, the actors indulged themselves loudly, jokes and stories flowing, impressions performed, anecdotes related. The sheer relief of being away from Berlin inspired a feverish jollity, a holiday atmosphere that had already prompted a couple of romantic liaisons amongst members of the cast and promised more nights of passion ahead. But none of the male actors had propositioned Clara. It was as though they divined something in her which told them their approaches would be rebuffed. As they revelled in the unaccustomed fine food and called loudly for more wine, Clara felt the restaurant's other clientele eyeing the Germans, in their expensive suits and scented furs, with wariness and resentment.

'To my magnificent cast!'

Willi Forst raised a glass and beamed. Sitting there, Clara thought back to the newspaper pictures in March, when Hitler entered Vienna in his six-wheeled bulletproof Mercedes, striking his familiar pose, upright, holding on to the windscreen with his left hand while raising the other in the Nazi salute. The crowd erupting in a volcano of feeling and the flowers raining down on him like ash. Would these Paris streets too be overtaken by tramping boots and thumping drums? Might France go the way of Austria? Austria wasn't even Austria any more, it was part of Greater Germany. It seemed countries could end, just as much as relationships.

A knock at her door made her turn. It was the bellboy, wearing a little navy cap and holding out a manila envelope.

'Pour vous, mademoiselle.'

'Merci.' She fished for a coin and opened the envelope curiously. Inside was a cream notecard, heavy and good quality, with a logo of Big Ben and a company name at the top. Beneath was spiky, academic handwriting.

Dear Miss Vine,

Please forgive me for approaching you directly, but I noticed from an article in Paris-Soir that you were in Paris and felt compelled to get in touch. We would be very interested in discussing a proposal with you. Would you be free to meet at the café Chez André in the Rue Marbeuf at 12 p.m. today? If you are able to come I shall be looking out for you,

Sincerely, Guy Hamilton,
Representative, London Films

London Films? Clara frowned. She had heard of it. From what she remembered it had been started by the Hungarian émigré Alexander Korda. It was based at Denham in Buckinghamshire and had hired Winston Churchill as a screenwriter. Hadn't they made *The Private Life of Henry VIII* and *Things To Come* and last year's *Fire Over England*, with Laurence Olivier and Vivien Leigh? Clara had taken a special interest in that one because a director had once casually referred to her as 'the German Vivien Leigh', so she had attended the first night at the Ufa Palast and sat in the cinema, closely studying the actress's classic, porcelain beauty, before concluding that the director, unfortunately, was exaggerating. Clara might have the same heart-shaped face, clear brow and dark eyebrows, but her cheeks were fuller, her skin more olive and her mouth had a rebellious purse to it which gave her looks a distinctive, less classic edge.

She checked her watch. It was already 11 a.m. She was suddenly, unaccountably excited. This proposal would almost certainly be the offer of a part – she was gradually becoming better known, and as many of the German Jewish actors and directors who had been forced to leave Berlin had now relocated to England, it was likely that one of them had mentioned her name. Evidently someone was looking out for her. And maybe, if this company was offering her a job, she should take it. What might it be like returning to London, picking up the threads of a life she had left five years ago and doing an ordinary job without risk or subterfuge? Seeing her father, sister and brother and other people who had been consigned firmly to the past?

Clanging the shutters to, she grabbed a short jacket to slip over her dress. Peering in the mirror she applied a thin layer of Elizabeth Arden's Velvet Red – always her first weapon of concealment – and gave her reflection an encouraging smile. Dabbing a trace of powder over the freckles that the sun had brought out, she pulled a brush through her hair and pinned it loosely at the nape of her neck with a diamanté clip. Then she donned her sunglasses. Evidently the idea of a day without business was just a fantasy after all.

*